D0299618

Iain Banks came to controversial public notice with the publication of his first novel, *The Wasp Factory*, in 1984. Since then he has gained widespread popular and critical acclaim with further works of both fiction and science fiction. He lives in Fife.

Also by Iain Banks

THE WASP FACTORY
WALKING ON GLASS
THE BRIDGE
ESPEDAIR STREET
CANAL DREAMS
COMPLICITY
WHIT

and by Iain M. Banks

CONSIDER PHLEBAS
THE PLAYER OF GAMES
USE OF WEAPONS
THE STATE OF THE ART
FEERSUM ENDJINN
EXCESSION

THE CROW ROAD

Iain Banks

An *Abacus* Book

First published in Great Britain by Scribners
This edition published by Abacus 1993
Reprinted 1993 (twice), 1994, 1995 (twice), 1996 (three times), 1997

Copyright © 1992 Iain Banks

The right of Iain Banks to be identified as
author of this work has been asserted by
him in accordance with the Copyright, Designs
and Patents Act 1988.

*All characters in this publication are fictitious
and any resemblance to real persons, living or dead,
is purely coincidental.*

All rights reserved.
No part of this publication may be reproduced,
stored in a retrieval system, or transmitted, in any
form or by any means, without the prior
permission in writing of the publisher, nor be
otherwise circulated in any form of binding or
cover other than that in which it is published and
without a similar condition including this
condition being imposed on the subsequent purchaser.

A CIP catalogue record for this book
is available from the British Library.

Typeset by Leaper & Gard Ltd, Bristol
Printed in England by Clays Ltd, St Ives plc

Abacus
A Division of
Little, Brown and Company (UK)
Brettenham House
Lancaster Place
London WC2E 7EN

Again, for Ann,
And with thanks to:

James Hale,
Mic Cheetham,
Andy Watson
and Steve Hatton

CHAPTER

It was the day my grandmother exploded. I sat in the crematorium, listening to my Uncle Hamish quietly snoring in harmony to Bach's Mass in B Minor, and I reflected that it always seemed to be death that drew me back to Gallanach.

I looked at my father, sitting two rows away in the front line of seats in the cold, echoing chapel. His broad, greying-brown head was massive above his tweed jacket (a black arm-band was his concession to the solemnity of the occasion). His ears were moving in a slow, oscillatory manner, rather in the way John Wayne's shoulders moved when he walked; my father was grinding his teeth. Probably he was annoyed that my grandmother had chosen religious music for her funeral ceremony. I didn't think she had done it to upset him; doubtless she had simply liked the tune, and had not anticipated the effect its non-secular nature might have on her eldest son.

My younger brother, James, sat to my father's left. It was the first time in years I'd seen him without his Walkman, and he looked distinctly uncomfortable, fiddling with his single earring. To my father's right my mother sat, upright and trim, neatly filling a black coat and sporting a dramatic black hat shaped like a flying saucer. The UFO dipped briefly to one side as she whispered something to my father. In that movement and that moment, I felt a pang of loss that did not entirely belong to my recently departed grandmother, yet was connected with her memory. How her moles would be itching today if she was somehow suddenly reborn!

'Prentice!' My Aunt Antonia, sitting next to me, with Uncle Hamish snoring mellifluously on her other side, tapped my sleeve and pointed at my feet as she murmured my name. I looked down.

I had dressed in black that morning, in the cold high room of my aunt and uncle's house. The floorboards had creaked and my breath had smoked. There had been ice inside the small dormer window, obscuring the view over Gallanach in a crystalline mist. I'd pulled on a pair of black underpants I'd brought especially from Glasgow, a white shirt (fresh from Marks and Sparks, the pack-lines still ridging the cold crisp cotton) and my black 501s. I'd shivered, and sat on the bed, looking at two pairs of socks; one black, one white. I'd intended to wear the black pair under my nine-eye Docs with the twin ankle buckles, but suddenly I had felt that the boots were wrong. Maybe it was because they were matt finish . . .

The last funeral I'd been to here – also the first funeral I'd ever been to – this gear had all seemed pretty appropriate, but now I was pondering the propriety of the Docs, the 501s and the black biker's jacket. I'd hauled my white trainers out of the bag, tried one Nike on and one boot (unlaced); I'd stood in front of the tilted full-length mirror, shivering, my breath going out in clouds, while the floorboards creaked and a smell of cooking bacon and burned toast insinuated its way up from the kitchen.

The trainers, I'd decided.

So I peered down at them in the crematorium; they looked crumpled and tea-stained on the severe black granite of the chapel floor. Oh-oh; one black sock, one white. I wriggled in my seat, pulled my jeans down to cover my oddly-packaged ankles. 'Hell's teeth,' I whispered. 'Sorry, Aunt Tone.'

My Aunt Antonia – a ball of pink-rinse hair above the bulk of her black coat, like candy floss stuck upon a hearse – patted my leather jacket. 'Never mind, dear,' she sighed. 'I doubt old Margot would have minded.'

'No,' I nodded. My gaze fell back to the trainers. It struck me that on the toe of the right one there was still discernible the tyre mark from Grandma Margot's wheelchair. I lifted the left trainer onto the right, and rubbed without enthusiasm at the black herring-bone pattern the oily wheel had left. I remembered the day, six months earlier, when I had pushed old Margot out of the house and through the courtyard, past the outhouses and down the drive under the trees towards the loch and the sea.

*

'Prentice, what *is* going on between you and Kenneth?'

The courtyard was cobbled; her wheelchair wobbled and jerked under my hands as I pushed her. 'We've fallen out, gran,' I told her.

'I'm not stupid, Prentice, I can see that.' She looked up at me. Her eyes were fierce and grey, as they always had been. Her hair was grey now, too, and thinning. The summer sun cleared the surrounding oaks and I could see her pale scalp through the wisps of white.

'No, gran, I know you're not stupid.'

'Well, then?' She waved her stick towards the outhouses. 'Let's see if that damn car's still there.' She glanced back at me again as I wheeled the chair round on its new heading, towards the green double doors of one of the courtyard garages. '*Well*, then?' she repeated.

I sighed. 'It's a matter of principle, gran.' Stopping at the garage doors, she used her stick to knock the hasp off its staple, pushed at one door till its planks bowed slightly, then, wedging her stick into the resulting gap, levered the other door open, a bolt at one corner scraping and tinkling through a groove worn in the cobbles. I pulled the chair back to let the garage door swing. Inside it was dark. Motes swirled in the sunlight falling across the black entrance. I could just make out the corner of a thin green tarpaulin, draped angularly about level with my waist. Grandma Margot lifted the edge of the tarp with her stick, and flicked it away with surprising strength. The cover fell away from the front of the car and I pushed her further into the garage.

'Principle?' she said, leaning forward in the chair to inspect the long dark bonnet of the car, and pushing the tarp back still further until she had revealed the auto up to its windscreen. The wheels had no tyres; the car rested on blocks of wood. 'What principle? The principle of not entering your father's house? Your own family home?' Another flick of the cane and the covering moved up the screen, then fell back again.

'Let me do that, gran.' I stepped to the side of the car and pulled the tarpaulin back until it lay crumpled on the boot, revealing that the car had a missing rear window. More dust revolved in the light from outside, turning Grandma Margot into a seated silhouette, her almost transparent hair shining like a halo.

She sighed. I looked at the car. It was long and quite beautiful, in a recently-old-fashioned way. Beneath the patina of dust it was a very dark green. The roof above the missing rear window was battered and dented, as was the exposed part of the boot lid.

'Poor old thing,' I whispered, shaking my head.

Grandma Margot sat upright. 'It or me?' she said sharply.

'Gran . . .' I said, tutting. I was aware that she could see me very well, sunlit from behind her, while all I could see of her was a dark shape, a subtraction of the light.

'Anyway,' she said, relaxing and poking at one of the car's wire wheels with her walking stick. 'What's all this nonsense about a matter of principle?'

I turned away, rubbing my fingers along the chrome guttering over a rear door. 'Well … dad's angry at me because I told him I believed in … God, or in something, anyway.' I shrugged, not daring to look at her. 'He won't … well, I won't … We're not talking to each other, so I won't come into the house.'

Grandma Margot made a clucking noise with her mouth. 'That's it?'

I nodded, glancing at her. 'That's it, gran.'

'And your father's money; your allowance?'

'I –' I began, then didn't know how to put it.

'Prentice; how are you managing to survive?'

'I'm managing fine,' (I lied.) 'On my grant.' (Another lie.) 'And my student loan.' (Yet another lie.) 'And I'm doing some bar work.' (Four in a row!) I couldn't get a bar job. Instead I'd sold Fraud Siesta, my car. It had been a small Ford and kind of lazy about starting. People used to imply it looked battered, but I just told them it came from a broken garage. Anyway, that money was almost gone now, too.

Grandma Margot let out a long sigh, shook her head. 'Principles,' she breathed.

She pulled herself forward a little, but the wheelchair was caught on part of the tarp. 'Help me here, will you?'

I went behind her, pushed the chair over the ruffled canvas. She hauled open the offside rear door and looked into the dull interior. A smell of musty leather wafted out, reminding me of my childhood and the time when there was still magic in the world.

'The last time I had sex was on that back seat,' she said wistfully. She looked up at me. 'Don't look so shocked, Prentice.'

'I wasn't –' I started to protest.

'It's all right; it was your grandfather.' She patted the wing of the car with one thin hand. 'After a dance,' she said quietly, smiling. She looked up at me again, her lined, delicate face amused, eyes glittering. 'Prentice,' she laughed. 'You're blushing!'

'Sorry, gran,' I said. 'It's just … well, you don't … well, when you're young and somebody's . . .'

'Past it,' she said, and slammed the door shut; dust duly danced. 'Well, we're all young once, Prentice, and those that are lucky get to be old.' She pushed the wheelchair back, over the toe of my new trainers. I lifted the chair clear and helped complete the manoeuvre, then pushed her to the door. I left her there while I put the tarpaulin back over the car.

'In fact some of us get to be young twice,' she said from the doorway. 'When we go senile: toothless, incontinent, babbling like a baby . . .' Her voice trailed off.

'Grandma, please.'

'Och, stop being so sensitive, Prentice; it isn't much fun getting old. One of the few pleasures that do come your way is to speak your mind . . . Certainly annoying your relatives is enjoyable too, but I expected better of you.'

'I'm sorry, Grandma.' I closed the garage door, dusted off my hands, and took up my position at the back of the wheelchair again. There was an oily tyre print on my trainer. Crows raucoused in the surrounding trees above as I pushed my gran towards the drive.

'Lagonda.'

'Sorry, Gran?'

'The car; it's a Lagonda Rapide Saloon.'

'Yes,' I said, smiling a little ruefully to myself. 'Yes, I know.'

We left the courtyard and went crunchily down the gravel drive towards the sparkling waters of the loch. Grandma Margot was humming to herself; she sounded happy. I wondered if she was recalling her tryst in the Lagonda's back seat. Certainly I was recalling mine; it was on the same piece of cracked and creaking, buttoned and fragrant upholstery – some years after my gran's last full sexual experience – that I had had my first.

This sort of thing keeps happening in my family.

*

'Ladies and Gentlemen of the family; on the one hand, as I don't doubt you may well imagine, it gives me no great pleasure to stand here before you at this time ... yet on the other hand I am proud, and indeed honoured, to have been asked to speak at the funeral of my dear old client, the late and greatly loved Margot McHoan ...'

My grandmother had asked the family lawyer, Lawrence L. Blawke, to say the traditional few words. Pencil-thin and nearly as leaden, the tall and still dramatically black-haired Mr Blawke was dressed somewhere in the high nines, sporting a dark grey double-breasted suit over a memorable purple waistcoat that took its inspiration from what looked like Mandelbrot but might more charitably have been Paisley. A glittering gold fob watch the size of a small frying pan was anchored in the shallows of one waistcoat pocket by a bulk-carrier grade chain.

Mr Blawke always reminded me of a heron; I'm not sure why. Something to do with a sense of rapacious stillness perhaps, and also the aura of one who knows that time is on his side. I *thought* he had looked oddly comfortable in the presence of the undertakers.

I sat and listened to the lawyer and in short order wondered (a) why Grandma Margot had chosen a lawyer to make the address, (b) whether he'd be charging us for his time, and (c) how many others of my family were wondering the same things.

'... long history of the McHoan family in the town of Gallanach, of which she was so proud, and to which she so ... usefully and, and industriously contributed throughout her long life. It was my privilege to know and serve both Margot and her late husband Matthew well, in Matthew's case first as a school friend, back in the twenties. I well remember ...'

*

'Grandma, I mean; good grief.'

'What?'

My grandmother drew deeply on the Dunhill, flicked her wrist to close the brass Zippo, then put the lighter back in her cardigan.

'Grandma, you're smoking.'

Margot coughed a little and blew the smoke towards me, a grey screen for those ash-coloured eyes. 'Well, so I am.' She inspected the cigarette closely, then took another drag. 'I always wanted to, you know,' she told me, and looked away, over the loch towards the hills and trees on the far side. I'd wheeled her down to the shore path at Pointhouse near the old cairns. I sat on the grass. A soft breeze disturbed the water; seagulls flew stiff-winged, and in the distance the occasional car or truck disturbed the air, making a lazy throat-clearing noise as they emerged from or disappeared into the channel the main road drove between the trees. 'Hilda used to smoke,' she said quietly, not looking at me. 'My elder sister; she used to smoke. And I always wanted to.' I picked up a handful of pebbles from the path-side and started throwing them at the waves, lapping against the rocks a metre below us, almost at high tide. 'But your grandfather wouldn't let me.' My grandmother sighed.

'But gran,' I protested. 'It's bad for you.'

'I know.' She smiled broadly. 'That was another reason I didn't ever take it up, after your grandfather died; they'd found it was unhealthy by then.' She laughed. 'But I'm seventy-two years old now, and I don't give a damn.'

I chucked a few more pebbles. 'Well, it isn't a very good example to us youngsters, is it?'

'What's that got to do with the price of sliced bread?'

'Eh?' I looked at her. 'Pardon?'

'You're not really trying to tell me that young people today look to their elders for an *example*, are you, Prentice?'

I grimaced. 'Well . . .' I said.

'You'd be the first generation that did.' She pulled on the cigarette, a look of convincing derision on her face. 'Best do everything they don't. That's what tends to happen anyway, like it or lump it.' She nodded to herself and ground the cigarette out on her cast, near the knee; flicked the butt into the water. I tutted under my breath.

'People react more than they act, Prentice,' she said eventually. 'Like you are with your dad; he raises you to be a good little atheist and then you go and get religion. Well, that's just the way of things.' I could almost hear her shrug. 'Things can get imbalanced in families, over the generations. Sometimes a new one has to ... adjust things.' She tapped me on the shoulder. I turned. Her hair was very white against the rich summer green of the Argyllshire hills and the brilliant blue of the sky beyond. 'D'you feel for this family, Prentice?'

'*Feel* for it, gran?'

'Does it mean anything to you?' She looked cross. 'Anything beyond the obvious, like giving you a place to stay ... well, when you aren't falling out with your father? Does it?'

'Of course, gran.' I felt awkward.

She leaned closer to me, eyes narrowing. 'I have this theory, Prentice.'

My heart foundered. 'Yes, gran?'

'In every generation, there's a pivot. Somebody everybody else revolves around, understand?'

'Up to a point,' I said, non-committally, I hoped.

'It was old Hugh, then your grandfather, then it was me, and then it got all confused with Kenneth and Rory and Hamish; they each seem to think they were it, but ...'

'Dad certainly seems to think he's paterfamilias.'

'Aye, and maybe Kenneth has the strongest claim, though I still think Rory was more clever. Your Uncle Hamish ...' She looked troubled. 'He's a bit off the beaten track, that boy.' She frowned. (This 'boy' was nearly fifty, of course, and himself a grandfather. It was Uncle Hamish who'd invented Newton's Religion, and who had taken me in when my father and I had fallen out.)

'I wonder where Uncle Rory is,' I said, hoping to divert my gran from areas that sounded portentous and daft with the familiar game that anybody in our family can play; making up stories, conjectures, lies and hopes about Uncle Rory, our one-time golden boy, professional traveller and some-time magician, whose most successful act had been his own disappearance.

'Who knows?' My gran sighed. 'Might be dead, for all we know.'

I shook my head. 'No, I don't think so.'

'You sound certain, Prentice. What do you know we don't?'

'I just feel it.' I shrugged, threw a handful of pebbles into the waves. 'He'll be back.'

'Your father thinks he will,' Margot agreed, sounding thoughtful. 'He always talks about him as though he's still around.'

'He'll be back,' I nodded, and lay back in the grass, hands under my head.

'I don't know, though,' Grandma Margot said. 'I think he might be dead.'

'Dead? Why?' The sky was deep, shining blue.

'You wouldn't believe me.'

'What?' I sat up again, swivelled to face her, looking over the much-scribbled-upon grey-white cast (as well as signatures, get-well-soon messages and silly drawings, there were at least two shopping lists, a recipe copied down from the radio and detailed instructions on how to get by car to the flat I shared in Glasgow).

Grandma Margot pulled up her sleeve to expose her white, darkly spotted right forearm. 'I have my moles, Prentice. They tell me things.'

I laughed. She looked inscrutable. 'Sorry, gran?'

She tapped her wrist with one long pale finger; there was a large brown mole there. Her eyes were narrowed. She leaned closer still and tapped the mole again. 'Not a sausage, Prentice.'

'Well,' I said, not sure whether to try another laugh. 'No.'

'Not for eight years, not a hint, not a sensation.' Her voice was low, almost husky. She looked as though she was enjoying herself.

'I give in, gran; what are you talking about?'

'My moles, Prentice.' She arched one eyebrow, then sat back with a sigh in her wheelchair. 'I can tell what's going on in this family by my moles. They itch when people are talking about me, or when something . . . remarkable is happening to the person.' She frowned. 'Well, usually.' She glared at me, prodded me in the shoulder with her stick. 'Don't tell your father about this; he'd have me committed.'

'Gran! Of course not! And he wouldn't, anyway!'

'I wouldn't be too sure of that.' Her eyes narrowed again.

I leant on one of the chair's wheels. 'Let me get this right; your *moles* itch when one of us is talking about you?'

She nodded, grim. 'Sometimes they hurt, sometimes they tickle. And they can itch in different ways, too.'

'And that mole's Uncle Rory's?' I nodded incredulously at the big mole on her right wrist.

'That's right,' she said, tapping the stick on one footrest of the wheelchair. She held up her wrist and fixed the raised brown spot with an accusatory glare. 'Not a sausage, for eight years.'

I stared at the dormant eruption with a sort of nervous respect, mingled with outright disbelief. 'Wow,' I said at last.

*

'. . . survived by her daughter Ilsa, and sons Kenneth, Hamish and Roderick.' The good lawyer Blawke had helpfully nodded at my dad and my uncle when he mentioned them. Dad kept on grinding his teeth; Uncle Hamish stopped snoring and gave a little start at the mention of his name; he opened his eyes and looked round – a little wildly, I thought – before relaxing once more. His eyelids started to droop again almost immediately. At the mention of Uncle Rory's name Mr Blawke looked about the crowded chapel as though expecting Uncle Rory to make a sudden and dramatic appearance. 'And, sharing, I'm sure, in the family's grief, the husband of her dear late daughter, Fiona.' Here Mr Blawke looked very serious, and did indeed grasp his lapels for a moment, as he nodded, gravely, at Uncle Fergus. 'Mr Urvill,' Mr Blawke said, completing the nod that had developed pretensions to a bow, I thought, and then clearing his throat. This genuflection completed, the reference to past tragedy duly made, most of the people who had turned to look at Uncle Fergus turned away again.

My head stayed turned.

Uncle Fergus is an interesting enough fellow in himself, and (of course) as Mr Blawke knew to his benefit, probably Gallanach's richest and certainly its most powerful man. But I wasn't looking at him.

Beside the thick-necked bulk of the Urvill of Urvill (soberly resplendent in what I assumed was the family's mourning tartan – blackish purple, blackish green and fairly dark black) sat neither of his two daughters, Diana and Helen – those long-legged visions of money-creamed, honey-skinned, globetrotting loveliness – but instead his niece, the stunning, the fabulous, the golden-haired, vellus-faced, diamond-eyed Verity, upwardly nubile scionette of the house of Urvill, the jewel beside the jowls; the girl who, for me, had put the lectual in intellectual, and phany in epiphany and the ibid in libidinous!

Such bliss to look. I feasted my eyes on that gracefully angular form, just this side of her uncle and sitting quietly in black. She had worn a white quilted skiing jacket outside, but now had taken it off in the unfittingly chilly crematorium, and sat in a black blouse and black skirt, black ... tights? Stockings? My God, the sheer force of joy in just imagining! and black shoes. And shivering! The slick material of the blouse trembling in the light from the translucent panes overhead, black silk hanging in folds of shade from her breasts, quivering! I felt my chest expand and my eyes widen. I was just about to look away, reckoning that I had gazed to the limits of decency, when that shaven-sided, crop-haired head swivelled and lowered, her calm face turning this way. I saw those eyes, shaded by her thick and shockingly black brows, blink slowly; she looked at me.

Small smile, and those diamond eyes piercing, marking me.

Then the gaze removed, refixed, directed somewhere else, once more facing the front. My neck felt un-oiled as I turned away, blasted and raddled by the urge of that directed consideration.

Verity Walker. Eating my heart out. Consuming my soul.

*

'And dad's mole?'

'Here,' Grandma Margot said, tapping her left shoulder. She laughed a little as we went along the path between the shore and the trees. 'That one itches fairly often.'

'And mine?' I asked, plodding after the wheelchair. I'd taken my biker's jacket off and it lay now on my gran's lap.

She looked up at me, her expression unreadable. 'Here.' She patted her tummy, looked forward again. 'Pivotal, wouldn't you say, Prentice?'

'Ha,' I said, still trying to sound non-committal. 'Could be. What about Uncle Hamish? Where's he at?'

'Knee,' she said, tapping the plaster on her leg.

'How *is* your leg, gran?'

'Fine,' she said tetchily. 'Plaster comes off next week. Can't happen soon enough.'

The wheels of the chair sighed through the grass on either side of the narrow path. I remembered something I'd been meaning to ask.

'What were you doing up that tree anyway, gran?'

'Trying to saw a branch off.'

'What for?'

'To stop those damn squirrels using it as a diving board to get to my bird table, that's what for.' She used her stick to whack a crumpled drinking-yoghurt bottle off the path and into the water.

'You could have asked somebody else.'

'I'm not totally incapable, Prentice. I'd have been all right if that hoodie hadn't started dive-bombing me; ungrateful wretch.'

'Oh, it was a bird's fault, was it?' I had a mental picture of some beetle-eyed carrion crow swooping on my gran, knocking her off her ladder. Maybe it had seen *The Omen.*

'Yes, it was.' Grandma Margot twisted in her wheelchair and raised both her stick and her voice. 'And a few years ago I'd only have been bruised, as well. Brittle bones are one of the things that make getting old such a damn nuisance, too, especially if you're a woman.' She nodded brusquely. 'So think yourself lucky.'

'Okay,' I smiled.

'Damn birds,' she muttered, glaring at a stand of ash trees on the edge of the plantation with such severity that I half expected to hear a parliament of crows cry out in answer. 'Ach well,' she shrugged. 'Let's head back to the house; I need to go.'

'Right you are,' I said, and wheeled the chair around. Grandma Margot lit another cigarette.

'That branch is still there, by the way.'

'I'll deal with it.'

'Good lad.'

A lark trilled, high overhead.

I wheeled my gran back along the path by the water, over the main road and up the gravel drive, through the sunlit cobbled courtyard towards the tall house with the crow-stepped gables.

I cut the offending branch down that afternoon, before I went back to Gallanach, to my Uncle Hamish's house, for tea. My dad arrived while I was up the ladder, sawing away at the sappy oak and swatting at flies. He stopped and looked at me when he got out of the Audi, then he disappeared into the house. I kept on sawing.

*

My great-great-great grandfather, Stewart McHoan, was buried in a coffin made from black glass by the craftsmen he had commanded in his capacity as manager of the Gallanach Glass Works (a post now filled by my Uncle Hamish). Grandma Margot had gone for the more conventional wooden model; it slid away into the wall as Bach's Mass reached one of its choral climaxes. A wood-fronted door slid back up to block the hole the coffin had disappeared into, then a little purple curtain lowered itself over the doorway.

The head honcho of the undertakers supervised us as we all formed up for what was obviously the important and formal business of Leaving The Chapel. My father and mother left first. 'I told you we sat in the wrong place, Tone,' I heard my Uncle Hamish whisper behind me. (Aunt Tone just went 'Ssh!')

Outside it was a calmly sombre day, chill and a little damp. I could smell leaves being burned somewhere. The view down the crematorium's birch-lined drive led towards the town and the ocean. In the distance, through the haze, North Jura was dark pastel and flat-looking on the unruffled grey blanket of sea. I looked around; dark-dressed people were everywhere amongst the parked cars, talking quietly. Their breath rose in clouds through the still air. Uncle Hamish was talking to the lawyer Blawke; Aunt Antonia to my mother. Dad was with the Urvills. The wonderful Verity was mostly hidden by my father, her snow-white ski jacket in eclipse behind the old man's tweed coat. I considered shifting my position so I could see her properly, but decided against it; somebody might notice.

At least, I thought brightly, she was here alone. For the last two years that I'd been worshipping Verity from afar she'd been going out with a gorm-free creature called Rodney Ritchie; his parents owned Ritchie's Reliable Removals in Edinburgh and were keen on alliteration. My father had met them once and coined a new collective noun: an embarrassment of Ritchies.

Anyway, Urvill family gossip had it that Verity might be coming to her senses regarding Rodney's removal, and it was a positive and encouraging sign that she had turned up here without the geek in tow. I thought about approaching her. Maybe when we got back to the castle.

I also thought about talking to James, but little brother was leaning against the crematorium wall looking bored but cool in his borrowed great-coat, earplugs in, getting his Walkman fix at last. Still mainlining The Doors, probably. For a moment I almost missed my elder brother, Lewis, who hadn't been able to make it back for the funeral. Lewis is better-looking, smarter and wittier than I am, so I don't miss him often.

I was standing beside Uncle Hamish's Jaguar. Maybe I should just get into the car. Or find somebody else to talk to. I could feel that an attack of awkwardness – the kind of episode I am unhappily prone to – was imminent.

'Hi, Prentice. You okay?'

The voice was deep and throaty but female. Ashley Watt strolled up, put her hand on the side of my shoulder, patting. Her brother Dean was just behind. I nodded.

'Yeah. Yeah; fine. How's yourself? Hi, Dean.'

'Hi, man.'

'You just back for this?' Ash asked, nodding her head at the low grey granite of the crematorium buildings. Her long fawn hair was gathered up; her strong, angular face, dominated by a blade of a nose and a pair of large round-lensed glasses, was concerned and sad. Ash was my age, but she always made me feel younger.

'Yeah; back to Glasgow on Monday.' I looked down. 'Wow, Ash; I don't think I've ever seen you in a skirt before.' Ash always wore jeans. We'd known each other since we'd used to crawl around on the same carpets together, but I couldn't remember seeing her in anything else but jeans. Yet there were her legs all right; pretty good-looking ones too, under a knee-length black skirt. She wore a big naval-looking jacket with the cuffs turned over, and black gloves; medium-high heels made her the same height as me.

She grinned. 'Short memory, Prentice. Recall school?'

'Oh, yeah,' I nodded, still looking at the legs. 'Apart from then, though.' I shrugged, smiled warily at her. I'd gone through a protracted Unbearable stage while I'd been at high school – it had lasted from my first day through to about fourth year – and the most vivid memory I had of Ash from that time was when I and her two brothers had carried out a highly successful snowball ambush on her, her sister and their pals as they'd walked back from school one dark evening. *Somebody's* snowball had broken that long sharp nose of Ashley's, and I suspected it had been one of mine if for no other reason than because as far as I knew nobody else had been deploying snowballs whose ballistic properties had been enhanced by the judicious reinforcement of their cores with moderately sizeable chuckie stones.

Her nose had been reset, of course, and we'd got on better since we'd each left school. Ash frowned a little, her slightly magnified grey eyes searching mine.

'I was sorry to hear about the old lady. All of us were.' She swivelled briefly to Dean, standing lighting up a Regal behind her. He nodded; black jeans and a dark blue crombie that looked like it had seen better decades.

I wasn't sure what to say. 'I'll miss her,' I said eventually. I'd been trying not to think about it, ever since I'd heard the news.

'Was it a heart attack, aye, Prentice?' Dean inquired through his cloud of smoke.

'No,' I said. 'She fell off a ladder.'

'I thought she did that last year,' Ash said.

'She did; off a tree. This time she was clearing the gutters. The ladder slipped and she went through the conservatory roof. She was dead by the time they got her to the hospital. Shock from blood-loss, apparently.'

'Oh, Prentice, I'm sorry,' Ash said, and put her hand on my arm.

Dean shook his head and looked mystified. 'Ah thought she had a heart attack.'

'She did have one,' I nodded. 'About five years ago; got a pacemaker fitted.'

'Maybe she had a heart attack while she was up the ladder,' Dean suggested. Ash kicked his shin. 'Oo-ya!' he said.

'Excuse Mr Sensitivity here,' Ash said. 'But like I said: we were all really sorry to hear, Prentice.' She looked around. 'Haven't seen Lewis here; could he not make it?'

'He's in Australia,' I sighed. 'Being funny.'

'Ah.' Ash nodded, smiling faintly. 'Well, that's a shame.'

'For the Australians, perhaps,' I said.

Ash looked sad, even pitying. 'Aw, Prentice –'

Dean prodded his sister in the back with the hand he wasn't rubbing his shin with. 'Hoi; what was that about yon guy ye bumped into in that jacuzzi in Berlin? Said ye were goantae tell –'

'Oh yeah ...' Ash turned from frowning at her brother to frowning at me, took a breath, then let it out. 'Hey; you fancy a pint later, Prentice?'

'Well, maybe,' I said. 'I think we're ordered up to the castle for drinks and a bite to eat.' I shrugged. 'This evening?'

'Okie-dokie,' Ash nodded.

'A *jacuzzi*?' I asked, looking at Dean and Ash in turn. '*Berlin*?'

Dean grinned broadly and nodded.

Ash said, 'Aye, Prentice; watchin the wa' come doon. And a shocking and decadent tale it is, too, let me tell you. See you in the Jacobite about eight?'

'Right you are,' I said. I leaned close and nudged her. 'What jacuzzi?'

I saw the expression on Dean's face, then heard the noise, then watched Ashley's gaze rise from my face to fasten somewhere over my left shoulder. I turned slowly.

The car came screaming up the crematorium drive, leaves swirling into the air behind. It was a green Rover, and it had to be doing sixty. Probably exceeding the previous speed record within the crematorium grounds by a factor of at least three. It was heading more or less straight for us, and braking distance was running out fast.

'That no Doctor Fyfe's car?' Dean said, as Ash grabbed my sleeve and started to pull me back, at the same time as the Rover's engine note fell from its wail, its nose dipped and the rear end wavered as the tyres tried to bite the moist tarmac.

'I thought he had an Orion,' I said, as Ashley pulled Dean and me past the rear of Uncle Hamish's car and onto the grass. Everybody in the crowd outside the crematorium was watching the green 216 as it skidded to a stop, avoiding a head-on collision with the Urvill's Bentley Eight by only a few centimetres. The tyres rasped on the tarmac. Doctor Fyfe – for indeed, that was who it was – jumped out of the driver's seat. He was as small, rotund and bewhiskered as ever, but today his face was red and his eyes were staring.

'Stop!' he yelled, slamming the door and running for the chapel entrance as fast as his little legs would carry him. 'Stop!' he shouted again; a little unnecessarily, I thought, as everybody had quite entirely stopped whatever they'd been doing some time before his car had even begun braking. 'Stop!'

I still insist that I heard a muffled crump at this point, but nobody believes me. That was when it happened, though.

The sensitive morticians who run the Gallanach Corporation Crematorium usually wait until night before they burn the bodies, to avoid the possibility of resulting smoke-plumes sending overwrought relations into unsightly paroxysms of grief, but Grandma Margot had specified that she wanted to be incinerated immediately; her cremation was therefore genuinely under way as we stood there.

'Ah!' said Doctor Fyfe, stumbling just before he was intercepted before the door of the chapel by a concerned undertaker. 'Ah!' he said again, and crumpled, first into the undertaker's arms and then to the ground. He was on his knees briefly, then turned and sat down, clutched at his chest, stared at the granite flagstones outside the chapel, and to the assembled, still stunned and quieted crowd of us announced, 'I'm sorry, folks, but I believe I'm having a coronary . . .' and keeled over on his back.

There was an instant when nothing much seemed to happen. Then Dean Watt nudged me with the hand holding his Regal and said quietly, 'There's a funny thing, eh?'

'Dean!' hissed Ashley, as people crowded round the doctor.

'Oo-ya!'

'Call an ambulance!' somebody shouted.

'Use the hearse!' yelled my dad.

'Och, it's only a bruise,' Dean muttered, rubbing vigorously at his shin. 'Oo-ya! Will ye *quit* that!'

They used the hearse, and got Doctor Fyfe to the local hospital in ample time to save his life if not his professional reputation.

The muffled crump – which I still maintain that I heard – was my grandmother exploding; Doctor Fyfe had neglected to ask the hospital to remove her pacemaker before she was cremated.

Like I say, this sort of thing keeps happening in my family.

CHAPTER
2

These were the days of fond promise, when the world was very small and there was still magic in it. He told them stories of the Secret Mountain and the Sound that could be Seen, of the Forest drowned by Sand and the trees that were time-stilled waters; he told them about the Slow Children and the Magic Duvet and the Well-Travelled Country, and they believed all of it. They learned of distant times and long-ago places, of who they were and what they weren't, and of what had and what had never been.

Then, every day was a week, each month a year. A season was a decade, and every year a life.

*

'But dad, Mrs McBeath says there is so a God, and you'll go to a bad place.'

'Mrs McBeath is an idiot.'

'No she's no, dad! She's a teacher!'

'No she's not, or better still, no she *isn't*. Don't use the word "no" when you mean "not".'

'But she's *no* a niddyott, dad! She *is* a teacher. Honest.'

He stopped on the path, turned to look at the boy. The other children stopped too, grinning and giggling. They were almost at the top of the hill, just above the Forestry Commission's arbitrary tree line. The cairn was visible, a lump on the sky-line. 'Prentice,' he said. 'People can be teachers and idiots; they can be philosophers and idiots; they can be politicians and idiots ... in fact I think they have to be ... a *genius* can be an idiot. The world is largely run for and by idiots; it is no great handicap in life and in certain areas is actually a distinct advantage and even a prerequisite for advancement.'

Several of the children giggled.

'Uncle Kenneth,' Helen Urvill sang out. 'Our daddy said you were a commie.' Her sister, alongside her on the path and holding her hand, gave a little squeal and put her free hand up to her mouth.

'Your father is absolutely correct, Helen,' he smiled. 'But only in the pejorative sense, and not the practical one, unfortunately.'

Diana squealed again and hid her face, giggling. Helen looked puzzled.

'But dad,' Prentice said, pulling at his sleeve. 'Dad, Mrs McBeath *is* a teacher, really she is, and she said there is so a God.'

'And so did Mr Ainstie, too, dad,' Lewis added.

'Yes, I've talked to Mr Ainstie,' McHoan told the older boy. 'He thinks we should send troops to help the Americans in Viet Nam.'

'He an idiot too, dad?' Lewis hazarded, decoding the sour expression on his father's face.

'Definitely.'

'So there isnae a God, eh no Mr McHoan?'

'No, Ashley, there isn't.'

'Whit aboot Wombles, Mr McHoan?'

'What's that, Darren?'

'The Wombles, Mr McHoan. Of Wimbledon Common.' Darren Watt was holding the hand of his little brother, Dean, who was staring up at McHoan and looking like he was about to burst into tears. 'Are they real, Mr McHoan?'

'Of course they are,' he nodded. 'You've seen them on television, haven't you?'

'Aye.'

'Aye. Well then, of course they're real; real puppets.'

'But they're no *really* real, naw?'

'No, Darren, they're not really real; the real creatures on the real Wimbledon Common are mice and birds and maybe foxes and badgers, and none of them wear clothes and live in nice well-lit burrows with furniture. A lady made up the Wombles, and made up stories about them, and then people made the stories into television programmes. That's what's real.'

'See, ah told ye,' Darren said, shaking his little brother's hand. 'They're no real.'

Dean started to cry, face screwing up, eyes closing.

'Oh, good grief,' McHoan breathed. It never ceased to amaze him how quickly a small child's face could turn from peach to beetroot. His own youngest, James, was just leaving that stage, thank goodness. 'Come on, Dean; up you come up here and we'll see if we can get to the top of this hill, eh?' He lifted the howling child up – after he'd been persuaded to let go of his brother's hand – and put him on his shoulders. He looked at the little up-turned faces. 'We're nearly there, aren't we? See the cairn?'

There was a general noise of agreement from the assembled children.

'Come on, then! Last one there's a Tory!'

He started off up the path; Dean was crying more quietly now. The other children ran round and past him, laughing and shouting and scrambling straight up the hillside, over the grass towards the cairn. He quit the path and started after them, then – holding

Dean's legs – turned to look back at Diana and Helen, who were still standing quietly, hand-in-hand, on the path. 'You two not playing?'

Helen, identically dressed to her sister in little new green dungarees and staring out from under her precisely-trimmed black fringe, shook her head, frowned. 'We better go last, Uncle Kenneth.'

'Oh? Why?'

'I think we're Tories.'

'You might well turn out to be,' he laughed. 'But we'll give you the benefit of the doubt for now, eh? On you go.'

The twins looked at each other, then, still hand-in-hand, started up the grassy slope after the rest, earnestly concentrating on the business of clumping one foot in front of the other through the long rough grass.

Dean was starting to cry loudly again, probably because he thought his brother and sister were leaving him. McHoan sighed and jogged up the hill after the kids, shouting encouragement and making sure he trailed the last of them to the top and the cairn. He made a great show of being out of breath, and wobbled as he sat down, collapsing dramatically on the grass after setting Dean to one side.

'Oh! You're all too fit for me!'

'Ha, Mr McHoan!' Darren laughed, pointing at him. 'You're the toerag, so ye are!'

He was mystified for a moment, then said, 'Oh. Right. Toe-rag, Tuareg, Tory.' He made a funny face. 'Tora! Tora! Tory!' he laughed, and so did they. He lay in the grass. A warm wind blew.

'What for are all these stones, Mr McHoan?' Ashley Watt asked. She had climbed half-way up the squat cairn, which was about five feet high. She picked up one of the smaller rocks and looked at it.

Kenneth rolled over, letting Prentice and Lewis climb onto his back and kick at his sides, pretending he was a horse. The Watt girl, perched on the cairn, bashed one rock against another, then inspected the struck, whitened surface of the stone she held. He grinned. She was a tyke; dressed in grubby hand-me-downs like the rest of the Watt tribe, she always seemed to have a runny nose, but he liked her. He still thought Ashley was a boy's name (wasn't it from *Gone With The Wind*?), but then if the Watts wanted to call their children Dean and Darren and Ashley, he supposed that was up to them. Could have been Elvis and Tarquin and Marilyn.

'D'you remember the story of the goose that swallowed the diamond?'

'Aye.'

It was one of his stories, one he'd tried out on the children. Market research, his wife called it.

'Why did the goose eat the diamond?'

'Please, Uncle Kenneth!' Diana Urvill said, holding up one hand and trying to click her fingers.

'Yes, Diana.'

'It was hungry.'

'Naw!' Ashley said scornfully from the cairn. She blinked furiously. 'It wiz fur teeth!'

'It *swallowed* it, smarty-pants, so there!' Diana said, leaning towards Ashley and shaking her head.

'Hey!' McHoan said. 'You're both ... sort of right. The goose swallowed the diamond because that's what geese do with things like pebbles that they find; they swallow them so that they go into their ... anybody know?' He looked round them all as best he could without disturbing Lewis and Prentice.

'*Gizzurd*, Mr McHoan!' Ashley shouted, waving the stone she held.

Diana squealed and put her hand to her mouth again.

'Well, a gizzard is part of a bird, too, that's right Ashley,' he said. 'But the diamond actually went into the goose's crop, because, like lots of animals and birds, geese need to keep some wee stones, like pebbles or gravel, in their crop, down here,' he pointed. 'So that they can grind their food up small and digest it better when it goes into their tummy.'

'Please, Mr McHoan, Ah remember!' Ashley shouted. She clutched the stone to her chest, getting her ragged, thin grey jumper a little dirtier.

'Me too, dad!' Prentice shouted.

'And me!'

'Me too!'

'Well,' he said, rolling slowly over and letting Lewis and Prentice slide off his back. He sat up; they sat down. 'Way back, a long long time ago, there were these big enormous animals that used to live in Scotland, and they –'

'What did they look like, dad?' Prentice asked.

'Ah.' McHoan scratched his head through his brown curls. 'Like ... like big hairy elephants ... with long necks. And these big huge animals –'

'What were they called, please, Uncle Kenneth?'

'They were called ... mythosaurs, Helen, and they would swallow rocks ... big rocks, way down into their crops, and they used these rocks to help crunch up their food. They were very very big animals, and very heavy because of all the rocks they carried around inside them, and they usually stayed down in the glens because they were so heavy, and didn't go into the sea or the lochs because they didn't float, and they stayed away from marshes, too, in case they sank. But –'

'Please, Mr McHoan, did they up climb trees, naw?'

'No, Ashley.'

'Naw, ad didnae think so, Mr McHoan.'

'Right. Anyway, when they were very very old and they were going to die, the mythosaurs would come to the tops of hills ... hills just like this one, and they'd lie down, and they would die peacefully, and then after they were dead, their fur and their skin would disappear, and then their insides would disappear too af –'

'Where aboots did their fur and their skin go, please, Mr McHoan?'

'Well, Ashley ... they turned into earth and plants and insects and other wee animals.'

'Oh.'

'And eventually there would just be a skeleton left –'

'Eek,' said Diana, and put her hand over her mouth again.

'Until even that crumbled away and became dust, and –'

'And their tusks, Mr McHoan?'

'Pardon, Ashley?'

'Their tusks. Did they go intae dust as well?'

'Umm ... yes. Yes, they did. So after a while everything was dust ... except for the stones that the big animals had carried in their crops; those lay in a big pile where the mythosaurs had laid down to die, and that,' he turned and slapped one of the larger stones protruding from the base of the rock pile behind him. 'That,' he grinned, because he liked the story he had just thought up and told, 'is where cairns come from.'

'Ah! Ashley! You're standing on stuff that's been in a animal's gizzurd!' Darren shouted, pointing.

'Eaurgh!' Ashley laughed and jumped down, throwing the stones away and rolling on the grass.

There was a deal of general tomfoolery and wee high squealing voices for a while. Kenneth McHoan looked at his watch, and wound it up as he said, 'All right, kids. Time for your dinner. Anybody hungry?'

'Me!'

'Me, dad!'

'We are, Uncle Kenneth.'

'Ah could eat a missasore, so ah could, Mr McHoan!'

He laughed. 'Well, I don't think they're on the menu, Ashley, but not to worry.' He took his pipe out and stood up, filled the bowl and tamped it down. 'Come on, you horrible rabble. Your Aunt Mary's probably got your dinner ready for you by now.'

'Will Uncle Rory be doing tricks, Uncle Kenneth?'

'If you're good, and eat up your vegetables, Helen, aye, he might.'

'Oh good.'

They trooped down. Dean had to be carried because he was tired.

'Dad,' Prentice said, falling back to talk to him while the rest whooped and yelled and capered on the slope. 'Are miffasores real?'

'As real as Wombles, kiddo.'

'As real as Dougal in *The Magic Roundabout*?'

'Every bit. Well, almost.' He drew on the pipe. 'No; just as real. Because the only place anything is ever real is inside your head, Prentice. And the mythosaur exists inside your head, now.'

'Does it, dad?'

'Yes; it used to just exist in my head but now it exists in your head too, and the others'.'

'So is God in Mrs McBeath's head, then?'

'Yep, that's right. He's an idea in her head. Like Father Christmas and the Tooth Fairy.' He looked down at the child. 'Did you like the story about the mythosaur and the cairns?'

'Was it just a story then, dad?'

'Of course it was, Prentice.' He frowned. 'What did you think it was?'

'I don't know, dad. History?'

'Histoire, seulement.'

'What, dad?'

'Nothing, Prentice. No, it was just a story.'

'I think the story about you meeting mum's more better, dad.'

'Just "better" will do, Prentice; the "more" isn't required.'

'Still a better story, dad.'

'Glad you think so, son.'

The children were entering the forest, funnelling into the path between the pines. He looked away then, across the rough geography of bough and leaf, to the village and the station, just visible through the trees.

*

The train chuffed off into the evening, the red light on the final carriage disappearing round the bend in the cutting through the forest; the steam and smoke climbed into the sunset skies beyond. He let the feeling of return wash over and through him, looking across the deserted platform on the far side of the tracks, down across the few lights of Lochgair village to the long electric-blue reflection that was the loch, its gleaming acres imprisoned between the dark masses of the land.

The noise of the train faded slowly, and the quiet susurration of the falls seemed to swell in recompense. He left his bags where they lay and walked to the far end of the platform. The very edge of the platform dropped away there, angling down to the deck of the viaduct over the rushing water beneath. A chest-high wall formed the furthest extent of the rest of the platform.

He rested his arms on the top of the wall and looked down the fifty feet or so to the tumbling white waters. Just upstream, the river Loran piled down from the forest in a compactly furious cataract. The spray was a taste. Beneath, the river surged round the piers of the viaduct that carried the railway on towards Lochgilphead and Gallanach.

A grey shape flitted silently across the view, from falls to bridge, then zoomed, turned in the air and swept into the cutting on the far bank of the river, as though it was a soft fragment of the train's steam that had momentarily lost its way and was now hurrying to catch up. He waited a moment, and the owl hooted once, from inside the dark constituency of forest. He smiled, took a deep breath that tasted of steam and the sweet sharpness of pine resin, and then turned away, went back to pick up his bags.

'Mr Kenneth,' the station master said, taking his ticket at the gate. 'It's yourself. Back from the varsity, are you?'

'Aye, Mr Calder; that's me done with it.'

'You'll be coming back then, will you?'

'Aye, maybe. We'll see.'

'Indeed. Well, I'll tell you now; your sister was here earlier, but wi' the train bein late an that . . .'

'Ach, it's not far to walk.'

'Indeed not, though I'll be shutting up shop very soon now, and I could offer you a lift on the back of my bike if you liked.'

'I'll just walk, thank you.'

'As you will, Kenneth. It's good to see you back.'

'Thank you.'

'Ah . . . that might be her, actually . . .' Mr Calder said, looking down the curve of the station approach. Kenneth heard a car engine, and then headlights swung white light across the iron railings holding the rhododendrons back from the tarmac road.

The big Super Snipe growled into the car park, heeling as it turned and stopping with the passenger's door opposite Kenneth. 'Hello again, Mr Calder!' a voice called out from the driver's seat.

'Evening, Miss Fiona.'

Kenneth threw his bags onto the back, settled into the passenger seat and accepted a kiss from his sister. He was pressed back into the seat as the Humber accelerated off down the road.

'Okay, big brother?'

'Just grand, sis.' The car skidded briefly as it swung onto the main road. He clutched at the grab handle on the door pillar, looked at his sister, sitting hunched over the big steering wheel, dressed in slacks and blouse, her fair hair tied back. 'You have passed your test, haven't you, Fi?'

'Course I have.' A car, coming in the opposite direction, honked at them and flashed its lights. 'Hmm,' she said, frowning.

'Try the dip switch.'

'Ah hah.'

They swept off the main road and into the house drive, roared up between the dark masses of the oaks. Fiona took the car grinding over the gravel, past the old stable block and round the side of the house. He looked back over his shoulder. 'Is that a wall?'

Fiona nodded as she brought the car to a halt in front of the house. 'Dad wants a courtyard, so he's building a wall by the stables,' she said, turning off the engine. 'We're going to have a conservatory overlooking the garden, if mum has her way, which I dare say she will. I think your room's all right, but Hamish's is being redecorated.'

'Heard from him?'

'Getting on famously with the piccaninnies, apparently.'

'Fi; really. They're Rhodesians.'

'They're little black Rhodesians and I shall always think of them as piccaninnies. Blame Enid Blyton, say I. Come on, Uncle Joe; you're just in time for supper.'

They got out; there were lights on in the house, and a couple of bikes lying against the steps curving up to the front door. 'Whose are those?' he asked, taking his bags from the back of the car.

'Couple of lassies camping over there,' Fiona pointed, and he could just make out a dim orange shape, lit from inside, under the elms on the west side of the lawn.

'Friends of yours?'

Fiona shook her head. 'No; just turned up, asked to camp; think they thought we were a farm. They're from Glasgow, I think.' She took his briefcase from him and bounded up the steps to the opened double doors of the porch. He hesitated, reached into the car and took the keys out of the ignition, then glanced at the tent. 'Ken?' Fiona called from the door.

He made a tutting noise and put the keys back, then shook his head and pulled them out again. Not because there were strangers around, and certainly not just because they were from Glasgow, but just because it was irresponsible to leave keys in the car like that; Fiona had to learn. He pocketed the keys and picked up his bags. He glanced over at the tent, just as it flared with light.

'Oh!' he heard Fiona say.

And that was when he first saw Mary Lewis, running out of a tent in her pyjamas with her hair on fire, screaming.

'Christ!' He dropped the bags, ran across the gravel drive towards the girl haring across the grass, hands beating at the blue and orange flames crackling round her head. He leapt down to the lawn, pulling off his jacket as he went. The girl tried to run past him; he tackled her, bringing her down with a ragged thump; he had the jacket over her head before she properly started struggling. After a few seconds, while she whimpered, and the stink of burning hair filled his nostrils, he pulled the jacket away. Fiona came running; another girl, dressed in too-big pyjamas and a fawn duffle coat, and holding a small flat kettle, followed her from the house, wailing.

'Mary! Oh, Mary!'

'Nice tackle, Ken,' Fiona said, kneeling by the girl with the burned hair, who was sitting quivering. He put one arm round her shoulders. The second girl fell to her knees and put both arms round the girl she'd called Mary.

'Oh, hen! Are you all right?'

'I think so,' the girl said, feeling what was left of her hair, and then burst into tears.

He extracted his arm from between the two girls. He brushed his jacket free of grass and burned hair, and put it round the shoulders of the crying girl.

Fiona was pulling bits of hair away and peering at her scalp in the gloom. 'Think you've been lucky, lassie. But we'll call the doctor anyway.'

'Oh no!' the girl wailed, as though this was the worst thing in the world.

'Now, now, Mary,' the other girl said, her voice shaking.

'Come on, let's get into the house,' Kenneth said, rising. 'Take a look at you.' He helped the two girls to their feet. 'Maybe get you a cup of tea, eh?'

'Oh, that's what caused all this in the first place!' Mary said, standing pale and shaking, eyes bright with tears. She gave a sort of desperate laugh. The other girl, still hugging her, laughed too. He smiled, shaking his head. He looked into the girl's face, finally seeing it properly, and thought how bizarrely beautiful she looked, even with half a head of frizzy, whitened hair, and eyes red raw with crying.

Then he realised he was seeing her – and seeing her better all the time – in the light of a flickering glow that was blooming in the west of the garden, under the elms. Her eyes widened as she looked past him. 'The tent!' she howled. 'Oh *no*!'

*

'And I *missed* it! Damn damn damn! I *hate* going to bed this early!'

'Shush. I've told you; now go to sleep.'

'No! What happened next? Did you have to take all her clothes off and put her to bed?'

'No! Don't be ridiculous! Of course not!'

'Oh. That's what happened in this book I read. 'Cept the girl was wet from being in the sea ... she's fallen in the water!' Rory completed the latter part of this sentence in his Bluebottle voice. 'She's fallen in the water!' the wee voice said again, in the darkness of the room.

Kenneth wanted to laugh, but stopped himself. 'Please shut up, Rory.'

'Go on; tell me what happened next.'

'That's it. We all came into the house; mum and dad hadn't even heard anything. I got the hose going eventually but by that time it was too late to save much of the stuff in the tent; and anyway then the primus really blew up, and –'

'What? In an explosion?'

'That's the way things normally blow up, yes.'

'Holy smoke! Oh damn, hell and shite! I missed it.'

'Rory; mind your language!'

'Weeeellll.' Rory turned over in the bed, his feet prodding Kenneth in the back.

'And mind your feet, too.'

'Sorry. So did the doctor come or not?'

'No; she didn't want us to call him, and she wasn't badly hurt; just her hair, really.'

'Waa!' Rory gave a squeal of excitement. 'She's not *bald*, is she?'

'No, she isn't bald. But she'll probably have to wear a scarf or something for a while, I expect.'

'So they're staying in the house, are they? These two lassies from Glasgow? They're in the house?'

'Yes, Mary and Sheena are staying in my room, which is why I've got to sleep with you.'

'Ffworr!'

'Rory, shut up. Go to sleep, for Pete's sake.'

'Okay.' Rory made a great bouncing movement, turning over in bed. Kenneth could feel his brother lying still and tense beside him. He sighed.

He remembered when this had been his room. Before his dad had unblocked the fireplace and put a grate in it, the only heating during the winter had been that ancient paraffin heater they hadn't used since the old house, back in Gallanach. How nostalgic he had felt then, and how distant and separated from Gallanach at first, even though it was only eight miles away over the hills, and just a couple of stops on the train. That heater had been the same height as him, at first, and he'd been told very seriously never ever to touch it, and been slightly frightened of it at the start, but after a while he had grown to love the old enamelled heater.

When it was cold his parents would put it in his room to heat it up before he went to bed, and they would leave it on for a while after they'd said good-night to him, and he'd lie awake, listening to the quiet, puttering, hissing noise it made, and watching the swirling pattern of flame-yellow and shadow-dark it cast on the high ceiling, while the room filled with a delicious warm smell he could never experience after that without a sense of remembered drowsiness.

It had been a precious light, back then; must have been during the war at first, when his dad was using the probably illegal stockpile of paraffin he'd built up before rationing began.

Rory nudged him with one foot. He ignored this.

He ignored another, slightly stronger nudge, and started snoring quietly.

Another nudge.

'What?'

'Ken,' Rory whispered. 'Does your tassel get big sometimes?'

'Eh?'

'You know; your tassel; your willy. Does it get big?'

'Oh, good grief,' he groaned.

'Mine does. It's gone big now. Do you want to feel it?'

'No!' he sat up in the bed, looking down at the vague shape of his brother's head on the pillow at the other end of the bed. 'No, I do not!'

'Only asking. Does it, though?'

'What?'

'Your willy; get big?'

'Rory, I'm tired; it's been a long day, and this isn't the time or the place –'

Rory sat up suddenly. 'Bob Watt can make stuff come out of his; and so can Jamie McVean. I've seen them do it. You have to rub it a lot; I've tried but I can't get any stuff to come out, but twice now I've got this funny feeling where it's like heat; like heat coming up as if you're getting into a bath, sort of. Do you get that?'

Kenneth sighed, rubbed his eyes, rested his back against the low brass rail at the foot of the bed. He drew his legs up. 'I don't think it's really up to me to have to go into all this, Rory. You should talk to dad about it.'

'Rab Watt says it makes you go blind.' Rory hesitated. 'And he wears glasses.'

Kenneth stifled a laugh. He looked up at the dim roof, where dozens of model aircraft hung on threads and whole squadrons of Spitfires and Hurricanes and ME 109s attacked Wellingtons, Lancasters, Flying Fortresses and Heinkels. 'No, it doesn't make you go blind.'

Rory sat back, legs drawn up too. Kenneth couldn't make out his brother's expression; there was a soft glow from the small nightlight candle on Rory's desk, near the door, but it was too weak to let him see the boy's face clearly.

'Ha; I told him he was wrong.'

Kenneth lay back down. Rory said nothing for a while. Then Rory said, 'I think I'm going to fart.'

'Well, you'd better make damn sure it goes out the way.'

'Can't; got to keep it under the covers or it might ignite on the nightlight and blow the whole house up.'

'Rory; shut up. I'm serious.'

'. . . 'sall right.' Rory turned over, settled down. 'It went away.' There was silence for some time. Ken fitted his legs round Rory's back, closed his eyes, and wished that his father had concentrated on restoring more rooms in the old house rather than building courtyard walls.

After a while, Rory stirred again and said sleepily, 'Ken?'

'Rory; please go to sleep. Or I'll kick you unconscious.'

'No, but Ken?'

'Whaaat?' he breathed. *I should have beaten him up when we were younger; he isn't scared of me at all.*

'Have you ever shagged a woman?'

'That's none of your business.'

'Go on; tell us.'

'I'm not going to.'

'Please. I won't tell anybody else. Promise. Cross my heart and hope to die I won't.'

'No; go to sleep.'

'If you tell me, I'll tell you something.'

'Oh, I'm sure.'

'No, really; something dead important that nobody else knows.'

'I'm not buying it, Rory. Sleep or die.'

'Honest; I've never told anybody, and if I do tell you you mustn't tell anybody else, or I might get put in the jail.'

Kenneth opened his eyes. *What's the kid talking about?* He turned over, looked to the head of the bed. Rory was still lying down. 'Don't be melodramatic, Rory. I'm not impressed.'

'It's true; they'd put me in jail.'

'Rubbish.'

'I'll tell you what I did if you tell me about shagging.'

He lay there, thought about this. Apart from anything else, the horrible and ghastly truth was that at the ripe old age of practically twenty-two, he had never made love to a woman. But of course he knew what to do.

He wondered what Rory's secret was, what he thought he had done, or what story he had made up. They were both good at making up stories.

'You tell me first,' Kenneth said, and felt like a child again.

To his surprise, Rory said, 'All right.' He sat up in bed, and so did Kenneth. They waggled closer until their heads were almost touching, and Rory whispered, 'You remember last summer, when the big barn burned down on the estate?'

Kenneth remembered; it had been the last week of his vacation, and he had seen the smoke rising from the farm, a mile away along the road towards Lochgilphead. He and his dad had heard the bell sound in the ruined estate chapel, and had jumped into the car, to go and help old Mr Ralston and his sons. They'd tried to fight the fire with buckets and a couple of hoses, but by the time the fire engines arrived from Lochgilphead and Gallanach the old hay barn was burning from end to end. It stood not far from the railway line, and they'd all assumed it had been a spark from an engine.

'You're not going to tell me –'

'That was me.'

'You're joking.'

'Promise you won't tell, please? Please please please? I've never told anybody and I don't want to go to jail, Ken.'

Rory sounded too frightened to be lying. Kenneth hugged his young brother. The boy shivered. He smelled of Palmolive.

'I didn't mean to do it, Ken, honest I didn't; I was experimenting with a magnifying glass; there was this wee hole in the roof, and this beam of sunlight, and it was like a sort of searchlight falling on the straw, and I was playing with my Beaufighter; not the Airfix one, the other one, and I was melting holes in the wings and fuselage 'cos they look dead like bullet holes and you can melt a big long line of them and they look like twenty millimetre cannon holes, and I pretended the sunshine really was a sort of searchlight, and the plane crashed, and I'd thought I'd see if I could make the straw go on fire, just a little bit, round where the plane had crashed, but I didn't think it would all burn down, really I didn't; it just all went up dead sudden. You won't tell, will you, Ken?'

Rory pulled back, and Kenneth could just make out the boy's eyes, shining in the gloom.

He hugged him again. 'I swear; on my life. I'll never tell anybody. Ever.'

'The farmer won't have to sell his car to buy a new barn, will he?'

'No,' he laughed quietly. 'It's old Urvill's farm anyway, really, and being a good capitalist, I'm sure he had it well insured.'

'Oh ... okay. It was an accident, honest it was, Ken. You won't tell Mr Urvill, will you?'

'Don't worry; I won't. It was only a barn; nobody hurt.'

'It was an accident.'

'Sssh.' He held the boy, rocked him.

'I was that frightened afterwards, Ken; I was going to run away, so I was.'

'There now; sssh.'

After a while, Rory said, groggily, 'Going to tell me about shagging, Ken, eh?'

'Tomorrow, all right?' he whispered. 'Don't want you getting all excited again.'

'You promise?'

'I promise. Lie back; go to sleep.'

'Mmmm. Okay.'

He tucked the boy in, then looked up at the dull crosses of the planes, poised overhead. *Young rascal*, he thought.

He lay back himself, toyed briefly with his own erection, then felt guilty and stopped. He closed his eyes and tried to sleep, but couldn't stop thinking of the girl whose hair had gone on fire. He'd seen quite far down her pyjama top when he'd put his arm round her shoulders.

He forced himself to stop thinking about her. He reviewed the day, the way he often had since childhood, trying to fill the time between the light going out and his brain finally relaxing, letting him go to sleep.

Well, so much for his plan to tell his parents as soon as he got home that he too wanted to travel, that he didn't want to stay here, or get a job at the factory, managerial or not, or become a teacher like Hamish. Maybe something settled and bourgeois like that could come later, but he wanted to taste the world first; there was more to it than this wee corner of Scotland, more to it than Glasgow and even Britain. The world and his life were opening up before him and he wanted to take full advantage of both (apart from anything else, there was always the Bomb, that lurking presence forever threatening to close it all back down again with one final, filthy splash of light that heralded the long darkness, and made a nonsense of any human plan, any dream of the future. Eat, drink and be merry, because tomorrow we blow up the world).

He had intended to tell his parents all this as soon as he got in, but the incident with the girls and their tent and that poor, shocked, bonny lassie with her hair on fire had made it impossible.

It would have to wait until tomorrow. There would be time. There was always time.

He wondered what her skin would feel like. It had been the colour of pale honey. He wondered what it would feel like to hold her. He had touched her – he had been sprawled on top of her, dammit – but that wasn't the same thing, not the same thing at all. She had been slim, but her breasts, soft globes within the shadows of those silly pyjamas, had looked full and firm. There had been something fit and limber about the way she'd moved, even when she'd been shivering after her ordeal. He would have believed she was an athlete, not a student of – what had she said? – geography. He smiled in the darkness, touching himself again. He'd like to study her geography, all right; the contours of her body, the swelling hills and deep dales, her dark forest and mysterious, moist caves . . .

*

The girls stayed at Lochgair for another six days. The McHoans were used to keeping open house, and wouldn't hear of the girls just packing up what was left of their possessions and cycling or taking a train back to Glasgow.

'Och, no; you must stay,' Margot McHoan said, at breakfast the next morning. They were all sat round the big table; Mary with a towel round her head, looking prettily embarrassed, her friend Sheena, big-boned, blonde and apple-cheeked, happily wolfing down sausage and eggs, Fiona and Kenneth finishing their porridge, Rory searching for the plastic toy concealed somewhere in the Sugar Smacks packet. Dad had left for the glass factory earlier.

'Oh, Mrs McHoan, we couldn't,' Mary said, looking down at the table. She had only nibbled at her toast.

'Nonsense, child,' Margot said, pouring Rory another glass of milk and smoothing the *Herald* on the table in front of her. 'You're both very welcome to stay, aren't they?' She looked round her three children.

'Certainly,' Fiona said. She had already found Sheena to be a kindred spirit when it came to Rock 'n Roll, which might provide her with a valuable ally when it came to displacing dad's folk songs and Kenneth's jazz on the turntable of the family radiogram.

'Of course.' Kenneth smiled at Mary, and at Sheena. 'I'll show you around, if you like; much better to have a local guide, and my rates are very reasonable.'

'Muuuum, they've forgotten to put the wee boat in this box,' Rory complained, arm deep in the Sugar Smacks packet, face dark with frustration and ire.

'Just keep looking, dear,' Margot said patiently, then looked back at the two girls. 'Aye; stay by all means, the two of you. This big house needs filling up, and if you feel guilty you can always help with a bit of decorating, if there's any wet days, and if my husband gets round to it. Fair enough?'

Kenneth glanced at his mum. Margot McHoan was still a striking-looking woman, though her thick brown hair was starting to go grey over her forehead (she had dyed it at first, but found it not worth the bother). He admired her, he realised, and felt proud that she should be so matter-of-factly generous, even if it might mean that he had to keep sleeping in the same bed as his young brother.

'That's awful kind, Mrs McHoan,' Sheena said, wiping her plate with a bit of fried bread. 'Are you sure?'

'Totally,' Margot said. 'Your parents on the phone?'

'Mine are, Mrs McHoan,' Mary said, glancing up.

'Good,' Margot said. 'We'll call them, tell them you'll be here, all right?'

'Oh, that's awfully nice of you, Mrs McHoan,' Mary said, and flickered a wee nervous smile at the older woman. Kenneth watched her and the smile ended up, albeit briefly, directed at him, before Mary looked down, and crunched into her toast and marmalade.

He drove the two girls round the area in the Humber when his dad wasn't using it; sometimes Fiona came too. The summer days were long and warm; they walked in the forests south of Gallanach, and in the hills above Lochgair. A puffer captain let them travel through the Crinan canal on his boat, and they took the family dory puttering over to Otter Ferry for lunch one day, over the smooth waters of Lower Loch Fyne, one windless day when the smoke rose straight, and cormorants stood on exposed rocks, wings held open like cloaks to the warm air, and seals popped up, black cones of blubber with surprised-looking faces, as the old open boat droned slowly past.

There was a dance on in Gallanach Town Hall that Saturday, the day before the two girls were due to return to Glasgow; Kenneth asked Mary to go with him. She borrowed one of Fiona's dresses, and a pair of his mother's shoes. They danced, they kissed, they walked by the quiet harbour where the boats lay still on water like black oil, and they sauntered hand-in-hand along the esplanade beneath a moon-devoid sky full of bright stars. They each talked about their dreams, and about travelling to far-away places. He asked if she had given any thought of maybe coming back here some time? Like next weekend, for example?

There is a loch in the hills above Lochgair; Loch Glashan, reservoir for the small hydro power station in the village. Matthew McHoan's friend, Hector Cardle, a Forestry Commission manager, kept a rowing boat on the loch, and the McHoans had permission to use the boat, to fish the waters.

*

Rory was bored. He was so bored he was actually looking forward to school starting again next week. Back in the spring, he had hoped that Ken being back home would make the summer holidays fun, but it hadn't worked out that way; Ken was either up in Glasgow seeing that Mary girl, or she was here, and they were together all the time and didn't want him around.

He had been in the garden, throwing dry clods of earth at some old model tanks; the clouds of dust the clods made when they hit the hard, baked earth looked just like proper explosions. But then his mum had chased him out because the dust was getting the washing dirty. He hadn't found anybody else around to play with in the village, so he'd watched a couple of trains pass on the railway line. One was a diesel, which was quite exciting, but he'd soon got bored there, too; he walked up the track by the river, up to the dam. It was very warm and still. The waters of the loch were like a mirror.

He walked along the path between the plantation and the shore of the loch, looking for interesting stuff. But you usually only found that sort of thing down at the big loch. There was a rowing boat out in the middle of the little loch, but he couldn't see anybody in it. He was banned from making rafts or taking boats out. Just because he'd got a bit wet a few times. It was unfair.

He sat down in the grass, took out a little die-cast model of a Gloster Javelin, and played with it for a while, pretending he was a camera, tracking the plane through the grass and over the pebbles and rocks by the loch side. He lay back in the grass, looked at the blue sky, and closed his eyes for a long time, soaking up the pinkness behind his eyelids and pretending he was a lion lying tawny and sated under the African sun, or a sleepy-eyed tiger basking on some rock high over a wide Indian plain. Then he opened his eyes again and looked around, at a world gone grey, until that effect wore off. He looked down at the shore; little waves were lapping rhythmically at the stones.

He watched the wavelets for a while. They were very regular. He looked along the nearby stretch of shore. The waves – hardly noticeable, but there if you looked – were coming ashore all along the lochside. He followed the line they seemed to indicate, out to the little rowing boat near the middle of the loch. Now he thought about it, it was *very* odd that there was nobody in the boat. It was moored; he could see the wee white buoy it was tied to. But there was nobody visible in the boat.

The more carefully he looked, the more certain he became that it was the rowing boat that all these little, rhythmic waves were coming from. Hadn't Ken and Mary been going fishing today? He had thought they'd meant sea-fishing, in Loch Fyne, but maybe he hadn't been paying attention. What if they had been fishing from the rowing boat and fallen overboard and both been drowned? Maybe that was why the boat was empty! He scanned the surface of the loch. No sign of bobbing bodies or any clothing. Perhaps they'd sunk.

Anyway, what was making the boat make those waves?

He wasn't sure, but he thought he could see the boat moving, very slightly; rocking to and fro. Maybe it was a fish, flopping about in the bottom.

Then he thought he heard a cry, like a bird, or maybe a woman. It made him shiver, despite the heat. The boat seemed to stop rocking, then moved quite a lot, and then went totally still. The little waves went on, then a few slightly bigger, less regular ones lapped ashore, then the water went still, and was as flat as a pane of glass.

A gull, a white scrap across the calm sky, flapped lazily just above the blue loch; it made to land on the prow of the little rowing boat, then at the last second, even as its feet were about to touch, it suddenly burst up into the sky again, all panic and white feathers, and its calls sounded over the flat water as it flapped away.

What sounded very like laughter came from the little rowing boat.

Rory shrugged, put the model plane in the pocket of his shorts and decided to go back down to the village and see if there was anybody around to play with yet.

Kenneth and Mary held hands at tea that evening, and said they wanted to get married. Mum and dad seemed quite happy. Fiona didn't seem in the least surprised. Rory was nonplussed.

It was years before he made the connection between those tiny, rhythmically lapping waves, and that blushing, excited announcement.

CHAPTER
3

Gaineamh Castle, home of the Urvills once again, stands amongst the alders, rowans and oaks that cover the northern flanks of the Cnoc na Moine, due south of the carbuncular outcrop that supports the First Millennium fort of Dunadd, and a little north-west of the farm rejoicing in the name of Dunamuck. The castle, a moderately large example of the Scottish Z-plan type, with cannon-shaped stone waterspouts, has a fine view through the trees and across the parkland and fields to the town of Gallanach, which spreads round the deep waters of Inner Loch Crinan like some slow but determined beach-head of architecture somehow landed from the sea.

The sound of gravel crunching beneath a car tyre has always meant something special to me; at once comforting and exciting. Of course the one time I tried to explain this to my father he suggested that what it really signified was the easy rolling pressure the middle and upper classes thought it was their right to exert upon the multitudinous base of the workers. I have to confess that the entire counter-revolution in world affairs has come as something of a personal relief to me, making my dad seem no longer quite so remorselessly well-clued-up, but rather – if anything, any more – just quaint. It would have been sweet to tackle him on that subject at the time, especially given that Gorby's unleashed restructuring had just resulted in the spectacular and literal deconstruction of one of the age's most resonantly symbolic icons, but at the time we weren't talking.

'Prentice,' rumbled the slightly bloated Urvill of Urvill, taking my hand and briefly shaking it, as if weighing my mitt. I felt for a moment the way a young bull ought to feel when the man from McDonalds slaps its haunch . . . but then probably doesn't. 'So very sorry.' Fergus Urvill said. I wondered whether he was referring to Grandma Margot's death itself, her detonation, or Doctor Fyfe's apparent attempt to up-stage the old girl. Uncle Fergus let my hand go. 'And how are your studies going?'

'Oh, just fine,' I said.

'Good, good.'

'And the twins; are they both well?' I asked.

'Fine, fine,' Fergus nodded, presumably allocating his two daughters a word each in his reply. Ferg's gaze went smoothly to my Aunt Antonia; I took the hint, and (like Margot) passed on. 'Antonia,' I heard behind me. 'So very sorry . . .'

Helen and Diana, Uncle Ferg's two lusciously lissom daughters, sadly couldn't be here; Diana spent most of her time either in Cambridge or the least touristy part of Hawaii, which is the bit thirty kilometres away from the beaches – four of them vertically – at the Mauna Kea observatory, studying the infra-red. Helen, on the other hand, worked for a bank in Switzerland, dealing with the ultra-rich.

'Prentice, are you all right?' My mother took me in her arms, held me to her black coat. Still splashing on the *No. 5*, by the smell of it. Her green eyes looked bright. My father had been at the head of the reception line; I had ignored him and the compliment had been returned.

'I'm fine,' I told her.

'No, but are you really?' She squeezed my hands.

'Yes; I'm really really fine.'

'Come and see us, please.' She hugged me again, said quietly, 'Prentice, this is silly. Make it up with your father. For me.'

'Mum, please,' I said, feeling like everybody was looking at us. 'I'll see you later, okay?' I said, and pulled away.

I walked into the hall, taking off my jacket, blinking hard and sniffing. Coming from cold into warmth always does this to me.

The entrance hall of Gaineamh Castle sports the business end of a dozen or so beheaded male red deers, perched so high up on the oak-panelled walls that attempting to utilise them for their only conceivable practical purpose in such a location – hanging coats, scarves, jackets, etc. on their impressively branched antlers – only exposes them as the venue for a kind of non-returnable sport rather than a sensible amenity. Rather more prosaic brass hooks, like smooth unsuitable claws beneath the glass-eyed stares of the stags, accepted our garments in their stead. My much be-zippered black leather pretend-biker's jacket seemed a little out of place amongst the sober wools and furs; Verity's snow-white skiing jacket looked ... well, just sublime. I stood and stared at it for a second or two longer than was probably fit; but it really did seem to glow in the dark company. I sighed, and decided to keep my white silk Möbius scarf on.

*

I entered the hammer-beamed Solar of the castle; the great hall was filled with a quietly chattering crowd of McHoans, Urvills and others, all nibbling canapés and vol-au-vants, and sipping whisky and sherries. I suspect my grandmother would have preferred pan-loaf sarnies and maybe a few slices of ham-and-egg pie, but it had, I suppose, been a kind gesture of the Urvill to ask us back here, and one should not carp. Somehow the McHoan home, still bearing the scars of grandma's sudden, unorthodox and vertical re-entry into the conservatory following her abortive attempt to de-moss the gutters, seemed unfitting as our post-cremation retreat.

There! I caught sight of Verity, standing looking out of one of the Solar's tall mullioned windows, the wide grey light of this chill November day soft upon her skin. I stopped and looked at her, a hollowness in my chest as though my heart had become a vacuum pump.

Verity: conceived beneath a tree two millennia old and born to the flare and snap of human lightning. Emerging to emergency, making her entrance, and duly entrancing.

Whistling or humming the first phrase of Deacon Blue's *Born In A Storm* whenever I saw her had become a sort of ritual with me, a little personal theme in the life lived as movie, existence as opera. See Verity; play them tunes. It was in itself a way of possessing her.

I hesitated, thought about going over to her, then decided I'd best get a drink first, and started towards the sideboard with the glasses and bottles, before I realised that offering to refresh Verity's glass would be as good a way as any of getting talking to her. I turned again. And almost collided with my Uncle Hamish.

'Prentice,' he said, in tones of great import and sobriety. He put one hand on my shoulder and we turned away from the window where Verity stood, and away from the drinks, to walk up the length of the hall towards the stained-glass height of the gable-end window. 'Your grandmother has gone to a better place, Prentice,' Uncle Hamish told me. I looked back at the vision of wonderfulness that was Verity, then glanced at my uncle.

'Yes, Uncle Hamish.'

Dad called Uncle Hamish 'The Tree' because he was very tall, moved in a rather awkward way – as though made out of something less flexible than the standard issue of bone, sinew, muscle and flesh – and (so he claimed, at any rate) because he had seen him act in a school play once, and he had been very, well, wooden. 'Anyway,' my dad had insisted when he'd originally confided this private piece of nomenclature, only half a decade earlier, on the occasion of my sixteenth birthday, when we'd got drunk together for the first time, 'he just lumbers about!'

'She was a good woman, and did little that was bad and much that was good, so I'm sure she has gone to a reward rather than a punishment, living amongst our anti-creates.'

I nodded, and as we strolled amongst them, looked around at the various members of my family, the McGuskies (Grandma Margot's maiden-family) the Urvill clan, and sundry worthies from Gallanach, Lochgilphead and Lochgair, and pondered, not for the first time, what on Earth (or anywhere else for that matter) had given Uncle Hamish the idea for his bizarre, home-made religion. I really didn't want to go into all this right now, and anyway found the whole subject a little awkward, because I wasn't actually quite as gung-ho for Hamish's personal theology as he seemed to think I was.

'She was always very kind to me,' I told him.

'And therefore your anti-create will be kind to her,' Uncle Hamish said, still with one hand on my shoulder, as we stopped and looked up at the stained-glass monstrosity at the far end of the hall. This showed in graphic form the story of the Urvills from about the time of the Norman conquest, when the family of Urveille, from Octeville in Cotentin, had crossed into England, percolated northwards, swirled briefly around Dunfermline and Edinburgh, and finally come to rest – perhaps afflicted by some maritime memory of their ancestral lands on the seam of the Manche – in what had been the very epicentre of the ancient Scots kingdom of Dalriada, losing only a few relatives and a couple of letters on the way. Swearing allegiance to David I, here they have stayed, to mingle their blood with that of the Picts, the Scots, the Angles, the Britons and the Vikings who have all variously settled, colonised, raided and exploited this part of Argyll, or maybe just arrived at one time and forgotten to leave again.

The peregrinations and subsequent local achievements of the clan Urvill make interesting history, and would make fascinating viewing if the giant window telling the tale wasn't so badly done. The fashionable but untalented son of one of the previous head Urvill's school pals had been commissioned to execute the work, and had taken the brief all too literally. Deadly dull and eye-squintingly garish at the same time, the stained glass window made me want to grit my teeth.

'Yes, I'm sure you're right, uncle,' I lied.

'Of course I am, Prentice,' he nodded slowly. Uncle Hamish is balding, but of the school that believes long wisps of hair grown on one side of the head and then combed delicately across the pate to the other edge look better than naked sin exposed to the elements. I watched the coloured light from the stained glass window slide over shiny skin and hardly less luminescent oiled hair, and thought what a prat he looked. I inadvertently found myself humming the appropriate piece of music from the Hamlet cigar adds and thinking of Gregor Fisher.

'Will you join me in worship this evening, Prentice?'

Oh shit, I thought. 'Perhaps not, actually, uncle,' I said, in tones I hoped sounded regretful. 'Have to pop down the Jac to talk to a girl about a jacuzzi. Probably go straight from here.' Another lie.

Uncle Hamish looked at me, the grain-like lines on his forehead bunching and tangling, his brown eyes like knots. 'A *jacuzzi*, Prentice?' He pronounced the word the way the lead in a Jacobean tragedy might pronounce the name of the character who has been his nemesis.

'Yes. A jacuzzi.'

'That's a form of bath, isn't it?'

'It is.'

'Not meeting this young lady *in* a bath, are you, Prentice?' Uncle Hamish's lips twisted slowly into what was probably meant to be a smile.

'I don't believe the facilities of the Jacobite Bar run to such a thing, uncle,' I told him. 'They've only recently got round to installing hot water in the gents. The relevant jacuzzi is in Berlin.'

'The German city?'

I thought about this. Could I have mis-heard Ash and she have been talking about the briefly famous chart-topping band of the same name? I thought not. 'Yes, uncle; the city. Where the wall was.'

'I see,' Uncle Hamish nodded. 'Berlin.' He stared up at the violently clashing leaden imagery of the great stained-glass window. 'Isn't that where Ilsa is?'

I frowned. 'Aunt Ilsa? No, she's in Patagonia, isn't she? Incommunicado.'

Uncle Hamish looked suitably confused as he contemplated the garish gable glass. Then he nodded. 'Ah yes. Of course.' He looked back down at me. 'However. Shall we see you for supper, Prentice?'

'I don't know,' I admitted. 'Just as likely to end up with a kebab, I imagine. Or a fish supper.'

'Well, you have your key with you?'

'Oh yes. Thanks. And I'll be . . . you know; quiet, when I come in.'

'Right.' Uncle Hamish gazed back up at the crass glass. 'Right. We'll probably be off in a half-hour or so; let us know if you do want a lift.'

'Surely.'

'Right you are, then.' Uncle Hamish nodded, turned, then looked back with an intensely puzzled expression. 'Did I hear somebody say mother *exploded*?'

I nodded. 'Pacemaker. That's what Doctor Fyfe was rushing to tell us; told dad in the ambulance. But it was too late by then, of course.'

Uncle Hamish looked more baffled than ever, but nodded eventually and said, 'Of course,' and walked off over the parquet with a startlingly tree-like creaking noise which I realised – with a small but welcome surprise – was issuing from his black brogues.

I made straight for the sideboard with the drinks, but a quick inspection of the casement of the relevant window on my way there revealed that Verity the Comely had gone.

*

Fortingall is a modest hamlet in the hills north of Loch Tay, and it was there in the winter of 1969 that my Aunt Charlotte was determined to consummate her marriage. Specifically, she wanted to be impregnated beneath the ancient yew tree that lies in an enclosure within the graveyard of the small church there; she was convinced that the tree – two thousand years old, according to reliable estimates – must be suffused with a magical Life Force.

It was a dark and stormy night (no; really), the grass under the ancient, straggling, gnarled yew was sodden, and so she and her husband, Steve, had to settle for a knee-trembler while Charlotte held onto one of the overhanging boughs, but it was there and then – despite the effects of gravity – that the gracile and quiveringly prepossessing Verity was conceived, one loud night under an ink black sky obscuring a white full moon, at an hour when all decent folk were in their beds and even the indecent ones were in somebody's, in a quaint little Perthshire village, back in the fag end of the dear old daft old hippy days.

So my aunt says, and frankly I believe her; anybody wacko enough ever to have bought the idea that there was some sort of weird cosmic energy beaming out of a geriatric shrub in a back-end-of-nowhere Scottish graveyard on a wet Monday night probably hasn't the wit to lie about it.

*

'Naw, she's great, I mean really *really* great. I'm in love. I love her; I'm hers. Verity; take me; put me out of my misery. O God . . .'

I was drunk. It was getting on towards midnight in the Jacobite bar and at my normal rate of drinking that meant I'd had about ten pints of export. Ash and Dean Watt, and another couple of old pals, Andy Langton and Lizzie Polland, had all drunk about the same as I had, but then they'd been home for their tea and they hadn't been swilling back the Urvill's whisky for a significant part of the afternoon.

'So have you told her, Prentice?' Ash said, putting down another set of pints on the pocked copper table we were hunched around.

'Ah, Ash,' I said, slapping the table. 'I admire a woman who can carry three pints at the same time.'

'I said, have you told this lassie you love her, Prentice?' Ash said, sitting down. She took a bottle of strong cider from one breast pocket of her navy shirt, and a glass of whisky from the other.

'Wow!' I said. 'Ash! I mean, like; wow! Wicked.' I shook my head, took up my old pint and finished it.

'Answer the lassie,' Dean said, nudging me.

'No, I haven't,' I confessed.

'Ya coward,' said Lizzie.

'I'll tell her for you if you like,' Droid offered (there is an entire generation of Andrews with the shared nickname of Droid, post *Star Wars*).

'Na,' I said. 'But she is just fabulous. I mean –'

'Why not tell her?' Liz asked.

'I'm shy,' I sighed, hand on heart, eyes heaven-ward, lashes fluttering.

'Get out a here.'

'So tell her,' Ash said.

'Also,' I sighed. 'She's got a boyfriend.'

'Ah-ha,' Ash said, looking at her pint.

I waved one hand dismissively. 'But he's a wanker.'

'That's all right, then,' Liz said.

I frowned. 'Actually, that's the only flaw Verity seems to have; her lousy taste in men.'

'So you *are* in with a chance then?' Liz said brightly.

'Yeah,' I said. 'I think she's going to chuck him.'

'Prentice,' Ash insisted, tapping the table. '*Tell* her.'

'I can't.'

'Why not?'

'Because I wouldn't know how to,' I protested. 'I've never told anybody I love them before. I mean, how do you? The words sound so corny, so devalued. It's so . . . it's just such a cliché.'

Ash looked scornful. 'What rubbish.'

'Well, smarty-pants,' I said, leaning over to her. 'Have *you* ever told anybody you love them?'

'Hundreds of times, darling.' Ash said in a deep voice, pouting. Dean guffawed. Ash drank from her pint, then shook her head. 'Well, actually, no.'

'Ha!' I said.

Ash leaned over to me, her long nose almost touching mine. '*Tell* the girl, you idiot.'

'I can't,' I said, sitting back. 'I just can't. She's too perfect.'

'*What*?' Ash frowned.

'Infallible. Too perfect; ideal.'

'Sounds like misogynist romantic shite to me,' snorted Liz, who's always taken a hard line on such things.

'It is,' I admitted. 'But she's just incredible. D'you know where she was conceived?'

Dean and Ash exchanged looks; Andy spluttered into his beer while Lizzie rolled her eyes. 'Aw yeah,' Dean said, nodding and looking quite serious. 'Doesn't everybody?'

I was shocked, and almost cut short my next gulp of beer. 'You don't really, do you?'

'Course not, Prentice,' Ash said shaking her head. Her long fair hair spilled from over one shoulder. 'What diff –'

'Aw, it's just incredible,' I told them. 'Her mum told me; Aunt Charlotte. Bit of a nutter, but okay. I mean totally aff her heid really, but anyway –' I took another gulp of beer, '– she had this thing about psychic energy or some crap like that ... and about Scottish history –'

'Aw; runs in the family, does it, Prentice?' Dean asked.

'Naw; she's not a McHoan ... anyway; she'd married this English guy called Walker and they hadn't consummated the marriage, right, not on their wedding night; she wanted to wait, and when they did get it together she made sure it was in this wee village called Fortingall, right? Near Loch Tay. Thing is, she'd heard something about Fortingall being where Pontius Pilate –'

'Wait a minute,' Dean said. 'How long was it between them getting married and them humping?'

'Eh?' I scratched my head. 'I don't know; a day or two. Oh! I mean, they'd done it before, like. It wasn't their first time or anything. It was just Aunt Charlotte's idea that it'd be more special if they hadn't done it for a while, and then did it under this tree. But they had been fucking before. I mean; good grief, this is the love generation we're talking about here.'

'Right,' Dean said, apparently mollified.

'Anyway; Fortingall is where some people say Pontius Pilate was born, and –'

'Whit?' Andy said, wiping his beard. 'Away ye go.'

'So they say,' I insisted. 'His dad was in the ... shit ... the seventh legion? The ninth? Damn ...' I scratched my head again, looked down at my trainers (and thought with some relief that at least tonight I would not have the long struggle to undo the buckles and untie and then loosen the laces on the Docs, which were my usual drinking gear these days). 'Or *was* it the seventh legion?' I pondered, still staring at my Nikes.

'Never mind if it was the fuckin' foreign legion,' Droid said, exasperated. 'You're no trying to tell us Pontius fucking Pilate was born in Scotland!'

'Well maybe!' I said, spreading my arms wide and almost spilling Ash's whisky. 'His dad was in the legion stationed there! Apparently! I mean, the Romans had a military camp and Pontius

Pilate's pa was stationed there, maybe, and so young Pontius could have been born there! Why not?'

'You're making this up,' laughed Ash. 'You're just like your dad; I remember those stories on a Sunday afternoon.'

'I am not like ma dad!' I yelled.

'Hey, shoosh,' Lizzie said.

'Well, I'm not! I'm telling the truth!'

'Aye, well,' Ash said. 'Maybe. People get born in funny places. David Byrne was born in Dumbarton.'

'Anyway; Pontius Pi –'

'Whit?' Dean grimaced. 'The guy that wrote *Tutti Frutti*?'

'Listen; Pontius –'

'Na; that was John Byrne,' Lizzie said. '*David* Byrne; the guy in Talking Heads, ya heidbanger.'

'Look, anyway, forget Ponti –'

'Anyway, it was Little Richard.'

'Will you shut up? This isn't about Pon –'

'What? In Talking Heads?'

'Shut up! I'm telling you; Po –'

'Na; that wrote *Tutti Frutti*.'

'I give in,' I said, sitting back. I sighed, supped my export.

'Aye, the song; but no the film.'

'It wasnae a fillum; it was a series.'

'Ah *know*; you knew what ah meant.'

'I hate these drunken, rambling conversations,' I breathed.

'Aye, but I've heard worse.' Ash nodded.

'Anyway, it wasnae fillum at all; it was video.'

'It was naawwwt!' Dean drawled scornfully. 'Ye could *see* it was fillum! What sort a telly have *you* got?'

I crossed my legs, crossed my arms and swivelled to look at Ash. I rubbed my rather greasy face and focused on her. 'Hi. Come here often?'

Ashley pursed her lips and studied the ceiling. 'Just the once,' she said, frowning at me. 'In the toilets.' She gathered my shirt lapels in her fist and pulled me close to her face. 'So who talked?'

'Fnarr fnarr,' I breathed over her. Ash's face wrinkled, quite attractively, actually. But then it was late.

'Hi youse,' a deep voice said, bending over us. 'Yer oan.'

'On what?' I asked the very large fellow with very long hair who had spoken.

'The pool table; PM and AW; that's youse, is it no?'

'Shit, aye, right enough.'

Ash and I went to play pool.

I'd been just about to ask her about the jacuzzi in Berlin, but now didn't seem like the right time.

*

Uncle Fergus had the observatory built back in 1974 (when the heavenly Verity was four). The idea was two-fold. First of all – according to my father – Fergus wanted a bigger and better telescope than he had. Dad had a three-inch refractor in a shed in the garden at Lochgair. Fergus ordered a six-inch reflector. Also, it was a business sample. The lenses and mirror were to be made in the new Specialist Glass Division of the Gallanach Glass Works, the Urvill-owned factory which even yet provides the town with a significant proportion of its employment. Not only, therefore, would Uncle Fergus have a fascinating and unique additional feature for his not-long restored castle, it would be both an advertisement for his Glass Works *and* tax-deductible!

The fact the telescope was a wee bit close to Gallanach itself, and so possibly prone to light pollution from the town's sodium vapour lamps, was less of a problem than it might appear; with Uncle Fergus's connections he could have the offending lamps shaded at the council's expense. So Uncle Fergus was prepared if necessary – and only selectively, of course – to dim his home town.

(His niece had already bettered that; when the diminutive, bloody and bawling form of Verity Walker had appeared on the scene, the lights had actually gone out.)

I'd met the sublime Verity for the first time in some years in the observatory, one coal-sack-black moonless night in 1986, a few days before I left to go to University, when I was already full of the exhilaration and fear of departure and independence, and the whole huge world seemed to be opening up before me, like some infinite blossom of opportunity and glamour. The twins had taken to having star-gazing parties in the cold, cramped hemisphere which protruded from the summit of the compact castle, and I'd arrived late after being out on the hill with little brother James during the afternoon and then suffering a delayed tea because some friends of dad's had showed up unannounced and had to be catered for.

'Aye, it's yourself, Prentice,' boomed Mrs McSpadden, informatively. 'And how are you?' Mrs McSpadden was the Urvill's housekeeper; a rotundly buxom lady of perpetual middle-age with a big baw-face that gave the impression of being freshly scrubbed. She had a very loud voice and dad always told people that she hailed from Fife. A ringing noise in one's ears after a close encounter with the lady tended to enforce the impression this was literally true. 'The rest are up there. Will you take this tray up? There's coffee in these pots; you just turn the wee spot to the front here, ken, and –' She lifted the corner of a heavy napkin smothering a very large plate. '– there's hot sausage rolls under here.'

'Right, thanks,' I said, lifting the tray. I'd come in through the castle kitchen; entering through the main door after it had been shut for the night could be a performance. I made for the stairs.

'Here, Prentice; take this scarf up to Miss Helen,' Mrs McSpadden said, flourishing the article. 'That lassie'll catch her death of cold up there one night, so she will.'

I bowed my head so that Mrs S could put the scarf over my neck.

'And mind them there's plenty of bread, and some chicken in the fridge, and cheese, and plenty of soup forbye, if you get hungry again.'

'Right, thanks,' I repeated, and jogged carefully upstairs.

'Anybody got any roach paper?'

I squeezed into the brightly-lit dome of the observatory; it was about three metres in diameter, made from aluminium, the telescope took up a lot of it, and it was cold, despite a wee two-bar electric heater. A modestly proportioned ghetto-blaster was playing something by the Cocteau Twins. Diana and Helen, bundled in enormous Mongolian quilted jackets, were crouched round a small table with Darren Watt, playing cards. My elder brother, Lewis, was at the telescope. We all said our hellos. 'This is cousin Verity. Remember her?' Helen said, as she draped the scarf I'd brought her over Darren's head. Helen pointed at a cloud of smoke, and as it blew towards me and cleared I saw her.

There was a sort of cubby-hole in the non-rotating part of the observatory, built into the attic of the castle's main block. It was just a long cupboard really, but you could coorie down into it to make more space in the dome proper. Verity Walker was lying in a sleeping bag there, only her upper half protruding into the dome; she was smoking one joint and rolling another, on the cover of a pictorial atlas of the universe. 'Evening,' she said. 'Got any roach paper?'

'Yeah; hi,' I said. I put the tray down, searched my pockets, pulled out some stuff. The last time I'd seen Verity Walker, maybe five or six years earlier, she'd been a scrawny tyke with a mouth full of orthodontic brace-work and a serious Shakin' Stevens habit. Now – once seen through the smoke – she had short, pure blonde hair, and a delicate, almost elfin face which tapered to an exquisite chin that looked like it had been made to be grasped lightly in three fingers and pulled closer to your lips ... well, to my lips, anyway. Her eyes were the blue of old sea-ice, and when I saw her complexion all I could think was: *Wow; Lloyd Cole city!* Because she had perfect skin.

'That'll do.' She took something from my hand. 'Thanks.'

'Hey! That's a library ticket!' I grabbed it back. 'Here.' I handed her half a book token my mother had given me.

'Thanks.' She started cutting it with a little pair of scissors.

'It's just a tokin' token,' I told her, squatting down beside her.

She grunted with laughter, and my heart performed manoeuvres that the connecting plumbing makes topologically impossible.

'All set for the big move, bro?' Lewis grinned down from the wee seat under the eye-piece of the telescope. He reached over to the table where I'd set the tray down and started pouring coffee into the mugs. My big brother has always seemed more than two years older than me; a little taller than my 1.85, and a little more thick-set, he looked bigger still at the time thanks to a beard of the burst-sofa persuasion. Back then, it was his turn to be in disgrace with my father, because he'd just dropped out of University.

'Yeah, all set,' I told him. 'Found a place to stay.' I nodded at the telescope. 'Anything interesting tonight?'

'Got it on the Pleiades just now. Take a look.'

We took turns star-gazing, playing cards, crouching round the little electric heater, and constructing joints. I'd brought a half bottle of whisky, and the twins had some brandy, which we used to beef up the coffee. The munchies struck again an hour or so after we'd polished off the last of the sausage rolls; the twins mounted an expedition into the depths of the castle in search of the mythical Soup Dragon (we spoke in Clanger while they were gone) and returned with a steaming tureen and a half-dozen bowls.

'Where're you staying in Glasgow, Prentice?' Darren Watt asked.

'Hyndland,' I said, slurping my soup. 'Lauderdale Gardens.'

'Ah, that's no far from us. Going to be around on the thirtieth? We're having a party.'

'Oh, ah, yeah; probably.' (Actually, I'd been going to come home that weekend, but I could juggle things.)

'Ah well, come along; should be fun.'

'Thanks.'

Darren Watt was in his last year at Art School and – for me, at least – had been the epitome of cool since New Year two years earlier. After the bells, mum had driven Lewis and me into Gallanach; we went to a party Droid and his chums were giving. Darren had been there; blond, lean, drop-dead bone structure, and exuding style. I'd admired the looped silk scarf he'd worn over a red velvet jacket that would have looked silly on most people but in which he looked totally poised. He'd given me the scarf, and – when I'd tried to demur – explained he was growing bored with it; better it went to somebody who would appreciate it, though he hoped I'd hand it on too, if I ever tired of it.

So I took it. It was just an ordinary silk scarf, given a half twist and the ends carefully sewn together, but that, of course, made it a Möbius scarf, the very idea of which I just thought was wonderful. I thought Darren was pretty wonderful, too, and for a while wondered if maybe I was gay, too, but decided against it. In fact, a large part of the attraction of an invite to a party at Darren's place was due to the fact his flat-mates were three salivatingly attractive and reputedly enthusiastically heterosexual female arts students (I'd met them when he'd brought them to Gallanach on a day trip the previous year).

'You still making models of these wave-powered hoodjie-ma-flips?' I asked him, finishing my soup. Darren was wiping his plate with a bit of bread, and I found myself copying him.

'Aye,' he said, looking thoughtful. 'Looks like I've found a sponsor for the real thing, too.'

'What? Really?'

Darren grinned. 'Big cement company's interested; talking about a serious money grant.'

'Wow! Congratulations.'

For the last eighteen months or so, Darren had been making these tenth-scale wood and plastic models of sculptures he wanted to build full size in concrete and steel one day. The idea was to construct these things on a beach; he'd need planning permission, lots of money, and waves. The sculptures were wave-powered mobiles and fountains. When a wave struck them a giant wheel would revolve, or air would be forced through pipes, producing weird, chest-shaking, cathedral-demolishing bass notes and uncanny howls and moans, or the water in the waves themselves would be channelled, funnelled, and emerge in a whale-like spout of spray, bursting from the top or sides of the sculpture. They sounded great, perfectly feasible, and I wanted to see one work, so this was good news.

I went downstairs for a pee, and came back to a good-natured but confused argument. 'What do you mean, no it doesn't?' Verity said from her sleeping-bagged cubby-hole.

'I mean, what is sound?' Lewis said. 'The definition is; what we hear. So if there's nobody there to hear it . . .'

'Sounds a bit anthro-thingy to me,' Helen Urvill said, from the card table.

'But how can it fall without making a sound?' Verity protested. 'That's crazy.'

I leaned over to Darren, who was sitting looking amused. 'We talking trees falling in forests?' I asked. He nodded.

'You're not listening –' Lewis told Verity.

'Maybe you're not making a sound.'

'Shut up, Prentice,' Lewis said, without bothering to look at me. 'What I'm saying is, What is a sound? If you define it as –'

'Yeah,' interrupted Verity. 'But if the tree hits the ground that must make the air move. I've stood near a tree when it's felled; you feel the ground shake. Doesn't the ground shake either, when there's nobody there? The air has to move; there must be . . . movement, in the air; its molecules, I mean . . .'

'Compression waves,' I provided, nodding to Verity, and thinking about Darren's wave-powered organ-pipe coast sculptures.

'Yeah; producing compression waves,' Verity said, with an acknowledging wave at me (oh, my heart leapt!). 'Which birds and animals and insects can hear –'

'Ah!' Lewis said. 'Supposing there aren't –'

Well, it got silly after that, dissolving into the polemical equivalent of white noise, but I liked the robustly common-sensical line Verity was taking. And when she was talking, of course, I got to stare at her without anybody thinking it odd. It was wonderful. I was falling in love with her. Beauty *and* brains. Wow!

More sounds, more spliffs, more star-gazing. Lewis did his impression of a radio being tuned through various wavelengths; fingers at his lips to produce the impressively authentic between-stations noises, then suddenly putting on silly voices to impersonate a news reader, compère, quiz contestant, singer ... 'ttttrrrrsssshhhh ... reports that the London chapter of the Zoroastrians have fire-bombed the offices of the *Sun* newspaper for blasphemy ... zzzoooowwwaaannggggg ... athangyou, athangyou, laze an ge'men, andenow, please put your hands together for the Siamese Twins ... kkkkrrrraaasshhhwwwaaaasssshhhaaa ... uh, can you eat it, Bob? Ah, no, you can't. I'm afraid the answer is; a Pot Nooddle ... bllbllbllbl ... Hey hey, we're the junkies! ... zpt!'

And so on. We laughed, we drank more coffee, and we smoked.

The gear was black and powerful like the night; the hollow aluminium skull of the observatory tracked the 'scope's single eye slowly over the rolling web of stars, or – hand-cranked – swivelled the universe about our one fixed point. Soon my head was spinning, too. The music machine played away – far away – and when I started to understand the lyrics of a Cocteau Twins song, I knew I was wrecked. The stars shone on in mysterious galactic harmonies, constellations like symphonies of ancient, trembling light; Lewis told weird and creepy stories and bizarrely apposite jokes, and the twins – hunkered over the little card-table in their quilted jackets, their night-black hair straight and shining and framing their broad-boned beautiful faces – looked like proud Mongolian princesses, calmly contemplating creation from the ribbed dome of some fume-filled yurt, midnight-pitched on the endless rolling Asian steppe.

Verity Walker – professed sceptic though she was – read my palm, her touch like warm velvet, her voice like the spoken ocean, and in her eyes each iris like a blue-white sun stationed a billion light years off. She told me I'd be sad and I'd be happy and I'd be bad and I'd be good, and I believed all of it and why not, and she told me the last part in Clanger, the tin-whistle pretend language from one of the children's programmes we'd all watched as youngsters, and she was trying to keep a straight face, and Lew and Dar and Di and Hel were snorting with laughter and even I was grinning, but I'd been singing happily along to the Cocteau Twins' other-worldly words for the past hour, and I knew exactly what she said even though she might not have known herself, and fell completely in love with her iris-blue eyes and her wheat-crop hair and her peat-dark voice and the peach-skin fuzz of infinitesimally fine hairs on her creamy skin.

*

'What was all that stuff about Pontius Pilate, anyway?' Ash said.

'Aw . . .' I waved my hand. 'Too complicated.'

Ash and I stood on a low little mound overlooking what had been the Slate Mine wharf, at the north-west limit of Gallanach where the Kilmartin Burn flows out of the hills, meanders without conviction, then widens to form part of Gallanach Bay before finally decanting into the deeper waters of Inner Loch Crinan. Here was where the docks had been, when the settlement had exported first coal then slate then sand and glass, before the railway arrived and a subtle Victorian form of gentrification had set in the shape of the railway pier, the Steam Packet Hotel and the clutch of sea-facing villas (only the fishing fleet had remained constant, sporadically crowded amongst its inner harbour in the stony lap of the old town, swelling, dying, burgeoning again, then falling away once more, shrinking like the holes in its nets).

Ashley had dragged me out here, now in the wee small hours of what had become a clear night with the stars steady and sharp in the grip of this November darkness, after the Jacobite Bar and after we'd trooped (victorious at pool, by the way) back to Lizzie and Droid's flat via McGreedy's (actually McCreadie's Fast Food Emporium), and after consuming our fish/pie/black pudding suppers and after a cup of tea and a J or two, and after we'd got back to the Watt family home in the Rowanfield council estate only to discover that Mrs Watt was still up, watching all-night TV (does Casey Casen *never* sit down in that chair?), and made us more tea, and after a last wee numbrero sombrero in Dean's room.

'I'm going for a walk, guys, okay?' Ash had announced, coming back from the toilet, cistern flushing somewhere in the background, pulling her coat back on.

I'd suddenly got paranoid that I had over-stayed my welcome and – in some dopey, drunken excess of stupidity – missed lots of hints. I looked at my watch, handed the remains of the J to Dean. 'Aye, I'd better be off too.'

'I wasn't trying to get rid of you,' Ash said, as she closed the front door after us. I'd said goodbye to Mrs Watt; Ash had said she would be back in quarter of an hour or so.

'Shit. I thought maybe I was being thick-skinned,' I said as we walked the short path to a wee garden gate in the low hedge.

'That'll be the day, Prentice,' Ash laughed.

'You really going to walk at this time of night?' I looked up; the night was clear now, and colder. I pulled on my gloves. My breath was the only cloud.

'Nostalgia,' Ash said, stopping on the pavement. 'Last visit to somewhere I used to go a lot when I was a wean.'

'Wow, really? How far is it? Can I come?' I have a fascination with places people think powerful or important. If I hadn't been still fairly drunk I'd have been a lot more subtle about asking to accompany Ash, but, well, there you are.

Happily, she just laughed quietly, turned on her heel and said, 'Aye; come on; isn't far.'

So here we stood, on the wee mound only five minutes from the Watt house, down Bruce Street, through a snicket, across the Oban road and over the weedy waste ground where the dock buildings stood, long ago.

The dock-side was maybe ten metres away; the skeletal remains of a crane stood lop-sided a little way along the cancered tarmac, its foundations betrayed by rotten wooden piling splaying out from the side of the wharf like broken black bones. Mud glistened in the moonlight. The sea was a taste, and a distant glittering that all but disappeared if you looked at it straight. Ash seemed lost in thought, staring away to the west. I shivered, un-studded the wide lapels of the fake biker's jacket and pulled the zip up to my right shoulder so that my chin was encased.

'Mind if I ask what we're doing here?' I asked. Behind and to our left, the lights of Gallanach were steady orange, like all British towns, forever warning the inhabitants to proceed with caution.

Ash sighed, her head dropped a little. She nodded down, at the ground we stood upon. 'Thought you might know what this is, Prentice.'

I looked down. 'It's a wee lump of ground,' I said. Ash looked at me. 'All right,' I said, making a flapping action with my elbows (I'd have spread my hands out wide, but I wanted to keep them in my pockets, even with my gloves on). 'I don't know. What is it?'

Ash bent down, and I saw one pale hand at first stroke the grass, and then dig down, delving into the soil itself. She squatted like that for a moment, then pulled her hand free, rose, brushing earth from her long white fingers.

'This is the Ballast-Mound, the World-Hill, Prentice,' she said, and I could just make out her small thin smile by the light of the gibbous moon. 'When the ships came here, from all over the world, for whatever it was they were shipping from here at the time, they would sometimes arrive unladen, just ballast in them; you know?'

She looked at me. I nodded. 'Ballast; yeah, I know what ballast is; stops ships doing a *Herald of Free Enterprise*.'

'Just rocks, picked up from wherever the ship last set sail from,' Ash said, looking to the west again. 'But when it got here they didn't need it, so they dumped it –'

'Here?' I breathed, looking at the modest mound with new respect. 'Always here?'

'That's what my grampa told me, when I was a bairn,' Ash said. 'He used to work in the docks. Rolling barrels, catching slings, loading sacks and crates in the holds; drove a crane, later.' (Ashley pronounced the word 'cran', in the appropriate Clyde-side manner.) I stood amazed; I wasn't supposed to be getting ashamed at my lack of historical knowledge until Monday, back at Uni.

'"Hen," he'd say, "There's aw ra wurld unner yon tarp a grass."'

I watched from one side as Ashley smiled, remembering. 'I never forgot that; I'd come out here by myself when I was a kid, just to sit here and think I was sitting on rocks that had once been a bit of China, or Brazil, or Australia or America . . .'

Ash squatted down, resting on her heels, but I was whispering, '. . . Or India,' to myself just then, and for one long, swim-headed instant my veins seemed to run with ocean-blood, dark and carrying as the black water sucking at the edges of the tumbledown wharf beneath us. I thought, *God, how we are connected to the world!*, and suddenly found myself thinking about Uncle Rory again; our family connection to the rest of the globe, our wanderer on the planet. I stared up at the broken face of moon, dizzy with wonder and a hunger to know.

*

When he was younger than I am now, my Uncle Rory went on what was supposed to be a World Trip. He got as far as India. Fell in love with the place; went walk-about, circulating; to Kashmir from Delhi, then along the hem of the Himalayas, crossing the Ganga at Patna – asleep on the train – then zig-zagging from country to coast and back again, but always heading or trying to head south, collecting names and steam trains and friends and horrors and adventures, then at the very hanging tip of the sub-continent, from the last stone at low tide on Cape Comorin one slack dog-day; reversing; heading north and west, still swinging from interior to coast, writing it all down in a series of school exercise books, rejoicing in the wild civility of that ocean of people, the vast ruins and fierce geography of the place, its accrescent layers of antiquity and bureaucracy, the bizarre images and boggling scale of it; recording his passage through the cities and the towns and villages, over the mountains and across the plains and the rivers, through places I had heard of, like Srinagar and Lucknow, through places whose names had become almost banal through their association with curries, like Madras and Bombay, but also through places he cheerfully confessed he'd visited for their names as much as anything else: Alleppey and Deolali, Cuttack and Calicut, Vadodara and Trivandrum, Surendranagar and Tonk ... but all the while looking and listening and questioning and arguing and reeling with it all, making crazed comparisons with Britain and Scotland; hitching and riding and swimming and walking and when he was beyond the reach of money, doing tricks with cards and rupees for his supper, and then reaching Delhi again, then Agra, and a trek from an ashram to the great Ganga, head fuddled by sun and strangeness to see the great river at last, and then the long drift on a barge down to the Farakka Barrage a train to Calcutta and a plane to Heathrow, half dead with hepatitis and incipient malnutrition.

In London, after a month in hospital, he typed it all out, got his friends in the squat where he lived to read it, called it *The Deccan Traps And Other Unlikely Destinations*, and sent it to a publisher.

It very nearly sank without trace, but then it was serialised in a Sunday newspaper, and suddenly, with no more warning or apparent cause than that, *Traps* just was the rage, and he was there.

I read the book when I was thirteen, and again four years later, when I understood it better. It was hard to be objective – still is – but I think it is a good book; gauche and naïve in places, but startling; vivacious. He went with his eyes open, and, not having taken a camera, just tried to record everything on the pages of those cheap exercise books, straining to make it real for himself, as though he could not believe he had seen and heard and experienced what he had until it was fixed somewhere other than in his stunned brain, and so he could describe walking towards the Taj Mahal – ho-hum, thinks the reader, immediately in the realm of the tacky postcard – and still give you a wholly fresh impression of the exact scale and actual *presence* of that white tomb; delicate but powerful, compact and yet boundlessly imposing.

Epic grace. With those two words he encapsulated it, and you knew exactly what he meant.

And so our Rory became famous, at that moment on the very lip of the escarpment of his fame, the rosy cliffs forever at his back as he wandered on.

*

Ash squatted down, resting on her heels. She tore a piece of grass from the mound, ran it through her fingers. 'And I'd come here when my daddy-paddy was beating the living shit out of my mum, and sometimes us too.' She looked up at me. 'Stop me if you've heard this one before, Prentice.'

I hunkered down too, shaking my head as much to clear it as to deny. 'Well, not exactly, but I knew it wasn't all sweetness and light, *chez* Watt.'

'Fuckin right it wasn't,' Ash said, and sounded bitter. The blade of grass ran through her fingers, was turned round, passed through again. She looked up, shrugged. 'Anyway, sometimes I came out here just because the house smelled of chip-fat or the telly was too loud, just to remind myself there was more to the world than 47

Bruce Street and endless arguments about fag money and which one of us got a new pair of shoes.'

'Aye, well,' I said, at a loss really to know what to say. Maybe I get uncomfortable being reminded there are worse backgrounds than coming from a family of mostly amiable over-achievers.

'Anyway,' she said again. 'They're levelling the lot tomorrow.' Ash looked back over her shoulder. I followed her gaze. 'That's what all that plant's for.'

I remembered the Triffid jokes we used to make about Heavy Plant Crossing, and only then saw the dim outlines of a couple of bulldozers and a JCB, a little way off down the piece of waste ground.

'Aw, shit,' I said, eloquently.

'An exclusive marina development with attractive fishing-village-style one- and two-bedroom flats with dedicated moorings, double garages and free membership of the private health club,' Ash said, in a Kelvinside accent.

'Fffuck,' I shook my head.

'What the hell,' Ashley said, rising. 'I suppose the Glasgow middle classes have to go somewhere after they've braved the treacherous waters of the Crinan canal.' She gave her hands one final dust. 'Hope they're happy there.'

We turned to leave the mound, me and the Ash, then I grabbed her arm. 'Hi.' She turned to me. 'Berlin,' I said. 'The jacuzzi; I just remembered.'

'Oh yeah.' She started walking down the slope, back to the weeds, the junk and the ankle-high remains of old brick walls. I followed her. 'I was in Frankfurt,' she said. 'Seeing this friend from college? We heard things were happening in Berlin so we hitched and trained it; met up with ... Well, it's a long story, but I ended up in this fancy hotel, in the swimming pool; and had a big whirlpool bath in a wee sort of island at one end, and this drunken English guy was trying hard to chat me up, and making fun of my accent and –'

'Cheeky basturt,' I said as we got to the main road.

We waited while a couple of cars sped north out of town.

'That's what I thought,' Ashley nodded, as we crossed the road. 'Anyway, when I told him where I came from he started saying he knew the place well and he'd been shooting here, and fishing, and knew the laird and –'

'Do we have a laird? I didn't know. Perhaps he meant Uncle Fergus.'

'Maybe, though when I asked him that he got cagey and said no ... but the point is he was acting all mysterious about something, and he'd already said there was somebody here who was having the wool pulled over their eyes, and had been for a long time, and he thought their name was ...' Ash stopped at the snicket that led up to Bruce Street. My route back to Uncle Hamish's house went straight along the main road.

I looked up the wee path, lit by a single yellow street lamp, half way up. Then I looked back into Ashley Watt's eyes.

'Not McHoan, by any chance?' I asked.

'Yep,' Ash nodded.

'Hmm,' I said. Because McHoans are fairly thin on the ground around here. Or anywhere, for that matter.

'Who was this guy?'

'Journalist. There to cover the big knock-down.'

'What was his name?'

'Rudolph something, I think somebody called him. He wouldn't say.'

'You might have used your feminine wiles.'

'Well, at the time they were more or less fully employed on a systems analyst from Texas with shoulders wide as the prairie sky and a gold company Amex card, to be perfectly honest, Prentice.' Ash smiled sweetly.

I shook my head. 'Saucy bitch.'

Ash grabbed my balls through my 501s and squeezed gently. My breath baled out.

'Language, Prentice,' she said, then released, covered my mouth with hers, wiped my teeth with her tongue, then swivelled, walked away.

'Wow,' I said. The old testes were complaining, but only slightly. I cleared my throat. 'Night, Ashley,' I said, cool as I could.

Ash turned, grinning, then reached into her big, naval-looking jacket with the brass buttons and fished something out; threw it.

I caught the projectile; a little lump of grey concrete, smooth and dark on one side.

'Die Mauer,' she said, walking backwards. 'Actually from the section near the Brandenburg Gate where it said, "Viele viele bunte Smarties!". The red paint on one surface used to be in the middle of the dot in the last "i". Bit of the world that used to be between Germanies.' She waved. 'Night, Prentice.'

I looked at the grainy chunk of concrete in my hand. 'Wow,' I breathed. Ash's fair hair flared briefly under the street light, then dimmed as she walked away. 'Wow!'

CHAPTER

He looked round the Solar of the castle. The big new window at the gable end of the hall was still covered with a translucent plastic sheet which rustled in the wind and crackled as the rain blew onto it. A shifting grid of dark lines was the shadow of the scaffolding outside. The high-ceilinged hall smelled of paint, varnish, new wood and drying plaster. He walked over to one of the mullioned windows, and stood there, looking out at the low clouds as they drifted over Gallanach, soaking the dull town with the curving veils of rain they dragged beneath them, like the train of some vast grey gown.

'Daddy, daddy! Uncle Fergus says we can go up on the roof with mum if we're careful! Can we? Please can we? Promise we won't jump off!' Lewis skipped into the hall, dragging little Prentice behind him. Lewis had his anorak back on, and Prentice was dragging his behind him over the shining parquet floor.

'Aye son, I suppose so,' Kenneth said, sitting on his ankles to pull the younger boy's jacket on and zipping it up. Lewis went leaping and whooping round the hall while this was going on. 'Not so loud, Lewis,' Kenneth said, without much conviction.

Prentice smiled at his dad. 'Daddy,' he said in his slow, croaky voice. 'Need the toilet.'

Kenneth sighed, pulled the child's hood up, then pushed it back down again. 'Aye well; your mum will take you. Lewis!' he shouted. Lewis darted guiltily away from the paint pots he'd been examining at the other end of the hall, and came running over.

'This is great, daddy! Can we get a castle too, aye?'

'No. We can't afford it. Take your brother back to his mum; he needs the toilet.'

'Aww,' whined Lewis, staring accusingly at his young brother, who just grinned at him and wiped his nose on one cuff of his anorak. Lewis prodded Prentice in the back. 'You're always spoiling things!'

'Do as you're told, Lewis,' McHoan said, straightening. His knees complained as he did so. 'On you go. And be careful on that roof.' He waved them both towards the double doors they'd entered through.

Lewis made a show of plodding off, clumping one foot in front of another, body swaying exaggeratedly. He was pulling Prentice by one toggle of his anorak hood.

'By the *hand*, Lewis,' Kenneth said wearily.

'You're a pest, boy,' Lewis told his younger brother as they reached the doorway.

Prentice turned and waved to his dad with his free hand. 'Bye, daddy,' the wee voice said. Then he was pulled out of the room.

'Bye, son,' McHoan said, and smiled. Then he turned back to the window and the rain.

*

'It's a bit damp still.'

'Ach, yer no afraid of a bit a wet, ur ye? Yer no a girrul ur ye?'

'No I'm *not* a girl. But if I get my clothes mucky –'

'Your dad's rich; he can buy you new clothes.'

'Aye; yer paw's rich. You could probably have new claes every day if you wantit.'

'Don't be ridiculous. All I'm saying –'

Kenneth could see both points of view; Lachy, in a grimy shirt held together by odd buttons and a safety pin, and tattered, patched short trousers that drooped below his knees and had probably belonged to at least two elder brothers, was already grubby (and sporting the vivid remains of a black eye no one had mentioned because it had probably been his dad who gave it him). Fergus had nice, well-fitting clothes on: grey serge short trousers, a new blue jersey and a tweed jacket with leather patches sewn on the elbows. Even Kenneth felt a little dowdy in comparison. His shorts had been darned at the back, though he was getting a new pair when the next clothes rations came through. The girls all wore skirts, blouses and jerseys; their socks were white, not grey. Emma Urvill had a coat with a little hood that made her look like a pixie.

'Are we playing this game or not?' she asked.

'Patience,' Lachy said, turning to the girl, still standing holding her bike. 'Patience, lassie.'

Emma looked skywards and made a tutting noise. Beside her, Kenneth's sister, Ilsa, also on her bike, shook her head.

The castle stood on the side of the hill. The tall trees around it were still dripping, and its rough, uneven stones were dark and wet from the rain that had not long stopped. A watery sun gleamed on the dark leaves of the ivy that clung to one side of the ruin, and in the forest behind, a wood pigeon cooed softly.

'Oh, what the heck,' Fergus Urvill said, and rested his bike against a tree.

Lachy Watt let his bike fall to the ground. Kenneth lowered his to the damp grass alongside. The girls propped theirs against the wooden rails at the start of the bridge. The short wooden bridge, about wide enough for a cart, crossed a steep, bush-choked gully about thirty feet deep. At the bottom of this tiny, dank glen a burn splashed and foamed; it rushed out of the woods, curled round three sides of the rock and grass knoll the roofless castle stood upon, fell over a small waterfall, then progressed gently afterwards, joining the River Add near the main road, so that eventually its waters flowed through and beneath the town of Gallanach and into the bay near the railway pier.

Sun came suddenly, making the grass bright and the ivy leaves sparkle; the wind pushed through the forest with a quiet roar, releasing drops of water all around. Kenneth watched a train on the viaduct at Bridgend, about a mile away; the west wind was keeping its noise from them, but he could see the steam rising quickly from the dark locomotive and whipping back over the half-dozen burgundy coaches in little white clouds that spread and were torn apart and flung away by the wind.

'Right,' Lachy said. 'Who's het?'

'Het?' Fergus said. 'You mean "it"?'

'You know what ah mean; who's goin het first?'

'Do One potato, Two potato,' suggested Emma.

'Oh Goad, all right,' Lachy said, shaking his head.

'And you shouldn't take the Lord's name in vain,' Emma told him.

'Christ, Ah'm sorry,' Lachy said.

'You did it again.'

'You a Tim or sumhin?'

'I'm a Christian,' Emma said primly. 'And I thought you were, too, Lachlan Watt.'

'Ah'm a Protestant,' Lachy said. 'That's what am are.'

'Can we get on with this, please?' Ilsa said.

They all lined up, fists clenched; Lachy ended up being it, much to his own annoyance.

Kenneth had never been inside the old castle; you could just see it from the house, if you knew what you were looking for, and you could see it quite well if you used dad's binoculars, but it was on the Urvill estate, and even though their families had been friends for years – generations, dad said, which meant even longer – Mr Robb, on whose farm the castle stood, didn't like children, and chased them off his fields and out of his woods whenever he could, threatening them with his shotgun. He couldn't chase Fergus and Emma Urvill off though, so they were all safe. Kenneth had wondered if Mr Robb was secretly a fifth columnist or even a Nazi, and was hiding men washed up from a sunken U-boat, or preparing a place for paratroopers to land, but despite him and some of the other children watching Mr Robb very carefully from the woods a few times, they had never been able to prove anything. But they had explored the hidden garden a bit, and decided the castle looked worth investigating.

The castle had dark, intact dungeons at ground level, and a stone stair-case in a circular tower that rose to the open heart of the ruin, where a few jumbled stones and a floor of earth and weed looked up to the sky. The stairs wound further up inside the corner tower, pausing at each long-collapsed floor above, where a doorway looked out onto the central well. Another stairway pierced the walls themselves on the far side of the shell of the keep, rising through their thickness past another three doorways hanging like internal balconies, to a couple of small rooms at the top of dark chimneys which led to the base of the walls outside.

The castle held a variety of other dark nooks and shadowy crannies you could hide in, as well as windows and fireplaces set high in the thick walls, where you could climb if you were good at climbing, and if you were really good you could climb up from the circular stairs to the very summit of the ruin, where you could walk, if you dared, right round the thick tops of the walls, over the weeds and the ivy, sixty feet or more above the ground. From there you could look out to sea, over Gallanach, or into the mountains to the north and the forested hills to the south. Closer, there was the overgrown walled garden, across another bridge behind the castle, where tangles of rhodies crowded under monkey-puzzle trees and a riot of exotic flowers attracted buzzing clouds of insects in the summer.

The rules were that you could hide anywhere in the castle; Kenneth and the others left Lachy at the track side of the bridge, counting slowly. They laughed and squealed, bumping into each other and shushing each other as they tried not to shout too loudly while they dithered and giggled over where to hide.

Kenneth climbed up into a high window and crouched down.

Eventually, Lachy came into the open hall of the castle, looking around. Kenneth watched him for a moment, then ducked back in, flattened himself down as close to the stone sill of the window as he could.

He was the last to be found, and for a while delighted in the fact that none of them could find him, even after Lachy had caught the rest and they were all shouting at him to come out so they could have another go. He lay there, feeling the damp breeze coming through the window and tickling the hairs on his bare legs. He listened to the shouts of the others, echoing in the castle's emptied shell, and to the voices of the crows and the wood pigeons in the trees, and he smelled the dark, wet smell of the moss and weeds that had found a foothold amongst the ruin's grey stones. He kept his eyes tightly closed, and as he listened to them search for him and call on him, there came a strange, tight, quivery feeling in his tummy which made him want to clench his teeth and bring his knees together and made him worry about wetting his pants.

I love this here, he thought to himself. I don't care if there is a war on and Fergus's uncle got killed in North Africa, and Wullie Watt got killed in the North Atlantic and Lachy gets hit by his dad and we might have to move to another house because Mr Urvill wants ours back and I don't understand trigonometry and the Germans do invade us; I love this. If I died right now I wouldn't care; wouldn't care at all.

Lachy climbed right up onto the top of the walls eventually, and only then did he see Kenneth. Kenneth came down, yawning widely and rubbing his eyes and claiming he had fallen asleep. He'd won, had he? Oh, jolly good.

They played some more, and made fun of Fergus after he'd won a game because Kenneth had worked out what the two little rooms at the top of the second set of stairs were; they were toilets, and that was why the chimneys led down and went out of the castle; it was so all the number one and numbers twos could fall down there. Fergus had hidden down a latrine! And him worried about getting his clothes dirty, too! Fergus denied they were toilets; they were completely clean and didn't smell at all and they must be chimneys.

'Chimneys, ma arse!' Lachy laughed. 'They're shite-holes!'

(Emma tutted, but couldn't help smiling.)

'Chimneys!' Fergus insisted desperately, blinking hard. He looked at Kenneth as though expecting him to agree. Kenneth looked down at the tramped-down earth under his feet.

'They're shite-holes, so they are,' laughed Lachy. 'And you're just a big jobbie!'

'Chimneys,' Fergus protested, his voice rising, his face going red.

'Big jobbie, big jobbie; big smelly jobbie!' Lachy chanted.

Kenneth watched Fergus shake with anger while Lachy danced round the interior of the keep, singing out, 'Big jobbie, big jobbie; big smelly jobbie!'

Fergus stared angrily at his sister and at Kenneth, as though betrayed, then just stood and waited for Lachy to get bored with his taunting, and as Kenneth watched, a blank, emotionless expression gradually replaced the anger on Fergus's face.

Kenneth had the fleeting, extraordinary impression of seeing something buried alive, and felt himself shake suddenly, almost spastically, shivering.

'... jobbie, jobbie; big smelly jobbie!'

*

In the last game, Kenneth hid with Emma Urvill in one of the dungeons, showing her how to turn her back to the light and put the hood of her coat up to hide her face, and sure enough when Ilsa came to the door of the dungeon – and he felt that quivering, scary, glorious feeling in his tummy again – she didn't see them, and they hugged each other once she had gone, and the hug was warm and tight and he liked it and she didn't let go, and after a while they put their mouths together and kissed. He felt a strange echo of that terrifyingly wonderful sensation in his belly and his heart, and he and Emma Urvill held onto each other for ages, until all the others were caught.

Later, they played in the tangling undergrowth of the walled garden, and found an old over-grown fountain with the stone statue of a naked lady in it, and an old shed at one corner where there were ancient tins and jars and bottles with Victorian-looking writing on them. The rain came on for a while and they all stayed in there, Fergus complaining about his bike rusting, his sister and Kenneth exchanging the occasional sly look, Ilsa staring out at the rain and saying there were places in South America where it hadn't stopped raining for hundreds of years, and Lachy mixing various sticky, treacley subtances together from the shelves of old bottles and tins, trying to find a combination that would explode, or at least burn, while the rain hammered then whispered then dripped on the tarred roof overhead, and plopped through holes onto the springy wooden floor of the shed.

*

'Of course, we haven't moved all the bottles yet,' Fergus said, pointing with his pipe at the still unfilled racks that covered the wall of the cellar. The cellar was painted white, and lit by naked bulbs; wires hung and there were un-plastered holes for cables and plumbing leading through the walls and up to other floors. The wood and metal wine racks gleamed, as did the two hundred or so bottles that had already been stored.

'Should keep you going for a bit, eh, Fergus?' he grinned. 'Once you've filled this lot up.'

'Mmm. We were thinking of touring a few vineyards next summer,' Urvill said, scratching his thick chin with his pipe. 'Bordeaux; the Loire, that sort of thing. Don't know if you and Mary fancy making a foursome or not, hmm?'

Fergus blinked. Kenneth nodded. 'Well, perhaps. Depends on holidays and that sort of thing. And the kids, of course.'

'Oh,' Fergus said, frowning as he picked a little sliver of tobacco off his Pringle sweater. 'We weren't thinking of taking the children.'

'Ah, well, no; of course not,' Kenneth said, as they went to the door. Fergus switched the lights out in the various cellars and they went up the stone-flagged steps towards the utility room and kitchen.

It was that cellar, he thought to himself as he followed Fergus's Hush Puppies up the steps. That was where I hid with Emma Urvill, and kissed her. That cellar; I'm sure it was that one. And that window I was looking out earlier; that was the one I hid in that day, nearly thirty years ago; I'm certain.

He felt a terrible weight of time and loss settle on him then, and a slight feeling of resentment at the Urvills in general and Fergus in particular, for having – with so little thought – stolen part of his memories from him. At least malice might have acknowledged the value of his nostalgia.

'Ferg, this dishwasher's like a Chinese Puzzle,' Fiona stood up from the recalcitrant machine, then saw her brother and smiled broadly, came towards him, hugging.

'Hiya, Ken. Been getting the guided tour, have you?'

'Yes; very impressive.' Kenneth kissed his sister's cheek. How old had she been when he'd come out here with Fergus and the rest? About two, he guessed. Not old enough to come all this way on a bike. He must have been eight or nine. He wondered where

Hamish had been; ill, maybe. He'd always been taking colds.

Fiona Urvill, née McHoan, wore old flared Levis and a loose green blouse knotted over a white T-shirt. Her copper-coloured hair was tied back. 'How're you?'

'Oh, I'm well,' Kenneth nodded; he kept an arm round her waist as they walked over to the dishwasher, where Fergus crouched, consulting the instruction booklet. The door of the dishwasher was hinged open like a drawbridge.

'Appears to be written in code, my dear,' Fergus said, scratching the side of his head with his pipe. Kenneth felt a smile form on his face as he looked down at the man. Fergus seemed old before his time: the Pringle jumper, the Hush Puppies, even the pipe. Of course, Kenneth could remember when he used to smoke a pipe; but that had been different. Looked like Fergus was losing his hair already, too.

'How's school?' Fiona asked her brother.

'Och, getting on,' he said. 'Getting on.' He had been promoted to Principal Teacher in English the previous autumn. His sister always wanted to know how things were going at the high school, but he usually felt reluctant to talk about work around her and Fergus. He wasn't sure why, and he suspected he probably wouldn't like acknowledging the reason, if he ever did work it out. He was even more chary about revealing he was writing down some of the stories he'd told the kids over the years, hoping to publish them some day. He was worried people might think he was trying to out-do Rory, or – worse still – think he hoped to use him as a contact, an easy way in.

'No, I tell a lie,' Fergus admitted. 'Here's the English bit. Well, American, anyway.' He sighed, then looked round. 'Talking about English-speaking furriners, McHoan; you still all right for the International next Saturday?'

'Oh aye,' Kenneth nodded. They were meant to be going to the Scotland–England rugby game in a week's time. 'Who's driving?'

'Umm, thought we'd take the Morgan, actually.'

'Oh God, Fergus, must we? I'm not sure I can find my bobblehat.'

'Oh, come on man,' Fergus chuckled. 'Thought we'd try a new route: down to Kintyre; across to Arran, Lochranza to Brodick; Land Ardrossan and then the A71 to the A of the N. Strikes and power cuts permitting, of course.'

'Fergus,' Kenneth said, putting one hand to his brow. 'It sounds enormously complicated.' He refused to rise to the bait about strikes and power cuts. He guessed that 'A of the N' meant Athens of the North. 'Are you sure the Lochranza ferry runs outside the high season, anyway?'

Fergus looked troubled, stood up. 'Oh, it must, mustn't it? Well, I think it does.'

'Might be best to check.'

'Righty-oh, will do.'

'Anyway, couldn't we take the Rover?' Kenneth wasn't keen on the Morgan; its stiff ride hurt his back and gave him a headache, and Fergus drove too fast in the ancient open-top. Maybe it was the sight of all that British Racing Green paint and the leather strap across the bonnet. The Rover, 3.5 though it was, seemed to calm Fergus a little.

'Oh, come on man, where's your sense of occasion?' Fergus chided. 'The hotel won't let us into the car park if we show up in the *Rover*,'

'Oh God,' Kenneth sighed, and squeezed his sister's waist. 'The Morgan it is then.' he looked at Fiona. Those green eyes sparkling. 'I'm getting old, sis. Do you think I'm getting old?'

'Positively ancient, Ken.'

'Thanks. How're the twins?'

'Oh, glowing.'

'Still taking them to Windscale for their hols then, are you?'

'Ha! Oh, Ken, you're still so comparatively witty.'

'Have you tried switching it on?' Fergus suggested, squatting on the floor in front of the dishwasher again. His voice echoed inside the machine as he tried to stick his head inside amongst the racks.

'Don't be catty, Ferg,' Fiona told him. She smiled at her brother. 'Haven't seen young Rory out here for a while, and he never calls us; he okay?'

'Still in that squat in Camden, last we heard, living off his ill-gotten sub-continental gains.'

'A *squat*?' Fergus said, words muffled. 'Thought he made a packet on that . . . travel book thingy.'

'He did,' Ken nodded.

'About India, wasn't it?'

'Yep.'

'Ferg,' Fiona said, exasperated. 'You bought the book, remember?'

'Of course I remember,' Fergus said, reaching into the dishwasher to fiddle with something. 'Just haven't read it, that's all. Who needs to read a book to find out about India? Just go to bloody Bradford . . . What's he doing living in a *squat*?'

Ken ground his teeth for a second, looking appraisingly at Fergus's ample rear. He shrugged. 'He just likes living with the people there. He's a social animal, Ferg.'

'Have to be a bloody animal to live in a squat,' Fergus muttered, echoing.

'Hoi, don't be horrible about my brother,' Fiona said, and tapped Fergus's backside with her foot.

Fergus glanced quickly round and glared at her, his plump, slightly reddened face suddenly grim. Kenneth felt his sister stiffen next to him. Then Fergus gave a little wavering smile, and with a quiet grunt turned back to the opened machine and its instruction booklet. Fiona relaxed again.

Kenneth wondered if things were really all right with the couple. He thought he sensed a tension between them sometimes, and a couple of years earlier, not long after the twins had been born, he'd thought Fergus and Fiona had seemed distinctly cold towards each other. He had worried for them, and he and Mary had discussed it, wondering what might have caused this unhappiness, and if there was anything they could do (they had decided there wasn't, not unless they were asked). Still, he had tried broaching the subject with Fergus once, after a dinner party, while they nursed whiskies in the conservatory of the old Urvill house and watched the lights of the navigation buoys and lighthouses scattered around and through the Sound of Jura as they winked on and off.

Fergus hadn't wanted to talk. Mary had had no more success with Fiona. And anyway it had all seemed to come gradually right again.

Maybe I'm just jealous, he thought to himself, as Fiona pulled away from him and went to the big new Aga, sitting squat, cream and gleaming against one wall of whitewashed stone. She put a hand over part of the cooker's surface, gauging the heat. The silence in the kitchen went on.

Kenneth had never given Freud much credence; mainly because he had looked as honestly into himself as he could, found much that was not to his taste, found a little that was even just plain bad, but nothing much that fitted with what Freud's teachings said he ought to find. Still, he wondered if he did resent Fergus, at least partly because he had taken his sister away, made her his.

Well, you never knew, he supposed. Maybe everybody's theories were right, maybe the whole world and every person, and all their relationships within it were utterly bound up with one another in an intricate, entangled web of cause and effect and underlying motive and hidden principle. Maybe all the philosophers and all the psychologists and all the theoreticians were right ... but he wasn't entirely sure that any of it made much difference.

'Mary and the kids with you?' Fiona said, turning from the Aga to look at him.

'Taking in the view from the battlements,' Kenneth told her.

'Good,' she nodded. She glanced at her husband. 'We're getting an observatory, did Ferg tell you?'

'No.' He looked, surprised, at the other man, who didn't turn round. 'No, I didn't know. You mean a ... a telescope; an astronomical observatory?'

'Bloody astronomically expensive,' Fergus said, voice echoing in the dishwasher.

'Yes,' Fiona said. 'So Ferg can spend his nights star-gazing.' Mrs Urvill looked at her husband, still squatting in front of the opened machine, with an expression Kenneth thought might have been scorn.

'What's that, my dear?' Fergus asked, looking over at his wife, an open, innocent expression on his face.

'Nothing,' his wife said brightly, voice oddly high.

'Hmm,' Fergus adjusted something inside the dishwasher, scratched above his ear with his pipe again. 'Jolly good.'

Kenneth looked away then, to the windows, where the rain spattered and ran.

*

Conceived in a howling gale, Verity was born – howling – in one, too. She came into the world a month before she was due, one windy evening in August 1970, by the shores of Loch Awe – a birth-place whose title, Prentice at least had always thought, could hardly have been more apt.

Her mother and father had been staying at Fergus and Fiona Urvill's house in Gallanach for the previous two weeks, on holiday from their Edinburgh home. For the last night of their holiday the young couple decided to visit a hotel at Kilchrenan, an hour's drive away to the north east up the side of the loch. They borrowed Fergus's Rover to make the journey. The bulging Charlotte had that week developed a craving for salmon, and duly dined on salmon steaks, preceded by strips of smoked salmon and followed by smoked salmon mousse, which she chose in preference to a sweet. She complained of indigestion.

Well – if in Charlotte's case rather monotonously – fed, they began the return journey. The evening was dull, and although there was no rain a strong warm wind was blowing, waving the tops of the trees and stroking lines of white breakers up the length of the narrow loch. The gale increased to storm force as they drove south west into it, down the single-track road on the western shore.

The narrow road was littered with fallen branches; it was probably one of those that produced the puncture.

And so, while her husband struggled with over-enthusiastically-tightened wheel-nuts, Charlotte went into labour.

Barely half an hour later a stunning blue flash – the colour of the moon and brighter than the sun – burst over the scene from the hill above.

The noise was thunderous.

Charlotte screamed.

Above, on the hillside, stood the lattice forms of two electricity pylons, straddling the heather like grey gigantic skeletons wreathed in darkness. The black wind howled and there was another blinding flash and a titanic concussion; a line of violet incandescence split the night mid-way between the two huge pylons as energy short-circuited through the air between the wind-whipped power-lines.

Charlotte screamed again, and the child was born.

*

The tail end of Hurricane Verity passed over the British Isles that night; it had been born in the doldrums, cut its teeth flooding bits of the Bahamas, flirted with the coast of North Carolina, and then swept off across the North Atlantic, gradually losing energy; a brief encounter with the angle between a cold front and a warm front just off Ireland refreshed it unexpectedly, and it trashed numerous pleasure boats, rattled a few acres of windows, played frisbee with a multitude of slates and broke many a bough as it passed over Scotland.

The stretch of the national electricity grid down the western shore of Loch Awe towards Gallanach was one of the storm's more spectacular victims, and Charlotte always claimed that it was right on the stroke of the final massive arc between the thrashing cables – which tripped circuit breakers in the grid to the north and plunged all of Gallanach into darkness – that her child (wrinkled, blood-flecked and salmon pink) finally slid out into her father's hands.

They named her Verity, after the hurricane.

*

When she was eighteen, Fergus Urvill gave his niece Verity a very special present made from one of the exhibits in the museum attached to his glass factory. For the child born to the blaze and crack of human lightning, her entry into this world marked by the same brilliant arcs of short-circuited energy that plunged Gallanach into powerless gloom, he had a necklace fashioned which was made from fulgurite.

Fulgurite is a natural glass, like another of the museum's minor treasures, obsidian. But while obsidian is born purely of the earth, formed in the baking heat and furious pressure of volcanic eruptions, fulgurite is of the earth and of the air, too; it is made when lightning strikes unconsolidated sand, and fuses it, vitrifies it in long, zig-zag tubes. God's glass, Hamish McHoan called it.

The Gallanach Glass Works Museum contained a collection of tubular fulgurites, plucked from the sands of Syria by Walter Urvill – Fergus's grandfather – on a visit there in 1890, and transported back to Scotland with great care and not a little luck so that they arrived intact. One of the crinkled, gnarled little tubes was over a metre long; another just a fraction shorter. Fergus had the smaller of the two sent to a jeweller in Edinburgh, to be broken, the pieces graded and ground and polished and threaded together like dark little pearls, to create a unique necklace for his niece.

He presented the result to the lightning-child during her birthday party, at her parents' house in Merchiston, in Edinburgh, in August 1988 (it was, perhaps unfittingly, a perfectly fine, warm, clear and calm night, on that anniversary). Fergus – always a rather dour, prematurely elderly figure, characterised by those collar-contacting jowls – improved immensely in the eyes of both Kenneth and Prentice McHoan with that single, elegant, and rather unexpectedly poetic act.

Verity had the grace to accept the necklace with a particular gratitude that acknowledged the thought behind the gift, and the taste to make it a regular, even habitual, part of her wardrobe.

The upholstery of Fergus's Rover was cleansed of the debris and stains associated with Verity's birth and the car continued to serve the Urvill family for another five years or so until 1975, when it was traded in (for what Prentice would thereafter maintain was a scandalously small sum, considering that the thing ought to have been preserved as some sort of internationally-recognised shrine to Beauty) for an Aston Martin DB6.

It was once Prentice's dream, shortly after he'd passed his driving test, to find that old Rover – lying in a field somewhere, perhaps – and to buy it; to own the car his beloved had been born in; to drive it and to cherish it. He realised, of course, that it had almost certainly been scrapped long before, but that had not prevented him harbouring the perhaps irrational notion that somehow a little of its recycled metal must have found its way into at least one of the three old bangers he'd owned.

The defiantly thunderous and lightning-fast Aston Martin DB6 was the car that Fergus and Fiona Urvill were travelling in on the night they were involved in a crash at Achnaba, just south of Lochgair, in 1980.

CHAPTER
5

Right, now this isn't as bad as it sounds, but ... I was in bed with my Aunty Janice.

Well, actually, in one sense it's *exactly* as bad as it sounds because when I say I was in bed with her, I don't mean I was in bed with her because we'd gone hill-walking together and been caught out in a snow storm and eventually found shelter in some exceptionally well-appointed bothy that just so happened to have only one bed and we had to get into it together to keep warm; nothing like that. We were fucking.

But (phew), she wasn't a real aunt; not a blood relation, not even an aunt by marriage. Janice Rae had been Uncle Rory's girlfriend, and I just called her Aunty. However she *had* been my father's brother's lover, and – perhaps more embarrassingly – it had been her daughter, Marion, who had initiated me into the whole sticky, smelly, noisy, potentially fatal, potentially natal, sordid and sublime act in the first place, on the dry, cracked green leather surface of the garaged Lagonda Rapide Saloon's back seat, one hot and musty summer's afternoon, eight years earlier.

(We brought the house down.)

Blame Lewis.

*

The voice has gone quiet, deep, almost gravelly now. A light – harsh and white – shines from one side, so that his lean, clean-shaven face looks hard and angular, even cruel.

'I have this door in my house,' he breathes, then pauses. 'It's a very special door.' He looks to one side. The way he does it, you get the urge to look that way too, but you don't. 'Do you know what I keep on the other side of that door?' He raises one eyebrow, but there is silence in the darkness. You wait. 'Behind the door I keep ...' (He leans forward now, towards us, somehow confiding and threatening together.) '... the rest of the Universe.' A wintery smile, and if you were prone to that sort of thing, your skin might crawl.

There is a little nervous laughter. He waits patiently for it to subside. 'I have a special name for that door,' he says, eyes narrowing. 'Do you know what I call it?' (This is the dangerous bit, where it could all end in disaster, but he holds the pause, and the silence is eloquent.) 'I call it ...' he pauses again, looks into the darkness to one side, then towards the light again. '... my Front Door.'

There is more laughter, like relief. He smiles for the first time; a thin, unimpressed expression. 'Perhaps you have one like it, in your house.' He steps back, the lights go up, and he makes a sort of half nod, half bow. 'My name is Lewis McHoan. Good night.'

He walks off to loud applause; cheers, even.

I look from the television to my flatmates.

'Aye, he's no bad,' Gav says, pulling open another can of cider.

'He's okay,' agrees Norris, and drinks from his. 'That last bit was a bit weird but. He really your brother, aye?'

I glare at the screen as the MC appears, signing off. Lewis had been the last act. 'Yes.' I say, taking my empty Export can between both hands, and crushing it. 'Yes, he is.' The credits roll. I throw the squashed can at the litter bin, but it misses, hits the wall, rolls across the floor and dribbles flat beer onto the threadbare carpet.

*

I stood in the bookshop, reading the story about the magic dressing gown, tears in my eyes.

A hand tapped me on the shoulder. I put the book down quickly on the pile and hauled my hanky from my pocket, bringing it up to my face as I turned. I blew my nose.

'Come on, slow-coach,' mum said, smiling down at me. Her gaze flicked to the book-pile. 'Reading your dad's stories at last, eh? What's brought this on?' Not waiting for an answer, she put one arm round my shoulders and guided me out onto the Departures concourse. 'Come on; let's go and wish your Uncle Rory *bon voyage*, shall we?'

'All right,' I said, sniffing.

Mum frowned down. 'Prentice, have you been crying?'

'No!' I said vehemently, shaking my head and stuffing the hanky back into my trousers. Mum just smiled. I felt the tears try to come again, prickling behind my eyes.

'Prentice!' Uncle Rory said, picking me up. 'God, you're getting big. I'll soon not be able to lift you.'

Good, I thought; this is embarrassing. I hugged him, as much to get my face out of sight as to express any regret at his leaving.

'Aye,' I heard my mum saying. 'I think we had a wee tear or two, there.'

'We didn't, did we?' Uncle Rory laughed, bringing me back round in front of him, holding me there. His big face, entirely framed by curly auburn hair, looked happy and kindly. I wanted to hit him and my mum, or maybe burst into tears and hug them;

either would do. 'Ah, dinnae greet, laddy,' he laughed, lapsing into the working-class Scots I had grown ashamed of because my beautiful cousins Diana and Helen didn't speak like that, and those coarse Watt children did.

Stop it! I beamed at him (I was trying to develop a technique for aiming my thoughts at people to get them to do things for me; there were promising developments, but it was early days still, and I was suffering a lot of teething problems. That bastard George Lucas hadn't had the decency to reply to my letter about The Force yet, either).

'I have not been crying, honest I haven't, Uncle Rory,' I said, sniffing.

'Of course you haven't,' Uncle Rory grinned, winking at my mum.

'That's right,' I said. *Now put me down!*

Uncle Rory put me down with a grunt. 'That's better,' he said, roughing up my hair. 'Ah; a wee smile!'

Of course I'm smiling, you big fool; you are prey for my thoughts!

'Will you be away awful long, Uncle Rory?' I asked.

'Yes, I dare say I will, Prentice,' Uncle Rory said. The PA system shouted that the Heathrow flight was boarding. The voice mentioned something about a gate, but I doubted it would be anything as interesting as a stargate. Uncle Rory picked up his shoulder bag and the three of us started to walk towards a big crowd of people. A loud roar outside the glass expanse of one wall sounded excitingly like a crash . . . but it was only a plane landing.

'If you're in Hollywood and bump into George Lucas –'

Uncle Rory laughed mightily, and exchanged one of those infuriatingly knowing adult looks with my mum. 'I don't think that's very likely, Prentice, but if I do . . .'

'Will you ask him if he got my letter?' I said. We reached the place where everybody was standing around and hugging, and we stopped. 'He'll know what it's about.'

'I certainly will.' Uncle Rory laughed, squatting down. He made a worse mess of my hair and gripped both shoulders of my blazer. 'Now you be a good boy and I'll see you all in a few months.' He stood up. Him and mum had a brief cuddle, and she kissed him on the cheek. I turned my face away. I was glad my father wasn't here to see this. How could they do that sort of thing in public? I had a look round to see if my dad was watching from behind a potted palm or through holes cut in a newspaper, but he didn't seem to be.

'Bye, Rory; safe journey.'

'Bye, Mary. Tell Ken I'll call when I can.'

'Will do. Take care now.'

Uncle Rory grinned. 'Yeah.' He squeezed one of her shoulders and winked at her *again*! 'Bye love; see you.'

'Bye.' We watched him show his ticket to the man at the gate, then with one last wave he was gone.

I turned to mum. 'Mum, can I have some more money for the Star Wars machine?' I pointed at the video games. 'I got through three stages last time and I almost got to the fourth; I think I know how to deal with the big towers now and I'm getting really good at –'

'I think you've had quite enough of that machine, Prentice,' mum said, as we walked away through the people. We were heading for the stairs. I tried to pull her towards the row of video games.

'Aw, mum, please; come on; I'll let you watch if you like.'

You will let me play the machine. You will let me play the machine.

She had the nerve to laugh. 'That's very kind of you, Prentice, but I'll pass on that. We have to get back home.'

'Can I go home on the train mum, please can I?'

You will let your son take the train home. You will let your son Prentice take the train home.

'Something wrong with my driving, you wee rascal?'

'No mum, but can I please?'

'No, Prentice; we'll take the car.'

'Aww, but mum . . .'

'Will I buy you a book?' Mum stopped near the bookshop. 'Would you like that?'

'There's a Judge Dredd annual out,' I said helpfully.

She *tss*ked. 'Oh, I suppose, if it'll keep you quiet . . .'

While she paid for it, I went to the pile of dad's books, and when nobody was looking I tore a couple of pages in one book, then put a load of somebody else's books over the top of dad's, so that nobody could see them.

How *dare* he take the stories he'd told me and Lewis and James and the others and tell them to other people, to strangers? They were ours; they were *mine*!

'Come on, terror,' mum said.

A hand between my shoulder blades propelled me from the shop. But at least it wasn't the Vulcan Death Grip.

You will change your mind about letting your son take the train.

Mrs Mary McHoan, you will change your mind about letting your son Prentice take the train home . . . and about playing the Star Wars machine . . .

*

'I mean, nobody tells you sex is going to be so *noisy*, do they? I mean, they can be quite specific about the actual act itself; there is no gory detail, no technical nuance that is not gone into, by teachers or parents or books about sex or the Joy of LURVE or television programmes or just the boys or girls in the year above you at school telling you behind the bike sheds, BUT NOBODY TELLS YOU ABOUT THE NOISE!

'They don't! The first time I ever got laid it was the summer, it was hot, we were doing it naked in the old missionary position, and there I was, trying to pretend I'd been doing this for years, and thinking am I doing this right? Was that enough foreplay, did I devote sufficient time to going down on her or did it look like I was doing it because I read you ought to in *Cosmopolitan* ... and I did want to spend more time down there, but my neck was getting sore ... and I'm thinking should I start chewing the other earlobe now, and should I sort of pull back so I can get my mouth to her nipples, because I'd like to suck them; I would, but my neck's still sore, and just as I'm thinking about all this, and *still* trying to think about putting this MFI kitchen unit together to stop myself from coming too soon but it isn't working any more more because I keep thinking of screws and pre-drilled holes and male and female parts and I'm stroking her and it's great and she's panting and I'm panting and then, just then, from in between our two naked, heaving bodies, THERE IS A NOISE LIKE A RHINOCEROS FARTING!

'There is the noise of a fart the like of which you have never heard in your life before; it echoes off nearby tall buildings; it leaves your ears ringing; little old half-deaf ladies three streets away run to the broom cupboard and start hammering on the ceiling and threatening their upstairs neighbours with the Noise Abatement Society. I mean, a Loud Fart, okay?

'And she is laughing and you don't know what to do; you try to keep going but it happens again and she's in hysterics and it is all deeply, deeply, *deeply* embarrassing, and you keep going but there's this constant farting noise caused by all the sweat and it just isn't the same any more and you're thinking why didn't they tell me about this? Why wasn't I told? I mean, do other people put a towel in between them, or what?

'... And you come eventually and after a cuddle and you've whispered a few sweet somethings, you withdraw, holding the old johnny on because that's what it says on the packet after all, and you go to the loo to dispose of the horrible dangly greasy thing and you have a very full bladder by now and you think you'll have a pee ... Ha ha ha ha ha; WRONG! You *think* you'll have a pee, but you *can't*! ...'

I shook my head, remembering the times Lewis had ranted away like this in the past; in pubs, amongst friends, at parties. I'd enjoyed it usually, back then; I'd felt almost privileged to witness these chaotic fulminating tirades, and even been proud that Lewis was my brother ... But then I'd come to my senses and decided that my elder sibling was in fact a vainglorious egomaniac with a runaway sarcasm-gland problem. Now he was taking what had been relatively amusing examples of a private wit and exposing them to everybody, to make money and amass praise. My family are always doing this sort of thing to me.

I looked at Gav. Gav was standing at my side, clutching his pint glass up near his shoulder and howling with laughter. He was sweating. He had tears in his eyes and his nose was running. He was having a great time. Gavin – one of my two flatmates – is a chap of the world; he has been there, he has done all this, he has had everything that Lewis was describing happen to him, too, and he didn't mind who knew it; this was the comedy of recognition; it was mature, it was happening, it was ideologically correct in terms of sexual politics, but it was also extremely *rude*, and Gav just thought it was all totally hilarious. He was spilling what was left of his pint down his coat, but I suspected he wouldn't have cared even if he had noticed.

I shook my head again and looked back at the low stage, where Lewis was still stalking back and forth like a caged hyena, grinning and sweating and gleaming under the lights and shouting into the microphone and flinging one arm about and smiling wickedly and striding side to side, side to side, talking to individuals at the front, to the people at the side and in the middle of the crowded audience, talking to us standing here at the back, talking to everybody.

Lewis was dressed in black jeans and a white tuxedo over a white T-shirt which had three enormous black letters on it; FTT. In much smaller letters underneath, it read: (have carnal knowledge of the conservative and unionist party and their supporters). You could buy these T-shirts at the door. Gav had one, wrapped in polythene and stuffed in one pocket of his coat.

We were upstairs in Randan's, the latest incarnation of a bar that had previously traded under the name Byre's Market, and before that had been called Paddy Jones's; premises forever apostrophised. That original appellation was before my time, and I confess to a degree of yearning for an age when bars had, in the main, sensible names, and did not pride themselves on serving their own creakingly-titled cocktails, a Choyce Selection of Our Eftimable Home-Made Pies, Hotpottes And Other Fyne Dishes, and twenty different designer lagers, all of which taste identical, cost the earth and are advertised on the tellingly desperate Unique Selling Points of having a neat logo, a top that is difficult to open or a bottle neck whose appearance is apparently mysteriously enhanced by having a slice of citrus fruit rammed down it.

But if this is the price we have to pay for all-day opening and letting women into public bars, then I admit it may well be churlish to carp. I used to think dad was kidding about bars closing in the afternoon, and at ten in the evening (TEN, for Christ's sake; I don't go *out* until midnight sometimes!), and about some not having women's toilets at all ... but apparently it's all true, and scarcely a decade and a half gone.

I looked at my watch, wondering how long Lewis was going to keep this up. Telling conventionally-structured jokes uses up material appallingly quickly and if that had been what Lewis was up to I might not have had the prospect of enduring too much more challenging, non-sexist, politically aware, near-the-bone (well, near the bone-head, at any rate) alternative humour, but this observational stuff – telling people things they already know and getting them to pay you for the privilege (sort of the light entertainment equivalent of psychoanalysis) – can go on virtually indefinitely. Indeed, I felt like it already had.

Lewis was moderately big all of a sudden, after a series of appearances on that late-night TV show. The programmes had been recorded at a Comedy Festival in Melbourne, Australia, which Lewis had been invited to (hence his inability to make old Margot's funeral). Tonight was the première date on his first solo UK tour, and it looked depressingly likely that it would be totally sold out, thanks to the advertising power of television. If he hadn't given me the complimentary tickets I doubted that Gavin and myself would have stood any chance of getting in (but then if he hadn't given me the complimentary tickets a troop of wild Clydesdales on speed wouldn't have dragged me here).

I looked at my watch again. Half an hour gone. So far he had said exactly one thing I found even slightly amusing, and that was right at the start: 'At one stage I thought I was a complete asshole.' (There followed the inevitable pause for effect). 'But I passed through that.'

Laugh? I almost.

'... about my family, ladies and gents, because I come from this very strange family, you know; very strange family indeed ...' Lewis said.

Gav turned, big red face beaming; he nudged me. I didn't turn to look at him. I was staring – glaring – at the stage. My mouth felt dry. He wouldn't dare, would he?

'There's my Uncle Alfred –'

I started to relax. We do not have an uncle Alfred. Still, maybe he was going to use some true or embroidered slice of family history and just disguise it with a false name.

'Uncle Alfred was a very unlucky man. He was so unlucky we actually called him Unlucky Uncle Alfred. We did. Unlucky Uncle Alfred was so unlucky, he's the only man in history ever to have been killed by an avalanche on a dry ski-slope.'

I relaxed a bit more. He hadn't dared. This was just a joke.

'No, really. He was skiing down when it sort of started to come undone at the top and roll down ... crushed to death by three hundred tones of nylon tufting. Haven't been able to look at a Swiss Roll the same way since.'

Another nudge from a highly amused Gavin. 'That true, Prentice, aye?'

I gave what I hoped was a suitably withering look, then turned back to the stage. I drank my heavy and shook my head.

'Prentice,' Gav insisted from my side, missing the first part of Lewis's next mirth-infused effusion. 'Zat true, aye?'

Obviously my withering look needed more work in front of the mirror. I turned to Gavin. 'Every word,' I told him. 'Except his real name was Uncle Ethelred.'

'Aw aye.' Gav nodded wisely, took a sip from his beer without significantly moving the glass from near his right shoulder, and frowned as he tried to catch up with what Lewis was saying, only to succeed in catching the predictably below-the-belt punch-line. Everybody else laughed, so so did Gav, no less enthusiastically than anybody else, and, interestingly, no less enthusiastically than he had at any other part of Lewis's act, when he'd heard every word. Remarkable. I watched Gav for a while from the corner of my eye, wondering, not for the first and – barring serious accidents and justifiable homicide – almost certainly not for the last time, what I was doing sharing a flat with somebody whose cogitative powers I had last had cause to ponder only a few hours earlier, when I had discovered – while watching the news with Gav – that he had believed up until then that the Intifada was an Italian sports car.

In a way I envied Gav, just because he found life such a hoot. He also seemed to think that it was – like himself, perhaps – comparatively uncomplicated. As is the way with such things, these subjectively positive qualities tend to have precisely the opposite effect on the temperaments of those in close proximity to the person concerned.

This was a man, after all, who had not yet mastered something as fundamental and as linear in its properties (for the most part) as running a bath at the correct temperature. How many times had I gone into the bathroom in our flat to find that the bath was full almost to the brim of hot, steaming water? This was an indication that Gav was planning to bathe in an hour or so. Gavin was of the opinion that the way to draw a bath was to fill it entirely from the tap that had the little 'H' on it (thereby reducing the flat's supplies of immediately available hot water to zero), then leaving the resulting body of liquid to cool to something approaching a state in which a human body could enter it without turning instantly the colour of a just-boiled lobster. This normally took about thirty minutes in the depths of winter, and sometimes well over an hour in high summer, during which time Gav was inclined to amuse himself watching television – soap operas and the less intellectually taxing game shows, preferably – or eating, say, banana and Marmite sandwiches (just one example from Gavin's extensive repertoire of unique snackettes that entirely substituted culinary originality for anything as boring as tasting pleasant).

My attempts to explain the subtle dialectics of utilising both hot and cold taps – consecutively or concurrently – to produce a bath that could be used immediately without recourse to the Western General's burns unit (with the resulting benefits of freeing the bath for the use of others earlier and in the process using a great deal less electric power, which both we and the planet could ill afford), fell not so much on deaf ears as on open-plan ones. In automotive terms, if Lewis was a motor-mouth, then Gavin was a cross-flow head.

I drained my glass, studied the flattening dregs of foam at the bottom.

'Nuther beer, big yin?'

'No thanks, Gav; I'll buy my own.'

Gavin, I had long ago concluded, believed that life revolved around rugby and beer, and that – especially under the influence of too much of the latter – sometimes it just revolved. Perhaps it might be a mistake to match him pint for pint.

'Ah; go on. Heavy, aye?' He grabbed my empty glass, and with that he was gone, shouldering his way through the pack of bodies for the distant dream that was the bar. He was still grinning inanely. Probably a good point for him to mount an expedition to the bar. Lewis was in the middle of a long, right-on, faux-naïve spiel about post-isms which Gav probably found a little bewildering. ('I mean, what is post-feminism? Eh? Answer me that? What do they mean? Or have I missed something? I mean, was there a general election last week and nobody told me about it and half the MPs are now women? Are fifty per cent of the directors of all major industries female? Is it no longer the case that the only way to hold on to your genitals if you're brought up in Sudan is to be born a boy? Don't Saudi Arabian driving licences still have a section that says Title: Mr, Mr or Sheik, please delete?')

I really had been going to buy my own drink; anybody who has ever been hard-up will tell you it's the easiest way to regulate one's finances while still remaining nominally sociable, but Gav, profligate though he may have been with the heat plumes from his baths (and kettles; Gavin's determination to wreck the ecosphere through the generation of copious volumes of unnecessary hot water extended to never boiling a kettle that was less than brim-full, even if only a single cup was required), was equally generous when it came to buying drink. At such moments it was almost possible to forget he was also the inventor of custard and thousand-island dressing pudding.

My brother seemed to be thinking along the same epicurean lines. However, to my horror (emulsified with a small amount of schadenfreudian delight), he appeared to be proposing to sing.

I closed my eyes and looked down, ashamed not just for Lewis but for my whole family. So this was the cutting edge of British alternative humour. Finishing with a song. Good grief.

I shall draw a veil over this performance, but let history record that this pretended paean of praise for Mrs Thatcher – comparing her to various foods, with only a hint of sarcasm most of the way through ('as English as Blueberry pie') – ended with the couplet 'Maggie, you're a Spanish omelette, like an egg you just can't be beaten, / Maggie, you're all the food that I eat ... twenty-four hours after it's eaten.'

The puzzled patrons of Randan's, who had been worriedly thinking that perhaps Lewis wasn't quite so right-on after all, and had had his head turned by a sniff of fame and a glimpse of the flexible stuff, suddenly realised their man was still okay (phew), and it had all been an elaborate joke (ha!) as well as a knowing dig at more conventional comedians (nudge), and so duly erupted with applause (hurrah!).

I breathed a sigh of relief that at last it was all over – barring encores, of course – clapped lightly, looking at my watch as I did so. A glance revealed that the besieged bar was under further pressure now that the attacking forces had been reinforced following the end of Lewis's act. I suspected that for all my scorn I might yet be grateful for Gav's rugbying skills that evening, not to mention his Neanderthal build (perhaps that was why he found rugby so attractive; he was a throw-back!)

I looked at my watch again, wondering if Lewis would be unduly insulted, and Gav overly disappointed, if we didn't go back-stage to see the great performer afterwards. Things had gone so appallingly well that Lewis would undoubtedly be on a high and hence unbearable.

Perhaps I could plead a headache, if that wasn't too un-butch for Gav to accept. ('Ach, have another few beers and a whisky or two and it'll soon go away, ya big poof,' would be the sort of reply my flat-mate would favour, as I knew to my cost.)

'Excuse me, are you Prentice? Prentice McHoan?'

I'd noticed the woman sidling through the crowd in my direction a few seconds earlier, but paid no real attention, assuming I just happened to be on her route.

'Yes?' I said, frowning. I thought I recognised her. She was short, maybe early forties; curly brown hair and a round, attractive face that looked run-in without being worn out. I coveted her leather jacket immediately, but it wouldn't have fitted me. A glint in her eyes could have been animal lust but was more likely to be contact lenses. I tried to remember where I'd seen her before.

'Janice Rae,' she said, offering her hand. 'Remember?'

'Aunty Janice!' I said, shaking her hand. I suspected I was blushing. 'Of course; you used to go out with Uncle Rory. I'm sorry I knew I recognised you. Of course. Aunt Janice.'

She smiled, 'Yeah, Aunt Janice. How are you? What are you doing?'

'Fine,' I told her. 'At Uni; last year. History. And yourself?'

'Oh, keeping all right,' she said. 'How are your parents, are they well?'

'Fine. Just great,' I nodded. I looked round to see if Gav was on his way back; he wasn't. 'They're fine. Umm ... Grandma Margot died last month, but apart from that –'

'Oh no!' she said. 'Margot? Oh, I'm sorry.'

'Yes,' I said. 'Yes, well, we all were.'

'I feel terrible; if only I'd kept in touch ... Do you think it would be all right if I, if I wrote ... to your mum and dad?'

'Oh, sure; yeah; fine. They'd be delighted.'

'Even if I'd just made the funeral ...' she said, downcast.

'Yes ... Big turn-out. Went ... not with a whimper.' I nodded at the empty stage. 'Lewis couldn't make it, but everybody else was there.'

Her eyes widened; it was like a light went on beneath her skin, then started to go out even as she said, 'Rory, was he –?'

'Oh,' I said, shaking my hand quickly in front of her, as though rubbing something embarrassing out on an invisible blackboard. 'No; not Uncle Rory.'

'Oh,' she said, looking down at her glass. 'No.'

''Fraid we haven't heard anything for, well, years.' I hesitated 'Don't suppose he ever got in touch with you, did he?'

She was still looking at her glass. She shook her head. 'No; there's been nothing. No word.'

I nodded my head, looked around for Gav again. Janice Rae was still inspecting her glass. Broke or not I'd have offered to buy her another drink, but her glass was full. I was aware that I was sucking in my lips, trapping them between my teeth. This is something I do when I'm feeling awkward. I wished she would say something more or just go away.

'I always felt,' she said, looking up at last, 'that your dad knew more than he was letting on.'

I looked into her bright eyes. 'Did you?'

'Yes. I wondered if Rory was still in touch with him, somehow.'

'Well, I don't know,' I said. I shrugged. 'He does still talk about him as though ...' I had been going to say as though he were still alive, but that might have hurt her. 'As though he knows where Uncle Rory is.'

She looked thoughtful. 'That was the way I felt, when I was down there, after Rory ... left. There was one time when ...' She shook her head again. 'I thought he was going to tell me how he knew; let me in on his secret, but ... well, at any rate, he never did.' She smiled at me. 'And how is Lochgair? Your parents still in that big house?'

'Still there,' I confirmed, catching sight of Gav making his way through the scrum of bodies, concentrating on the two full beer glasses in front of him.

Janice Rae looked warm and happy for a moment, and her eyes narrowed a little, her gaze shifting away to one side. 'It was a good place,' she said softly. 'I have a lot of happy memories of that house.'

'I guess we all do.'

*

Uncle Rory had met Janice Rae at some literary do in Glasgow. She was ten years older than him, a librarian, divorced, and had a ten-year-old daughter called Marion. She lived with her mother, who looked after Marion while Aunt Janice was at work. I could remember the two of them coming to the house for the first time. Uncle Rory had brought various women to the house before; I'd ended up calling them all aunty, and I was calling Janice that by the end of the first weekend they spent at Lochgair.

Despite the fact that Marion was a girl and a couple of years older than me, I got on well enough with her. Lewis – also two years older than me – was going through an awkward stage during which he wasn't sure whether to treat girls with scorn and contempt, or sweeties. James, born the year after me, liked what and who I liked, so he liked Marion. She became one of The Rabble, the generic and roughly affectionate term my father applied to the various kids he would tell stories to on a Family Sunday.

A Family Sunday was one when either the McHoans or the Urvills played host to the other family, plus that of Bob and Louise Watt. Aunt Louise had been born a McHoan; her father was the brother of Matthew, my paternal grandfather and husband of Grandma Margot, she of the heart that broke only after she was safely dead. Bob Watt was brother of Lachlan, whose taunting of Uncle Fergus concerning the matter of hiding inside a medieval lavatory led to the unfortunate incident with the display case and resulted in Lachlan becoming the man with four eyes, but who did not wear glasses.

Bob Watt never turned up for Family Sundays, though Aunt Louise did, often wearing thick make-up and sometimes dark glasses. Sometimes the bruises showed through, all the same. Now and again there'd be something she didn't even try to hide, and I can recall at least two occasions when she turned up with her arm in a sling. I didn't think very much about this at the time, just assuming that my Aunt Louise was somehow more fragile than the average person, or perhaps excessively clumsy.

It was Lewis who eventually told me that Bob Watt beat up his wife. I didn't believe him at first, but Lewis was adamant. I puzzled over this for a while, but at length just accepted it as one of those inexplicable things that other people did – like going to the opera or watching gardening programmes – which seemed crazy to oneself but made perfect sense to the individuals concerned. Maybe, I thought, it was a Watt family tradition, just as Family Sundays and at least one person in each generation of our family managing the Gallanach Glass Works seemed to be two of our traditions.

Mum and Aunt Janice became friends; she and dad were much closer in age to Janice than Rory, and they were parents, too, so perhaps it was no surprise they got on. Whatever; after Uncle Rory disappeared, Aunt Janice and Marion still came down to the house every now and again. It was the year after Rory vanished that Marion, then about fifteen, got me into the garage where the car was. We'd been out on our bikes, riding round some of the forestry tracks one hot and dusty September day; everybody else was in Gallanach, shopping, or – in Lewis's case – playing football.

Marion Rae had the same curly brown hair her mother did. She had a round, healthy-looking face which even I could see was quite pretty, and was about the same height as I was, though a little heavier (I was of that age and body-type concerning which adults help to ease the difficult journey through the age of puberty by making remarks about disappearing if you turned sideways, and running around in the shower to get wet). We'd seen some old burnt-out wreck of a car abandoned in a ditch, up in the hills; I'd said something about the sports car under the covers in the courtyard garage back at the house; Marion wanted to see it.

I still maintain I was seduced, but I suppose I was inquisitive as well. Girls were still less interesting to me than models of the Millennium Falcon and my Scalextric set, but I had conducted a couple of masturbatory experiments which had set me thinking, and when Marion, exploring the warm, dim, tarpaulin-green gloom of the old car with me, said, Phew she was hot, wasn't I? and started unbuttoning her blouse, I didn't say No, or run away, or suggest we get out of the stuffy garage.

Instead I blew on her.

Well, she was sweaty, and I could see moisture on the top of her chest, above the little white bra she was wearing, trickling between the white swells of her breasts. She seemed to appreciate the gesture, and lay back and closed her eyes.

I remember her asking if I wasn't hot, and feeling my leg, and her hand running up to my thigh, then there was some silly line like, 'Oh, what's this?' as she felt inside my shorts, expressing what even then I thought was probably fake surprise at what she discovered there. My own words were no less inane, but something – either the heat of the moment or just retrospective embarrassment – seems to have wiped them and most of the subsequent relevant details from my memory. Still, I recall being pleased that everything seemed to fit, and work as well, and if our (now I think about it, ridiculously fast) mutual thrusts hadn't unsettled the car on its blocks, that sense of having successfully risen to the occasion and worked out what to do with relatively little guidance would have been my abiding impression of the proceedings.

Instead, just as I was both coming and going (going; 'Wow!'), and Marion was making some extremely interesting noises, the car collapsed under us.

It shuddered and fell onto the concrete floor of the garage with an apocalyptic crash. We'd shaken it off its blocks. Some bizarre sense of symmetry had made me insist that we should not lie across the back seat, but that I should instead squat on the transmission tunnel, with Marion half on the rear seat, and half on me. As a result, the Rapide fell backwards off its wooden supports and its boot rammed into a load of drums and cans stored behind it, crushing them in turn against an old Welsh dresser that had been consigned to the garage years earlier; this – loaded up with tins and tools and spare parts and junk until it was top heavy – proceeded to over-balance. It leant, creaking, towards the car, and – although it did not actually fall over – distributed most of its load of paint, spanners, plugs, bolts, spare bulbs, bits of trim, hammers, wrenches and assorted boxes and tins all over the tarpaulin-covered boot, rear window and roof of the Lagonda.

The noise was appalling, and seemed to go on forever; I was dead still, my orgasm – more quality than quantity – completed, and my mouth hanging open as the cacophony reverberated through the garage, the car and my body. Dust filled the car's interior; Marion sneezed mightily and almost squeezed me out of her. Something heavy hit the rear window, and it went white all over, crazed into a micro-jigsaw of tiny glass fragments.

Eventually the noise stopped, and I was about to suggest that we ran away very soon and to some considerable distance before anybody discovered what had happened, when Marion grabbed both my buttocks with a grip like steel, stuck her panting, sweat-streaked face against mine, and snarled those words with which I – in common with most men, I suspect – would eventually become relatively familiar, in similar, if rather less dramatic situations: '*Don't Stop.*'

It seemed only right to comply, but my mind wasn't really on what I was doing. Another precedent, perhaps.

Marion seemed to have some sort of fit; it coincided with – or perhaps was the cause of – the rear window falling in. It showered us both with little jagged lumps of glass, green under the tarpaulin-light, like dull emeralds. We both stayed like that for a bit, breathing heavily and brushing crystalline fragments out of each other's hair and laughing nervously, then started the delicate business of disengaging and trying to dress in the back of a tarpaulin-covered car full of gravelly glass.

We completed dressing outside the car, in the garage, shaking bits of glass out of our clothes as we did so. I had the presence of mind to put these fragments back into the car, and spread the glass more evenly over the seat, removing the shard-shadow of Marion from the cracked green leather (there was, I noticed with a little pride and considerable horror, a small stain there – probably more Marion than me, to be honest – but there was nothing I could do about that beyond wiping it with my hanky). We closed the garage, grabbed our bikes and headed for the hills.

It was a week before dad discovered the disaster scene in the garage. He never did work it out.

Lewis threatened to tell him, but that was only because I'd been stupid enough to blab to my brother, and then been incensed to discover he'd screwed Marion too, twice; on the two previous weekends she'd been down. I immediately threatened to tell the police because Lewis was older than she was and that made it Statue-Tory Rape (I'd heard of this on TV); he said if I did that he'd tell dad about the car ... and so there we were, me barely a teenager and already arguing over a woman with my brother.

*

'It was good to meet you again, Janice,' Lewis said, shaking Aunt Janice's hand, then taking her elbow in the other hand, kissing her on the cheek. 'You should get in touch with Mary and Ken again; I'm sure they'd love to hear from you.'

'I will,' she said, smiling, then fastened the collar of her glove-leather jacket.

Lewis turned to me. 'Bro; sure we can't tempt you?'

'Positive,' I said. 'Got a lot of work to do. Enjoy yourselves.'

'Aw, come on, ya big poof,' Gav said, breathing beer. He put one arm round my shoulders and hugged. From the amount of pressure involved, I gathered he was trying to fold me in half. ''Sno even wan yet!'

'Yes, Gavin, the night is yet senile; but I have to go. You have fun, all right?'

'Aye, okay.'

'Taxi!' shouted Lewis.

We were standing on Byres Road, outside Randan's, which would be closing soon. Lewis, some guy he'd been friendly with at Uni, a girl who may or may not have been Lewis's girlfriend, and Gav had all decided to head for some bar in the centre of town. I had demurred, as had Janice.

'Prentice; see you at the weekend.' Lewis hesitated as he pulled the taxi door open for the maybe-girlfriend, then came up to me, hugged me. 'Good to see you, little brother.'

'Yeah; you take care,' I said, patting his back. 'All the best.'

'Thanks.'

They left in the taxi; Janice and I walked up Byres Road to where she'd left her car. It started to rain. 'Maybe I will take that lift,' I told her.

'Good,' she said. She pulled a small umbrella from her shoulder bag, opened it as the rain came on heavier. She handed it to me. 'Here; you'd better hold this; you're taller.' She took my arm and we had to lean towards each other to keep even our heads dry under the little flimsy umbrella.

She smelled of *Obsession* and smoke. She, Gav and I had gone to meet Lewis, holding court in the small dressing room. Later we had all gone to the downstairs bar, then Lewis had announced he wanted to keep on drinking after they called time. Janice had had a couple of fizzy waters, and seemed totally sober, so I reckoned it was safe to accept a lift.

'You don't really like your brother that much, do you?' she asked.

'Yes, I do,' I told her. The traffic hissed by, heading up Byres Road. 'He just . . . annoys me sometimes.'

'I thought you seemed a bit reluctant when he suggested going back home this weekend.'

I shrugged. 'Oh, that's not Lewis; that's dad. We aren't speaking.'

'Not speaking?' She sounded surprised; maybe amused. 'Why not?'

'Religious differences,' I said. It had become my stock reply.

'Oh dear.' We turned onto Ruthven Street, away from the bright shop fronts and traffic. 'Still a bit further to go,' she said.

'Where are you parked?'

'Athole Gardens.'

'Really? Not a good place to live if you had a lisp.'

She laughed, squeezed my arm.

Hello, I thought. I switched the umbrella from one hand to the other and put my arm lightly round her waist. 'I hope I'm not taking you out of your way. I mean, I could walk. It isn't far.'

'No problem, Prentice,' she said, and put her arm round my waist. *Hmm.* I thought. She gave a small laugh. 'You were always thoughtful.' But somehow, the way she said it, I thought, *No, she's just being friendly.*

We got into the Fiesta; she dumped the brolly in the back. She put both hands on the wheel, then turned to me. 'Listen, I've got some ... some papers Rory left with me. I did mean to send them to your father, but to be honest I lost track of them, and then didn't find them again until mum died and I was clearing stuff out ... I don't suppose it's anything ... you know, that the family needs, is it?'

I scratched my head. 'Dad has all Rory's papers, I think.'

'It's just old poems and notes; that sort of thing.' She started the car; we put our belts on. She took a pair of glasses from her shoulder bag. 'All a bit confusing, really.'

'Hmm,' I said. 'I suppose dad might want a look at them. Wouldn't mind looking at them myself, come to think of it.'

'Do you want to pick them up now?' She looked at me, her round face soft-looking in the orange blush of the sodium vapour. Her hair was like a curly halo. 'It isn't far.'

'Yeah, okay. I guess so.'

I watched her face. She smiled as we pulled away. 'You sound just like Rory sometimes.'

*

Janice Rae was the last person known to have seen Uncle Rory, one evening in Glasgow. Rory had been staying with friends in London for the previous fortnight. He had talked to his agent and seen some television people about doing some travel series, but whatever deal he'd been trying to set up with the BBC, it had fallen through.

At the time Rory was still – just – living off *Traps*, which was attracting a trickle of money even then, when he'd spent everything he'd got for later travel books and occasional articles. He was sharing a flat with an old pal called Andy Nichol who worked in local government; according to Andy, Rory had moped around their flat for a couple of days, shut in his room mostly, supposedly writing, then when Andy had come back from work one day, Rory had asked if he could borrow Andy's motorbike for the night. Andy had given him the keys, and Rory had set off; he'd stopped briefly at Janice Rae's mum's place, and said something about having an idea; some way of saving the project he'd been working on; adding some new ingredient.

He'd given Janice the folder that she now wanted to give me, eight years later, and then rode off into the sunset, never to be seen again.

*

Her flat was on Crow Road, not all that far away, down near Jordanhill. As she showed me into the place, down a hall lined with old movie posters, I asked her if she'd ever heard Grandma Margot use the saying: away the Crow Road (or the Craw Rod, if she was being especially broad-accented that day). It meant dying; being dead. 'Aye, he's away the crow road,' meant 'He's dead.'

Janice looked away from me when I said those words, mumbled about the papers and went to get them.

Idiot, I told myself. I stood in the living room; it was full of heavy old furniture that looked as though it belonged somewhere else, and some limited edition modern prints. On a sideboard, there was a photograph of Janice Rae's dead mother, and another of her daughter Marion and her husband. Marion was a policewoman in Aberdeen. I shook my head, grinning and feeling very old and very young at once.

'Here,' Aunt Janice said. She handed me a cardboard folder stuffed with loose papers. On the spine it said *CR* in black felt-tip. The folder was burgundy but the spine was faded to grey.

'CR?' I said.

'*Crow Road*,' Janice said quietly, looking down at the folder in my hands.

I wasn't sure what to say. While I was still thinking, she looked up, bright-eyed, glanced around at the walls of the flat and shrugged. 'Yeah; I know. Sentimental of me, eh?' She smiled.

'No,' I said. 'It's . . . it's –' The words *sweet* and *nice* suggested themselves, but didn't seem right. '– fitting. I guess.' I stuck the folder under my arm, cleared my throat. 'Well . . .' I said.

She had taken off her jacket; she wore a blouse and cords. She shrugged. 'Would you like some coffee? Something stronger?'

'Umm . . .' I said, taking a deep breath. 'Well . . . aren't you tired?'

'No,' she said, folding her arms. 'I usually read way past this time of night. Stay; have some whisky.'

She took my jacket, poured me a whisky.

I sat down on a huge, surprisingly firm old couch. It looked like brown leather, but any smell it had had was gone. I held the whisky glass up. 'Won't you?' I said. *This is like playing chess*, I thought.

'Well, not if I have to drive you home, Prentice.'

'Oh . . . I could . . . walk,' I smiled bravely. 'Can't be more than three or four miles. Less than an hour. You'd lend me a brolly, wouldn't you? Or there might be a night bus. Please; have a whisky; sit down, make yourself at home.'

She laughed. 'Okay, okay.' She went to the table where the bottles were, poured herself a whisky. Somewhere in the distance, that sound of the city: a siren warbling.

'Stay here, if you like,' she said, slowly putting the top back on the bottle. She turned, leaning back against the table, drinking from her glass, looking down at me. 'That's if you want to ... I don't want you to think I'm seducing you or anything.'

'Shit,' I said, putting my glass down on a rather over-designed coffee table. I put my hands on my hips (which is rather an unnatural thing to do when you're sitting down, but what the hell). 'I was kinda hoping you were, actually.'

She looked at me, then gave a single convulsive laugh, and right until then I think it might still have gone either way, but she stood there, her back to the table, set her glass down upon its polished surface, put her hands behind her back, and looked down, her head forward and a little to the left. Her weight was on her left leg; her right leg was relaxed, knee bent in slightly towards the left. I could see she was smiling.

I knew I'd seen that stance before, and even as I was getting up from the couch to go over to her I realised she was standing just the way Garbo does in *Queen Christina*, during the Inn sequence, when she's sharing the best room with John Gilbert, playing the Spanish ambassador who doesn't realise until that point the disguised Garbo is a woman, not a man. She starts to take her clothes off eventually, and gets down to her shirt; then Gilbert looks round, does a double take and looks back; and she's standing just like that, and he knows.

It had – I recalled, even as I went over to her – been one of Uncle Rory's favourite old films.

*

It was one of those wonderful first nights when you never really do more than drowse between bouts of love-making, and even when you do think no more; that's it, finito ... you still have to say goodnight, which itself means a kiss, and a hug; and each touch begets another touch more sweet, and the kiss on the cheek or neck moves to the lips, the lips open, the tongues meet ... so every touch becomes a caress, each caress an embrace, and every embrace another coupling.

*

She turned to me, during that night, and said, 'Prentice?'

'Mm-hmm?'

'Do you think Rory's ... away the crow road? Do you think he's dead?'

I turned on my side, stroked her flank, smoothing my hand from thigh to shoulder, then back. 'I really don't know,' I admitted.

She took my hand, kissed it. 'I used to think, sometimes, that he must be dead, because otherwise he'd have been in touch. But I don't know.' There was just enough light seeping in past the curtains to let me see her head shaking. 'I don't know, because people sometimes do things you'd never have thought they would ever do.' Her voice broke, and her head turned suddenly; she pushed her face into the bedclothes; I moved over to hold her, just to comfort her; but she kissed, hard, and climbed on top of me.

I had, up until that point, been performing an agonising re-appraisal of the indignant signals of total, quivering, painful exhaustion flooding in from every major muscle I possessed. My body's equivalent of the Chief Engineer was screaming down the intercom that the system just wouldn't take any more punishment, Jim, and there was no doubt that I really should have been pulling out and powering down just then ...

But, on the other hand, what the heck.

*

'"... all your nonsenses and truths, your finery and squal-adoptions, combine and coalesce, to one noise including laugh and whimper, scream and sigh, forever and forever repeating, in any tongue we care to choose, whatever lessened, separated message we want to hear. It all boils down to nothing, and where we have the means and will to fix our reference within that flux; there we are. If it has any final signal, the universe says simply, but with every possible complication, 'Existence,' and it neither pressures us, nor draws us out, except as we allow. Let me be part of that outrageous chaos ... and I am."'

Her voice was sleepy; the hand that had been quietly ruffling my hair had now gone limp. The litany subsided, the quiet words not echoing in the dark room.

Uncle Rory's words, apparently. At first just thought; a mantra to delay ejaculation – a slightly more civilised, if narcissistic, alternative to brother Lewis's thoughts about constructing MFI kitchen units. Then, once, she had asked him what he thought of when they made love (and smoothed over his protestations of eternal in-head fidelity) to discover that – purely to prolong her pleasure – he sometimes recited a piece of his own poetry to himself. He was persuaded to repeat it, for her, and it became a shared ritual.

'Always ... always liked that,' she said quietly, shifting a little to fit her body to mine. 'Always ...'

'Hmm,' I said, and felt her breathing alter. 'Good-night, Janice,' I whispered.

'Night, Rore,' she murmured.

I wasn't sure what to feel. Eventually I yawned, pulled the duvet over the two of us, and smiled into the darkness.

I went to sleep wondering what on earth had possessed Uncle Rory to write a miserable, incomprehensible line 'your finery and squal-adoptions'.

What in the name of hell was a squal-adoption, for goodness' sake?

There was something else nagging me; my conscience. The embarrassing truth was that despite having taken a sort of policy decision years ago, the gist of which was: no condom, no sex, Janice and I had not been using one. She'd emplaced a cap, but that, as the leaflets will tell you, don't provide no AIDS protection. So here I was indulging in casual – if intensive – sex with a woman I hadn't even heard anything about for eight years; hell, she could have been up to anything! But she had claimed the opposite, and I'd believed her. It was probably the truth, but it was exactly such instances of casually misplaced trust that were undoubtedly going to kill better men and women than me over the next decade or so.

Still, it was done. I drifted away.

I swear I was asleep when my eyes flicked on their own and in a burst of dark certainty I thought: *squalid options*! that's what he wrote: *Squalid options*, before going instantly back to sleep again.

CHAPTER
6

They sat, stood or lay within the shattered cone-stump of the old broch, looking out over the more recent, but just as empty, equally abandoned, and even more forlorn square crater of the never-used production-platform yard. Above, a lark – just a speck against the blue – sang, its shrill voice jetting fluid bursts of song.

'Aw, tell us, Mr McHoan; please.'

'Yeah, dad; what is it?'

'Please, Uncle Ken. Pleeease.'

'Yeah, come on, Mistur McHoan. Tell us. Whit is it?'

'What's what?'

'The sound you can see!' Prentice shouted, jumping down from the broken wall of the broch; Ashley was climbing higher.

'The sound you can see?' he said thoughtfully. He leant back on the sun-warmed stones, looking across the grass circle inside the old ruin, over the spray of grey stones downhill where the broch had fallen or been torn away, over the sharp green tops of the pines to the waters of Loch Fyne. A white-hulled yacht ran gull-winged before the wind, heading north-east up the loch towards the railway bridge at Minard point; perhaps heading for Inveraray. In the distance, a few miles behind, he could see another boat, its spinnaker a tiny bright bulb of pure yellow, like a flower on a gorse bush.

'Well,' he said. 'You can't see it from here.'

'Aw naw!'

'Where can you see it from then, uncle?'

'Well, where we were when I told you about it; we could see it from there.'

'In the Old House?' Diana said, looking puzzled.

'That's right.'

'It isn't the wind, then,' Helen Urvill said, and sat down beside him.

Lewis snorted derisively. 'The wind!' he said. 'Don't be so stupid.'

'Aunt Ilsa said it might be breeze block, but I wasn't to say anything until ... aw ... *heck*!' Prentice flattened his hand and struck it off his forehead with a loud slap; he fell over backwards into the long grass.

'Very amusing, Prentice,' Kenneth sighed.

'Hi, Mr McHoan; look at where I am!'

'Good grief, Ashley; be careful.' She was at the top of the wrecked broch wall, rising into the sky like a grey sine on a sheet of blue paper; Ashley a point.

'I'm no scairt, Mr McHoan!'

'I bet you aren't, but I didn't *ask* you whether you were scared or not, Ashley; I told you to be careful. Now get down here.'

'I'll come down if ye tell us whit the sound ye can see is, so ah will, Mr McHoan.'

'Get down here, you wee monkey!' he laughed. 'I was about to tell you, before you started hollering. Down; now.'

'Aw, dinnae get yer knickers in a twist, Mr McHoan,' Ashley

said, shaking her blonde-haired head and starting to climb down the curved edge of the wall.

'I won't, young lady,' he said. Diana and Helen looked shocked, then giggled. Lewis and Prentice sniggered quietly.

'She said knickers, Mr McHoan,' Dean Watt said.

'Ah'm tellin mum,' Darren told his sister as she made her way, feet and bum first, down the slope of stone.

'Ach, away and bugger yourself, Darren Watt,' the girl said, checking on her next footstep.

'Haaaw!' gasped Diana.

'Ashley!' Kenneth said, exasperated.

'Oh, Mr McHoan, did you hear whit she said! Did ye! Yur a wee bissum, so ye are, Ashley.'

'Yes, I did, and –'

'That's very rude you know, young lady,' Prentice said, wagging his finger at the girl. ('Oh shut up, Prentice,' said Lewis.)

'Ah'm no a bissum –'

'Uncle Ken: what's a bu –'

'Waa! She said –'

'Knickers knickers kni –'

' –buggerlugs.'

'All right, all right!' Kenneth said, raising his voice over a high-pitched babble of Childish. 'That's enough! Do you want to hear the answer or not, you horrible rabble?'

'But –'

'She –'

'Ah'm –'

'Stop it!' he roared. He jumped to his feet and shook one fist in the air, dramatically pirouetting so that the gesture included each of them. 'You're all acting like children! If I'd wanted this sort of treatment I'd have stayed a teacher!'

'But dad, we *are* children,' Prentice said, rolling his eyes and shaking his head and falling over in the grass again, sighing loudly.

'Innocence is no excuse, Prentice McHoan!' he roared, shaking one finger at the prone child. 'That was the motto of my old school and you'd all better remember it!'

Lewis was the only one not amused by the performance. He played with a bit of grass. The others were either laughing outright or sat, bunched up, heads down between shoulders, arms tense by sides, making snorting, guffawing noises and exchanging nodding, wide-eyed looks.

'Oh dear lord!' Kenneth shouted to the bare blue sky, his arms wide, head thrown back. 'Look down upon this awful stupid bairn of mine and teach him some common sense before the world gets him!'

'Ha, Mr McHoan! You dinnae believe in the lord!' Ashley roared from half-way up the wall, almost level with his head.

He swivelled to her. 'And that's enough of your old buck, Ashley Watt! I don't believe in Santa Claus but Prentice still gets presents at Christmas, doesn't he?'

'Ah!' Ashley said, pointing at him. 'That's different, Mr McHoan; there's hunners of them!'

He took a step back, looked shocked. 'You little barrack-room barrister; what sort of extra-mural comment is that?' He threw his arms out wide again. To his shock, Ashley jumped right into them, yelling,

'Jurmonimo!'

The girl slammed into his chest, clunked her head off his chin, little arms whacking round his neck, knees hoofing into his stomach. He put his arms out to hold her, staggered back, almost fell, aware that behind him were the twins, sitting on the grass.

He bent his knees, flexed his back, and did not collide with or fall over the twins. He wobbled upright with Ashley still clinging to him, legs round his waist now. She smelled ... sweaty, was probably kindest. 'Well,' he wheezed, winded. 'Thank you for that contribution, Ashley.' The others were relatively quiet. Ashley was rubbing her forehead vigorously with one hand. He frowned, lifted the girl away from his chest so he could look at her face. Apart from being grubby, it looked all right. '*What* did you shout, Ashley?'

'Please, Mr McHoan,' the wee rough voice said, 'Ah said JURMONIMO!'

He started to laugh and had to put her down. He went to his knees, then sat down and rolled over. All the rest joined in except Ashley, who stood, arms folded, bottom lip stuck out fiercely.

'This isnae funny,' she said, turning away. 'Ah'm away tae get fed.'

'Ha ha ha ha,' Kenneth McHoan said, holding his tummy. 'Ha ha.'

'Were your classes this hilarious?'

Kenneth opened his eyes.

'Uncle Rory!' Prentice said, and ran for the man; the boy jumped up onto him rather the way Ashley had leapt down onto his father. Rory laughed and caught him, swung him around, let go an arm and grabbed a leg, whirling the boy round once. 'Wheee!' Prentice yelled. Rory landed him one-handed.

Kenneth went to Rory, hugged him. 'God, man, it's good to see you.'

'You too, Ken.'

'You just get back?' Kenneth laughed.

'Ten minutes ago.'

The two men separated; Kenneth looked his brother up and down.

'Uncle Rory! Uncle Rory! Do some magic; do a trick!'

Rory's chestnut curls had been cut back to what was almost a crew-cut; his face was tanned, clean-shaven. Rory pursed his lips, took a coin from his pocket, bent down to the children, made the coin progress across the knuckles of one hand, then disappear into his fist; he waved over it, and when the fist became hand, the coin was gone. Squeals.

Rory looked lean and a little tired; his jeans were white with wear, and frayed at one knee. He wore a cheesecloth shirt and smelled vaguely of patchouli.

The coin re-appeared behind Diana's ear. She put one hand to her mouth, eyes wide. The others went, 'Yaaayy!'

Kenneth grinned, shook his head, as Rory straightened, a little stiffly. 'More! More! Do it *again*!'

'Later,' Rory said, looking serious, mysterious, and winking.

'So,' Kenneth said. 'How's the world?'

Rory shrugged, 'Still there.'

'Back for long?'

Another shrug, and an easy smile. 'Dunno. Maybe.'

'Well,' Ken said, putting one arm round his brother's shoulders and starting to walk towards the path, where the still-frowning form of Ashley Watt stood, arms crossed tight as her brows. Ken smiled broadly at her, glanced at Rory. 'Better get all the family in the one place before you start answering questions; otherwise you'll get fed up telling the same stories all the time.' Kenneth turned round, waved to the rest of the children. 'Come on, rabble; your Uncle Rory's back from exotic places and he's got much better stories than me!'

The children started after them. The two men came up to Ashley; Rory ruffled her hair. She frowned. Kenneth lifted her up with a grunt, held her dangle-legged in front of him. 'Sorry if I upset you, Ashley,' he told her.

'Huh, okay, Mr McHoan,' she said. 'Ah'm sorry ah swore.'

'Okay,' he set her down.

She looked down the hillside to the forestry track that led back to Lochgair, glanced up at him, then back at the other children, and said loudly, 'Ah bet ah can be back at the hoose first, though but.' She turned and ran.

The rest raced after her, whooping and hollering past Kenneth and Rory.

Kenneth shook his head. 'Preprandial stampede; traditional,' he told his brother. He made a show of squeezing Rory's boney shoulder. 'Woa; feels like you could do with a bit of feeding up yourself.'

'Yeah,' Rory said, looking down at the heather. 'Well, my stories might be a bit thin, too; maybe I should tell them to you first. Let you re-tell the kids.' He gave a small laugh. 'You're the professional fictioneer in the family. I'm just a glorified hack.'

'Hey, is that false modesty or even a note of *jealousy* there, young Rore?' Kenneth laughed, squeezing his brother's shoulder again. 'Come on, man; I stayed here and had weans and taught weans and you were off getting famous; consorting with tigers and wandering through the Taj Mahal and then wowing us all; fucking celebrity; toast of the town and plenty of bread; literary festivals, awards –'

'*Travel* writing awards,' Rory sighed.

'Nothing wrong with that. Jeez; last time I *saw* you, you were on TV. What was that line? "Better lionised than mauled."?' Ken laughed as they walked down the hill.

Rory made an exasperated noise, shook his head. 'Ken, don't you remember anything?'

Ken looked nonplussed. 'What? Did I get it wrong?'

'No, but that was *your* line. *You* said that. Years ago. One night. We were drunk; I don't know . . . but you said it, not me.'

'*Did* I?'

'Yes.'

Ken frowned. 'You sure?'

'Positive,' Rory snapped.

'Good grief. I'm wittier than I thought.' Ken shrugged. 'Well; you're welcome to it. But anyway; let your poor old brother have his turn. Don't begrudge me for being able to distract the odd pre-adolescent from the TV for the odd half-hour.'

Rory shook his head. 'I don't, Ken,' he said, and sighed again. 'I'm not jealous.' He looked at his brother; bearded, hair still dark, face cheerfully lined but still young-looking. 'Just those end-of-ramble blues.' Rory shrugged, the thin shoulders moving under Kenneth's arm. 'But it's good to be back.'

Ken smiled. They saw Prentice walking back up through the

grass and fern towards them, panting. The others were kicking up a cloud of dust on the forestry track; a small and highly noisy storm heading Lochgair-ward.

'What is it, Prentice?' Kenneth called.

'Dad!' the boy gasped from some distance off.

'What?'

'What *was* the sound . . .' He took a deep breath. 'You can see?'

'The Sound of Jura!' he yelled. 'Now keep running or you'll get no dinner!'

'Okay!' Prentice called. He jogged off, shaking his head.

*

The rain fell with that impression of gentle remorselessness west coast rain sometimes appears to possess when it has already been raining for some days and might well go on raining for several more. It dissolved the sky-line, obliterated the view of the distant trees, and continually roughened the flat surface of the loch with a thousand tiny impacts each moment, every spreading circle intersecting, interfering and disappearing in the noise and clutter of their successors. It sounded most loud as it pattered on the hoods of their jackets.

'Ken, are you sure fish are going to bite in this weather?'

'Course they will, Prentice. Have some faith.'

'Well that's good, coming from you.'

Kenneth McHoan looked at his son, sitting looking suitably miserable in waterproofs in the bows of the little boat. 'Just a phrase. I could have said, "Trust me," I suppose.'

'Huh.' Prentice said. 'That's no better. Who was it used to say "If someone says 'Trust me' . . . don't"?'

'Na,' Kenneth said, shaking his head. 'That was Rory. I never said that.'

'You did!' Prentice said, then seemed to realise he was sounding petulant, and looked away again. He plonked the rear end of the fishing rod down in the bottom of the boat, watched the thin end waggle up and down for a while. He folded his arms, leaned forward, hunching up. 'God, I'm depressed.'

'Cheer up,' Kenneth said, falsely hearty. 'Have some more coffee.'

'I don't want coffee.'

'Well, you forced me into it; I was saving this for later, but ...' Kenneth opened the poppers on the Berghaus jacket, unzipped and dug into the deep internal pocket, pulled out a hip-flask. He offered it to Prentice.

Prentice looked at it, looked away. 'I don't think that's going to solve anything.'

Kenneth sighed, put the flask away again, completed reeling in, cast again, and slowly wound the lure in once more. 'Prentice; look, we're all sorry about –'

Darren Watt was dead.

He'd been on his motorbike, driving to Glasgow one bright day. He was overtaking a truck on the long straight at the start of Glen Kinglas; a car pulled out onto it from the Cowal Road. Darren had assumed the driver had seen him, but the driver had only looked one way; hadn't thought to check there was nothing overtaking on his side of the road. Darren's bike hit the wing of the car doing eighty; he might have survived being thrown into the open road or the heather and grass at the road-side, but he had started to turn as he saw the car coming out in front of him, so hit it at a slight angle; he was catapulted across the road and into a lay-by; he hit the big concrete litter bin full on, and was dead by the time the ambulance arrived.

'It's not just Darren,' Prentice said. 'It's everything; it's ... it's Uncle Rory; Aunt Fiona, and ... shit, it's even doing History, dad. Jesus; do human beings *ever* just get on with each other? Why are we always at each other's throats?'

'Well, I wouldn't worry about Rory,' Kenneth said quietly.

'Why shouldn't I? He's dead. He must be; it's been six years; we could probably have him legally declared dead.' Prentice kicked the rod. 'Good excuse for a wake; and we wouldn't even have the expense of a coffin or anything.'

'Prentice . . .' Kenneth said.

'Well!' Prentice shouted. 'You're always so fucking smug about Rory being alive! What do you know? What makes you so smart?'

'Prentice, calm down.'

'I will not! Christ, dad, do you realise how insufferable you can be? Mr Omniscience. Jeez.' Prentice looked away at the grey landscape of water, cloud and dripping trees.

'Prentice, I don't know for certain Rory's alive, but I'm fairly sure. In a round-about sort of way, he keeps in touch. I think. That's all I can say.' He started to say something else, then stopped himself. 'Oh, I don't know what to say. I want to say, "Trust me," but . . . looks like Rory himself has ruled that out. Can't say he isn't right about that . . . It's true, most of the time. But I'm not lying to you.'

'Maybe not,' Prentice said. He looked back at Kenneth. 'But you might be wrong about the things you're so busy telling us the truth about.'

'I did say I wasn't certain.'

'Yeah? What about Darren?'

Kenneth looked puzzled. He shook his head. 'No, you've lost me; what do you –'

'I can't believe he's just . . . gone, like that, Ken. I can't believe there isn't something left, some sort of continuity. What was the point of it all, otherwise?'

Kenneth put the rod down, clasped his hands. 'You think Darren's . . . personality is still around, somewhere?'

'Why not? How can he be such a great guy, and clever and just . . . just a good friend, and some fuckwit forgetting to look both ways cancels out all that . . . probably not even a fuckwit; probably some ordinary guy thinking about something else . . . How . . .'

Prentice shoved his hands under his oxters, rocked forward, head down. 'God, I hate getting inarticulate.'

'Prentice, I'm sorry. Maybe it sounds brutal, but that's just the way it is. Consciousness ... goodness, whatever; they haven't got any momentum. They can stop in an instant, just snuffed out. It happens all the time; it's happening right now, all over the world; and Darren was hardly an extreme example of life's injustice, death's injustice.'

'I know!' Prentice put his hands up to the jacket hood, over his ears. 'I know all that! I know it's happening all the time; I *know* the death squads are torturing children and the Israelis are behaving like Nazis and Pol Pot's preparing his come-back tour; you keep telling us; you always told us! And people just scream and die; get tortured to death because they're poor or they help the poor or they wrote a pamphlet or they were just in the wrong place at the wrong time; and nobody comes to rescue them, and the torturers never get punished; they retire, they even survive revolutions sometimes because they have such fucking useful skills, and no super-hero comes to save the people being tortured, no Rambo bursts in; no retribution; no justice; nothing ... and *that's just it*! There *has* to be something more than that!'

'Why?' Kenneth said, trying not to sound angry. 'Just because we feel that way? One wee daft species, on one wee daft planet circling one wee daft star in one wee daft galaxy; us? Barely capable of crawling into space yet; *capable* of feeding everybody but ... nyaa, can't be bothered? Just because we think there must be something more and a few crazy desert cults infect the world with their cruel ideas; *that's* what makes the soul a certainty and heaven a must?' Kenneth sat back, shaking his head. 'Prentice, I'm sorry, but I expected better of you. I thought you were smart. Shit; Darren dies and you miss Rory, so you think, "Bugger me; must be a geezer with the long flowing white beard after all."'

'I didn't say –'

'What about your Aunt Kay?' Kenneth said. 'Your mum's

friend; she *did* believe; must be a God; prayed every night, went to church, practically claimed she had a vision once, and then she gets married, her husband dies of cancer within a year and the baby just stops breathing in its cot one night. So she *stops* believing. Told me that herself; said she couldn't believe in a God that would do that! What sort of faith is *that*? What sort of blinkered outlook on the world is it? Didn't she *believe* anybody ever died "tragically" before? Didn't she ever read her precious fucking Bible with its catalogue of atrocities? Didn't she believe the Holocaust had happened, the death camps ever existed? Or did none of that matter because it had all happened to somebody else?'

'That's all you can do, isn't it?' Prentice shouted back. 'Shout people down; skim a few useful anecdotes and bite-sized facts and always find something different to what they've said!'

'Oh I'm sorry! I thought it was called argument.'

'No, it's called being over-bearing!'

'Okay!' Kenneth spread his arms out wide. 'Okay.' He sat still for a time, while Prentice remained hunched and tense-looking in the bows. When Prentice didn't say anything, Kenneth sighed. 'Prentice; you have to make up your own mind about these things. I . . . both your mother and I have always tried to bring you up to think for yourself. I admit it pains me to think you . . . you might be contemplating letting other people, or some . . . some doctrine start thinking for you, even for comfort's sake, because –'

'Dad,' Prentice said loudly, looking up at the grey clouds. 'I just don't want to talk about it, okay?'

'I'm just trying –'

'Well, stop!' Prentice whirled round, and Kenneth could have wept to see the expression on the face of his son: pained and desperate and close to tears if he wasn't crying already; the rain made it hard to tell. 'Just leave me alone!'

Kenneth looked down, massaged the sides of his nose with his fingers, then took a deep breath. Prentice turned away from him again.

Kenneth stowed the fishing rod, looked round the flat, rain-battered waters of the small loch, and remembered that hot, calm day, thirty years earlier, on another fishing trip that had ended quite differently.

He took up the oars. 'Let's head back in, all right?'

Prentice didn't say anything.

*

'Fergus, darling! You're soaked! Oh; you've brought some little friends with you, have you?'

'Yes, mother.'

'Good afternoon, Mrs Urvill.'

'Oh, it's young Kenneth McHoan. Didn't see you under that hood. Well, jolly good; come in. Take off your coats. Fergus, darling; close that door.'

Fergus closed the door. 'This is Lachlan Watt. His dad works in our factory.'

'Oh, really? Yes. Well ... You've all been out playing, have you?'

Mrs Urvill took their coats, handling Lachy's tattered and greasy-looking jacket with some distaste. She hung the dripping garments up on hooks. The rear porch of the Urvill's rambling house, at the foot of Barsloisnoch hill, beyond the north-west limits of Gallanach, smelled somehow cosy and damp at the same time.

'Now, I dare say you young men could do with some tea, am I right?'

Mrs Urvill was a tall, aristocratic-looking lady Kenneth always remembered as wearing a head-scarf. She wasn't that day; she wore a tweed skirt, sweater, and a pearl necklace which she kept fingering.

She made them tea, accompanied by some slices of bread and bramble jelly. This was served at a small table in Fergus's room, on the first floor.

Fergus had one slice of bread, and Kenneth managed two before Lachy wolfed all the rest. The war was only over a few months, and rationing was still in force. Lachy sat back, belched. 'That was rerr,' he said. He wiped his mouth on the frayed sleeve of his jumper. 'See the breed in our hoose; it's green, so it is.'

'What?' said Kenneth.

'What rot,' Fergus said, sipping his tea.

'Aye it is,' Lachy said, pointing one grubby finger at Fergus.

'Green bread?' Kenneth said, grinning.

'Aye, an' ah'll tell ye why, tae, but ye've goat tae promise no tae tell anybudy.'

'Okay,' Kenneth said, sitting forwards, head in hands.

'Hmm, I suppose so,' Fergus agreed unenthusiastically.

Lachy glanced from side to side. 'It's the petrol,' he said, voice low.

'The petrol?' Kenneth didn't understand.

'Load of absolute rot, if you ask me,' Fergus sneered.

'Na; it's true,' Lachlan said. 'See the Navy boys, oot oan the flyin boat base?'

'Aye,' said Kenneth, frowning.

'They pit this green dye in thur petrol, an if yer foun wi that in the tank uv yer motor car, ye get the jile. But if ye pit the petrol through breed, the dye comes oot, an ye can use the petrol an naebudy kens a thing. It's true.' He sat back. 'An that's why we huv green breed in oor hoose, sometimes.'

'Woof,' Kenneth said, fascinated. 'Bet it tastes horrible!'

'That's illegal,' Fergus said. 'My mother knows the C.O. at the base; if I told her she'd tell him and you'd probably all be arrested and you *would* get the jail.'

'Aye,' Lachy said. 'But you promised no tae tell, didn't ye?' He smiled thinly over at Fergus, sitting on the other side of the small table. 'Your maw always call ye "Darlin". aye?'

'No,' Fergus said, sitting straight and drawing a hand across his forehead, moving some hair away from his eyes. 'Only sometimes.'

Kenneth got up and went to stare at a big model ship in a glass case on the far side of the room. It was an ordinary steamer, not a warship, unfortunately, but it looked magnificent, like one of the ones he'd seen in the big museum in Glasgow when his dad had taken him there. The ship was wonderfully detailed; every stanchion and rail was there; every tiny port-hole, even the oars in the tiny shore-boats behind the tall funnel, their seats and internal ribs thinner than match-sticks.

'You her darlin, ur ye?' Lachy said, wiping some crumbs from the plate. 'You her wee darlin, that right, Fergus?'

'Well, what if I am?' Fergus said sniffily.

'Weyl, whort if a eym?' Lachy mimicked. Kenneth looked round from the gleaming, perfect model.

Fergus's face looked pinched. 'At least my mum and dad don't hit me, *Master* Watt.'

Lachy sneered, stirred in his seat. 'Aye, great fur some,' he said, standing up. He walked round the room, looking at some wooden aircraft models on a desk, tapping them. 'Very fancy carpet, Fergus darling,' he said, going up and down on his heels on the thick pile of the intricately-patterned rug. Fergus said nothing. Lachy picked up some lead soldiers from a couple of trays ranked full of them, then stood inspecting some maps on the wall, of Scotland, the British Isles, Europe and The World. 'They red bits aw ours, are they?'

'No, they're the King's actually,' Fergus said. 'That's the Empire. They're not red because they're *commie* or anything.'

'Ach,' Lachy said, 'Ah ken that; but ah mean they're British; they're ours.'

'Well, I don't know about "*ours*", but they belong to Britain.'

'Well,' Lachy said indignantly. 'Ah'm British, am ah no?'

'Hmm. I suppose so,' Fergus conceded. 'But I don't see how you can call it yours; you don't even own your own house.'

'So whit?' Lachy said angrily.

'Yes, but, Fergus,' Kenneth said. 'It is the British Empire and we're all British, and when we're older we can vote for MPs to go to parliament, and they're in power, not the King; that's what the Magna Carta says; and we elect them, don't we? So it is our Empire, really, isn't it? I mean you when think about it.'

Kenneth walked into the middle of the room, smiling at the other two boys. Fergus looked unconvinced. Lachlan rolled his eyes, looked at the small single bed, then at a couch in one corner. 'You got this room all tae yerself?' Lachy said, voice high.

'Yes, so?' Fergus replied.

'Bi Christ, it's all right for some, eh, Ken?' Lachy said, winking at Kenneth and walking over to the model ship in the glass case. 'Aye,' he said, tapping the glass, then twisting a little key in a lock at one end of the case; the side panel of the case opened. 'Ah bet ye can get up tae all sorts aw things in here by yourself at nights.' He started trying to haul the model out of the case.

'Stop that!' Fergus shouted, standing up.

Lachy shifted the whole glass on its stand, reached in and lifted the model out of its two wood and brass cradles. Kenneth saw the rear mast bend against the top of the case. The black threads of the radio wires sagged.

'How can ye play with it in here?' Lachlan protested, straining to pull the model out.

'Lachy –' Kenneth said, starting over to him.

'It's not a toy!' Fergus said, running over. He swatted Lachy's arm. 'Stop it! You'll break it!'

'Ach, all right,' Lachy said. He slid the model ship back in. Kenneth noticed with some relief that the mast flexed back into shape, hauling the radio antennae taut again. 'Keep yer hair on, *darling*.'

Fergus locked the door of the case and pocketed the key. 'And don't call me that!'

'Sorry, *darling*.'

'I said stop it!' Fergus shrieked.

'Ach, dinnae wet yer knickers, ya big lassie.'

'You disgusting little –'

'Oh, come on, you two; act grown-up,' Kenneth said. 'Fergus,' he pointed over to the window, and a slope-topped display case standing under it. 'What's all this stuff?'

'That's my museum,' Fergus said, glaring at Lachy and walking to the window.

'Oo, a museum,' Lachy said in a pretend posh voice, but came over too.

'Things I've found, locally,' Fergus explained. He stood over the case, pointing. 'That's a Roman coin, I think. And that's an arrow-head.'

'Whit's that green thing?' Lachy said, pointing to one corner.

'That,' Fergus told him, 'is a fossilized pear.'

Lachy guffawed. 'It's a bit aw bone, ya daft bugger. Where'd ye get yon? Back a the butcher's shop? Find it in the dug's bowl, aye?'

'No I did not,' Fergus said indignantly. 'It's a fossilized pear; I found it on the beach.' He turned to Kenneth. 'You've got some education, Kenneth; you tell him. It's a fossilized pear, isn't it?'

Kenneth looked closer. 'Hmm. Umm, I don't know, actually.'

'Fuckin bit a bone,' Lachy muttered.

'You filthy-mouthed little wretch!' Fergus shouted. 'Get out of my house!'

Lachy ignored this, bent down, face over the cabinet.

'Go on; get out!' Fergus screamed, pointing to the door.

Lachy looked sourly at the pitted, vaguely green exhibit labelled 'Fossilized Pear, Duntrunne Beach, 14th of May 1945.'

'I'm not kidding! Out!'

'Fergus –' began Kenneth. He put a hand on the other boy's arm. Fergus hit it away, face white with fury.

Lachy wrinkled his nose, which was almost touching the glass of the cabinet. 'Still, whit dae ye expect frae a laddy that hides in a lavvy?'

'You *pig*!' Fergus screamed, and brought both fists thudding down on the back of Lachy's head. Lachy's face crashed through the glass, into the display case.

'Fergus!' Kenneth yelled, pulling him away as Fergus kicked at Lachy's legs. Lachy screamed, jerked back, spilling glass, arms flailing, face covered in blood.

'Aah, ya basturt!' he wailed, staggering. 'Ah canny see!'

'Lachy!' Kenneth shouted, hauling his hanky out of his pocket. He went to Lachy, grabbed his shoulders. 'Lachy; stand still! Stand still!' He tried to wipe the blood from the other boy's eyes; it was all over his jumper, dripping onto the carpet.

'But ah canny see! Ah canny see!'

'What on *earth* is going on in he – Oh my God!' Mrs Urvill said, from the doorway. 'Fergus! What have you been letting him do? And get him off that carpet; it's Persian!'

*

Lachlan lost an eye. The Gallanach Glass Works, Ornaments Division, made him an artificial one. Fergus was soundly beaten by his father, and not allowed out for a fortnight. The Urvills granted the Watt family the sum of one thousand guineas in full and final settlement of the matter, the papers drawn up by the firm of Blawke, Blawke and Blawke.

Lachlan was still growing, and perhaps because of that during his mid-teens the eye kept falling out, so another, slightly larger, was made; Lachlan was allowed to keep the old one. He had a third glass eye, which he'd got from the hospital when the first one had been lost for a week (it was eventually discovered, months later, under a chest of drawers in Lachy and Rab's bedroom, where presumably it had rolled during the night), but it was of inferior quality; duller and less lifelike, and he kept it as a spare.

He was the boy with four eyes, and he didn't even need glasses. Or rather a monocle.

'Keep an eye out for us, Lachy!' and variations thereof became a popular phrase amongst his school-mates, though not to his face after the first boy to say it within Lachy's earshot, if not sight, was held down by a half-dozen powerful young Watts and forced to swallow the brown-irised orb, and then to bring it back up.

*

Mary McHoan sniffed the air. 'Prentice, you smell of petrol.'

Prentice collapsed into a seat in the living room. 'Sorry,' he said.

His mother looked over the top of the *Guardian* at him. On the television, a game of snooker was proceeding silently. Prentice sat and looked at it. Mary put the paper down, took off her reading glasses.

'Where's Ken?' Prentice asked. He still had his black leather jacket on.

'In bed, reading,' Mary told him. She folded the paper, went over to her son, and sniffed the air above him. 'And smoke! You smell of ... of non-pub smoke,' she said, going back to her seat. 'What have you been up to?'

Prentice leaned towards her. 'Promise you won't tell dad?'

'No, Prentice,' she said, smoothing her skirt. She took a coffee mug from the small table at her side and sipped from it. 'You know I'm terrible with secrets; not like your father.'

'Hell's teeth. Oh, well,' Prentice said. 'Whatever; we got let off, so –'

'Let off what?' Mary said, alarmed.

'We were in the Jac and Bill Gray said he'd heard the Watts saying – well, it was Ashley, he said, which was why I didn't believe him at first – but he'd heard them ... they were all sitting, all the young ones; the Watts, anyway, sitting there being anti-social and morose, cause of Darren getting killed, and anyway, Bill heard Ash saying there was only one way to deal with it, or they'd never get over it properly, and they should all get sledgehammers and stuff –'

'Sledgehammers!' Mary said, clutching at her elbows.

'That's what I said!' Prentice said, sitting forward, unzipping his jacket. 'Sledgehammers? And Bill said yeah, he was sure; and crowbars, that sort of stuff; they were going to get it out of their system, and I believed Bill because he's so straight; no side at all, and I looked over and they were all standing up and putting their coats on and drinking up, and I tried to talk to Ashley, but they were out the door, and Ash said something about coming along too, and it was Bill had the car, and he'd dashed for a pee, and by the time we got out to the car park they were tearing off in Dean's Cortina, and then Bill couldn't get his car started and we headed for the Watts' house, but by then they'd been there and they passed us; we turned round, followed their lights, caught up with them at those new houses out by Dalvore, but they were just throwing stuff in the boot. I shouted to them, but they got back in and screamed off again, so we followed.

'Jeez, I thought they knew where that guy lived that hit Darren, but Bill said he was from East Kilbride, and I said but we're heading that way! And they just kept going; past here and up to Inveraray, and then I thought, God, I hope I know what they're really going to do, and I told Bill, and he said Shit, let's hope so.'

'Prentice.'

'Sorry. Anyway, I was right. They drove to Kinglas; Glen Kinglas, with us following, and they got parked in the lay-by, and we did too, and we all got out, and we all stood there for a while, and nobody said anything. Then they got the sledgehammers and the crowbars out, and we turned the cars and left the engines running so we had plenty of light, then Bill and I sat on the bank and watched them ... Oh, wow! Mum; you should have seen them! They smashed that fucking litter bin –'

'Prentice!'

'Sorry. But they did; they pulverised the mother. They whacked and smashed and blasted the damn thing to smithereens then tore them to shreds too; hammered the metal bins inside flat, turned the concrete shell of the thing to dust, and I'd asked Bill if it was okay, and he'd said, In the circumstances ... so I went to his car and got his spare can of petrol, because Bill's really organised that way, and said, Was it all right? And they were all standing there, sweating and panting and looking just so *drained*, and Ash just sort of nodded, and I emptied the petrol all over the remains of the bin and Dean threw a match at it and Whumph! up it went, and we just stood there.

'And then this cop stopped! I couldn't believe it! What were the chances? And like only a couple of cars had passed; hadn't stopped, though one had slowed down, certainly, but it had gone off again. And this enormous fu – great sergeant got out and he was, like *incandescent*! The bin was nothing on this guy! And we all just stood there, and I thought, Oh no, this really could end badly, because there was just him by himself, and he was cursing us up and down and the Watts weren't taking it too well and I thought I could hear Dean starting to growl, and I finally managed to get a word in edgeways when he said who'd set it on fire and I said me and stepped forward, showing him the petrol can, and told him what it was all about; about Darren hitting the thing and it being like – well I tried not to use too many long words, but like, expiation ... and he listened, and I was like in that way when you're really nervous where once you've started you can't stop, and I was probably repeating myself all over the place and rambling and not making much sense, but I just kept on going, and he just stood there with this look like thunder on his face, all lit by the fire, and I stopped and said we knew it was wrong and we'd accept having to be punished for it – even though I heard Dean growling when I said it – but even so, although we might be sorry we'd done it, we were glad too, and that was just the way it was, and if we didn't normally have respect for public property, it wouldn't mean so much to us to destroy it like we had.'

Prentice swallowed. 'And I shut up at last, and nobody said anything, and the fire was nearly out by this time, and the big sergeant just says, 'Get on your way and pray I never haul any of you up for anything else.' And I'm like, Yessuh, massa, and kicking dirt over the wee bits of the fire that's left and the Watts are still surly but they're putting all the stuff back in the boot of the Cortina and the big guy's just standing with his arms folded watching us, and I'm thinking; Guildford Four, Birmingham Six, hell; there's still a few good apples left, and we just got into our cars and drove away, with the big sergeant still standing there glowering like Colossus in our tail lights.' Prentice spread his hands. 'That's it.'

'Well,' Mary said. 'Good grief.' She shook her head, glanced at the snooker, then put her glasses on and took up her paper again. 'Hmm, well, I probably won't tell your father that. Away and wash your hands, try to get rid of that smell. There's plenty of milk in the fridge if you want cereal.'

'Right-oh, mum.' He came over to her, kissed her hair.

'Yuk; what a stink. Go and wash, you vandal.'

'Thanks for listening, mum,' he said, on his way to the door.

'Oh, I had a choice, did I?' she said, pretending primness.

Prentice laughed.

CHAPTER
7

We passed the lay-by near the Cowal Road junction doing about ninety. I watched as we went by. Nothing; it was just a damp, deserted parking place with a big new concrete litter bin (replaced with unusual alacrity, in less than six months). We swept past, trailing light spray. It was a dim, grey day; light drizzle from the overcast, mountains hidden past about a thousand feet. We were on dipped-beam; the instruments glowed orange in front of the delicious, straight-armed, black-skirted, Doc-shoed, crop-blonde, purse-lipped Verity; my angelic bird of paradise, driving like a bat out of hell.

*

'Yo; Prentice. Get you out of bed?'

'Oh, you guessed.'

'It's a gift. Pick you up at one?'

'Umm . . . Yeah. Where are you, Lewis?'

'At the Walkers', in Edinburgh.'

'Oh . . . Is Verity there?'

'Yeah; she's coming.'

'Eh?'

'She's coming; to Lochgair. Charlotte and Steve are off to the States this morning, skiing, and Verity –'

'Skiing, to the States? Sheesh, that pack-ice gets –'

'Shut up, Prentice. The upshot is Verity's going to be Festival Perioding with the Urvills. She's going to drive us there.'

And me insane, I thought.

'Great,' I said. 'No Rodney?'

Lewis laughed. 'No Rodney. Verity is finally a Rod-free zone.'

'Couldn't have happened to a nicer chap.'

'Agree grade and comments. See you thirteen hundred hours.'

'Yeah; see you then.' I put the phone down.

There was a dartboard above the phone with a picture of Thatcher taped over it. I kissed it. 'Yeeeeee-HA!' I shouted, leaping back into the bedroom.

'Shut up, Prentice,' Gav moaned, muffled, from his bed. He was invisible under a heap of duvet. My bed was on the other side of the room, away from the window, and so not quite as cold as Gav's in the winter. I fell into it, bounced. (Technically I should have Norris's solo room because I've been in the flat longest, but that room's small and noisy; also, Gav doesn't snore and he's quite happy to retreat to the living room couch if I have female company . . . That's another thing; there's only room for a single bed in Norris's room). 'Put the heater on, ya bastard,' Gav mumbled.

I leapt up, ninja'd over to Gav's bed and wheeched the duvet off.

'Aw ya –!' He grabbed the duvet back, cocooned himself again. '– bastard!'

'Gavin,' I told him. 'You are a skid-mark on the lavatory bowl of life. But I respect you for it.' I turned, grabbed my dressing gown and made for the door; with one mighty ninja kick, the side of my right foot connected with all three switches of the fan heater at the same time and it hummed into life. 'I shall make some tea.'

'Dunno about tea; fuckin good at makin a noise.'

'Thank you for sharing that with us, Gav. I shall return.'

'What's the weather like?'

'Hmm,' I said, staring at the ceiling, one finger to my lips. 'Good question,' I said. 'The weather's like, a manifestation of the energy-transfer effected between volumes of the planet's gaseous envelope due to differential warming of the atmosphere at various latitudes by solar radiation. Surprised you didn't know that, actually, Gavin.'

Gavin stuck his head out from under the duvet, giving me cause once more to marvel at the impressive way the lad's shoulders merged into his head with no apparent narrowing in between (this appeared to be the principal physical benefit bestowed by the game of rugby; the acquisition of an extremely thick neck, just as the most important thing one could take to the sport was a thick skull, and from it an intact one still in satisfactory two-way communication with one's spinal cord).

Gav – who probably epitomised thick-skulledness, though admittedly would not be amongst one's first fifteen when it came to offering proof of heavy traffic within the central nervous system – opened one bleary eye and focused on me with the same accuracy one has grown to expect from security forces aiming baton rounds at protesters' legs. 'What the fuck's made you so unbearable this morning?'

I clasped my hands, smiled broadly. 'Gavin, I am in a transport of delight, or at least shall be shortly after one o'clock this afternoon.'

There was a pause while Gavin's duty-neuron struggled to assimilate this information.

The intense processing involved obviously exhausted too much of Gav's thinly-stretch grey matter to allow speech in the near future, so he contented himself with a grunt and submerged again.

I boogied to the kitchen, singing, 'Walking On Sunshine'.

*

I watched the orange-white needles swing across their calibrated arcs. Ninety. Jeez. I was sitting behind Lewis, who was in the front passenger seat. I kind of wished I'd sat behind Verity; I wouldn't have seen so much of her – not even a hint of that slim, smooth face, frowning in concentration as she barrelled the big black Beemer towards the next corner – but I wouldn't have been able to see the speedometer, either. Lewis seemed unperturbed.

I shifted in my seat, a little uncomfortable. I pulled the seat belt tight again. I checked Verity wasn't watching and adjusted my jeans a little. The folder containing Rory's work lay on the seat by my side; I lifted the file onto my lap, concealing a bulge. There was a reason for this.

We'd been on the bit of fast dual carriageway between Dumbarton and Alexandria, not long after Verity and Lewis had picked me up. Verity made a sort of wriggling motion a couple of times, straining back against her seat. This force was applied by those long, black-nyloned legs, and though most of the pressure was provided by her left limb, some residual effort pushed her right foot down as well, and on each occasion we speeded up, just momentarily, as her amply-soled Doc Marten pressed against the accelerator.

'You okay?' Lewis had asked, sounding amused.

She'd made a funny face. 'Yup,' she'd said, shifting down to fourth as a car she'd been waiting to pass pulled back into the slow lane. We were all pressed back into our seats. 'Problem of wearing sussies, sometimes; they sort of pull a bit, you know?' She flashed a smile at Lewis, then me, then looked forward again.

Lewis laughed, 'Well, no, can't claim I do know, but I'll take your word for it.'

Verity nodded. 'Just getting things sorted out here.' She strained against the back-rest again, her bum lifting right off the seat. The car, already doing eight-five, roared up to over a hundred. The rear of a truck was approaching rapidly. Verity wiggled her bottom, plonked it back down, calmly braked and shifted up to fifth, dawdling along behind the green Parceline truck while she waited for it to overtake an Esso tanker. 'Parceline, parceline ...' she breathed, tapping her fingers on the thick steering wheel. She made it sound French, pronouncing the word so that it rhymed with 'Vaseline'.

'That better?' Lewis inquired.

'Mm-hum,' Verity nodded.

Meanwhile I was fainting in the back seat, just thinking of what that tight black mid-thigh skirt concealed.

It had taken until the long, open left-hander that leads down into Glen Kinglas before my erection had finally subsided, and that had been mostly naked fear; Verity had lost it just for a second, the rear of the car nudging out towards the wrong side of the road as we whanged round the bend. Sitting in the rear, maybe it had felt worse, but I'd been petrified. Thankfully, there'd been no traffic coming; the concept of striking up an intimate – indeed potentially penetrative – relationship with the rocks on the far side of the road had been bad enough; but even the prospect of a head-on with another lump of metal travelling at anything remotely like the sort of speed we were sustaining might have resulted in me making my mark in the most embarrassing fashion on the leather upholstery of the Bavarian *macht-wagen.*

Verity just went 'Whoa-yeah!' like she'd accomplished something, jiggled the steering wheel once and accelerated cleanly away.

Anyway, it's one of the minor unfortunate facts of life that a detumescing willy is prone to trap stray pube hairs under the foreskin as it scrolls forward again, and that was why I was adjusting my clothing as we braked for the bend above Cairndow.

I opened the *Crow Road* folder lying on my lap and leafed

through some of the papers. I'd read the various bits and pieces a couple of times now, looking for something deep and mysterious in it all but not finding anything; I'd even done a little research of my own, and discovered through mum that dad had some more of Rory's papers in his study; she'd promised she'd try and look them out for me. I took a sheet of paper out of the folder and held the page of scribbled, multi-coloured notes up, resting it on one raised knee, gazing at it with a critical look, wondering if Verity could see what I was doing. I cleared my throat. I'd rather been hoping Lewis or Verity might have asked me what the file contained by now, and what I was doing, but – annoyingly – neither of them had.

'Sounds?' Lewis asked.

'Sounds.' Verity nodded.

I sighed. I put the sheet back in the folder and the folder back on the other rear seat.

We rounded the top of Upper Loch Fyne listening to an old Madonna tape, the Material Girl singing 'Papa Don't Preach,' which raised a smile from me, at least.

... Back to Gallanach, for Christmas and Hogmanay. I felt a strange mixture of hope and melancholy. The lights of on-coming cars glared in the dull day. I watched the lights and the drizzle and the grey, pervasive clouds, remembering another car journey, the year before.

'Sounds daft to me, Prentice,' Ashley said, lighting another cigarette.

'It sounds daft to *me*,' I agreed. I watched the red tip of her cigarette glow; white headlights streamed by on the other side of the motorway, as we headed north in the darkness.

Darren had been dead a couple of months; I had fallen out with my father and I'd been in London for most of the summer, staying with Aunt Ilsa and her long-term companion, whose only name appeared to be Mr Gibbon, which I thought made him sound like a cat for some reason ... Anyway, I'd been staying with them in darkest Kensington, at Mr Gibbon's very grand, three-storeyed town-house in Ascot Square, just off Addison Road, and working at a branch of Mondo-Food on Victoria Street (they were trying a new line in Haggisburgers at the time and the manager thought my accent would help shift them. Only trouble was, when people said, 'Gee, what's in these?' I kept telling them. I don't believe they're on the menu any more). I'd saved some money, grown heartily sick of London, fast food and maybe people, too, and I was getting out.

Ash had been in London for a programming interview with some big insurance company and had offered me a lift back home, or to Gallanach anyway, as I'd exiled myself from Lochgair. Her battered, motley-panelled 2CV had looked out of place in Ascot Square, where I think that anything less than a two-year old Golf GTi, Peugeot 209 or Renault 5 was considered to be only just above banger status, even as a third car, let alone a second.

'Sorry I'm late, Prentice,' she'd said, and kissed my cheek. She and Lewis had been out for a meal the night before. Big brother was staying in Islington, making a living from TV comedy shows by being one of the twenty or so names that zip up the screen under where it says Additional Material By:, and trying to be a stand-up comic. I'd been invited to dinner too, but declined.

I'd hoped she'd just pick me up and we'd be on our way, but Ash hadn't seen Aunt Ilsa for a long time and insisted on exchanging more than just pleasantries with her and Mr G.

*

Aunt Ilsa was a large, loud woman of forbiddingly intense *bonhomie*; I always thought of her as being the most remote outpost of the McHoan clan (unless you counted the still purportedly peripatetic Uncle Rory); a stout bulwark of a woman who – for me at least – had always personified the dishevelled ramifications of our family. A couple of years older than dad, she had lived in London for three decades, on and off. Mostly, she was off; travelling the world with Mr Gibbon, her constant companion for twenty-nine of those thirty years. Mr Gibbon had been an industrialist whose firm had employed the ad agency which Aunt Ilsa had worked for when she'd first moved to London.

They met; he found her company agreeable, she found his a new slogan. Within a year they were living together and he had sold his factory to devote more time to the rather more demanding business of keeping Aunt Ilsa company on her peregrinations; they had been on the move more or less ever since.

Mr Gibbon was a grey-haired pixie of a man, ten years older than Aunt Ilsa, and as tiny and delicate as she was tall and big-boned. Apparently he was quite charming, but as the basis of his charm seemed to rest upon the un-startling stratagem of addressing every female he encountered by the fullest possible version of her name (so that every Julie became a Juliana, every Dot extended to a Dorothea, all Marys became Mariana, Sues Susanna, etc. Sorry; etcetera) as well as the slightly perverse habit of calling all young girls 'madam' and all old women 'girls,' it was a charm to which I at least was quite prophylactically immune.

'And you are ...?' he asked Ashley as he welcomed her in the hallway.

'Ash,' she said. 'Pleased to meet you.'

I grinned, thinking Mr Gibbon would have a hard job finding a convincing embellishment for Ash's uncommon monicker.

'Ashkenazia! Come in! Come in!' He led the way to the library.

Ash turned back to me as we followed, and muttered, 'He's a pianist, isn't he?'

Totally misunderstanding what she meant, I sneered slightly at Mr Gibbon's back, and nodded. 'Yeah; isn't he just.'

Aunt Ilsa was in the library; she had a heavy cold at the time and I am tempted to say we discovered her poring over a map, but the inelegant truth is that she was searching the shelves for a misplaced book when we entered.

She spent most of the next half hour or so talking about the extended holiday to Patagonia she was planning, in an extremely loud voice and with an enthusiasm that would probably have embarrassed the Argentinian Tourist Board.

I sat fretting, wanting to be away.

*

By some miracle, the 2CV hadn't been towed away when I'd finally dragged Ash out; we'd made it to the M1, picked up a hitcher and – rather beyond the call of duty, I'd have said – dropped him where he was going, in Coventry. We got lost in Nuneaton trying to get back on the M6, and were now heading through Lancashire at dusk, still an hour or more from the border.

'Prentice, there are a lot of better reasons for not talkin to your dad, believe me.'

'I believe you,' I said.

'What about your mother?'

'No, she's still talking to him.'

She tutted. 'You know what I mean. You're still seeing her, I hope.'

'Yeah; she came to Uncle Hamish's a couple of times, and she drove me back to Glasgow once.'

'I mean, what's the big argument? Can't you just agree to disagree?'

'No; we disagree about that.' I shook my head. 'Seriously; it doesn't work that way; neither of us can leave it alone. There's almost nothing either of us can say that can't be taken the wrong way, with a bit of imagination. It's like being married.'

Ash laughed. 'What would you know? I thought your mum and dad were pretty happy.'

'Yeah, I suppose. But you know what I mean; when a marriage or relationship is going wrong and it's like everything that one person says or doesn't say, or does or doesn't do, seems to rub the other one up the wrong way. Like that.'

'Hmm,' Ash said.

I watched the red tail lights. I felt very tired. 'I think he's angry that having given me the freedom to think for myself, I've not followed him all down the line.'

'But, Prentice, it's not as though you even believe in Christianity or anything like that. Shit, I can't work out what it is you *do* believe in . . . God?'

I shifted uncomfortably in the thin seat. 'I don't know; not God, not as such, not as a man, something in human form, or even in an actual thing, just . . . just a field . . . a force –'

'"Follow the Force, Luke," eh?' Ash grinned. 'I remember you and your Star Wars. Didn't you write to Steven Spielberg?' She laughed.

'George Lucas.' I nodded miserably. 'But I don't even mean anything like that; that was just background for the film. I mean a sort of interconnectedness; a field effect. I keep getting this feeling it's already there, like in quantum physics, where matter is mostly space, and space, even the vacuum, seethes with creation and annihilation all the time, and nothing is absolute, and two particles at opposite ends of the universe react together as soon as one's interfered with; all that stuff. It's like it's there and it's staring us in the face but I just can't . . . can't access it.'

'Maybe it isn't accessible,' Ash said, fag in mouth, holding the steering wheel with her knees and making a stretching, circling motion with her shoulders (we were on a quiet stretch of motorway, thankfully). She took her cigarette from her mouth again, put her hands back on the wheel. I hoped she wasn't getting sleepy; the drone of the wee Citroën's engine was cataleptically monotonous.

'How not?' I said. 'Why shouldn't it be accessible?'

'Maybe it's like your particle; inevitably uncertain. Soon as you understand one part of what it means, you lose any chance of understanding the rest.' She looked over at me, brows furrowed. 'What was that routine Lewis used to do? About Heisenberg?'

'Oh,' I said, annoyed now. 'I can't remember.'

'Something about being at school and bursting into this office and saying, look, are you Principal here or not, Heisenberg? And him going, weellll . . .' She gave a small laugh. 'Mind, it was funnier the way Lewis told it.'

'A little,' I conceded. 'But –'

'Lewis seems to be making it in the old alternative comedy scene, doesn't he?' Ash said.

'So we're told,' I said, looking away. 'I don't imagine Ben Elton or Robin Williams have considered early retiral quite yet, though.'

'Aye, but good for him, though, eh?'

I looked at Ash. She was watching the road as we roared down a slight incline at all of seventy. Her face was expressionless; that long, Modigliani nose like a knife against the darkness. 'Yeah,' I said, and felt small and mean-spirited. 'Aye, good for him.'

'It true you've not seen much of him in London?'

'Well, he has his own friends, and I was usually too tired after work.' (A lie; I wandered art galleries and went to films, mostly.) 'And I couldn't have paid my way, either.'

'Ach, Prentice,' Ashley said, chiding. She shook her head (the long mane of fair hair was tied up, so it did not swish and fall over her shoulders). 'He'd have liked to have seen you more often. He's missed you.'

'Oh, well,' I said.

I watched the lights again for a while. Ashley drove and smoked. I felt myself nodding off, and shook myself awake. 'Ah, dear . . .' I rubbed my face with both hands, asked, 'How do you keep awake?'

'I play games,' she told me.

'Oh yeah?'

'Yeah,' she nodded, licking her lips. 'Like Name That Tail-Light.'

'What?' I laughed.

'True,' she said. 'See that car up ahead?'

I looked at the two red lights. 'Yeah.'

'See how high up the lights are, not too far apart?'

'Yo.'

'Renault 5.'

'No kidding!'

'Mm-hmm. One it's over-taking?'

'Yeah?'

'Horizontally divided lights; that's an old Cortina; mark 3.'

'Good grief.'

'Here's a Beemer. New five series, I think ... about to pass us; should have lights that slant in slightly at the bottom.'

The BMW passed us; its rear lights were slanted in slightly, at the bottom. We overtook the old Ford and the 5 a little later.

'Course,' Ash said. 'It's more fun in a fast car when you're doing all the overtaking, but even just sitting at seventy you'd be surprised how much you pass, sometimes. Now.' She held up one finger. 'Listen and feel as we pull back into the slow lane.'

Ash swung the ancient 2CV to the left, then straightened.

'What?' I said.

'Nothing.' She grinned. 'Missed all the cats' eyes. Bump-free lane-changing. A great skill, you know.' She glanced at me, mock-serious. 'Not so easy in a Ferrari, or whatever; the tyres are too wide. But skinny wee tyres like this thing's got are just about ideal.'

'Allow me to sit back in amazement, young Ashley,' I said, crossing my arms and twisting in my seat to face her. 'I had no idea it was possible to extract such multifarious enjoyment from a simple night-time car journey.'

Ashley laughed. 'Cobbled streets are even more fun, if you're a girly.'

'Huh. Trust you to lower the tone of the whole conversation *and* introduce a note of clitoris envy at the same time.'

Ash laughed louder, ground the cigarette butt out in the ashtray, flipped it closed. 'Och, it's a gift; I'd be ashamed of myself if I wasn't just so fucking nice with it.' She put her head back and roared with laughter at this, before shaking her head and restoring her attention to the road. I laughed a little too, then stared out of the side window, wondering suddenly if Ash had slept with Lewis last night.

She clicked the indicator on. 'Ye Olde Motorway Services. Come on; yer Aunty Ashley'll buy you a coffee and a sticky bun.'

'Gee, you sure know how to show a boy a good time.'

Ash just smirked.

*

When I woke, about mid-day in the flat on Crow Road, Janice Rae had gone. To work, I assume. There was a note, on a small blue sheet of writing paper: 'You're the better stand-up. Call me, sometime, if you want. J.'

I looked at that qualified second sentence with an odd feeling of sadness and relief.

Drying off after a shower, I stood looking at two framed movie posters on the bathroom wall. *Paris, Texas* and *Dangerous Liaisons.*

I had a coffee and some toast, washed up and let myself out. I'd put the *Crow Road* folder in a Tesco bag, and walked back to our flat under grey skies and through a mild and swirling wind, swinging the carrier to and fro, and whistling.

Our flat was in Grant Street, near St George's Cross (and just off Ashley Street, funnily enough). My flat-mates were out when I got back, which was fine by me; I did not relish the prospect of facing the single-entendres that were Gav's best approximation of wit, and which inevitably followed any sexual adventure of mine or Norris's – real or imagined – Gav ever found out about. If I was lucky, Gav would be so shocked at the very idea I had had carnal knowledge of an aunt – even one of the not-really-an-aunt variety – that he would just pretend it hadn't happened. Hell, if I was *really* lucky he might stop talking to me altogether, I thought ... but that didn't seem likely. Or preferable, to be honest; part of me rather looked forward to such taunting. I'd caught a glimpse of my face in the hall mirror once, when Gav was berating me for such rakish tendencies, and I'd been smiling.

I made myself another coffee, extended myself on the sofa – my legs quivery with fatigue – opened the folder, pulled out the sheets of paper and started to read.

Crow Road seemed to be the title of Uncle Rory's Big Idea. From the notes, he seemed unsure whether its final form would be a novel, a film, or an epic poem. There were even some pages discussing the possibility of it being a concept album. I lay there on the couch and shuddered at the very thought. So *seventies.*

The material in the folder seemed to fall into three basic categories: notes, bits of descriptive prose, and poems. A few of the notes were dated, all between the early and late seventies. The notes were on a mixture of papers, mostly loose-leaf; ruled, plain, squared, graph. Some were on cartridge paper, some on pages torn from what looked like school exercise books, and some on folded, green-lined computer print-out. Napkins and old cigarette packets did not, sadly, put in an appearance. The notes were scribbled in a no-less motley variety of different-coloured pens (ball, felt and micro-liner) and used a lot of abbreviations and compressions: *H crshd twn carige & tr? Erlier proph. by Sr: 'kld by t. livng & t. ded((?)) H Chrst-lk figr (chng nm to start with T!!???); fml Chrst fr new times? Scot mrtyr? Or Birnam wd idea – disgsd army??? (2 silly?)* . . . and that was one of the more comprehensible bits.

2 silly, indeed.

The prose was mostly about places Rory had been; they read like out-takes from his travel pieces. *San José, Ca: Suddenly, the Winchester House itself seemed like a emblem for the restless American soul.* . . . about some weird house Rory wanted to use in his story, judging by some cryptic notes at the end of the passage.

Then there was the poetry:

. . . We know this life
is merely a succession

of endless brutal images,
punctuated,
for effect,
by relative troughs
whose gutsy heaves
at first disguised
but power us to the next disgrace.

'Not applying for a job with Hallmark cards, then,' I muttered to myself, sipping at my coffee.

But I kept on reading.

My head wasn't really in the right state for assimilating all this stuff, but as far as I could gather, Uncle Rory had been trying for years to come up with something *Creative* (his capital, his italics). Something that would establish him as a Writer: script-writer, poet, lyricist for a rock band, novelist, playwright ... it didn't matter. Being recognised for having kept a glorified diary while wandering through India when he was young and naïve wasn't enough for him. It wasn't *serious.* This work, *Crow Road*, would be Serious. It would be about Life and Death and Treachery and Betrayal and Love and Death and Imperialism and Colonialism and Capitalism. It would be about Scotland, (or India, or an 'Erewhon???') and the Working Class and Exploitation and Action, and there would be characters in the work who would represent all of these things, and the working out of the story *would itself prove the Subjectivity of Truth.*

... There were pages of that sort of stuff.

There were also pages of poems forced into some sort of rhyming structure so that they might conceivably have worked as songs, several paragraphs of references to critical works (Barthes, especially; *Death of the Author!* shouted what looked like a headline over one entire page of notes devoted to ideas about a *loose-leaf novel/poem??* There were location notes for a film and sheets about the physical appearance of the characters and the sort of actors who might play them, these surrounded by doodles, mazes and uninspired drawings of faces. There was a list of bands that might be interested in doing an album (a musical tone-scale running all the way from Yes to Genesis), and a sheaf of sketches for the sets in a stage presentation. What there wasn't was any indication whatsoever that Rory had actually written any part of this great work. The only things that might have been classed as narrative were the poems, and they didn't seem to have anything to do with each other, apart from the fact a lot of them seemed to be vaguely about Death, or Love. Tenuous, was the word that came to mind.

I looked in the folder again to see if I'd missed anything.

I had. There was another small sheet of blue writing paper, in Janice Rae's hand. 'Prentice – had a look at this –' (then the word 'while', crossed out heavily, followed by the word 'before', also nearly obliterated) '– Can't find any more; R had another folder. (?) If you find it and work out what it's all about, let me know; he said there was something secret buried in it. (Gallanach)?'

I bobbled my head from side to side. 'Gallanach?' I said, in a silly high-pitched voice, as though quoting. I stretched, grunting with pain as my leg muscles extracted their revenge for having been ignored twelve hours earlier.

I reached for my coffee, but it was cold.

*

'Dear God, we beseech ye, visit the reactive wrath of their own foulness upon those nasty wee buggers in the Khmer Rouge in general, and upon their torturers, and their leader Pol Pot, in particular; may each iota of pain they have inflicted on the people of their country – heathen or not – rebound upon their central nervous system with all the agony they originally inflicted upon their victims. Also, Lord God, we ask that you remember the dark deeds of any communistic so-called-interrogators, in this time of great upheaval in eastern Europe; we know that you will not forget their crimes when their day of reckoning comes, and their guttural, Slavic voices cry out to ye for mercy, and ye reward them with all the compassion they ever showed to those unfortunate souls delivered unto them. Prentice?'

I jumped. I'd almost fallen asleep while Uncle Hamish had been droning on. I opened my eyes. The Tree was looking expectantly at me.

'Oh,' I said. 'Umm ... I'd just like to put in a word for Salman Rushdie. Or at least take one out for old Ayatollah Ruhollah Khomeini ...' I looked at Uncle Hamish, who was making quiet signals that I should clasp my hands and close my eyes. We were in the front lounge of Uncle Hamish and Aunt Tone's Victorian villa in the attractive Gallanach suburbette of Ballymeanoch, facing each other over a card table. I closed my eyes.

'Ah,' I said. 'Dear God, we pray that as well as suffering whatever part of the general physical unpleasantness involved in the Iran–Iraq war you may judge to be rightly his, you can find a spare area in his suffering, er, anti-create, for Mr R. Khomeini, late of Tehran and Qom, to experience at least some of the, umm, despair and continual worry currently being undergone by the novelist Mr S Rushdie, of Bombay and London, heathen and smart-alec though he may well be. Amen.'

'Amen,' echoed Uncle H. I opened my eyes. Uncle Hamish was already rising from his seat, looking positively twinkly with health and good cheer. He rubbed his hands. 'Very good,' he said, moving in that oddly stiff and creaky way of his for the door. 'Let us repair for some repast,' he chuckled as he held the door open for me. 'I believe Antonia has prepared something called Cod Creole.' He sniffed the fishy air in the hall; we crossed to the dining room.

'Not Lobster Creole? Or Kid?' I inquired.

But I don't think Uncle Hamish heard me. He was humming something sombre and looking pleased with himself.

Uncle H has developed a fascinating heresy based on the idea that exactly what you did to other people while you were alive gets done right back to you once you're dead. Torturers die – in agony – hundreds, maybe thousands of times, before their ravaged souls are finally dropped from the jaws of a fearsome and vengeful God. Those who authorise the dreadful deeds carried out by the torturers (or whoever) also share whatever proportion of this retrospective agony the deity – or his angelic cost-benefit-calculating representatives – deem they deserve. Having quizzed The Tree on the details of this scheme, it would appear that said burden of transferred pain is debited from the account of the guy at – or rather wielding – the sharp end of the original action, which seems only fair, I suppose.

Apparently Uncle Hamish is awaiting divine inspiration on the knotty problem of whether the good things one has accomplished in one's life are also re-lived from the other side (as it were), or simply subtracted from the nasty stuff. At the moment he seems to be veering towards the idea that if you did more good than bad during your life you go straight to Heaven, an arrangement which at least processes the merit of simplicity; the rest sounds like something dreamt up by a vindictive bureaucrat on acid while closely inspecting something Hieronymus Bosch painted on one of his bleak but imaginative days.

Still, it has its attractions.

Aunt Tone and the family's two children, Josh and Becky, and Becky's infant daughter, Iona, were already in the dining room, filling it with bustle and chat.

'Said your prayers?' Aunt Tone said brightly, depositing a steaming dish of potatoes on the table.

'Thank you, yes,' Hamish replied. My uncle worships alone these days, and has done ever since his son left home to become a devout Capitalist (neither his wife nor his daughter had ever bothered with my Uncle's unique brand of condemnationist Christianity; as a rule, the McHoan women, whether so by blood or marriage, have displayed a marked reluctance to take their menfolk's passions seriously, at least outside the bedroom). I think that was why Uncle Hamish had been so delighted when I'd come to stay with the family, and also – perhaps – why he was in no hurry to help effect a reconciliation between me and my father.

We dined on spicy fish which repeated on me for most of the evening in the Jac, meeting pals, until I drowned it in an ocean of beer.

*

'Happy New Year!' Ashley yelled, flourishing a bottle of generic whisky with more enthusiasm than care; she cracked the bottle off the oak-panelled wall of the castle's crowded entrance hall, but without, apparently, causing damage to either. Clad in a sparkly jacket and a long black skirt, wreathed in silly string and clumps and strands of paper streamers from party poppers, her long hair bunned, she enveloped me in a very friendly kiss, breathing whisky and wine fumes. I kissed right back and she pushed away, laughing. 'Wo, Prentice!' she shouted over the noise. The hall was packed with people; music spilled out from the main hall beyond; pipes and fiddles, tabors and accordions, guitars and a piano, several of them playing the same tune.

'I thought you gave up,' I said, pointing at the cigarette she had stuck behind one ear. Josh and Becky were still at the doors, greeting people they knew.

'I did,' she said, taking the fag from behind her ear and putting it in her mouth. She left it there for a few seconds, then restored it to its previous position. 'See? Still given up; no temptation at all.'

Ash and I levered our way through the press of people while I undid my jacket and struggled to extricate my half-bottle of whisky from a side pocket. We made it into the hall, which was actually less crowded, though still full. A huge fire roared in the grate; people balanced on the fire-seat which ran around the hearth, and on every other available perch, including the stairs and the piano.

A few enthusiasts within the midst of the crowd were trying to dance the Eightsome Reel, which in the circumstances was a little like trying to stage a boxing match in a telephone box; not totally impossible, just pointless.

Ash and I found a space over near the piano. She reached over the piano to a pile of little plastic cups, grabbed one and shoved it into my hand. 'Here; have a drink.' She sloshed some whisky into the cup. 'How've you been?'

'Fine,' I said. 'Broke, and I can see that 2.1 disappearing over the event horizon, but fuck it; I've still got my integrity and my Möbius scarf, and a boy can go a long way with those things. You got a job yet?'

'What?'

'Let's stand away from this fucking piano.'

'What?'

'*Have you got a job yet*?

'Na. Hey.' She put one hand on my shoulder. 'Heard what David Bowie's latest film's called?'

'This sounds Lewisian,' I shouted.

'No,' she shook her head. '"Merry Christmas, Mister Ceausescu"!' Ashley laughed like a drain; a teetotaller might have said her breath smelled like one.

'Very funny,' I yelled into her ear. 'Haven't laughed so much since General Zia got blown up. Where is Lewis, anyway? We were waiting for them to turn up at Hamish and Tone's but they never showed. He and James here?'

Ash looked concerned for a second, then her smile returned. She put her arm round my shoulders. 'Saw James over by the accordion earlier. Hey; you want to take a stroll round the battlements?' She pulled a spliff half out of her breast pocket, let it fall back. 'Got a number here, but Mrs McSpadden keeps wandering through, and I seem to remember she took inordinate and *extremely* loud interest in one of these last year when wee Jimmy Calder stoked up. You comin?'

'Not right now,' I said, looking around the crowd, acknowledging a few waves and some distant mouthings that were probably shouts. I stood on tip-toes to look round the hall; a paper-plane battle seemed to be taking place at one end. 'You seen Verity?'

'Not for a bit,' Ash said, pouring herself more whisky. I refused. 'Hey.' Ash nudged me. 'There's dancing upstairs.'

'Verity there?'

'Maybe,' Ash said, raising her eyebrows.

'Let's check it out.'

'Way to go, Prent.'

... No Verity in the Solar, loud with sounds and dark with light, and less crowded still. Ash and I danced, then cousin Josh asked her, and I sat watching the people dance for a while – the best way to extract any real enjoyment from dancing, I've always thought, but I seem to be unusual in not gaining any real pleasure from performing the movements – and then saw Helen Urvill, entering the hall holding a lager can. I went over to her, through the dancers.

'Happy New Year!'

'Hey, Prentice. Same to you ...'

I kissed her, then lifted her up and spun her round; she whooped.

'How are *you*?' I yelled. Helen Urvill, elegantly tall and judiciously lean, straight thick hair obsidian black, dress combat-casual, back on holiday from Switzerland and looking as thoroughly kempt as ever, passed the lager can to me.

'I'm fine,' she said.

I looked at the tin she'd handed me. '*Carling Black Label*?' I said, incredulous. Somehow this did not quite seem Helen's style.

She smirked. 'Try some.'

I tried some; the stuff foamed, went up my nose. I spluttered, stepping back, dripping, while Helen took the can back and stood grinning. 'Champagne?' I said wiping my chin.

'Lanson.'

'What else? Oh you're so *stylish*, Helen,' I said. 'Wanna dance?'

We danced, and shared the can of champagne. 'How's Diana?' I shouted above the music.

'Couldn't get back,' Helen yelled. 'Still out in Hawaii.'

'Poor thing.'

'Yeah.'

Helen continued to circulate; I decided it was time for a pee and then maybe some food, which took me via the garden (there was a queue for the downstairs loo, and the upper part of the castle was locked) to the kitchen.

Mrs McSpadden was in command, over-seeing a production line of sandwiches, sausage rolls, bowls of soup and chilli, slices of black bun and Christmas cake and accompanying slices of cheese.

'Prentice!' Mrs McSpadden said.

'Mthth MnThpndn!' I replied, mouth full of cake.

She shoved a set of keys into my hand. 'Will ye pop down to the cellar, for us?' Mrs S shouted. 'Get another litre of whisky; it's the second archway on the left. Dinnae let anybody down with you, mind; keep that door locked.' The microwave chimed and she hauled a still half-frozen block of chilli out on a big plate; she started breaking it up with a large wooden spoon.

I swallowed. 'Okay,' I said.

I went through to the utility room, cool and dark after the noise and chaos of the kitchen. I turned the light on, sorted through the keys for one that looked like it might match the door to the cellar. A movement outside caught my eye and I peered through the window; looked like I'd put on an outside light, too.

Verity Walker, clad in a short black dress, was dancing sinuously on the roof of Uncle Fergus's Range Rover. Lewis sat cross-legged on the bonnet of the car, watching her. He glanced over, shading his eyes, and seemed to see me, looking through the window from the utility room. Verity pirouetted. Holding her shoes in one hand, she ran the other down over her body to one thigh, then back to her head and through her cropped blonde hair.

The floodlight outside – harsh and white – lit her like she was on stage. Her hair glowed like pale flame.

Lewis jumped off the Range Rover (Verity wobbled a little as the car bounced on its springs, but recovered); he stood at the side of the car, between me and it, and held one hand up to Verity. She danced on, oblivious, then he must have said something, and she danced seductively, fluidly, to the edge of the roof, hips moving slow, a big smile on her face as she looked down at Lewis, then she threw herself off the roof. Lewis caught her, staggered back a couple of steps, then forward, as Verity wrapped her arms round his neck and her legs round his waist; white glances of thigh against the black. Lewis put his arms round her as he pitched forward.

They thumped together into the Range Rover. I thought the impact must have hurt her back, but it didn't look like it had. Her arms and legs stayed where they were, and Lewis's head bent down to hers. Her hands started to stroke and caress the nape of his neck and the back and sides of his head.

After a while, one of Lewis's arms disengaged, waving behind him. One finger pointed up to the bright flood-light that was showing me all this. His hand made a cutting, chopping motion.

When he did it a second time, I put the light out.

I let myself into the cellar, locked the door behind me. The cellar was cold. I found the whisky, let myself out of the cellar and locked it, turned all the lights out, gave Mrs McSpadden the bottle, accepted a belated new-year kiss from her, then made my way out through the kitchen and the corridor and the crowded hall where the music sounded loud and people were laughing, and out through the now almost empty entrance hall and down the steps of the castle and down the driveway and down to Gallanach, where I walked along the esplanade – occasionally having to wave or say 'Happy New Year' to various people I didn't know – until I got to the old railway pier and then the harbour, where I sat on the quay-side, legs dangling, drinking my whisky and watching a couple of swans glide on black, still water, to the distant sound of highland jigs coming from the Steam Packet Hotel, and singing and happy-new-year shouts echoing in the streets of the town, and the occasional sniff as my nose watered in sympathy with my eyes.

CHAPTER 8

Rory stood on the dunes, facing the sea. Lewis stomped away along the tide-line, kicking at the odd piece of driftwood and the occasional plastic bottle. His hands were stuffed into the pockets of his camouflage jacket; his head – short-haired, these days – was down.

South Uist. Lewis seemed to be taking it as a personal insult that the family had come to the Hebrides for their summer holiday. People kept asking him what he was doing on Uist; Lewis was further north, ha ha.

'He's awful moody, isn't he, Uncle Rory?'

Rory watched Lewis walk away along the beach. 'Yeah.' He shrugged.

'Why do you think he doesn't want to walk with us?' Prentice's thin face looked genuinely puzzled. Rory smiled, looked once more at Lewis's retreating back, then started down the far side of the dune heading for the narrow road. Prentice followed. 'I think,' Rory said, 'it's called being at an awkward age.'

Kenneth, Mary and the boys had come holidaying to the Hebrides, as they did most years. Rory had been invited along too, as he usually was, and for a change had accepted. So far, they'd been lucky; the Atlantic weather systems had been kind, the days bright and warm, the nights calm and never completely dark. The big rollers boomed in, the wide beaches lay mostly empty, and the machair – between dunes and cultivation – was a waving ocean of bright flowers thrown across the rich green waves of grass. Rory loved it, somewhat to his surprise; a holiday from holidays. A place to stay where he didn't have to take notes about flights and ferries and hotels and restaurants and sights. No travel book to think about, no articles, no pressure. He could laze.

He volunteered to take the boys on a walk after breakfast that Sunday. James had stayed behind and Lewis had been sullen for the half-hour or so they'd been walking before suddenly announcing he wanted to be alone.

Rory and Prentice walked on together, their short shadows preceding them. The road would be turning east soon, and taking them back to the main road so that they could turn south and walk back to the house. Lewis knew his way about the area, so Rory was happy to let him wander off alone.

A car passed them on the single track road, heading north; they stood aside to let it pass, waving at the single occupant when he waved at them. The surf was a distant wash of noise, rolling over the sparkling machair in invisible waves. Larks warbled, points of sound in the sweep of blue sky and small puffy clouds.

'Is it all right to walk on a Sunday, Uncle Rory?'

'All right?' Rory said, glancing at the boy. In shorts and a short-sleeved shirt, he looked almost painfully thin. Rory wore an old cheesecloth shirt and cut-off jeans.

'Aye; dad was saying you're not even allowed to walk in some islands on a Sunday!' Prentice rolled his eyes and puffed his cheeks out.

'Well, yeah,' Rory said. 'I think they're like that in Lewis and

Harris. But that's the hard-line prods up there. Down here they're Catholics; bit more relaxed about that sort of thing.'

'But not being able to *walk*!' Prentice protested, shaking his head at his shadow on the grey-black tarmac.

'I think you're allowed to walk to church and back.'

'Ho! Big deal!' Prentice didn't sound impressed. He was silent for a while. 'Mind you,' he said, sounding sly. 'I suppose you could always take a very long way round.'

Rory laughed, just as his attention was caught by a little white blossom lying on the road surface in front of them. Prentice looked up, at first surprised, then smiling, when Rory laughed. Prentice stood on the flower, then jumped, shrieking with pain.

'Ah; my foot! My foot! Oh! Oh!'

Rory stood, open mouthed for a second, watching Prentice hop around on the tarmac, clutching at one ankle, his face contorted. Rory thought for a second Prentice was pretending, but the boy's expression convinced him he was in real pain. Prentice hopped onto the grass and fell over, still clutching at his foot; Rory could see something white stuck to the sole of the boy's sandshoe.

'What is it?' he said, crouching down by Prentice's side. The boy was shaking, and when he looked up at Rory there were tears in his eyes.

'I don't know,' he sobbed. 'Stepped on something.'

'Let me see.' Rory sat on the grass in front of Prentice and held his foot. The little white blossom he'd seen on the road's surface was stuck to the boy's sandshoe; it wasn't a flower, it was a little paper charity flag for the Royal National Lifeboat Institution, the sort you secured to your lapel with a pin. The flag was still attached to its pin, which was buried in the sole of Prentice's shoe. Rory sucked his breath in when he saw it; most of the pin must be inside the boy's foot, near the middle of the broadest part of the sole.

Prentice's foot and leg shuddered as he rolled on the grass. 'It's awful sore, Uncle Rory,' he said, voice trembling.

'It's just a wee pin,' Rory said, trying to sound encouraging. 'I'll have it out in a second.'

He licked his lips, rubbed his right index finger and thumb together for a couple of seconds and held Prentice's foot steady with his left hand. He used the nails of his finger and thumb to find the head of the pin, itself almost buried in the tan rubber sole of the sandshoe. He grasped it. Prentice whimpered, foot trembling in Rory's grip. Rory gritted his teeth, pulled.

The pin slid out; an inch of it, shining in the sunlight. Prentice cried out, then relaxed. Rory put the boy's foot down gently.

Prentice sat up, face quivering. 'That's better,' he said. He used one shirt sleeve to wipe at his face. 'What was it?'

'This.' Rory showed him the pin.

Prentice grimaced. 'Ouch.'

'You're probably going to need a tetanus injection,' Rory told him.

'Aw no! More needles!'

They took his shoe and sock off. Rory sucked at the tiny wound and spat, trying to remove any dirt. Prentice, eyes still watering, laughed nervously. 'Is that not a horrible smell, no, Uncle Rory?'

Rory threw the boy's white sock at him, grinning. 'I've been to India, kid; that ain't nuthin.'

Prentice put his shoe and sock back on and got to his feet, obviously in some pain when he stood. 'Here; I'll give you a carry-coal-bag,' Rory said, turning his back to the boy and putting his arms out from his sides as he crouched.

'Really, Uncle Rory? You sure? Will I not be awful heavy?'

'Hop on; you're a bean-pole, laddie. I'll probably go faster with you on my back; you walk too slow. Come on.'

Prentice put his arms round Rory's neck and got up onto his back; Rory set off at a run. Prentice whooped.

'See?' Rory said, slowing to a fast walk.

'I'm not too heavy, honest, Uncle Rory?'

'What? A skelf like you? Never.'

'Do you think this is a punishment from God for talking about walking on a Sunday, Uncle Rory?'

Rory laughed. 'Certainly not.'

'Do you not believe in God either, Uncle Rory?'

'No. Well; not in the Christian God. Maybe something else.' He shrugged his shoulders and shifted Prentice into a more comfortable position on his back. 'When I was in India, I thought then I knew what it was I might believe in. But when I came back it all seemed to go away again. I think it was something to do with the place.' He looked to one side, at the dazzling expanse of machair; endless emerald green scattered thick with flowers so bright they seemed lit from inside. 'Places have an effect on people. They alter your thoughts. India does, anyway.'

'What about when you went to America? Did that effect what you thought?'

Rory laughed gently. 'Yeah; it did that all right. Kind of in the opposite way, though.'

'Are you going to go away again?'

'I expect so.'

Prentice clapsed his hands in front of Rory's chin. Rory glanced at his wrists; thin and fragile looking. Prentice was still holding the little Lifeboat flag, twirling the pin between his fingers.

'When did you stop believing in God?' Prentice asked.

Rory shrugged. 'Hard to say; I think I started to think for myself when I was about your age, maybe a bit younger.'

'Oh.'

'I tried to imagine how the world had been created, and I imagined Sooty – you know; the glove puppet –'

'I know; they still have him. Sooty and Sweep.' Prentice giggled.

'Well, I imagined him standing on a wee planet about the size of a football –'

'But he hasn't got any legs!'

'Ah, but he did in the annuals I got for Christmas. Anyway, I imagined him waving a wand, and the world came into existence.

Like, I'd been to church, been to Sunday School, so I knew all the stuff in the Bible, but I guess I needed to envisage it . . . see it, in my own terms.'

'Uh-huh.'

'But then I thought; wait a minute; where does the planet Sooty's standing on come from? I thought Sooty could have waved his wand and made that appear too, but where would he stand while he was doing it? I mean, I didn't think, Well, he could float in space, and it never occurred to me to ask where Sooty himself had come from, or the wand, but I was already heading towards not believing, I suppose. It was like the dragons.'

'Dragons?' Prentice said, sounding excited and wary at once. Rory felt the boy tremble.

'Yeah,' Rory said. 'I used to hide under the covers of my bed at night, imagining there were dragons out there; in the room when the light was out, when there was nobody else there. I'd hunch down under the covers with just an air-hole to breath through, and shelter there. The dragons couldn't get you through the air-hole; they could only get you if you put out a foot or a hand, or worst of all your head; that was when they struck; bit it off, or pulled you right out and ate all of you.'

'Waa! Alien!' Prentice said. His arms squeezed Rory's neck.

'Yeah,' Rory said. 'Well, I guess a lot of horror films come from that sort of background. Anyway; I used to be petrified of these dragons, even though I knew they probably didn't exist; I mean I knew there was no Santa Claus, and no fairies and elves, but still thought ghosts and dragons were a possibility, and it only took one to kill you . . . I mean how did I really know I could trust adults? Even mum and dad? There were so many things I didn't really understand about people, about life. Most of the time you could just ignore a lot of the stuff you didn't know; it'd come in time, you'd be told when you needed to know . . . But how did you know that there wasn't some big secret, some big, evil deal going down that involves you but had been kept secret from you?

'Like, maybe your parents were just fattening you up until you would make a decent meal for these dragons, or it was an intelligence test; the kids smart enough to have sussed out the fact there were dragons around were the ones that would survive, and the ones that just lay there, trusting, each night, deserved to die, and their parents couldn't tell them or the dragons would eat *them*, and stories about dragons were the only clues you were ever given; that was all the adults could do to warn you ... I was pretty paranoid about it. I used to be frightened to fall asleep at night sometimes, afraid I'd stick my head out from under the clothes while I was asleep and wake up to find my head in a dragon's mouth, before I died.'

'Wow!'

Rory grunted, shifting Prentice's weight again. Kid wasn't so feather-light after all. 'But then one night, under the covers – I was just getting older, I guess, but anyway – I was sort of reviewing the day, and I was thinking about school, and what we'd learned, and we'd been doing the Second World War, and I hadn't liked the sound of this Hitler guy at all; and I'd asked dad, just to double-check, and –'

'So he was still alive? When you were ten?'

'Oh yeah; didn't die until I was twelve. Anyway; he brought down this book; history of the War in pictures, and it had like all these photos of the death camps, where the Nazis murdered millions of Jews, and communists, and homosexuals, and gypsies and anybody else they didn't like ... but mostly Jews, and there were like just piles of bodies; incredibly thin bodies, like bones; skeletons wrapped with tissue paper, and piled higher than a house ... and pits; long pits full of bodies, and the metal stretchers they were put onto to be shoved into the ovens, and the piles of wedding rings and spectacles; glasses, and even artificial legs and weird stuff like that ...

'Anyway, that night they put a night-light in my room, in case I had nightmares, but the shadows were even worse than the darkness, and so I just lay there, under the covers, quivering with fear thanks to these damn dragons, and I wished Ken was back from University because sometimes I was allowed to sleep in his room, and I wished I was allowed a torch in my room, but I wasn't, and I was wondering about crying really loudly, because that would bring mum and dad in to see me, but then what did I say was wrong? And then I suddenly thought . . .

'The dragons might be there; they might be real and they might be every bit as vicious as I'd imagined, but I'm a *human being*; so was Adolf Hitler and he killed millions of people!

'And I threw back the bedclothes before I had any more time to think about it and burst out of the bed; threw myself into the middle of the bedroom, screaming and roaring and thrashing about.'

'Ha!' Prentice said, squirming.

'That brought mum and dad through; thought I was having a fit or something. But I just looked up from the carpet with this great big reassuring smile and said there was nothing to worry about.' Rory smiled at the memory, bringing his head up to look around. A break in the dunes let the sound of surf grow louder. There was a car in the distance coming towards them.

'Brilliant!' Prentice said.

Rory grunted, shifting Prentice's weight once more. 'Never had any trouble with dragons after that.'

'I'll bet you didn't!'

The car hummed nearer as the view to one side slowly opened up through the dunes to reveal the shining beach and blue-green ocean.

'Let's see if we can get a lift off this car, eh?' Rory said. 'You okay to get down?

'Yeah!' Prentice slid off onto the grass and stood there, favouring his good leg, while Rory stretched and rubbed at his lower back. He stuck one thumb out when the car was still a few hundred yards away. Prentice reached up and put something on the thin collar of Rory's shirt. It was the little paper Lifeboat flag. Rory held his collar out so that he could look at it. He looked down at the boy's grinning face. 'Thanks,' he said.

'That's your medal, Uncle Rory,' Prentice told him. 'For being a brilliant uncle.'

Rory ruffled the boy's hair. 'Thanks, Prentice.' He looked back at the car. Was it slowing?

'I used to worry about Darth Vader,' Prentice confessed, putting his arm round Rory's waist and lifting his foot to massage it with one hand. 'I'd lie under the covers and make the noise he makes when he's breathing, and then I'd stop, but sometimes it would go on after I'd stopped!' Prentice shook his head, and slapped one hand off his forehead. 'Crazy, eh?'

Rory laughed, as the approaching car started to slow down. 'Yeah, well, that's what stories do to you, sometimes. Your dad's always tried never to tell you lies, or stories that would scare you or make you superstitious, but –'

'Ha!' Prentice said, as the battered Cortina II drew to a stop just past them. 'I remember he tried to tell us clouds came from the Steam Packet Hotel, in the town. That's what they were: packets of steam from the Steam Packet Hotel. Ha!'

Rory smiled as they walked towards the car, him supporting the limping boy. Rory looked away for a second, towards the beach, where the long Atlantic rollers crashed against the broad expanse of gold.

*

He sniffed the glass; the whisky was amber, and there wasn't much of it. The smell stung. He put it to his lips, hesitated, then knocked it back in one go. The drink made his lips and tongue tingle; his throat felt sore and the fumes went up his nose and down into his lungs. He tried very hard not to cough like he'd seen people cough in westerns when they tried whisky for the first time, and got away with just clearing his throat rather loudly (he looked round at the curtains, afraid somebody might have heard). His eyes and nose were watering, so he pulled his hanky from his trousers, blew his nose.

The whisky tasted horrible. And people drank this stuff for *pleasure*? He had hoped that by trying some whisky he'd understand adults a bit better; instead they made even less sense.

He was standing between the curtains and the windows of the ballroom of the Steam Packet Hotel, on the railway pier at Gallanach. Outside, the afternoon was wet and miserable-looking, and what little light there had been – watery and grey – was going now. Sheets of rain hauled in off the bay, blew around the steamers and ferries moored round the windswept quay, then collapsed upon the dark grey buildings of the town. The street lamps were already lit, and a few cars crawled through the rough-mirror streets with their lights on and their wipers flapping to and fro.

Music played behind Rory. He balanced the empty whisky glass on the window-sill and gave his nose a last wipe, pocketing his hanky. He supposed he'd better go back into the ballroom. Ballroom; he hated the word. He hated the music they were playing – Highland stuff, mostly – he hated being here in this dull, wet town, with these dull people listening to their dull music at their dull wedding. They should be playing the Beatles or the Rolling Stones, and they shouldn't be getting married in the first place – modern people didn't.

'Heeee-*yooch*!' a voice shouted, startlingly nearby, making Rory jump. The curtains bowed in a few yards away, almost touching the window-sill, the movement like a wave. Rory could hear the stamping, slapping feet move in time to the fiddles and accordions as they played a jig. People were clapping, shouting out. God, it was all so provincial.

Rory straightened his tie, and with his whisky still burning in his throat, and now his stomach too, he moved along to the gap in the curtains and slid through, back into the ballroom, where people sat drinking at long wooden tables and groups of dancers went whirling round in complicated, ever-changing patterns, all flowing dresses and clasping hands and big red sweaty faces and white shirts and ties and narrow trousers or – even worse – kilts.

Rory moved near the stage, behind the tables where Kenneth and Mary sat, talking to mum. Boring Hamish and the horse-resembling Antonia were on the floor, him in a kilt, her still in her white bridal gown, both dancing badly and out of time, but seemingly thoroughly enjoying themselves.

'Well,' he heard his mum saying, 'you two had better get a move on, or Hamish and Antonia will beat you to it.' She laughed and drank from her glass. She wore a hat. Rory hated his mother in a hat. He thought she sounded drunk. Kenneth and Mary smiled uncertainly at each other.

'Well, mum,' Kenneth said, sitting back, filling his pipe. 'We have been practising.'

'Kenneth!' his wife said quietly.

Mum shook her head. 'Ah, don't mind me; plenty of time yet, I dare say.' She looked into her empty glass. 'I wouldn't be missing grandchildren so much, but ...' She shrugged. There was an awkward silence between the three people then, while the music played and the dancers whooped and shouted and clapped and stamped. Rory saw his mother's shoulders move once, and she put her head down for a second, sniffed. She reached down for her handbag on the floor. Kenneth handed her his hanky. He put his arm round his mum's shoulders. Mary moved her seat closer, reached out and took one of the older woman's hands in hers.

'God, I miss that old devil,' mum said, and blew her nose. Eyes bright with tears, she looked at Mary, and then saw Rory standing behind and to one side of them. 'Rory,' she said, trying to sound all right. 'We wondered where you were. Are you enjoying yourself, darling?'

'Yes,' he lied. He hated her calling him 'darling'. He stayed where he was because he didn't want to get close enough for them to smell his breath. His mother smiled.

'Good lad. See if you can find your cousin Sheila; you said you'd ask her to dance, remember?'

'Yeah, all right,' he said, turning away.

He didn't like boring cousin Sheila, either. She was about the only girl here who was his own age. It was horrible being this age when nobody else was; they were all either adults or children. He blamed his parents. Mostly he blamed his dad. If he'd looked after himself, not had a heart attack, he'd still be around. That was how thoughtless he'd been. Rory supposed it was the same thoughtlessness that had made dad and mum have him so much later than the rest of their children. People just didn't think, that was the trouble.

He didn't go looking for Sheila. He decided to go wandering. He would slip away. He had always liked slipping away from things. At parties he would just quietly leave when nobody was watching him, so that only much later would anybody wonder where he was. When he was out with a group of other kids, playing kick-the-can or soldiers, he would often sneak away, so that they would never find him, or think he had fallen down a hole or into a burn or a loch. It was a wonderful feeling, to disappear like that; it made him feel different and special. He gloried in the cunningness of it, the feeling of having outwitted the others, of knowing what they did not; that he was out and away and they were back there where he'd left them, ignorantly worrying where he was, searching; wondering.

He slunk out through the doors while they were clapping the band after finishing one of their noisy, interminable Highland dances.

It was cooler in the lobby. He drew himself upright and walked confidently through the bit of the lobby that gave onto the Cocktail Lounge, where ruddy-faced men stood panting and laughing, sleeves rolled up, ties loose, queuing for drinks or holding trays of them, laughing loudly in deep voices.

He went through another set of doors, down some steps, round a corner, and found the hotel's single small lift. He pulled both sets of gates open with an effort, entered, then closed them again. The lift was a little bigger than a phone box. He pressed the brass button for the top floor. The lift jerked into motion and set off, humming. The white-washed walls of the lift shaft moved smoothly downwards as the lift ascended. Stencilled letters painted inside the shaft said 1st Floor ... 2nd Floor ... God, he thought, Americans must think they're in the Stone Age when they come to stay in a place like this.

He felt ashamed.

The top floor was boring. He went from one end to the other of the U-shaped hotel, up and down steps that marked the boundaries of the three separate buildings that made up the Steam Packet Hotel. There were no windows; only skylights, each spattered with rain drops and lined with little rivulets of running water. He'd been hoping for windows, and a view over the bay or the town.

He trod the corridors again, looking for an unlocked door. Maybe the maids would have left some of the rooms open, if there was nobody staying in them just now. He tried a few handles. The only open door led to a broom cupboard.

Then at the next door he heard giggling. He looked at the number. It was room 48. 48 was a good number; not as good as 32 or 64, but better than, say, 49, and much better than 47 (though that was interesting too because it was a prime). The very best numbers were numbers like 20, 23, 30, 40, 57, 75, 105 and 155. Calibre numbers; gun numbers. Those were luckiest. But 48 was all right.

More giggling. He looked back down the corridor, then crouched and looked through the key-hole. It was a bit clichéd, but what did people expect in a boring hotel like this in a boring town like this in a boring country like this? It was all you could do.

There was no key in the lock, so he could see in through the big old-fashioned key-hole. He saw a large dressing table sitting in a broad bay window. The dressing-table held a big, tippable mirror, and most of the rest of the room was visible in it. In the mirror Rory saw his sister Fiona, and then Fergus Urvill. They were making the big double bed.

Fiona still wore her peach-coloured bridesmaid's dress, very long and smooth-looking. There were flowers in her hair, which made her look quite good. Rory suspected she looked so good because she didn't live here any more; she lived in London, and Aunt Ilsa had got her a job working for a television company. Fiona sold time to people. That was how she put it. She sold advertising space. She sold time. Rory thought that sounded pretty interesting.

Fergus Urvill was on the other side of the bed, dressed in a kilt, shirt and waistcoat. Rory knew Fergus was ages with Kenneth, but somehow he always seemed older. Maybe it was because he had gone to a private high school. Rory didn't really know Fergus Urvill very well; although he did sometimes visit Lochgair, he spoke differently – posher – and seemed to spend a lot of his time shooting at birds and animals with other rich people.

Rory had always found Fergus Urvill to be a little frightening. Kenneth had told him the story, years ago, about when Fergus put Lachy Watt's eye out; he'd stuck a fossil bone in it, or something. Rory thought now that his brother must have exaggerated the story, made it more horrific than it really had been, and he *certainly* didn't believe that Lachy had run away to sea just so that he could wear an eye-patch and pretend he was a pirate. He *had* joined the merchant navy – Rory had asked dad about that – but he had an artificial eye, not a patch. Rory knew because he'd been with mum once when they'd met Lachy and a woman in the street in Lochgilphead. Rory had looked very hard but hadn't been able to decide which was the false eye.

His own eye smarted, exposed to the draft coming through the key-hole. He blinked, then used his other eye.

Fiona and Fergus were making the bed, but doing it in a funny sort of way; the bottom sheet had been doubled up half-way down the bed. They were both chuckling to themselves, and talking in quiet, urgent whispers. Fiona glanced off to one side a couple of times. Rory worked out she was looking at the door he was crouched behind.

They made the bed up, so that it looked ordinary. Rory got ready to run away down the corridor. But they didn't leave the room; instead, Fiona and Fergus, still breathless with giggles, still chattering excitedly away, started to turn the furniture in the room upside down. They left the bed, of course, but they turned a table, a chest of drawers, two bedside cabinets, two chairs and an easy chair upside down. They carefully replaced lights and vases and other bits and pieces as they went along. They stood before the dressing table for a while, looking at it and discussing it, apparently, but eventually just turned it round so that it faced the wrong way, rather than turn it upside down.

Fiona leant back against the rear of the dressing table, breathing hard, and waved one hand, wafting air over her face. Her cheeks were pink, and a couple of coils of copper hair had fallen from her hairdo, one on each side of her head. She pulled at her bodice, blew down, went 'Whoo!' Rory couldn't see Fergus Urvill. Then he reappeared, stood by Fiona. He was holding a key and a couple of toilet rolls; he said something Rory didn't catch. 'Oh no,' Fiona said, touching Fergus's arm. Her face looked amused but concerned. 'No, that's naughty . . .'

Fergus stood there for a moment. Rory couldn't see his face, but Fiona's looked glowing and bright. 'I like being naughty,' he heard Fergus say, and then he stepped forward and took Fiona in his arms, still holding the key and the toilet rolls.

What? thought Rory. This really was something. Sister Fiona and big Fergus Urvill? Stupid girl; probably only after her body.

'Ferg!' Fiona said, breaking away. Her face looked surprised, cheeks even redder. She smiled broadly, held Fergus's elbows. 'Well, this is . . . unexpected.'

'I've always ...' Fergus lowered his voice as he bent to kiss her again, face in her hair and then his mouth on hers. Rory missed the exact words.

Go on, thought Rory. Go on. Do it. Let me see!

Fergus's hands dropped the key and the toilet rolls, grabbed Fiona's bum. She pushed away from him. 'Ferg ...' she said, breathless, lip-stick smeared.

'Fiona,' Fergus moaned, clutching her. 'I want you! I need you!'

'Well,' Fiona said, gulping. 'That's very, ah ... but not here, eh?'

Fergus pulled her close again. 'Let me drive you home tonight.'

'Umm, well, I think we were getting a taxi.'

'Please; let me. Please. Fiona. You don't know ...' Fergus stuck his nose into her hair again, made a sort of moaning noise. 'Feel me.' And he guided one of Fiona's hands to the front of his kilt.

Good God, thought Rory. He took another quick glance down the hall, then looked back through the key-hole.

Fiona took her hand away. 'Hmm. Yes; actually I already could, Fergus.'

'I need you!' He pulled her close again.

'*Not here*, Fergus.'

'Fiona; please ...'

'All right; all right, Fergus. I'll try. We'll see, okay?'

'Yes; yes, thank you!' Fergus gathered Fiona's hands in his.

'Right,' she laughed. 'Well, come on; let's get out of here before the happy couple arrive. Put those back in the loo.' She pointed at the toilet rolls. Fergus retrieved them. She busied herself with her hair, restoring it. Fergus turned and disappeared from Rory's view. 'And put some cold water on *that*,' Fiona said, grinning. 'Looks like your sporran's trying to levitate.'

She came towards the door. Rory leapt back, staggered on legs that had gone half to sleep, and only just scrambled into the broom cupboard and got the door shut before the bedroom door opened. The broom cupboard key-hole didn't let him see anything. He heard muffled conversation but no footsteps.

He waited, breathless, heart hammering in the darkness, one hand in his trouser pocket, stroking himself.

*

'Do you know where the twins were conceived?'

'No idea,' he said, and belched.

'Fucking McCaig's Folly, that's where.'

'What, Oban?'

'The very place.'

'Good grief.'

'You don't mind me saying this, I mean talking about Fiona like this, do you?'

'No, no.' He waved one hand. 'Your wife; you talk about her. No, no, that's bad, that sounds bad. I'm all for women's lib.'

'Might have bloody known. Might have bloody known you would be. Bloody typical, if you ask me. You're a Bolshie bastard, McHoan.'

'And you are the unacceptable face of Capitalism, Ferg.'

'Don't quote that fairy at me, you Bolshie bastard. And don't call me Ferg.'

'Beg your pardon. Some more whisky?'

'Don't mind if I do.'

Rory got up out of the creaking wooden seat and walked unsteadily over to where Fergus lay on the bare wooden floorboards, head against the ancient, burst couch. The fire crackled in the grate, its light competing with that of the little gas lamp. Rory unscrewed the top from the bottle of Bells carefully and topped up Fergus's little silver cup. Fergus had brought a leather case with him; it held three of the silver cups and a big hip flask. Rory had brought the bottle in his rucksack.

'There you go.'

'Ta much. You're a decent fellow for a Bolshie bastard.'

'One tries, old bean,' Rory said. He walked carefully to his seat,

picked his little cup up from the floor and went to the room's single window. It was black outside. There had been a moon when they'd first arrived, but the clouds had come while they were chopping wood, and the rain while they'd cooked dinner on the two little primus stoves.

He turned from the darkness. Fergus looked like he was almost asleep. He was dressed in plus fours, tweed waistcoat (the jacket, and his waxed Barbour were hanging behind the door of the bothy), thick socks, brogues, and a fawn country shirt with a button-down collar. God, he even had his tie on still. Rory wore cords, mountain-biking boots and a plain M&S shirt. His nylon waterproofs were draped over a chair.

What an odd pair we make, he thought.

He had been back from his travels for a while, staying first in London then at Lochgair, while he tried to work out what to do with his life. He had the impression things were sliding past him somehow. He'd made a good start but now he was faltering, and the focus of attention was drifting slowly away from him.

He had returned to discover that – like his brother before him – Ken had given up being a teacher. Hamish had taken up the managerial place at the factory that everyone had expected would be Kenneth's, when Kenneth had decided to teach. Now Ken too was quitting the profession to try something else: writing children's stories. Rory had always thought of Hamish as a sort of ponderously eccentric fool, and Ken a kind of failure because he had so much wanted to travel, and instead had settled down with Mary, stayed in the same wee corner of the world as he'd been born and raised in, and not only raised his own children, but chosen to teach others', too. Rory had felt slightly sorry for his elder brother, then. Now he felt envious. Ken seemed happy; happy with his wife, with his children, and now with his work; not rich, but doing what he wanted to do.

And why hadn't Ken told *him he was writing too? He might have been able to help him, but even if Ken had wanted to do it all without any assistance from his younger brother, he might at least have told him what he was doing. Instead Rory had found out only when Ken had had his first story published, and now it was as though they were passing each other travelling in opposite directions; Ken slowly but surely building up a reputation as a children's story-teller while his own supposed career as a professional recounter of traveller's tales sank gradually in the west. Books people forgot about and articles in Sunday supplements that were only one notch above the sort of shit tourist boards put out.*

And so he'd left London, to come here, hoping to lick the closing wise wound of whatever talent it was he had.

He'd spent a lot of time just wandering in the hills. Sometimes Ken came too, or one of the boys if they were in the mood, but mostly he went by himself, trying to sort himself out. What it boiled down to was: there was here, where he had friends and family, or there was London where he had a few friends and a lot of contacts, and it felt like things were happening, and where you could fill time with something no matter how mixed up and fraudulent you felt... or there was abroad, of course; the rest of the world; India (to take the most extreme example he'd found so far), where you felt like an alien, lumbering and self-conscious, materially far more rich and spiritually far more poor than the people who thronged the place, where just by that intensity of touching, that very sweating crowdedness, you felt more apart, more consigned to a different, echoing place inside yourself.

One day, on a long walk, he'd almost literally bumped into Fergus Urvill, crouching in a hide up amongst the folds in the hills, waiting with telescope and .303 for a wounded Sika deer. Fergus had motioned him to sit down with him behind the hide, and to keep quiet. Rory had waited with the older man – silent for quarter of an hour apart from a whispered hello and a quick explanation of what was going on – until the herd of deer appeared, brown shapes on the brown hill. One animal was holding the rest back; limping heavily. Fergus waited until the herd was as close as it looked like it was going to come, then sighted on the limping beast, still two hundred yards away.

The sound of the shot left Rory's ears ringing. The Sika's head jerked; it dropped to its knees and keeled over. The rest raced off, bouncing across the heather.

He helped Fergus drag the small corpse down the slope to the track, where the Land Rover was parked, and accepted a lift back to the road.

'Hardly recognised you, Roderick,' Fergus said, as he drove. 'Not seen you since Fi and I got shackled. Must be at least that long.'

'I've been away.'

'Of course; your travels. I've got that India book of yours, you know.'

'Ah.' Rory watched the trees slide past the Land Rover's windows.

'Done any others?'

'There was one about the States and Mexico. Last year.'

'Really?' Fergus looked over at him briefly. 'I didn't hear about that,'

Rory smiled thinly. 'No,' he said.

Fergus made a grunting noise, changed gear as they bumped down the track towards the main road. 'Ken said something about you living in a squat in London . . . or something ridiculous like that. That right?'

'Housing cooperative.'

'Ah-ha.' Fergus drove on for a while. 'Always wanted to take a look at India myself, you know,' he said suddenly. 'Keep meaning to go; never quite get around to it, know what I mean?'

'Well, it isn't the sort of place you can just take a look at.'

'No?'

'Not really.'

The Land Rover came down to the main road between Lochgilphead and Lochgair. 'Look, we've got a do on this evening, in the town –' Fergus glanced at his watch. ' – bit late already, to tell the truth. But how about coming round tomorrow for . . . In fact, d'you fish?'

'Fish? Yeah, I used to.'

'Not against your vegetarian principles, is it?'

'No. India didn't change me that much.'

'Well, then; come fishing with me tomorrow. Pool on the Add with a monster trout in it; been after the swine for months. Plenty of smaller stuff too, though. Fancy it? Course, I'll never talk to you again if you catch the big feller, but might make a fun afternoon. What do you say?'

'Okay,' he said.

So they became friends, after a fashion. Most of Rory's pals in London were in the International Marxist Group, but here he was; wandering the hills with an upper class dingbat who just happened to be married to his sister and who lived for huntin', shootin' and fishin' (and seemed to spend the absolute minimum amount of time in his castle with his wife), and who had just last year rationalised half the work force in the glass factory out of a job. Still, they got on together, somehow, and Fergus was an undemanding companion; company of a sort, but not taxing; none of Ken's garrulousness, Lewis's moodiness or Prentice or James's ceaseless questioning. It was almost like walking the hills on your own.

And a couple of days ago Fergus had suggested they go for a longer hike, up into the trackless hills where the Landy couldn't reach. They would take collapsible rods, a couple of guns, and have to fish and shoot to eat. They could stay in the old lodge; it would save taking a tent.

So here they were, on the first floor of the old lodge, which was now used just as a bothy. The room they were in contained a single big dormer window, a fireplace, a couch, a table and two seats, and two bunkbeds. There were other rooms with more beds, but keeping to one room meant only lighting one fire; the autumn weather had turned chilly early.

'No,' Fergus said, looking up from where he lay, slumped against

the couch. 'But you don't mind me talking about Fiona like this, do you? I mean, your sister. My wife. You sure you don't mind, do you?'

'Positive.'

'Good man.'

'McCaig's Folly, eh?'

'Hmm? Oh; well yes ... at least I think so. Got the idea from Charlotte, actually.'

'What, your sister?'

'Mmm. The one that married that chap Walker, from Edinburgh.'

'Oh yeah; I remember.' Rory went over to the seat that held his jacket.

'Funny girl, Charlie; had this thing about ... antiquity. Got Walker to deflower her under this ancient fucking yew tree in Perthshire. So she told me, anyway.'

'Uh-huh.' Rory rummaged in his jacket pockets.

'Fiona and I thought we'd try something like that, one time we were in Oban, for some do. You know; put a bit of sparkle back in ... You sure you don't mind me talking about your sister like this?'

'Yeah.' Rory took his tobacco tin from the jacket. He held the tin up. 'As long as you don't mind me having a little smoke?'

'Not at all, not at all. Bloody cold it was, in that damn folly. Had to sit on a – Oh,' Fergus said, suddenly realising. 'You mean the old wacky baccy.'

Rory smiled, sat down. 'That's the stuff.'

'Not at all,' Fergus said, waving one hand. 'Go ahead.' He watched carefully as Rory set out the papers. 'Mmm, go ahead.'

Rory looked up, saw Fergus's fascinated expression. 'Do you want any of this, Fergus?'

'Umm,' Fergus said, sitting back, blinking. 'Could do, I suppose. Never really tried it, to be honest. Couple of chaps at the school got booted out for that stuff and I never did get round to it.'

'Well, I'm not forcing you.'

'Not at all. Not at all.'

They smoked the joint. Fergus, used to the occasional cigar with his brandy now that he'd given up his pipe, pronounced the smoke quite cool, and objected more to the sweet taste of the Old Holborn than to the scent of resin.

'This any good for hanky-panky?' he said, passing the roach back to Rory, who took a last hot toke then flicked the remains into the heart of the fire.

'Can be,' he said.

'Might try it some time. God knows we could do with something to – Look, you absolutely sure you don't mind me talking about your sister this way?'

'Positive.'

'Good man – hey! Did you hear that?'

Rory looked up at the ceiling. Fergus was staring at the plaster-board expanse above them. Rory listened. Then, above the crackling of the fire, he did hear something; a quiet, scrabbling noise in the roof-space above them.

'Rats, I'll bet!' Fergus said, and rolled over to his pack.

Rory thought about it. They were here in a deserted old house in the middle of nowhere on a black and starless night in one of the more mysterious bits of Scotland, and there was a scrabbling, clawy sort of noise coming from the ceiling above him and this other drunk, stoned man. He shrugged. Yeah; probably rats. Or mice. Or birds.

Fergus pulled his pack gently to him, scraping over the floor-boards. He lifted the rucksack up. The .303 and the shotgun were in a waterproof bag strapped to the side of the pack. Fergus undid the straps. 'Ssh,' he said to Rory. Rory had started building another joint. He waved. He drank some more whisky.

He was just inserting the roach when Fergus rolled over to him and held the shotgun out to him. 'Here!' he whispered urgently.

'Hmm,' Rory said, nodding thanks. He heard some clicks.

Fergus held the ancient Lee Enfield at his side. He knelt close by Rory. 'Think the little bastard's over there.' He pointed. He reached up, touched the gun Rory held. It was hard doing the roach one handed. 'Put that down, man!' Fergus hissed. He took the tin from Rory's lap and put all the makings down on the floor. Rory felt peeved.

'There,' Fergus said. 'Safety's off. When I fire, aim where I do, all right?'

'Yup,' Rory said, forgetting about the J. He took the shotgun. Fergus walked on his heels, still hunkered down, across the room, eyes and gun pointed towards the plasterboard ceiling. He stopped. There was a noise like a spider running across a very sensitive microphone.

Bang! went the rifle. Rory almost dropped the shotgun. 'There!' yelled Fergus. Plaster was falling from a small hole in the ceiling; there was smoke in the air. Rory aimed at the small hole, pulled the trigger. The gun struck back against his shoulder, sending him falling back off his seat. He clattered to the floor.

'Well, pump it, man, pump it!' he heard Fergus shouting from somewhere.

Awful lot of smoke around. Ears seemed to be ringing. He pumped the gun. (Funny; he'd have thought Fergus would have been a side-by-side man.) There was another sharp crack of sound from the .303. He saw the hole appear in the plaster almost right above him. Great; he could get the little bastard without having to get up from the floor. The floorboards ought to provide extra firing stability, too. He pulled the trigger again. The gun went Blam! with a little less sonic enthusiasm than before, though it hurt his shoulder a little more.

A white waterfall of plaster burst down from the ceiling and slapped and pattered all over him. Rory spat bits out of his mouth, blinked the white dust out of his eyes. He heard Fergus colliding with something in the room. He pumped the gun, looked round. Fergus was lying on the couch, aiming at the centre of the ceiling. He fired the Lee Enfield again; Rory was getting the hang of this now, and aimed the shotgun at the same place and fired it, almost before the noise of Fergus's shot had stopped echoing. The room was getting a bit hazy, and there was probably blood coming from his ears, but what the fuck. Rory readied the gun again.

He tried to follow where Fergus was pointing his rifle. As he did so, still lying there with his legs up on the chair he'd fallen over, he started to over-balance to one side, towards Fergus.

'Aah!' Rory said. He tried to put one hand out to stop himself, but the gun was still in his grip. The long, blue-black barrel arced towards Fergus. Fergus looked, as Rory fell helplessly over, the gun barrel falling like some felled tree, wide muzzle pointed straight towards him.

Rory could tell exactly what was going to happen, and couldn't stop it.

Fergus's eyes widened. He jumped; fell over the back of the couch.

Rory fell onto his side; the shotgun roared and the rear of the couch blew open in a dusty horsehair explosion.

Rory let the gun down to the floor. The noise still rang in his ears. The room stank of smoke and the fire had gone strangely quiet. 'Ferg?' he said, tentatively. Couldn't hear himself speak. 'Ferg!' *he shouted.*

He sat upright, leaving the gun on the floorboards. Plaster tumbled off his body in clouds of dust.

'Hello?' Fergus said, appearing over the top of the couch, gunless.

Rory looked at him. They both blinked, eyes watering. 'Did we get it?' Rory asked.

'Don't know,' Fergus said. He staggered round the rear of the couch, feet crunching in plaster, and sat down. He looked at the still slightly smoking hole in the couch, just beside where he'd sat, then up at the holes in the ceiling.

He stayed looking at the holes in the ceiling for a while. Then he started crying.

Rory watched for a while, befuddled. 'What's the matter, man?' he said.

Fergus took no notice; he kept on crying, still staring up at the holes in the ceiling. He took big lungfuls of air and then let them out in great racking sobs that shook his whole body. After a while he put his head in his hands and sat there, rocking back and forward, clutching his hair just above his ears. The tears flowed, trickling off his nose and spotting the white plaster dust on the floorboards at his feet.

'Ferg,' Rory said, going over to him. He hesitated, then put his arm on the man's shoulders. 'Fergus; for God's sake man, what's wrong?'

Fergus looked up and suddenly Rory felt older than him. Fergus's heavy, ruddy face was puffed and bloated, and tears had streaked through the dust on his cheeks, disappearing in the bristles on his jaw-line and chin. When he spoke it was in the voice of a small, hurt boy.

'Oh God, Rory, I've got to tell somebody, but you must promise; you must give me your word you won't breathe a word to anybody else. On your life.'

'Hey, you haven't killed anybody or anything, have you?'

'No,' Fergus shook his head, screwed his eyes up. 'No! Nothing like that! It's not something I *did.'*

'Okay; my word. All that stuff.'

Fergus looked at him and Rory shivered. 'You swear?' Fergus said, voice hollow.

Rory nodded. 'I swear.' He felt dizzy. The smoke-filled room seemed to tip and waver. He wondered if they put something trippy in shotgun or rifle cartridges. And why did I mention killing somebody? That wasn't too sensible, way out here on this moonless night, etc., with a couple of lethal fire-arms lying around.

'All right,' Fergus said, sitting back, breathing deeply. He looked almost soberly at Rory. 'You sure you don't mind me talking about your sister?' he said slowly, with what might have been some sort of smile on his face.

Oh god, thought Rory, and felt sick.

But it was too late to go back now.

*

The way he told it, it took maybe five minutes. Fergus Urvill was crying like a baby again at the end of it. Rory cuddled him. And after as many tender words as he could think of, to try and lighten the load, to try and make it seem less of a confession, even to try and compensate for the shared and shaming confidence, he told Fergus that he had been responsible for the fire that had burned down the barn near Port Ann, fifteen years earlier.

They ended up laughing about that, but it was the uneasy laughter of desperation and displacement, and all they could do after that was finish the whisky and have the joint Rory had been working on, and it was almost a relief when Fergus was sick as a dog out of the window, hanging out barfing onto the slates and into the guttering while Rory tried to clean the plaster off the top bunk and stowed the guns out of harm's way.

They woke with raging hangovers to a wrecked room and the smell of black powder and vomit. There was a dead rat, blown almost in two, resting on the hearth of the fire.

They left the place as it was, picked up their gear and walked away. Neither of them mentioned anything that had been said during the night; they just agreed to head back to civilisation and not to mix whisky and cannabis like that again.

There were no more huntin' shootin' and fishin' trips. Rory went back to live in London that winter, and ended up – funnily enough – living in a squat.

He wrote poems.

CHAPTER

The train sat, wrapped in rain and rocked by gusts, waiting to join the main line. Sidelined again, I watched the cold wind flatten the grubby-looking grass of a weedy field outside Springburn. A man walked across the field, some mongrel dog padding ahead of him. Two paths crossed the rectangular field, forming a neat St Andrew's Cross of down-trodden grass. The dog stopped to sniff at something in the grass, then squatted, urinating. The man following behind was dressed in cheap looking jeans and a donkey jacket, there was a bonnet perched on his head, and his hands were stuffed in his pockets. He walked up behind the dog and kicked its arse. The animal loped away, putting more distance between them, then resumed its casual, padding walk along the path. It was getting dark. Street lights were starting to come on in the distance, crimson slivers slowly brightening to orange.

I looked at my watch. We'd been stuck here, waiting to join the main line into Queen Street, for about ten minutes. You often had to wait here while the Edinburgh trains came and went, but the delay didn't usually last this long. The station was only five minutes away; more importantly, *food* was only five minutes away. I'd forgone breakfast because I hadn't got to bed till four in the morning, lunch because I had a hangover and anyway I was late for the train, and due to the fact that it was – according to British Rail at any rate – still part of the extended Festive Period, there had been no buffet trolley on the train. I was starving. I was so hungry I'd have eaten pork scratchings. Queen Street station, a scant mile and a half away, had burgers, sandwiches, shell pies, french fries and french sticks, bridies and pasties and patties. My God, if all they had were Haggisburgers, I'd eat those.

'Ladies and gentulmun ...' crackled a gruff Glaswegian voice from the carriage loudspeakers. My heart sank. The perfect end to a perfect holiday. 'Due to a signalling failure ...'

I looked out of the wind-shaken carriage, where people were moaning and cursing and making vows to start going by bus, or take the car next time, or buy a car, or learn to drive ... looked out through the rain-spattered sheets of glass, watching the cold January day leach out of the grey skies above the drenched city, and witnessed the rain fall upon the tramped-on, pissed-on, shat-on grass of the narrow path in the scrubby field with a feeling of wry but nevertheless wretched empathy.

God, what did any of it matter, in the end? You lived; you died. You were as indistinguishable from a distance as one of these blades of grass, and who was to say more important? Growing, surrounded by your kin, you out-living some, some out-living you. You didn't have to adjust the scale much, either, to reduce us to the sort of distant irrelevance of this bedraggled field. The grass was lucky if it grew, was shone upon and rained upon, and was not burned, and was not pulled up by the roots, or poisoned, or buried when the ground was turned over, and some bits just happened to be on a line that humans wanted to walk on, and so got trampled, broken, pressed flat, with no malice; just effect.

And intelligence? Control? There were things that we had no more control over yet than the grass did over the developer who chose to plough it all under and build a factory on top. Perhaps some asteroid, nudged out of its place in the great gravitational gavotte, would fall to Earth; a bullet into a face, obliterating. Unwitnessed, for what would be visible, from even a nearby star? A blink of flame, like a match struck beside a search-light ... And then nothing.

But didn't there have to be something out there, just to witness, just to *know*? Hell, it didn't even have to *do* anything; it didn't have to act on prayers or have us singled out as a special species, or play any part in our history and development; it didn't even necessarily have to have created us, or created anything, all it had to do was exist and have existed and go on existing, to record, to *encompass.*

I watched as the rain battered the grass and the wind pummelled it, quick gusts flattening patches of the field like sudden bruises beneath the dull sky. I could just imagine my father jumping up and down on this argument, this need for meaning, for faith.

The train jerked. I started, too, shaken from my reverie. Then the train went into reverse, motors growling, occupants groaning, and trundled slowly back through the squalls of rain, passing Maryhill and looping down through Anniesland and over Great Western Road.

We paralleled Crow Road for a bit, and stopped, waiting for signals, outside Jordanhill station; I looked up at the rear of the flats which fronted Crow Road, trying to work out which was Janice Rae's.

I thought of Uncle Rory, then remembered that I had some more of his papers with me, and a load of his poems. Mum had found them for me in the house at Lochgair. I got my bag down from the rack. Uncle Rory could not be more depressing than reality was, just now.

*

Any hope I might have entertained that Lewis and Verity's little Hogmanay hug had been an aberration, something they would fail to follow through, or feel for some reason embarrassed about, was comprehensively quashed the next evening when they turned up together at Uncle Hamish and Aunt Tone's, bearing all the signs of new lovers (literally so in the case of Lewis's neck, which displayed a line of passion purpurae worthy of an industrial vacuum cleaner, and which were ill-concealed by Lewis's longish dark curls and a white shirt fastened with a bootlace tie).

Lewis and Verity kept exchanging looks, laughing at anything even remotely amusing each other said, sitting close together, finding a hundred small excuses to touch each other . . . I wanted to throw up. We had all gathered for Hamish and Tone's traditional Ne'erday partyette; a necessarily quietish affair during which people exchanged tales of drunkenness, broken resolutions and recipes for hangover cures, as well as taking advantage of the opportunity to compare notes regarding blank spots in the memories of any of the assembled penitents.

I was helping Aunt Tone prepare stuff in the kitchen but had to give up when Lewis and Verity volunteered to assist as well, and then spent most of the time feeding one another little bits of food, goosing each other and going into sardinely-intimate huddles punctuated by low whispers, bursts of baboon-like giggles and convincingly porcine snorts. I went through to the dining-room and helped myself to a pint of the neuron-friendly punch Uncle Hamish always made for the event.

Mum and dad turned up later. There were about twenty of us, all told; mostly McHoans but with a smattering of civilians. We sipped – or in my case gulped – the weak but tasty punch, nibbled on Aunt Tone's buffet-bits, and played Alternative Charades; an invention of my father's in which one first has to guess the category of the thing one is being asked to decipher. When it was my turn to mime, I tended to concentrate on Popular Communicable Diseases, Well-Known Poisons, Famous Mass Murderers and Great Natural Disasters.

My last memory is of trying to mime Rare Gynaecological Disorders, preparatory to attempting Toxic Shock Syndrome. But apparently people insisted that one stand up to do one's piece, and I – successfully acclimatised to the horizontal by this time – refused to pander to this sort of nit-picking, and so passed my turn on to Cousin Josh with as much good grace as I could muster.

'The congenitally odd-jeaned person to my left will take my place,' I mumbled, waving one hand in his direction before letting my head resume its communion with Hamish and Tone's lounge carpet.

The bit about odd jeans was totally accurate, by the way; Cousin Josh made his fortune firstly by dealing in cars, then by risking all on a jeans company which at the time was tottering on the very hem of bankruptcy; under Josh's regime, their jeans weren't any better or any cheaper than anybody else's, but he had the garments made in odd sizes; waists of 29, 31, 33 inches, and so on, as opposed to the products from all other companies, domestic and foreign, which tended to favour the even numbers.

It was one of those brilliantly simple ideas people always wish they had had themselves, and believe that somehow they *could* have had; no need to incur any extra expense or make any more sizes than anybody else, or necessarily to distinguish one's product in other way, yet just by the idea one has a potential market of half the jeans-buying public, or at least that proportion of it which has always felt that they are somehow perpetually between the usual sizes.

I vaguely remember dreaming about Verity's jeans that night; how graphically, geographically tight they were and how wonderful it must be to take them off her. Then I imagined Lewis, boots tied round his neck, for some reason suddenly resembling Shane MacGowan, skinning her jeans off, not me, and he turned into Rodney Ritchie, at home with his parents, unpicking the individual stitches of her jeans with a tiny knife, and the Ritchies all wore badly-fitting jeans and had denim curtains and denim carpets and denim light shades and denim wallpaper with the little rivets left on like poppers so you could just press paintings and photos onto the wall . . . except that Mr Ritchie looked like Claude Lévi-Strauss, which is when I think I started to get confused.

*

Either I had been put to bed, I thought, as I woke up next morning, in the wee cold room at the top of the house, or my standard drunk-person's on-board auto-pilot facility was improving with experience.

I bathed, dressed, and broke my fast with some left-overs from the fridge, a pint of water and a couple of brace of Paracetamol, all without encountering anybody else in the house. It was only eight o'clock; obviously I'd conked out some time before everybody else, and they were still asleep (I had heard appropriate log-sawing-like noises coming from Hamish and Tone's room on my way back from the bathroom). The day looked bright but cold; I laced up the Docs and went for a walk in the hills behind Gallanach.

I felt like shit and I was trying so hard not to think of Lewis and Verity that I couldn't think about anything else, but the day was fabulous; clear and cold, the sky crystal blue and reflecting in the waters of hill-cupped lochans and the glinting length of Loch Add. On such days the hills hold a mixture of azure and gold never seen at any other time of year; the cobalt sky is more intense than it ever is in summer, and the straw-coloured hills shine strong in the light from the low winter sun. Against the shifting mirror that is the surface of a loch, the colours shimmer and dance; they take your breath away, and – for a brief, relieving while – they can even take your thoughts away.

Up in the hills, at the place of marching water, I found Ashley Watt and one of her more exotic cousins.

The concrete spillway below the Loch Add reservoir comes down to a stepped slope above the confluence of several small burns draining nearby slopes. A short bridge carries the track over the spillway, and that was where Ashley and Aline were sitting, legs dangling over the stream in the concrete gully, arms resting on the lower bar of the bridge rails.

They were sitting side by side, watching the marching water.

What happened was that the water first backed up behind the lipped edge of the top step, then over-flowed, and spilled with increasing force, in a sort of hydro-chain-reaction, down each subsequent step to the bottom of the channel. There followed a period of comparative quiet, while the water built up again behind the top step and those beneath. You might guess it was my dad who first pointed out this odd (and classically Chaotic) phenomenon and brought it to the attention of us kids. None of us had ever been able to discover whether it was a deliberate effect, or the result of pure chance. Whatever, it was wonderfully restful, unpredictable and therapeutic.

'Hey, Prentice,' Ash said. She looked a little worn and bleary-eyed, though her long, lion-coloured hair shone like health itself in the brassy sunlight of mid-day.

'Hi.' I nodded to her and to Aline, who was Franco-Vietnamese and engaged to Hugh Watt, one of Ashley's multitudinous cousins from the branch of the family that seemed to favour consorts of an exotic provenance (Hugh's brother Craig was going out with a stunning, lanky Nigerian called Noor). Aline looked even smaller and blacker-haired than usual, beside Ashley. 'Aline; ça va?'

'Magic, Prentice,' Aline replied in fluent Glaswegian.

'Have some skoosh,' Ash said as I sat down next to her. She reached between her and Aline and handed me a half-finished bottle of Irn-Bru. I had, over the course of the morning, already gulped down about a gallon of teeth-achingly cold stream-water at various points up in the hills, but the traditional Scottish hangover treatment was probably just what I needed. I took a couple of mouthfuls, handed the bottle back, wiping my lips.

'You look terrible,' Ash said.

'Feel worse,' I said glumly, watching the water cascade down the concrete stair-case of the spillway.

'Lost track of you at the Urvills' party, Prentice,' Ashley said. 'You just slope off, or did you get a lumber?'

'Oh God,' I moaned, and lowered my head to the cool steel pipe of the bridge rail.

'Hey ...' Ash said gently, putting her hand on my head and patting me. 'There there, Prentice ma man. What's the matter?'

'Oh, nothing much,' I sighed, slowly raising my head again and gazing at the water. 'I saw the woman I love wrap herself round my older, smarter and wittier brother like clingfilm round a sandwich, and it looks like they're enjoying each other the way ... Oh, God, I'm so pissed off I can't even think of a decent comparison. Or even an indecent one, which would probably – certainly – be more to the point.'

'Part from that; everything okay, aye?' Ash said, putting her arm round my shoulders.

'Help me, Ashley,' I said, closing my eyes and putting my head on her shoulder. 'What am I to do?'

'You must think of her on the toilet,' Aline said, and giggled.

'Off-white woman speak truth,' Ash said, lowering her head to rest it on mine. 'The hots rarely survive an intense course of imagining the beloved on the cludgie.'

'No,' I sighed, opening my eyes as a series of splashes announced another chaotic event on the spillway. 'I'd probably only develop a fetish for coprophagy.'

'*Pardon*?'

'That as unpleasant as it sounds?'

'Unpleasanter.'

'*Merde*!'

'Yup.'

'You're a hopeless case, Prentice, so you are. Have you contemplated suicide?'

'Yeah; soon as it's finished, I'm going to throw myself off the Channel Tunnel.'

Ashley's shoulders moved once under my head. 'Plenty of time to set your affairs in order, then.'

'It's not *my* affairs I'm concerned with.'

'Ach, she wasn't your sort, anyway, Prentice.'

'What; you mean not good enough for me?'

'No, Prentice; I mean too much taste. You never stood a chance with a woman that choosy.'

I pulled away and looked dubiously at Ashley, who smiled sweetly. 'What is this?' I said. 'You auditioning for the Exit chapter of the Samaritans, or what?'

Ashley took my hands in hers. 'Ah, Prentice. Dinnae worry; maybe it's just an infatuation; hers, or Lewis's ... or yours. Whatever. Maybe she'll come to her senses. Maybe she wants to work her way through all the McHoan brothers in order of age –'

'Or weight.'

' – or weight. Maybe she'll get married to Lewis but have a lifelong affair with you.'

'Oh, great.'

'See? You don't know what might happen,' Ashley said happily, spreading her hands.

'Anyway, Prentice,' Aline said in her sing-song voice. 'There are plenty more fishes in the sea, yes?'

I looked over at Aline. 'Hey, can I quote you on that?'

Aline winked at me, tapped the side of her nose. 'The toilet,' she said conspiratorially.

I started to get up. 'It's no good,' I sighed. 'You two are cheering me up too much and I can't stand the excitement.' I got wearily to my feet, muscles aching from the effects of drink and walk.

'See you down the Jac tonight?' Ash said.

'Maybe,' I said. 'I keep trying to drown my sorrows but they appear to be marginally more buoyant than expanded polystyrene.' The water cascaded down the face of the spillway again, the noise like a million stamping feet heard from a long way off. I shrugged. 'Fuck it, though; worth another try. Gotta start working some time.'

'That's my boy.'

'See you, gals.'

'Bye-bye, Prentice.'

'Try not to fall in love with anybody else before tonight.'

'Yo.'

*

An hour or so later I saw my mother's green Metro, just about to turn out of the drive-way of Hamish and Tone's house. She stopped when she saw me, wound the window down. 'Here you are,' she said.

'Here I am,' I agreed.

'I was waiting for ages there.' She glanced at her watch. 'Oh well. Getting in?'

I got into the car; we started to reverse the fifty yards back up the drive. Actually, my legs were so tired I was quite grateful for the lift. 'I brought what I could find of Rory's stuff.' Mum nodded. 'Your dad thinks there's more, but it's buried in the filing.' I looked at the back seat, where a folder lay. 'Not that you deserve it,' she added.

'Oh, thanks,' I said. I picked the folder up; *CRII* said the lettering on the spine. It looked similar to the folder I already had, but perhaps a little thicker. I vaguely remembered reminding mum last night that I was looking for the rest of Uncle Rory's papers.

'Well?' she said.

I looked over, yawning. 'Well?' I repeated.

We drew to a stop outside the door of the house. 'You don't remember last night, do you?' mum said, turning the ignition off. She was dressed in angora and chunky cords; new perfume. She looked slightly unamused and not a little worried.

'Not . . . in its entirety, no,' I confessed.

She shook her head. 'God, you were drunk, Prentice.'

'Umm,' I said, weighing the folder in my hands. '. . . Yes.' I smiled my best 'but I'm still your wee laddy' smile.

She raised those delicate brown brows. 'My God, you don't remember embarrassing Lewis and Verity last night, do you?'

I looked at her.

'I mean, apart from embarrassing your father and me,' she added.

I felt the blood draining from my face like somebody had opened a valve in my ankle. Oh-oh.

I swallowed. 'I wasn't doing my impression of the Bradford City supporter, the King's Cross Disaster victim and the guy from Piper Alpha meeting up in Hell, was I?' (Requires three cigarettes; offends everybody.)

'It's not funny, Prentice; poor Verity was nearly in tears. You're lucky Lewis didn't throttle you.'

'Oh my God,' I said, feeling cold. 'What did I *say*?'

(Duck, and cover.)

'Told her – told everybody – you were madly in love with her!' she said, eyes flashing. 'Then, having declared undying worship of the poor girl, you proceeded to slag her off for taking up with Lewis.' Mum shook her head angrily, tears in her eyes. 'Prentice! What were you *thinking* of?'

'Oh my God,' I moaned. KYAG. I put the folder down in my lap and put my forehead on the folder.

'Then you followed that up with some fairly off-colour remarks about Lapland, and what you referred to, I believe, as "the old earth-moving equipment".'

'Oh my God.'

'And I think we all successfully worked out what "doing the Delta Foxtrot" was, as well, before you became totally incoherent.'

'Oh my God!'

'I don't think saying "Oh my God" will make it any better, Prentice. I think you should apologise to Verity and Lewis as soon as you can. They're up at the castle.' My mother brought her voice under control with an effort. 'Though you might also think about saying sorry to Hamish and Antonia, too, as you were their guest and it was their party you brought grinding to an embarrassing halt. Just as well you agreed to go quietly when Kenneth suggested it was time you went to bed; though apparently he and Hamish practically had to carry you upstairs, and the whole way up you were muttering something vile about Lewis being thrown naked into a tub of starving Elephant Leeches.'

And dad put me to bed! Oh no! Dad and the Tree! The shame of it!

'Mum, I want to die,' I mumbled into the folder.

'Just at the moment, Prentice, I don't think there'd be any shortage of volunteers to help you on your way, if you were serious.'

'I am.'

'Stop being melodramatic, Prentice; it doesn't suit you. Sarcasm's more your forte.'

'Oh my God.'

'Prentice,' mum said, putting her hand on my head and running her fingers through my hair. 'Prentice ...'

I looked up, straightened. Mum's eyes looked red. She shook her head. 'Prentice, why are you so stupid with your cleverness sometimes?'

I took a deep breath. 'Wish I knew, mum,' I said, and sniffed, eyes smarting. Best not to say anything about it running in the family.

She took me in her arms, hugged me. I was surprised, as I always was at such moments, how slim and small she felt.

After a bit we let go of each other. She glanced in the mirror and declared I had wrecked her eyes for the rest of the day. Then we went in to Hamish and Tone's for tea and apologies, and later drove to the castle for what would have been the most excruciating interval of my life if Verity and Lewis had still been there, but they weren't; they had taken off in the car to visit some friends of Verity's who lived in Ardnamurchan, and wouldn't be back until late tomorrow at the earliest.

Mum took me back *chez* Hamish and Tone; she agreed to pass on my expressions of contrition to my father. She'd wanted me to come to Lochgair and say sorry to him there, but I had begged for mercy, and – rather to my surprise – been granted it.

I had already decided that tomorrow I would take the train back to what was now your official European City of Culture for the following twelve months. In theory, Verity and Lewis were meant to be giving me a lift in four days time, but that was obviously out, now.

I had to promise mum I'd write to each of them, and apologise in person at the first possible opportunity, and also that I'd stop off at Lochgair before I returned to Glasgow, to see dad.

*

Ashley met me in the Jac that night, listened to my woes, bought me drink when I ran out of money (I'm sure I was short-changed at the bar) even though she probably had less dosh than I did, and listened to my woes all over again when we went back to her mum's and sat up till God knows when, talking low so we wouldn't wake Dean in the next room. She made me coffee, gave me hugs, and at one point I fell asleep, and was at peace for a while, and woke up sprawled on the floor, my head on her lap, one gentle hand stroking my head. 'Ash,' I croaked, 'you're a saint.'

She just smiled.

A last cup of coffee and I left; back to H and T's in time for a few hours' fitful sleep; then up and away, run to the station by Aunt Antonia. I only just caught the train, and when, a quarter of an hour later, we pulled in to Lochgair, and I should have got my bag and quit the Sprinter and walked to the house and finally have talked – sober, and not in the context of a game of Alternative Charades – to my father, and apologised, and spent the three hours until the next Glasgow train with my mother and father in some longed-for spirit of reconciliation, I did nothing of the sort.

Instead I put my head to one side so that it rested against the cold glass of the window, closed my eyes and let my mouth hang open a little. I stayed like that for the minute or so we waited at the Lochgair station platform, and didn't stir again – yawning convincingly for any other passengers who might be watching – until we were crossing the viaduct at Succothmore.

*

Still stuck on the track within sight of Janice Rae's flat, I got up out of my seat, took down my bag and fished out the file mum had brought from the house. I found some much-Tippexed poems typed on foolscap, plus about twenty or so printed A4 pages which looked like they were part of a play or film script. I selected a page at random and started reading.

> *Lord:* ... And I see them as they will be, dead and torn; shocked, mutilated and alone, on battlefields or by long roads, in ditches or against high walls, in echoing white corridors and misty woods, in fields, by rivers; dumped in holes, thrown in piles; neglected and absolved. Or, if living on, filled with petty, bitter memories, and a longing for the war they fought to end. Oh captain, I see in this my ending, what I think you didn't start to glimpse with your most cunning intuition; the soldiers are always the real refugees. Their first victim is themselves, their life taken from them well before – as though seeking a replacement from another freed –

But I couldn't take any more. I put the papers in the folder and the folder in my bag, then stuffed that under my seat.

I looked out at the rain instead; it was cheerier.

I'd avoided stopping off to see mum and dad. It made my eyes close, every time I thought about it. What was wrong with me?

Well, I thought; they made me. They produced me; their genes.

And they brought me up. School and university still hadn't changed me as much as they had; maybe even the rest of my life could never compensate for their formative effect. If I was too embarrassed, too full of shame to go and see them, it wasn't just my fault; it was theirs too, because of the way they'd brought me up (God, I thought I'd stopped using that excuse when I left Lochgair Primary School). But there *was* a grain of truth in there.

Wasn't there?

And hell, I thought; I *had* been tired; I *was* tired still, and I would phone that evening – definitely – and say I'd fallen asleep, and nobody would be too bothered, and after all a chap could only cope with so much sorrow-saying in one day ... of course I'd phone. A bit of soft soap, a bit of flannel, like dad would say.

No sweat; I could charm them. I'd make everything all right.

*

Still, it was the hangover of that piece of moral cowardice at Lochgair station, along with everything else, that led to me feeling so profoundly awful with myself that evening (after the train finally did get into Queen Street and I walked back, soaked and somehow no longer hungry, in the rain to the empty flat in Grant Street), that mum had to call me there, because I hadn't been able to bring myself to phone her and dad ... and I still managed to feign sleep and a little shame and a smattering of sorrow and reassure her as best I could that really I was all right, yes of course, not to worry, I was fine, thanks for calling ... and so of course after that felt even worse.

I made a cup of coffee. I was feeling so bad that I treated it as a kind of moral victory that I was able to empty most of the water out of the obviously Gav-filled kettle and leave the level at the minimum mark. I stood in the kitchen waiting for the water to heat up with a distinct feeling of eco-smugness.

It was just as I was sitting down in the living room with my cup of coffee that I realised I'd left my bag on the train.

I couldn't believe it. I remembered getting out of my seat, putting on my jacket, wondering about trying to get something to eat, deciding I didn't feel hungry, glancing at the empty luggage rack, and then heading through the station and up the road. With no bag.

How could I? I put the coffee down, leapt out of my chair and over the couch, ran to the phone, and got through, ten minutes later, to the station. Lost Property was closed; call tomorrow.

I lay in bed that night, trying to remember what had been in the bag. Clothes, toiletries, one or two books, a couple of presents ... and the folder with Uncle Rory's papers in it; both folders, including the one I hadn't read yet.

No, I told myself, as panic tried to set in. It was inconceivable that I'd lost the bag forever. It would turn up. I had always been lucky that way. People were generally good. Even if somebody had picked it up, maybe they had done so by mistake. But probably a guard had spotted it and it was right now sitting in some staff-room in Queen Street station, or Gallanach. Or maybe – in a siding only a mile or two from where I lay – a cleaner's brush was at this moment encountering the bag, wedged back under the seat ... But I'd get it back. It couldn't just disappear; it had to find its way back to me. It had to.

I got to sleep eventually.

I dreamt of Uncle Rory coming home, driving the old Rover Verity had been born in, the window open, his arm sticking out, him smiling and holding the missing folder in his hand; waving it. In the dream, he had a funny looking white towel wrapped round his neck, and that was when I woke up and remembered.

My white silk scarf; the irreplaceable Möbius scarf, the gift of Darren Watt, had been in the missing bag as well.

'Noooo!' I wailed into the pillow.

*

Waking up was a process of gradually remembering all the things I had to feel bad about. I rang Lost Property first thing. No bag. I got them to give me the number for the cleaners' mess-room and asked there. No bag. I tried Gallanach, in case the train had got back there before the bag had been discovered under the seat by some honest person. No bag.

I tried both stations again in the afternoon; guess what?

I did the only thing I could think of, and retired to bed; if I was to be a blade of grass doomed to be trampled flat, then I might as well accept it and lie down. I stayed in bed for the next twenty-four hours, sleeping, drinking a little water, not eating at all, and only rousing myself when Gav arrived back (from his parents', I wrongly assumed), loudly declaring himself to be of unsound liver but totally in love.

Oh, lucky ewe, I said, does she come from a respectable flock?

Ha ha, it's your au – fr ... parents' friend, Janice, Gav beamed, radiating unrepentant guilt; came round here the other day looking for you we got talking went for a curry had a few drinks ended up back here one thing led to another know how it is always liked older women they're more experienced know what I mean arf arf anyway spent an extremely enjoyable New Year at her place apart from the usual visit to my folk's of course oh by the way she's coming round here tonight I'm cooking lasagne can you swap rooms seeing Norris won't be back until tomorrow it's just I didn't expect you back until then either, that okay?

I stared at Gav from my bed, blinking and trying to take in this torrent of exponentially catastrophic information. I attempted desperately to convince myself that what I was experiencing was just a particularly cruel and hateful dream concocted by some part of my mind determined to exact due penalty from my conscience for my having behaved with such despicable lack of grace during the holidays ... but failed utterly; my sub-conscious' stock of nightmare-paradigms includes nothing so banally twisted as Gav.

Finally, scraping together the last microscopic filaments of my tattered pride to produce a quorum fit for emergency ego-resuscitation if not actual wit, I managed: 'Gav, I'm shocked.' (Gav looked defensive for all of a micro-second, a concession my lacerated self-respect fell upon with all the pathetic desperation of a humiliatingly defeated politician pointing out that well, things can only get better.) 'You never told me you could cook lasagne.'

CHAPTER 10

Once upon a time, long ago, there was a rich merchant who thought that the city where he lived was full of bad people, and especially bad children.'

'Were they Slow Children?'

'Some of them were, as a matter of fact, but at the time they didn't have the signs to tell them so.'

'Are the Slow Children only in Lochgair, dad?'

'No; there are Slow Children in various places; watch out for the road-signs. Now; back to the story. The rich merchant thought the children should always salute him and call him "sir" when they passed him in the street. He hated beggars and old people who couldn't work any more. He hated untidiness and waste; he thought that babies who threw things from their cradles should be punished, and children who wouldn't eat their food should be starved until they ate what they had been given in the first place.'

'Dad, what if it had gone rotten?'

'Even if it had gone rotten.'

'Aw, dad! Even if it had maggots and things in it and it was all horrible?'

'Yes; that would teach them, he thought.'

'Awwrr! Yuk!'

'Well, the rich merchant was very powerful, and he came to control things in the city, and he made everybody do as he thought they ought to do; snowball-throwing was made illegal, and children had to eat up all their food. Leaves were forbidden to fall from the trees because they made a mess, and when the trees took no notice of this they had their leaves glued onto their branches ... but that didn't work, so they were fined; every time they dropped leaves, they had twigs and then branches sawn off. And so eventually, of course, they had no twigs left, then no branches left, and in the end the trees were cut right down. The same happened with flowers and bushes too.

'Some people kept little trees in secret courtyards, and flowers in their houses, but they weren't supposed to, and if their neighbours reported them to the police the people would have their trees chopped down and the flowers taken away and they would be fined or put in prison, where they had to work very hard, rubbing out writing on bits of paper so they could be used again.'

'Is this story pretend, dad?'

'Yes. It's not real; I made it up.'

'Who makes up real things, dad?'

'Nobody and everybody; they make themselves up. The thing is that because the real stories just happen, they don't always tell you very much. Sometimes they do, but usually they're too ... messy.'

'So the rich merchant wouldn't like them?'

'That's right. In the city, nobody was allowed to tell stories. Nobody was allowed to hum, or whistle or listen to music, either, because the merchant thought that people should save their breath the way they saved their money.

'But people didn't like living the way the merchant wanted them to; most mums and dads wouldn't serve their children rotten food, and hated having to pretend that they did. People missed the trees and flowers . . . and having to walk around with one eye covered by an eye-patch.'

'Why was that, dad? Why did they have –'

'Because the merchant thought it was a waste of light to have both eyes open; why not save the light the way you save money?'

'Were they like Mr Lachy, dad?'

'Well, not exactly, no; Lachlan Watt only has one eye; the other one looks like a real one but it's glass. The people in the city could change from one eye to the other on different days, but Lachlan –'

'Aye, dad, but they're like him sort of, aren't they?'

'Well, sort of.'

'Why has Mr Lachy only got one eye, dad?'

'Uncle Fergus punched him! Eh, dad?'

'No, Prentice. Uncle Fergus didn't punch him. It was an accident. Fergus and Lachy were fighting and Fergus meant to hit Lachy but he didn't mean to put his eye out. Now; do you two want to hear this story or not?'

'Aye, dad.'

'Aye, dad.'

'Right. Well, the city wasn't a nice place to live because of all the silly laws the merchant had passed, and people started to leave it and go to other towns and other countries, and the merchant was spending so much time passing new laws and trying to make people obey the ones he'd already passed that his own business started to fail, and eventually the city was almost deserted, and the merchant found that he owed people much more money than he had in the bank, and even though he sold his house and everything he owned he was still broke; he was thrown out of his house and out of the city too, because he had become a beggar, and beggars weren't allowed in the city.

'So he wandered the countryside for a long time, starving and having to beg for food, and sleeping in barns and under trees, and eventually he found a little town where all the beggars and old people he'd had thrown out of the city had gone; they were very poor, of course, but by all helping each other they had more than the merchant had. He asked if he could stay with them, and eventually they agreed that he could, but only if he worked. So they gave him a special job.'

'What, dad?'

'What was the job, dad?'

'He had to make brooms.'

'Brooms?'

'Old fashioned brushes made from bundles of twigs tied to a wooden handle. You know up in the forest you sometimes see those things for beating out fires?'

'The big flappy things?'

'Yes; they're big bits of rubber – old tyres – attached to wooden handles, for beating out fires on the ground. Well, in the old days, those used to be made from twigs, and even longer ago people used to use brooms like that to sweep the streets and even to sweep their houses. Not all that long ago, either; I can remember seeing a man sweeping the paths in the park in Gallanach with a broom like that, when I was older than either of you are now.'

'Ah, but dad, you're ancient!'

'Ha ha ha ha!'

'That's enough. Now listen; about these brooms, right?'

'What?'

'What, dad?'

'The man who had been a rich merchant, and who was now a beggar, had to make brooms for the town. He had a little hut with a stone floor, and a supply of handles and twigs. But to teach the man a lesson they had given him a supply of twigs that were old and weak; poor twigs for making brooms with.

'So, by the time he had made one broom the floor of the hut was covered in bits of twigs, and he had to use the broom he'd just made to sweep the floor of his hut clean before he could start making the next broom. But by the time he'd cleaned the floor to his satisfaction, the broom had worn right away, right down to the handle. So he had to start on another one. And the same thing happened with that broom, too. And the next, and the next; the mess made making each broom had to be cleared up with that same broom, and wore it away. So at the end of the day there was a great big pile of twigs outside the hut, but not one broom left.'

'That's silly!'

'That's a waste, sure it is, dad?'

'Both. But the people had done it to teach the man a lesson.'

'What lesson, dad?'

'Ah-hah. You'll have to work that out for yourselves.'

'Aw, dad!'

'Dad, I know!'

'What?' Kenneth asked Prentice.

'Not to be so damn silly!'

Kenneth laughed. He reached up and ruffled Prentice's hair in the semi-darkness; the boy's head was hanging out over the top bunk. 'Well, maybe,' he said.

'Dad,' James said from the lower bunk. 'What happened to the merchant?'

Kenneth sighed, scratched his bearded chin. 'Well, some people say he died in the town, always trying to make a broom that would last; others say he just gave up and wasted away, others that he got somebody else to make the brooms and found somebody to provide better twigs, and got people to sell the brooms in other towns and cities, and hired more people to make more brooms, and built a broom-making factory, and made lots of money and had a splendid house made ... And other people say he just lived quietly in the town after learning his lesson. That's a thing about stories, sometimes; they have different endings according to who you listen to, and some have sort of open endings, and some don't actually have proper endings yet.'

'Aw, but dad ...'

'But one thing's definite.'

'What, dad?'

'It's light-out time.'

'Aw . . .'

'Night-night.'

'Night, dad.'

'Yeah; night.'

'Sleep tight.'

'Don't let the bugs bite.'

'Right. Now lie down properly; noddles on pillows.'

He made sure they were both tucked in and went to the door. The night-light glowed softly on the top of the chest of drawers.

'Okay . . . Dad?'

'What?'

'Did the man not have any family, dad?' Prentice asked. 'In the story: the merchant. Did he not have any family?'

'No,' Kenneth said, holding the door open. 'He did, once, but he threw them out of his house; he thought he wasted too much time telling his two youngest sons bed-time stories.'

'Aww . . .'

'Aww . . .'

He smiled, padded back into the room, kissed the boys' foreheads. 'But then he was a silly man, wasn't he?'

*

They left Margot to look after the children and set off in the car, heading for Gallanach. Kenneth smiled when he saw the hand-painted sign at the outskirts of the village that said, 'Thank You.'

'What are you grinning at?' Mary asked him. She was bending down in her seat, staring into the little mirror that hinged up from the glove-box flap, inspecting her lip-stick.

'Just that sign,' he said. 'The one that goes with the Slow Children sign at the other end of the village.'

'Huh,' Mary said. 'Slow children, indeed. I hope you weren't telling my bairns horrible stories that'll keep them awake all night.'

'Na,' he said. The Volvo estate accelerated down the straight through the forest towards Port Ann. 'Though maggoty meat and people with one eye did come into it at one point.

'Hmm,' Mary said. She snapped the glove-box closed. 'I heard Lachy Watt's back in the town; is that true?'

'Apparently.' Kenneth rotated his shoulders as he drove, trying to ease the nagging pain in them that too much drink the night before always seemed to give him these days.

They had spent Hogmanay at home, welcoming the groups of people roaming the village as they came round. The last revellers had finally been seen off at nine in the morning; they and Margot had done some cleaning up before going to bed, though Ken had anyway had a couple of hours' sleep between three and five, when he'd fallen into a deep slumber on the wicker couch in the conservatory. The boys had gone out to play on the forestry tracks with their new bikes on what had proved a bright but cold day; Mary had got three hours' sleep before they came back, noisily demanding to be fed.

'Haven't seem him for . . . what? Ten years?' Mary said. 'Has he been away at sea all that time?'

'Well, hardly,' Ken said. 'He was in Australia, wasn't he? Settled down there for a while. Had some sort of job in Sydney, I heard.'

'What was he doing?'

'Don't know; you could ask him yourself. Supposed to be coming to Hamish and Tone's shindig tonight.'

'Is he?' Mary said. The Volvo hissed along the dark road; a couple of cars went past, holes of white light in the night, scattering spray which the water jets and wipers of the Volvo swept away again. Mary took a perfume spray from her handbag, applied the scent to wrists and neck. 'Fergus and Fiona are coming tonight, aren't they?'

'Should be,' Ken nodded.

'Do you know if Lachy and Fergus still talk to each other?'

'No idea.' He laughed. 'Don't even know what they'd talk about; a member of the factory-owning Scottish gentry and a second mate – or whatever Lachy is these days – who's spent the last few years in Oz. What is there to say; aye-aye, captain of light industry?'

'Fergus isn't gentry, anyway,' Mary said.

'Well, good as. Might not have a title, but he acts like he does sometimes. Got a castle; what more do you want?' Kenneth laughed lightly again. 'Aye-aye. Ha ha.'

The lights of Lochgilphead swung into view ahead, just as rain started to spot the windscreen. Kenneth put the wipers on. 'Aye-aye!' he sniggered.

Mary shook her head.

*

'Going to the dogs, if you ask me.'

'Fergus, people like you have been saying that since somebody invented the wheel. Things get better. They're always looking up.'

'Yes, Kenneth, but you're basically Bolshie, so you would think so.'

Kenneth grinned, took a drink of his whisky and water. 'It's been a good year,' he nodded. Fergus looked suitably disgusted, and threw back the remains of his own whisky and soda in one gulp.

They stood in the lounge of Hamish and Antonia's house, watching the others help themselves to the buffet Antonia had prepared. Neither of the two men had felt hungry.

'You might not be saying that when the refugees come back from Australia,' Fergus said sourly. Kenneth glanced at him, then looked round for Lachlan Watt; he was sitting on a distant chair, a plate of food balanced on his knees, talking to Shona Watt, his sister-in-law.

Kenneth laughed as Fergus refilled his glass from one of the whisky bottles on the drinks trolley behind them. 'Fergus, you're not talking about the Domino Theory by any chance, are you?'

'Don't care what you call it, McHoan; not saying it'll be next, either, but you just watch.'

'Fergus, for God's sake; not even that asshole Kissinger believes in the Domino Theory any more. The Vietnamese have finally got control of their own country after forty years of war; defeated the Japs, the French, us, and the most powerful nation in the history of the planet in succession, with bicycles, guns and guts, been bombed back into the bronze age in the process and all you can do is spout some tired nonsense about little yellow men infiltrating the steaming jungles of the Nullarbor Plain and turning the Aussies into Commies; I think a Highland League side winning the European Cup is marginally more likely.'

'I'm not saying they won't pause to draw breath, Kenneth, but I can't help feeling the future looks black for those of us interested in freedom.'

'Fergus, you're a Tory. When Tories say freedom they mean money; the freedom to send your child to a private school means the *money* to send your child to a private school. The freedom to invest in South Africa means the *money* to invest there so you can make even more. And don't tell me you're interested in freedom unless you support the freedom of blacks to come here from abroad, which I know you don't, so there.' Kenneth clinked his glass against Fergus's. 'Cheers. To the future.'

'Huh,' said Fergus. 'The future. You know, I'm not saying your lot won't win, but I hope it doesn't happen in my lifetime. But things really are going to the dogs.' Fergus sounded genuinely morose, Kenneth thought.

'Ah, you're just peeved your lot have elected a woman leader. Even that's good news ... even if she is the milk snatcher.'

'We got rid of an old woman and replaced him with a younger one,' Fergus said, mouth turned down at the corners, staring over his whisky tumbler and across the room to where his wife was talking to Antonia. 'That's not progress.'

'It is, Fergus. Even the Tories are subject to change. You should be proud.'

Fergus looked at Kenneth, a wealth of sombre disdain in his slightly watery-eyed look. Kenneth gave him a big smile. Fergus turned away again. Kenneth looked at the other man's heavily jowled, prematurely aged face and shook his head. Chiang-Kai-Shek and Franco dead, Angola independent, Vietnam free at last ... Kenneth thought it had been a great year. The whole tide of history seemed to be quickening as it moved remorselessly leftwards. He felt vaguely sorry for Fergus. His shower had had their reign, he thought, and grinned to himself.

It had been a good year for Kenneth personally, too. The BBC, bless its cotton socks, had taken some of the stories from his first collection; a whole week of *Jackanory* to himself, just six weeks before Christmas! At this rate he could start thinking about giving up teaching in a year or two.

'I wish I shared your enthusiasm for change.' Fergus sighed, and drank deeply.

'Change is what it's all about, Ferg. Shuffling the genes; trying new ideas. Jeez, where would your damn factory be if you didn't try new processes?'

'Better off,' Fergus said. He looked sourly at Kenneth. 'We're just about making enough from traditional paperweights to keep the Specialist Division afloat. All this hi-tech stuff just loses us money.'

'Well, it must be making money for somebody; maybe you weren't able to invest enough. Maybe the big boys'll take over. That's the way things go; capitalists all want to have a monopoly. Only natural. Don't get depressed about it.'

'You won't be saying that if we have to close the factory and put everybody out of work.'

'God, Ferg, it isn't that bad, is it?'

Fergus shrugged heavily. 'Yes, it is. We've told them it might come to that; the shop-stewards, anyway. Another strike, or too big a pay rise, and we might go under.'

'Hmm,' Kenneth said, sipping at his whisky. He wondered how serious the other man was. Industrialists often made that sort of threat, but they rarely seemed to be carried out. Kenneth was a little surprised that Hamish hadn't said anything about the factory being in such dire straits, but then his brother did seem to put the church and the factory above family and friends.

'I don't know.' Fergus shook his head. 'If we weren't tied to this bit of the country, I'd almost think about chucking it all in and heading off somewhere different – Canada, or Australia, or South Africa.'

It was Kenneth's turn to look sour. 'Yes,' he said. 'Well, you'd probably get on fine in the RSA, Ferg. Though that's the one place I *wouldn't* recommend if you want to keep well away from the red tide.'

'Hmm,' Fergus nodded, still watching his wife, now talking to Shona Watt. 'Yes, you may be right.' He knocked back his drink, turned to the bottle-loaded table behind and poured himself another large whisky.

Antonia clapped her hands, singing out: 'Come on, you boring lot; let's all play charades!'

Kenneth drained his glass, murmured. 'God, I hate charades.'

*

'Henriss . . . never liked him either; fat lipped beggar . . . queer, y'know; thass wha he's singing you know; d'you know that? "Scuse me while I kiss this guy . . ." disgussin . . . absluley disgussin . . .'

'Fergus, do shut up.'

'"Scuse me, while I kiss this guy" . . . bloody poofter coon.'

'I'm sorry about this, Lachy.'

'That's okay, Mrs U. You no goin to put your seat belt on, no?'

'No; not for short journeys –'

'Lachy? Lachy . . . Lachy! Lachy; I'm sorry about your eye . . . really really sorry; never forgave myself, never . . . here, shake . . .'

Fergus tried to lever himself up from the rear bench seat of the old Rover, but failed. He got as far as lifting his head and getting one shoulder off the seat, but then collapsed back onto the leather, and let his eyes close.

The car rumbled about him . . . even more restful than the noise of train wheels in the old days; he tried to remember the old days . . .

'You sure you don't mind doing this, Lachy?' Fiona said, swinging the car off the main road and onto the drive that led to the castle. The headlights made a tunnel of the trees and rhododendrons.

'Na, it's okay.'

Lachlan Watt had been about to leave Hamish and Antonia's party when Fergus had fallen over and Fiona had decided it was time to take her husband home; she had offered Lachy a lift back to his brother's house, but when they'd got there Fergus had seemed fast asleep, snoring loudly and taking no apparent notice of Fiona shaking him and shouting at him; Lachy had volunteered to come back to the castle to help get Fergus out of the car and upstairs to bed; Fiona would run Lachy back afterwards.

'God that man's a nuisance,' Fiona said, as they turned the corner in the drive and the lights of the castle came into view against the coal-dark night. 'Like I say; I could have got the baby-sitter to help me with him, but she's just a skelf . . . not our regular girl. She's *built like a rugby player, could probably put Ferg over her shoulder, but not this girl. Leanne's her name . . . that's her car there; doesn't look old enough to drive if you ask me . . .'*

Fiona brought the Rover to a halt behind a beaten-up mini, standing on the gravel in front of the castle's main entrance.

'This really is awful good of you, Lachy.'

'Aye, it's no problem, Mrs U.'

Fiona turned to him. She smiled. 'Lachy; it's Fiona. You make me feel old when you call me Mrs U.'

'Sorry; Fiona.' Lachy grinned.

He had been a thin, light-framed boy, and he had grown to become a lean, wiry man; the years of life on merchant ships, and then in Australia, had left his skin looking well-used, like soft and fine-grained – but slightly distressed – leather. His hair was unfashionably short, and both eyes glittered. It was a spare, uncluttered, characterful face, especially compared to Fergus's.

'That's better.' Fiona smiled. She turned and looked in disgust at the body in the back seat, just as Fergus started to snore again. 'Well; better get this lump out of the car, I suppose.'

Fergus had gone back into a deep sleep. They couldn't wake him. Fiona went in to tell the baby sitter she was free to go, while Lachy tried to rouse Fergus.

'Hoi you; Fergus. Ferg; wake up, man.'

'Aarg . . . Henriss, bassard.'

'Fergus; wake up, Fergus.' Lachlan tried slapping the man's cheeks; his heavy jowls wobbled like jellies.

'Hhnn . . .'

'Wake up,' Lachlan said, slapping Fergus's cheeks again, harder. 'Wake up,' he said quietly. 'Ye upper class cunt ye.' He fairly walloped Ferg on one chop.

Fergus awoke suddenly; arms waving about, eyes wild and bright, making no sound other than a faint gurgling noise. Then he rolled off the seat into the footwell and immediately started snoring again.

'Any luck with the sleeping beauty?' Fiona said, coming down the steps alongside a slim, blonde-haired girl who was zipping up an anorak.

Lachlan turned round. 'Na; he's sound.'

'That'll be the day,' muttered Fiona. She glanced in at Fergus, then turned to the girl. 'Thanks, Leanne, dear; now drive carefully, won't you?'

'Aye, Mrs Urvill,' the girl said, taking out some keys and heading for the mini. 'Night-night.'

'Bye now.'

Fiona and Lachy took an end of Fergus each; Lachy held him under the shoulders, Fiona by the ankles. They struggled up the steps, through the entrance hall, rested in the main hall, then took him up to the first floor.

'In here,' Fiona said, nodding.

Lachy supported Fergus's shoulders with one knee while he twisted the handle of a darkly-stained wooden door. It swung open to darkness.

'There's a light, aye?'

'Just there; down a bit.'

The room was small and bright; there was a single bed, a dressing table and chair, and a wardrobe. There was a print of a hunting scene on one wall, opposite a small window.

'Guest room's good enough for him tonight,' Fiona grunted as they swung him onto the bed and dropped him.

'Shooch!' Fiona said, collapsing onto the floor. Lachy sat down on the pillow at the head of the bed, breathing hard. Fiona wiped her brow. She got up shakily.

'That was hard work,' she said. She pulled Fergus's shoes off and nodded to the door. 'Come on; let's break into the old bugger's best malt before we run you back. You deserve it.'

'Fair enough,' Lachy said, smiling. 'No takin his clothes off, no?'

'Ugh. Certainly not,' Fiona said. She drew back a little against the door to let Lachy go past her into the hallway. 'He's lucky we didn't leave him in the car.' She turned out the light.

*

Fergus woke in utter darkness, wondering where he was; he felt as though he was falling backwards forever into darkness. For an instant he thought perhaps he was dead, consigned to perdition and gloom until the end of time, his only sensation that of falling back and back and back, head over heels forever. He heard himself moan, and felt with his hands: bedclothes. He was still wearing his own clothes, too. Here was his shirt on his wrist; there his trousers, sweater ... shoes off. He flexed his feet, feeling his toes in his socks. His hands found the sides of the bed; it was a single, then.

It was still totally dark. He tried to remember where he'd been last.

The party; Hamish and Antonia McHoan's. Of course. He must still be there, as this wasn't his own bed. Put to bed. Bit bad, that; probably in the dog-house as far as the lady wife was concerned, too, but then what was new?

He put one hand out, feeling for a table; he found what felt like one, and then a long cold metal stem. Reaching up, he felt a switch.

The light clicked on and suddenly everything was white and horribly bright. He shielded his eyes. God, his head felt fuzzy, and sore. He needed a drink very badly; water would do.

He looked round the white-painted room, thinking that it looked somehow familiar. Perhaps he had slept here before. Or maybe he'd given the McHoans some bits and pieces of furniture.

He listened but couldn't hear anything. The door of the room looked familiar, too. Odd to find a door so comforting, somehow.

He got up, wobbled across to the door. He was quite cold. He opened the door; a dark hall. Funny; the place didn't smell like the McHoans' house did. It smelled of wood and a sort of quite pleasant mustiness. This place smelled of stone and polish. Bit like the castle.

He went out into the hallway, felt along the wall for a light switch; he found one, switched it on. Stairs led up; the wood-panelled hall led to another set of stairs going down. There were old paintings on the walls. He felt very dizzy, and sat down on the bottom step of the stairs. He was home. This was the castle.

He got up, walked up the stairs. The door to the short flight of stairs that led to the two topmost floors was locked. He didn't understand. He searched his pockets but could find no key.

He pushed at the door again. He gathered a chestful of air to shout at Fiona – dozy bitch had locked him out of his own fucking castle, his own bedroom – but then thought of the children. Might wake the little beggars up. Didn't want that.

He went down through the lower hall to the kitchen, drank some water. His watch said it was two o'clock; so did the kitchen clock. There ought to have been keys hanging by the door to the utility room, but they weren't there. Bloody fishy. Had Fiona hidden them? Did she think he was dangerous, was that it?

Maybe she thought he would get up in some drunken stupor and ravish her. 'Huh, that'll be right,' he said to himself. His voice sounded rough in the quiet kitchen; he cleared his throat, coughed, and felt the dull pounding of his headache suddenly sharpen.

Damn it all. Perhaps he was being punished. Maybe she was punishing him for getting drunk. Had he done anything disgraceful? He couldn't remember, but he doubted it. He usually held his drink well, and behaved like a gentleman even when he did have one too many.

He looked at his reflection in the window over the sink. He pulled one splayed hand through his hair. Maybe he ought to have a shower or something. There was always the bathroom on the first floor . . .

He felt bloody annoyed, Fi locking him out of their apartments like that.

Then he remembered the observatory.

You could get up to it by the stairs to the roof. He'd been up there, in the roof space when the men had been installing the dome. For that matter, he'd seen that loft being put together, knew it almost as well as that self-opinionated young architect had. He'd crawled around in there, him and the builder, with a torch, discussing where the observatory could be built; what joists and supports would have to go, what extra bracing would be needed.

He chuckled to himself, put down the cup he'd been drinking the water from, wiped his lips.

He padded through the hall, up the four flights of stairs to the little landing where you either went straight ahead and out onto the battlements, or ducked through the wee door into the observatory.

It was bitterly cold inside the aluminium hemisphere. He wished he'd thought to put shoes on before he'd started on this piece of nonsense; feet felt like blocks of ice. Still.

He opened the door that gave into the extended cupboard under the roof. Dark. Damn; should have thought to bring a torch, too.

'Sloppy, Urvill, bloody sloppy,' he breathed to himself.

He squeezed inside the little cupboard. Really must lose some weight. Well, festive period well and truly over now; time to go on a diet, or do a bit more exercise. He wriggled to the rear of the cupboard; felt for the wooden battens on the panel at the end of the dark space. The panel came away after a little while; he put it on the floor in front of him, and wriggled through on his elbows and knees into the darkness beyond.

'Getting too old for this sort of thing,' he told himself. It was very nearly totally dark in the roof space; only a little light came from behind him, through the cupboard from the dome of the observatory. He felt his way across the joists in front of him, got his legs free from the cupboard and was able to get up into a crouch, balancing on a joist, hands just above his head, holding on to rough, undressed wood.

He swung one foot out, to the next joist, then put out one hand and felt for the next rafter; he transferred his weight carefully. There; did it. He was aware of the lath and plaster clinging to the bottom of the joists; put a foot through that and you'd be right through the ceiling below; chap could fall slap into the bath from here, probably; or into the twins' room, maybe; perish the thought; daddy coming crashing through the ceiling, give the little perishers nightmares for the rest of their lives.

He swivelled from joist to joist, rafter to rafter, feeling horribly like a monkey and getting very cold feet in the process even though he was breaking out in a sweat at the same time. His knees and his neck were making ghastly creaking noises and protesting like hell.

He looked back at the light coming from the observatory cupboard, now a good twenty feet away, and thought about going back; this whole prank was becoming a bit much, really. But he'd started, so he'd finish.

He saw the faintest of glows ahead, from between two of the joists. He smiled. 'That's the ticket,' he breathed to himself. With the next joist it came closer; then he could see one edge of the little hatch; then he was over it. A soft light gave away the outline of the door. He heard voices. God, the silly woman had probably left the radio on.

He got down on his knees again, feet supported on the joist behind; his knees gave sharp twinges of pain, taking almost all his weight.

He felt for the edges of the square door, found them and lifted it gently. What a locked-room mystery this would present the old girl with, if he could get in without her hearing him, and get undressed and slide in beside her! She'd never be able to work it out. Of course, he thought, as he levered the hatch door open slowly, letting more soft light spill out from underneath, he'd have to cover his tracks in the morning; damn silly to have left the cupboard back there open, and the light on in the dome. But never mind. Fi hardly ever went up there anyway.

He'd lifted the near edge of the door up about three inches above the top of the joist in front of him. He held it there, lowered his head, peeped into the room, smiling, wondering if he could see Fi from this angle. Voices. Warm air and voices.

'Oh ... God, God, God, God; yes, yes, yes, yes ...'

It took him a moment to work out what was going on.

But then he realised.

That was Fiona, in the bed, on the bed, covers half off, the only light in the room coming from a little candle by the bedside, her hair spilled on the pillow (the other pillow was on the floor) ... and that was Lachlan Watt, wrapped round her, body bucking like some horse, his hands at her neck, at one breast, in her hair, cupping her neck; the covers sliding off, Fiona putting her arms wide, clutching at the bottom sheet of the bed at one side, clutching the edge of the bedside table with the other. Her head beat from side to side and she said, 'Yes, yes, yes, yes,' again, then Lachlan – wiry, athletic-looking, skinny shanks ramming back and forth like some skinny bull – reached under her, pulled her up, his legs spreading, kneeling; she hung onto him, arms round his neck, then after a few vertical stabs he threw her down, back onto the bed; she grunted, arms still tight round his back, then she brought her legs up, right up over his thin, plunging, globe-buttocked behind, until her ankles were in the small of his back, rocking to and fro, feet crossed one over the other, locked there; with one splayed hand she held onto his back, pressing him to her, and with the other hand she felt down the length of his body, over ribs and waist and hips, and with another grunt reached round and under, taking his balls in her hand, pressing them and kneading them and squeezing them.

'Aw Christ!' he heard Lachlan Watt say, body arching. Fiona shuddered, her voice almost a squeal as she took a series of sudden, deep in-rushing breaths, and buried her head in the hollow between Lachlan Watt's shoulder and neck.

*

Fergus let the little door down without making a noise.

He felt very cold, and he had pissed himself. The urine was warm around his balls and tepid down his leg, but it was cold at his knees. He knelt there in the darkness, listening to the sounds of the subsiding passion in the room below, then swivelled silently and with even greater care than before, and feeling far more sober, moved back towards the thin, escaping light at the far end of the chill, cramped roof space.

CHAPTER
11

If the year of our folly 1990 had started inauspiciously for me, then the Fates, Lady Luck, Lord Chance, God, Life, Evolution – whoever or whatever – immediately thereafter set about the business of proving that the entangled disasters distinguishing the year's first few days were but a mild and modest prelude to the more thorough-going catastrophes planned for the weeks and months ahead ... and this with a rapidity and even an apparent relish which was impressive – if also bowel-looseningly terrifying – to behold.

Gav and my Aunt Janice got on like a house on fire, a combined location and fate I occasionally wished on them as I lay awake listening to the sounds of their love-making, a pastime I sometimes suspected I shared with people in a large part of the surrounding community, not to say northern Europe.

I had made the mistake of volunteering to sleep on the couch in the living room on the nights that Janice stayed at our flat; this offer was made with what I thought was obvious sarcasm one evening while Gav and Norris were attempting to develop a technique for cooking poppadoms in the microwave. They were having an intense and appropriately heated discussion on the problems of cold-spots (as evinced by the fact that their first attempts came out looking like braille roundels), and on the unfortunate instability of three poppadoms balanced together – caused not so much by the jerk they received when the turntable started up as by their movements while they cooked and swelled – but eventually my flatmates settled on the concept of standing the things up individually on the glass turntable, and so instigated what they termed a 'brainstorming session' in an attempt to find a suitable support mechanism. (I suppressed the urge to point out that the chances of two such patently zephyr-grade minds producing anything remotely resembling a storm was roughly equivalent to the likelihood of somebody called Cohen landing a pork scratching concession in Mecca during Ramadan.)

'An alligator clip with the chrome bits removed.'

'Naw; still metal.'

'Maybe we could shield it.'

'Na; has to be plastic. Yer non thermosetting stuff, for preference.'

'Well, look, Gav,' I said from the kitchen doorway. 'I only overhang the couch by a foot or so at each end; why don't I attempt to curl up there when you and Janice are in residence, if not flagrante, in the bedroom?'

'Eh?' Gav said, swivelling that thick neck of his to look at me, his massive brows furrowing. He scratched at one rugby-shirt shrouded armpit, then nodded. 'Aw; aye.' He looked pleased. 'Thanks very much, Prentice; aye, that'd be grand.' He turned back to the microwave.

'Maybe we could suspend them from this bit in the middle with a length of thread,' Norris grunted, sticking his head almost right inside the appliance. Norris, still clad in his white lab coat, was one of those medical students whom fate has seemingly marked out to spend the bulk of their studies and initial training suffering from quite stupendous hangovers incurred through the intake of near-fatal levels of alcohol the night before, and their subsequent professional careers sternly finger-wagging at any member of the general public who dares to consume over the course of a week what they themselves had been perfectly happy to sink during the average evening.

'I mean, don't let the fact I'm the longest serving flat-dweller put you off; the last thing I want to do is embarrass you, Gav,' I said (just a tad tetchily).

'Na, it's all right, Prentice; ta,' Gav said, then crouched down by Norris and squinted into the lit interior of the microwave. 'Nowhere to attach it,' he told Norris. 'Anyway; wouldnae turn, would it?'

They both looked thoughtful, heads side by side at the open oven door, while I wondered what the chances were of both heads fitting – and jamming – inside and the door safety-catch somehow short-circuiting.

'Na,' Norris said. 'We're looking at some form of support from below, know what ah mean? Come on, Gav, you're the engineer ...'

'I mean, that old duvet's bound to cover most of the important parts of my body, and the chances of the pilot on the fire blowing out again and gassing me in my sleep can't really be *that* high,' I said.

'Hmm,' Gav said. He straightened, then bent forward and tapped at the white plastic strip on the kitchen window ledge which retained the cheaply horrid secondary double-glazing the flat's owners had fitted.

'Just a block of wood, maybe,' Norris said.

'Get hot,' Gav said, looking more closely at the white plastic strip. 'Depending on how much water there is in the wood; could warp. Still think plastic's your best bet.'

'After all, Gav, I can just stay up till your drinking pals have decided to head home, or Norris's card school chums finally drag themselves away, or crash out and snore on the Richter scale, whatever; the fun rarely extends beyond three or four o'clock in the morning ... why, that would leave me a good four or five hours' sleep before an early lecture.'

'Aye, that's great, Prentice,' Gav said, still closely inspecting the window sill. Then he stood up suddenly and snapped his fingers. 'Got it!' he said.

What, I thought? Had my tone of reason in the face of monstrosity finally registered? But no.

'Blu-tack!'

'What?'

'Blu-tack!'

'Blu-tack?'

'Aye; Blu-tack. You know: Blu-tack!'

Norris thought about this. Then said excitedly. 'Aye; Blu-tack!'

'Blu-tack!' Gav said again, looking wide-eyed and pleased with himself.

'The very thing!' Norris nodded vigorously.

I shook my head, quitting the kitchen doorway for the comparative sanity of the dark and empty hallway. 'You crack the Bollinger,' I muttered. 'I'll just phone the Nobel Prize Committee and tell them their search is over for another year.'

'Blu-tack, ya beauty!' I heard from the white-glowing crucible of cutting-edge technological advancement that our humble kitchen had become.

*

'You mean you haven't read them all?'

'I went off the idea,' I said. I was sitting in what had effectively become my boudoir; our living room. Aunt Janice seemed to prefer staying here with Gavin to travelling out to Crow Road most nights.

Gav and Janice sat on the couch, loosely attired in dressing gowns and watching a video.

I had been sitting at the table housed in the living room bay window, trying to write a paper for a tutorial the next day, but Gavin and Janice had chosen to punctuate their highly audible coupling sessions (in what the more tenacious core-areas of my long-term memory still sporadically insisted had once been my bedroom) with an almost equally noisy episode of tortilla chip eating. The corny raucousness which ensued of course meant that the television volume had to be turned up to window-shaking levels so that the happy couple could savour the exquisitely enunciated phrasing of Arnold Schwarzenneger's lines over the noise of their munching.

I had admitted defeat on the subject of the links between agricultural and industrial revolution and British Imperialism, and sat down to watch the video. Perhaps appropriately, given the inflammatory nature of the effect Gav and Janice seemed to have on each other's glands, it was called *Red Heat*.

'Oh,' I'd said. 'A Hollywood movie about two cops who don't get along at first but are thrown together on a case involving drugs, foreigners, lots of fights and guns and which ends up with them respecting each other and winning. Sheech.' I shook my head. 'Makes you wonder where these script-writer guys get their weird and zany ideas from, doesn't it?'

Gav had nodded in agreement, without taking his eyes off the screen. Janice Rae had smiled over at me, her hair fetchingly disarrayed, her cheeks flushed. 'Oh yes, Prentice,' she'd said. 'What did you think of Rory's work, in that folder?'

Hence the exchange above.

Janice looked back at the telly and stretched one leg out over Gavin's lap. I glanced over, thinking that she had much better legs than a woman of her age deserved. Come to that, she had much better legs than a man of Gav's mental age deserved.

'So you haven't found any hints about what it was Rory had hidden in there?' she said.

'I've no idea what he wanted to hide,' I said, wishing that Janice would hide a little more of her legs.

I was uncomfortable talking about the poems and Rory's papers; the bag lost on the train coming back from Lochgair at the start of the year had stayed lost, and – stuck with just the memory of the half-finished stuff that Janice had given me originally – I'd given up on any idea I'd ever had of trying to rescue Uncle Rory's name from artistic oblivion, or discovering some great revelation in the texts. Still, it haunted me. Even now, months later, I had dreams about reading a book that ended half-way through, or watching a film which ended abruptly, screen whiting-out ... Usually I woke breathless, imagining there was a scarf – shining white silk looped in a half-twist – tightening round my neck.

'It was something he'd seen, I think.' Janice watched the distant screen. 'Something ...' she said slowly, pulling her dressing gown closed. 'Something ... over-seen, if you know what I mean.'

'Vaguely,' I said. I watched Gavin's hand move – apparently unconsciously, though of course with Gav that could still mean it was fully willed – to Janice's polyester-and-cotton covered thigh. 'Something,' (I suggested, watching this,) 'seen voyeuristically, perhaps?'

'Mmm,' Janice nodded. Her right hand went up to Gav's short, brownish hair, and started to play with it, twirling it round her fingers. 'He put it in ... whatever he was working on.' She nodded. 'Something he'd seen, or somebody had seen; whatever. Some big secret.'

'Really?' I said. Gavin's hand rubbed up and down on Janice's lap. Gav's face gave no sign he was aware of doing this. I pondered the possibility that the lad possessed some dinosaur-like secondary brain which was controlling the movements of his hand. Palaeo-biological precedent dictated such an organ be housed in Gavin's ample rear, and have responsibility for his lower limbs – not to say urges – rather than his arms, but then one never knew, and I reckoned Gavin's modest forebrain – doubtless fully occupied with the post-modernist sub-texts and tertiary structuralist imagery of *Red Heat* – could probably do with all the help it could get. 'Really?' I repeated.

'Mmm,' Janice nodded. 'So he said.' She bit her lip.

Gavin had a look of concentration on his face now, as though two parts of his brain were attempting the tricky and little-practised operation of communicating with each other.

'Something about –' Janice moved her hips, and seemed to catch her breath. '– the castle.' She clutched at Gav's hair.

I looked at her. 'The castle?' I said. But too late.

Perhaps lent the final impetus necessary for successful reception by the proximity of the area of stimulus to that of cognition, this hair-pulling signal finally seemed to awaken Gavin to the perception that there might be something else going on in his immediate area other than the video, undeniably captivating though it was. He looked round, first at his hand, then at Janice, who was smiling radiantly at him, and finally at me. He grinned guiltily.

He yawned, glanced at Janice again. 'Bit tired,' he said to her, yawning unconvincingly once more. 'Fancy goin' to –?'

'*What*' Janice said brightly, slapping her hand down on Gavin's bulky shoulder, '– a good idea!'

'Tell us how it ends, eh Prentice?' Gav said, nodding back at the television as he was half hauled out of the room by Aunt Janice, en route to the land of nod after a lengthy detour through the territories of bonk.

'With you going "Uh-uh-uh-uh-uh!"' I muttered to the closed door. I glared at the screen. '"How it ends,"' I muttered to myself. 'It's a video, you cretin!'

*

I returned to the changes in British society required to bring about the Empire on which the light of reason rarely shone. It was going to be a long night, as I also had to finish an already over-due essay on Swedish expansion in the seventeenth century (it would have to be a goodish one, too; an earlier remark – made in an unguarded moment during a methodically boring tutorial – ascribing Swedish territorial gains in the Baltic to the invention of the Smorgasbord with its take-what-you-want ethic, had not endeared me to the professor concerned; nor had my subsequent discourse on the innate frivolity of the Swedes, despite what I thought was the irrefutable argument that no nation capable of giving a Peace Prize to Henry Kissinger could possibly be accused of lacking a sense of humour. Pity it was actually the Norwegians.

I remembered a joke about Kissinger ('no; fucking her.') and found myself listening to Gav and Janice. They were still at that stage of their coital symphony where only the brass section was engaged, as the old metal bed creaked to and fro. The wind section – essentially vox humana – would join in later. I shook my head and bent back to my work, but every now and again, as I was writing or just thinking, a niggling little side-track thought would distract me, and I'd find myself remembering Janice's words, and wondering what exactly Uncle Rory might have hidden within his later work (if he really had hidden anything). Not, of course, that there was much point in me wondering about it.

For about the hundredth time, I cursed whatever kleptomaniac curmudgeon had walked off the train with my bag. May the scarf unravel and do an Isadora Duncan on the wretch.

'Uh-uh-uh-uh-uh!' came faintly from what had been my bedroom. I ground my teeth.

*

'Married?' I gasped, aghast.

'Well, they're talking about it,' my mother said, dipping her head towards the table and holding her Paisley-pattern scarf to her throat as she nibbled tentatively at a large cream cake.

We were in Mrs Mackintosh's Tea Roomes, just off West Nile Street, surrounded by straightly pendulous light fitments, graph-paper pierced wooden screens, and ladder-back seats which turned my usual procedure of hanging my coat or jacket on the rear of the seat into an operation that resembled hoisting a flag up a tall mast.

'But they can't!' I said. I could feel the blood draining from my face. They couldn't do this to me!

My mother, neat and slim as ever, ploughed crunchingly into the loaf-sized meringue cream cake like a polar bear breaking into a seal's den. She gave a tiny giggle as a little dollop of cream adhered to the tip of her nose; she removed it with one finger, licked the pinky, then wiped her nose with her napkin, glancing round the restaurant through the confusing topography of slats and uprights of the seats and screens, apparently worried that this minor lapse in hand–mouth coordination was being critically observed by any of the surrounding middle-class matrons, perhaps with a view to passing on the scandalous morsel to their opposite numbers in Gallanach and having mother black-balled from the local bridge club. She needn't have worried; from what I had seen, getting a little bit of cream on your nose was practically compulsory, like getting nicked on the cheek in a ritualised duel before being allowed to enter a Prussian drinking sodality. The atmosphere of middle-aged ladies enjoying something wicked and nostalgic was quite palpable.

'Don't be silly, Prentice; of course they can. They're both adults.' Mother licked cream from the ice-cave interior of the meringue, then broke off part of the superstructure with her fingers and popped it into her mouth.

I shook my head, appalled. Lewis and Verity! Married? No!

'But isn't this . . .' My voice had risen a good half-octave and my hands were waggling around on the end of my arms as though I was trying to shake off bits of Sellotape. '. . . rather soon?' I finished, lamely.

'Well, yes,' mum said, sipping her cappuccino. 'It is.' She smiled brightly. 'I mean, not that she's pregnant or anything, but –'

'Pregnant!' I screeched. The very idea! The thought of the two of them fucking was bad enough; Lewis impregnating that gorgeous creature was infinitely worse.

'Prentice!' Mother whispered urgently, leaning closer and glancing round again. This time we were getting a few funny looks from other customers. My mother smiled insincerely at a couple of Burberried biddies smirking from the table across the aisle; they turned sniffily away.

My mother giggled again, hand to mouth, then delved into the meringue. She sat back, munching, face red but eyes twinkling, and with those eyes indicated the two women who'd been looking at us; then she raised one finger and pointed first at me, then at her. Her giggle turned into a snort. I rolled my eyes. She dabbed at hers with a clean corner of napkin, laughing.

'Mother, this is not funny.' I drank my tea, and attacked another chocolate eclair. It was my fourth and my belly was still growling. 'Not *at all* funny.' I knew I was sounding prissy and ridiculous but I couldn't help it. This was a very trying time for me, and the people who ought to be offering support were offering only insults.

'Well,' mother said, sipping at her coffee again. 'Like I say, there's no question of that. I mean, not that it makes much difference these days anyway, but yes, you're right; it is a bit soon. Your father and I have talked to Lewis and he's said they aren't going to actually rush into anything, but they just feel so ... right together that it's ... just come up, you know? Arisen naturally between them.'

I couldn't help it. My obsessed, starveling brain was conjuring up all sorts of ghastly images to accompany this sort of talk; things arising, coming up ... Oh God ...

'They've talked about it,' mother said, in tones of utmost reason, with a small shrug. 'And I just thought you ought to know.'

'Oh, thanks,' I said, sarcastically. I felt like I'd been kicked by a camel but I still needed food, so I polished off the eclair, belched with all the decorum I could, and started eyeing up a Danish pastry.

'They're in the States right now,' mother said, licking her fingers. 'For all we know they might come back married. At least if that happens it won't come as quite such a shock now, will it?'

'No,' I said miserably, and took the pastry. It tasted like sweetened cardboard.

It was April. I hadn't been back to Gallanach yet this year, hadn't spoken to dad. My studies weren't going so well; a 2.2 was probably the best I could hope for. Money was a problem because I'd spent all the dosh I'd got for the car, and I needed my grant to pay off the overdraft I'd built up. There was about a grand in the old account – my dad's money came by standing order – but I wouldn't use it, and what I regarded as my own finances were – judging from the tone of the bank's increasingly frequent letters – somewhere in the deep infrared and in serious danger of vanishing from the electromagnetic spectrum altogether.

I had paid my rent early on with the last inelastic cheque I'd written, hadn't paid my Poll Tax, had tried to find bar work but been unsuccessful, and was borrowing off Norris, Gav and a few other pals to buy food, which comprised mostly bread and beans and the odd black pudding supper, plus a cider or two when I could be persuaded to squander my meagre resources on contributing to the funds required for a raid on the local off-licence.

I spent a lot of time lying on the couch in the living room, watching day-time television with a sneer on my face and my books on my lap, making snide remarks at the soaps and quizzes, chat shows and audience participation fora, skimming the scummy surface of our effervescent present in preference to plumbing the adumbrate depths of the underlying past. I had taken to finishing off the flat beer left in cans by the members of Norris's itinerant card school after its frequent visits *chez nous*, and was seriously considering starting to steal from bookshops in an attempt to raise some cash.

For a while I had been ringing the Lost Property office at Queen Street station each week, still pathetically hoping that the bag with Uncle Rory's poems and Darren Watt's Möbius scarf would somehow miraculously turn up again. But even they weren't having anything to do with me any more, after I'd *definitely* detected an edge of sarcasm in the person's voice and lost my temper and started shouting and swearing.

Rejected by Lost Property; it seemed like the ultimate insult.

And Aunt Janice never did remember any more about whatever Rory had hidden in his later work.

Mum sipped her coffee. I tore the Danish to bits, imagining it was Lewis's flesh. Or Verity's underclothes – I was a little confused at the time.

Well, let them get married. The earlier the better; it would end in tears. Let them rush into it, let them repent at leisure. They weren't right for each other and maybe a marriage would last a shorter time than a more informal, less intense liaison; brief and bitter, both of them on proximity fuses with things coming rapidly to a crunch, rather than something more drawn out, where they might spend long periods apart and so forget how much they hated being together, and enjoy the fleeting, passionate moments of reunion . . .

I fumed and bittered away while my mother finished her coffee and made concerned remarks about how thin and pale I was looking. I ate another Danish; mother told me everybody else was fine, back home.

'Come back, Prentice,' she said, putting one hand out across the table to me. Her brown eyes looked hurt. 'This weekend, come back and stay with us. Your father misses you terribly. He's too proud to –'

'I can't,' I said, pulling my hand away from hers, shaking my head. 'I need to work this weekend. Got a lot to do. Finals coming up.'

'Prentice,' my mother whispered. I was looking down at my

plate, licking my finger and picking off the last few crumbs, transferring them to my mouth. I could tell mum was leaning forward, trying to get me to meet her eyes, but I just frowned, and with my moistened finger-tip cleared my plate. 'Prentice; please. For me, if not for your dad.'

I looked up at her for a moment. I blinked quickly. 'Maybe,' I said. 'I don't know. Let me think about it.'

'Prentice,' my mother said quietly, 'say you will.'

'All right,' I said, not looking at her. I knew I was lying but there wasn't anything I could do about it. I couldn't send her away thinking I could be so heartless and horrible, but I also knew that I wasn't going to go home that weekend; I'd find an excuse. It wasn't that this dispute between my dad and me about whether there was a God or not really meant anything any more, but rather the fact of the history of the dispute – the reality of its course, not the substance of the original disagreement – was what prevented me from ending it. It was less that I was too proud, more that I was too embarrassed.

'You promise?' mother said, a slight stitching of her brows as she sat back in the ladder-backed seat the only indication that she might not entirely believe me.

'I promise,' I nodded. I felt, wretchedly, that I was such a moral coward, such a sickening liar, that making a promise I knew I had no intention whatever of keeping was hardly any worse than what I had already done. 'I promise,' I repeated, blinking again, and set my mouth in a firm, determined way. Let there be no way out of it; let me really *make* this promise. I was so disgusted with myself that I wanted to make myself suffer even more when I did – as I knew I would – break my word. I nodded fiercely and smiled bravely, utterly insincerely, at my mother. 'I really do promise. Really.'

*

We said goodbye outside, in the street. I told her the flat was in too disgusting a state for her to come and visit. She hoisted her umbrella to ward off the light drizzle that had started to fall, gave me a couple of twenty-pound notes, said she'd look forward to seeing me on Friday, kissed my cheek, then went off to do her shopping.

I had dressed as well as I could that morning, in more or less the same stuff I'd worn for Grandma Margot's funeral. Minus the lost Möbius scarf, of course. I turned up the collar of my fake biker's jacket and walked off.

I gave the money to a thankfully dumb-struck fiddle-player on Sauchiehall Street and walked away feeling like some sort of martyred saint. As I walked, this mood was gradually but smoothly replaced by one of utmost depression, while my body – as though jealous of all the obsessive regard my emotions were receiving – came up with its own demands for attention, evidenced by an unsteady, fluid shifting in my guts, and a cold sweat on my brow.

I felt fainter and fainter and worse and worse and more and more nauseous, unsure whether it was the bitterness of sibling-thwarted love, or just too much starch and refined sugar. It felt like my stomach had decided to take a sabbatical; all that food was just sitting there, unprocessed, locked in, slopping around and making me feel horrible.

After a while I stopped telling myself I wasn't going to be sick, and – resigned to the fact that I was going to have to throw up at some point – kept telling myself instead that I'd manage to hold it in until I was back in the flat, and so do it in private, rather than into the gutter in front of people.

Eventually I threw up into a litter bin attached to a crowded bus shelter on St George's Road.

I was still gagging up the last few dregs when somebody punched me on the cheek, sending the other side of my head banging against the metal wall of the shelter. I spun round and sat down on the pavement, a ringing noise in my head.

A tramp dressed in tattered, shiny trousers and a couple of

greasy-looking, buttonless coats bent down, looking at me. He smelled of last year's sweat. He gestured angrily up at the litter bin. 'Ye wee basturt; there might a been somethin good in there!' He shook his head in obvious disgust and stalked off, muttering.

I got to my feet, supporting myself on the side of the shelter. A wee grey woman wearing a headscarf peered out at me from the end of the bus queue. 'You all right, sonny?' she said.

'Aye,' I said, grimacing. 'Missus,' I added, because it seemed appropriate. I nodded at the bin. 'Sorry about that; my stomach's on strike and my food's coming out in sympathy.'

She smiled uncomprehendingly at me, looking round. 'Here's ma bus son; you look after yoursel, okay?'

I felt the side of my head where it had hit the bus shelter; a bruise was forming and my eye felt sore. The wee woman got on her bus and went away.

*

'Oh, Prentice!' Ash said, more in despair than with disgust. 'You're kidding.' She looked at me in the candle-light. I was past caring about feeling guilt and shame and everything was collapsing anyway, so I just looked straight back at her, resigned, and after a while I shook my head. Then I picked up a bit of naan bread and mopped up my curry sauce.

The naan bread was big; we'd both stuffed ourselves with it during the meal but it was still big. When it had arrived it had needed a separate table just to accommodate it; luckily the restaurant wasn't busy. 'Not so much a naan bread, more a toasted duvet,' I'd said. Ash had laughed.

During the course of the meal we'd reduced the blighter to the proportions of a couple of pillows, not to mention disposing of portions of chicken kalija and fish pakora to start, followed by garlic chilli chicken, lamb pasanda, a single portion of pulao rice, and side dishes of Bombay potato and sag panir to accompany.

Two dry sherries and a couple of bottles of Nuit St Georges had washed it all down and now we were onto the coffee and brandy. It was Ashley Watt's treat, of course; I still couldn't afford to eat out unless it was in the street and out of a paper poke. Ash was passing through Glasgow and staying with us on her way to a new job down in London.

It was mid-summer, and unseasonably warm for Glasgow; Ash wore a long, rough silk shirt, and leggings. A light cotton jacket hung over the back of her chair. I was still wearing out the regulation Docs and the thick black jeans. I had borrowed one of Norris's big paramilitary-style fawn shirts to wear as a jacket over my anti Poll Tax T-shirt. I'd left it to the end of the meal before I said anything about being arrested.

'Aw, man,' Ash said, sitting back slackly in her seat. The candlelight reflected in her glasses. '*Why*, Prentice?' The Anarkali was dark and quiet and a lot of the light was coming from the candle between us. She looked sad; concerned for me, I thought.

I rather liked it. I liked the idea of other people feeling sorry for me, even though I also despised them for it, because I wasn't worth their sympathy and that made them fools.

Of course, I despised myself for despising them for showing such genuine and unselfish emotions, but that's just one of the things you have to get used to when you're in a serious self-destruction spiral. Mine was feeling rather like a power-dive right now. I shrugged. 'Why not? I needed the money.'

'But your family's rich!'

'No, they're . . . Well, they might be fairly well . . .' I smiled, sat closer, took up my brandy and cradled it in front of the candle flame. 'Actually, there's quite a good exchange on those lines in *Catch-22*, the movie – much underrated film – which isn't in the book, so Buck Henry must have written it, where Nately's been killed and Yossarian's been to Milo's whorehouse to see Nately's whore and Milo's picked him up in the half-track and he's saying Nately died a rich man; he had such-and-such a number of shares in M&M enterprises, and Yossarian says –'

Ashley was glaring at me over the candle flame the way a hawk must glare at a field mouse the instant before it parts mouse from field forever. I saw this predatory, outraged expression building on Ash's face like a line of dark clouds on the horizon, and stopped talking, though entirely out of inquisitiveness, not trepidation.

'Shut the fuck up about *Catch-22*, ya cretin;' Ash said, storming forward and planting both fore-arms on the table cloth. 'What the fucking hell are you doin stealing books for money when you've no need to, eh? Just what sort of dick-head are you, Prentice? I mean, what the fuck are your parents going to think if they hear? How are they goin to feel? Or is that it? Are they supposed to feel bad? Are you tryin to get back at your dad because of this stupit religious thing? Well, come on; are you?'

I sat back, amused.

I played with the dumpy stem of the brandy glass, smirking at Ashley through the candle flame. Ashley's long hair was tied back and she looked rather attractive, now I thought about it. I wondered what the chances were of bedding the girl. A little recreational fornication would go down quite well just now. I wondered if Ash was into rough sex. I had no idea whether I was into it myself, but for some reason just then the idea seemed rather intriguing. I smiled at her, gave a small laugh. 'Really, Ashley, I didn't think you'd take it all so melodramatically. It's only shoplifting, after all. Just one silly book, too; worse things happen at C & A's.' I sat back, still smiling; legs crossed, arms crossed.

Ash's face was close to the flame, its yellow oval glowing like some magical caste-mark on her forehead. Much closer and she'll melt her glasses, I thought. She appeared to be trying to out-stare me, but actually I'm rather good at that sort of thing when I want to be, and I didn't let my eyes flicker.

A waiter was approaching from behind her, I noticed, without taking my eyes off hers; I felt the grin broaden on my lips. The waiter would distract her, especially as she had ordered the meal and was obviously paying, and anyway she almost certainly hadn't heard the waiter approaching.

Ash reached one hand out across the table and spilled my brandy into my lap.

Just as I was reacting, going 'Wha –!' and jerking forward, Ash turned smoothly to the waiter and with a broad smile said,

'The bill, please.'

*

'It *does* look like I've pissed myself!' I protested as we walked back to the flat. 'Those people were definitely laughing at me.'

'Oh, shut up, Prentice.'

'You're telling *me* to shut up!' I laughed. The July night was warm and muggy and the traffic rumbled like thunder down Great Western Road. 'You throw drink all over me, expect to sleep in my flat tonight and *you* tell *me* to shut up!'

Ash paced purposefully on, long flinging strides I was having difficulty in keeping up with. She was still glaring, though straight ahead now. I noticed people coming towards us weren't getting in her way.

'I didn't throw the drink, I tipped it,' she told me. 'And I'm only coming back to the flat to get my bag, if that's the way you feel. I'll sleep in the car. Or find a hotel.'

'I didn't!' I protested, waving my arms and running after her as I saw the possibility of getting into Ashley's increasingly attractive body slipping away from me. 'I didn't say that! I just don't like being told to shut up! I'm sorry! I mean, I'm really sorry I'm annoyed that you spilled – or tipped – drink all over me!'

Ash stopped so suddenly I wondered where she'd gone for a moment. I turned, looked, and went back to her, standing looking furious in the light of a Spud-U-Like.

'Prentice,' she said calmly. 'You've practically exiled yourself from your family and your home and your friends, you think you've failed your finals but you say you've no intention of sitting your re-sits even if you have; you've no money and you haven't even been looking for a job; you're getting done for shop-lifting and you're acting like such a fucking dick-head you seem determined to get shot of the last few pals you do have left . . . and all you can do is make smart-ass remarks.'

I looked through her bright red glasses into her light grey eyes and said, 'Well, so far so good, certainly, but let's not count our –'

She stamped on my right big toe, forcing me to produce an involuntary and appallingly undignified yelp. She stormed off; I half limped, half hopped after her.

'Let's not count our vultures before they're hatched, eh?' I laughed. She powered on, ignoring me. I hopped after her. 'Spare a shekel for a healthy beggar?' I cackled. 'Able was I ere I saw Michael; where can you land a Palin? And in what?'

Ash kicked my other shin. Wonderful girl; didn't even seem to break stride.

She disappeared into an off-licence. I waited outside, rubbing my shin and inspecting the damage to my Docs; luckily the scuff on the right toe didn't show up the way it would have with polished boots.

Ash reappeared with a bag; she swept past me, briefly showing me the bottle of Grouse it contained. I skipped after her down the street. 'After trying the fluid on a small unnoticeable area, you now wish to wash all of my trousers the spirited way, am I right, madam? Now; will you swap these two bottles of warm urine for that one bottle of our product?'

She shook her head, not looking at me. 'You and I are going to get filthily drunk, Prentice, and if by the time we get to the bottom of this bottle I haven't got some sort of sense out of you I'm going to break it over your thick fucking skull.' She turned, beamed a toothy non-smile at me for about a micro-second, then strode determinedly on.

I tried to keep up. I looked at the bottle in the bag. 'Couldn't you just leave the whisky, I'll drink it all, wake up in the morning – no, make that the afternoon – with a head that *feels* like you hit me over the skull with the bottle, and you sleep in the car ready for that long and demanding journey down the notoriously dangerous A74 tomorrow?'

Ash shook her head.

*

We got back to Grant Street. I looked up, saw some lights on in the flat. Maybe, I thought, Ash would be so turned on by the sounds of frantic coupling emanating from Gav and Aunt Janice in the bedroom that she'd tear my clothes off. Or maybe Norris and his pals would distract her from this crazed idea of getting air-locked drunk by suggesting a friendly game of cards.

Ash followed my gaze. She held the bottle up in front of my eyes. 'Ready for this, Prentice?'

'Drink doesn't solve anything, you know,' I told her. 'Just dissolves brain cells.'

'I know,' she said. 'I'm working on the principle that most people are okay unless they get muroculous with drink, when they become arse-holes; you're behaving like an arse-hole now, so maybe drink'll make you okay.'

I tried to look as sceptical as I could. 'I bet you believe in crop circles, too.'

'Prentice, I believe you seem determined to fuck your life up, and I just want to know why.'

'Oh,' I said brightly. 'That's easy; my affections have been rejected by the one I love and her carnality is being most thoroughly investigated by my elder and smarter brother on a more or less hourly basis, so I am spurned and she is spermed; my father believes his children should be free to make up their own minds, but preferably only out of the spare-parts that he provides ... And apart from that ... I mean the exams and getting nicked and stuff

. . . Well,' I sighed, looking up to the night sky, where the clouds were starting to blot out the few stars that the city lights did not obscure. I spread my arms wide. '. . . I'm just a waster.'

Ash looked at me. I could see her chest move in and out inside the light cotton jacket. 'Naw, Prentice,' she said quietly, after a while. 'You're just a bairn.'

I shrugged. 'Maybe. Come on.' I indicated the close. 'Let's get as drunk as you think we have to, and you can tell me all the reasons I'm so childish.' I glanced at my watch as we headed for the stairs. 'Better get started, though; we've only got all night.'

We climbed the stairs, reached the flat.

'You know,' Ash was saying, breathing hard and looking down the stair-well as I opened the door. 'I don't know *anybody* who lives in a flat who doesn't live on the top floor.'

'Friends in high places,' I said, opening the door to Janice Rae.

Aunt Janice was clothed (shirt and jeans), which made rather a refreshing change, and standing in the hallway. She looked distraught. Her eyes were red and her mascara had left what appeared to be a diagram of the Los Angeles freeway system down her cheeks. Beyond her Gav stood looking awkward and sheepish. I glanced from Janice to Gav and back again, while Janice looked at me, lip trembling.

Let me guess, I thought; they've finally done it; they've broken the bed.

'Oh, Prentice!' Janice said suddenly, throwing herself at me and enveloping my upper torso in a hug that would have done credit to a grizzly. I wondered what had brought this on, and how to peel Aunt Janice off. What must Ashley be making of all this? (She'd be getting jealous, with any luck.)

Janice pulled away; I could breathe again, and promptly did so.

'Oh, Prentice,' she said again, holding my head in both hands and shaking her own. Her eyes closed, she turned her face away, released her hold on my cheekbones and let me go on into the hall. Gav stood by the hall table, shifting his weight from side to side and glancing nervously down at the phone now and again.

He avoided my eyes.

I took a couple of steps forward, then heard something whispered from behind me, and looked back to see Janice hugging Ash, almost violently.

They'd never met before. How shocking, I thought. Where was that traditional British reserve only abandoned for cloying camaraderie under the influence of injuriously vast quantities of alcohol? I wondered, if nervously.

Ash was looking over Janice Rae's shoulder at me, those grey eyes behind the bright red glasses filling with tears.

'Um; you've to phone home,' Gav mumbled, apparently addressing his trainers.

'ET or BT?' I heard myself say to him, though the different sections of my brain seemed to have slipped out of synch somehow, and I was aware of all sorts of different things at once, and time seemed to have slowed down and at the same time some part of my brain was racing, trying to come up with some logical explanation for what was going on that didn't involve calamity ... and failing.

'It's –' Gav said, this time seemingly directing his remarks to his rugby-shirted chest. 'It's your dad,' he whispered, and suddenly started to cry.

CHAPTER
12

'This is the Specialist Glass Division,' Hamish said, opening a door. They found themselves in a long corridor with one glass wall that looked out into a bright, modern, open-plan and spacious area. Everything gleamed and the few people visible wore white coats; apart from the exposed brickwork of a couple of rotund furnaces, linked to the ceiling by shining metal ductwork, the place looked more like a laboratory than a factory.

There was a silence none of the three brothers seemed inclined to fill. Hamish, an immaculate white coat over his three piece suit, gazed with a rapt expression at the almost static panorama on the far side of the glass. Kenneth looked bored. Rory stood at Janice Rae's side, humming something monotonous, one arm round Janice's waist and attempting to tickle her, just above her right hip.

'Very clean,' Janice said eventually.

'Yes,' Hamish said gravely. He nodded slowly, still observing the scene beyond the glass. 'It has to be, of course.' He turned to the tables against the wall behind them, on which lay various glassy-looking objects, some in display cabinets, most loose, all with explanatory notes stuck to the wall above them. From a wooden plinth on one table, Hamish picked up a dull black cone that looked a little like a Viking helmet without the horns.

'This is a missile nose-cone,' he said, turning the cone over in his hands. He held it out to Janice. She took it.

'Hmm. Quite heavy,' she said. Rory tickled her again and she nudged him.

'Yes, heavy,' Hamish said gravely, taking it back and carefully replacing it on its wooden block. 'Strictly speaking, this is a glass ceramic rather than ordinary glass,' he said, adjusting the precise position of the nose cone on the plinth. 'The basis is lithium aluminosilicate, which withstands heat very well. Cooker hobs are made from this sort of thing . . . and obviously missiles need to withstand a lot of heat from friction with the air.'

'Obviously,' Kenneth said. He and Rory exchanged looks.

Hamish turned to another exhibit; a broad bowl, also dull and dark, and over half a metre across, it was like a gigantic plate with no lip. He lifted an edge so that they could look underneath, where it was criss-crossed with a lattice of deep ribs.

'Satellite aerial?' Kenneth said.

'No,' Hamish said, though a hint of a smile crossed his dour face. 'No, this is a substrate for an astronomical telescope mirror.'

'Like the one Fergus has in the castle?' Rory asked.

'That's right. All the substrates and optics for Mr Urvill's telescope were made here. Though of course they were on a smaller scale than this piece.' Hamish lowered the edge of the bowl and flicked a bit of dust off one edge. 'This is made from the same type of material as the nose cone there. It resists distortion under thermal shock.'

'Hmm,' Janice in a tone that suggested thatshe was really trying to be interested as well as sound it.

'Over here,' Hamish said, plodding towards another table, 'we have what are called the passivation glasses, related to the Borate glasses but made from zinc-silicoborate ...'

'All I said was I'd like to see the factory,' Janice whispered to Rory as they moved to follow Hamish. 'The outside would have done.'

'Tough shit,' Rory said, and tickled her with both hands this time, producing a yelp.

Another man in a white coat came up to Hamish from the far end of the corridor. 'Excuse me a moment,' Hamish said to the others, and turned to talk to him.

Kenneth turned to Rory and Janice. He tugged on Rory's sleeve and in a low monotone said, 'Dad, I'm bored, dad; dad, are we nearly finished yet, dad? Dad, want to go home, dad.' He leant one hand against the glass wall, glanced back at Hamish – still deep in conversation, and nodding – and rolled his eyes. He looked at Janice. 'My elder brother,' he said quietly. 'The man who put the Bore in Boro-silicate.'

'You don't have to stay.' Rory grinned. 'We could get a train home.'

Kenneth shook his head. 'No; it's okay.' He glanced at his watch. 'Maybe we can drag the Tree out for lunch soon.'

'Sorry about that,' Hamish said, coming up behind them.

They all smiled at him. Hamish moved one arm up to indicate they should move down the corridor to where they could see the exciting zinc-silicoborates. He took a pristine white handkerchief out of his pocket and rubbed at the faint hand-print Kenneth had left on the glass partition as he said, 'These passivation glasses are of much use in the semi-conductor industry, and we have high hopes that with the burgeoning of the Scottish computer industry – Silicon Glen as it is sometimes jocularly called – we shall shortly be supplying ...'

*

'And to think, all that could have been mine.' Kenneth sighed with pretended regret, putting his feet up on the low wall of the terrace and rocking his seat back on its rear legs as he shaded his eyes with one hand. He brought his drink up to his lips with the other.

Janice and Rory were tucking into their salads; the terrace of the Achnaba Hotel was crowded with tourists, and on the road in front of the hotel cars, caravans and coaches hummed past, heading for Lochgilphead, Gallanach, or Kintyre. A brisk warm wind blew from the south west, laden with the vanilla smell of gorse blossom, mixed with pine off the forests and a salt hint from the sea.

'Well, that's just the way it goes, Ken,' Rory said. 'Hamish got to be manager of the factory and you didn't. No use crying over spilled boro-silicate . . .'

Kenneth grinned, staring out over the balustrade of the terrace towards the hills on the far side of Loch Fyne. 'I wonder where that saying comes from. I mean, why milk? If it means something not very valuable, why not water? Or –'

'Maybe crying over milk was unlucky,' Rory suggested.

'It was years before I realised it was even common parlance,' Kenneth said, still staring out to the loch. 'I used to think it was something only mum came out with. Like "I couldn't draw a herring off a plate." I mean, what the hell does *that* mean? Or, "Och aye; that's him away the Crow Road." Jeez. Opaque or what?'

'But they might all have some . . . some basis in reality,' Rory insisted. 'Like crying over milk was bad news; spoiled it.'

'Maybe it spoiled un-spilled milk,' Kenneth nodded. 'Some chemical reaction. Like they say thunder can curdle milk; ions or something.'

'Ah,' Rory said. 'Then maybe you were *supposed* to cry over milk, because it helped preserve it, or made it easier to turn into cheese. And so it was a waste crying over spilled milk.'

'I think this is where we came in,' Kenneth said. He squinted at a car on the road as it hurried north. 'Isn't that Fergus?' he said, nodding.

'Where?'

'Racing green Jag; heading north.'

'Is that what Ferg's driving these days?' Rory said, rising up in his seat a little to watch the car pass. It swept round the long bend that carried the road towards the forest. He sat back down and took up his fork again. 'Yeah, looked like Ferg.'

'This is Fergus Urvill, who owns the factory?' Janice asked. She sat back in the white plastic chair, fanning herself with her napkin.

Kenneth looked at her. 'Yep, that Fergus,' he said. 'Of course, you haven't had the dubious pleasure yet, have you?' He put his glass down on the circular table, and inspected the rolled up sun-shade that protruded from the centre of the table like an unopened flower.

'No,' Janice said. 'What's he like?'

Kenneth and Rory exchanged glances. 'Bearing up remarkably well,' Kenneth said.

Janice looked puzzled for a second, then said, 'Oh; yes, of course; Fiona ...' she looked embarrassed. Rory patted her hand on the table.

Kenneth looked away for a moment, then cleared his throat. 'Yeah; anyway.' He stretched his shoulders, sat back. 'Fergus ... Upper-class; huntin'-shootin'-fishin' type ... Could be worse, I suppose.'

'Still,' Rory said. 'Not what you'd call a happy man.'

'Well, of course,' Janice said quietly, and bit her lip.

Kenneth frowned. 'His precious factory's making a profit,' he said briskly, draining his glass. 'The Greedy Party's in power. What more does he want?'

'A wife?' Rory suggested, and then sucked on one finger.

Kenneth looked down, studying his glass. There was silence.

Rory rubbed a mark off the white table's surface. Janice lifted the scooped neck of her bright print dress and blew down.

'Want some shade?' Kenneth asked Janice. She nodded. Kenneth stood, lifted the stalk of the sun-shade and opened the big parasol, casting a shadow over Janice and Rory.

'Did you know,' Janice said to Rory, squeezing his hand. 'In the Dewey Decimal System, glass-making comes under the code six six six?'

'Woo,' Rory whistled. 'Number of the beast! Spooky, eh?'

'Not many people know that,' Janice said. She smiled.

Kenneth laughed. He sat back in his chair again, dragging it round so he was under the shade too. 'Shame Ferg isn't superstitious.' He chuckled. 'Mind you, Hamish is. Maybe we should tell him that. The Tree has some pretty weird ideas about religion; he might just swallow the idea he's been working for the devil all this time. Renounce the whole business, start going round smashing windows.'

'Really?' Janice said. 'What is he? I mean what religion?'

Kenneth shrugged. 'Oh, just Church of Scotland; but if they had a Provisional Wing, I think he'd be on it.'

'He's always had a soft spot for the royal family –' Rory began.

'Yes; his head,' Kenneth said.

'– Maybe he could start the Royal Church of Scotland.'

'Maybe he could start thinking like a rational human being instead of a cave-man frightened by lightning,' Kenneth said tartly.

'Oh, you're so cruel,' Rory told him.

'I know,' Kenneth sighed, rolling the base of his glass around on the table top. 'Time for another drink, I think.'

'My round,' Janice said, rising.

'No,' Kenneth said, 'Let –'

'Sit down,' Janice told him, taking his glass from his hand. 'Same again?'

Kenneth looked glum. 'No; Virgin Mary this time. Gotta drive.'

The two men watched Janice head for the bar.

'What *did* Fergus ever say to you?' Kenneth asked Rory.

'What?' Rory said, blinking. 'What about?'

'God, I hate it when you're mysterious!' Kenneth shook his head. 'You know damn well. Before the crash; way before. What did Fergus ever tell you? Was it after you came back from India that second time; before you went back to London? You two went hill-walking a lot then, didn't you? Old Ferg spill some beans up in them there hills?'

'We talked,' Rory said awkwardly, using his fork to push bits of lettuce around his plate. 'He told me things, but . . . I don't want to go into it, Ken, it would only complicate matters. It's nothing that directly touches you.'

'What about Fiona?' Kenneth said, voice low, staring at his brother. 'Did it touch her?'

Rory looked away, across the loch. He shrugged. 'Look, Ken, it isn't something you'd benefit by knowing, all right? Just leave it at that.' The fork continued to shift the lettuce leaves around the plate.

Kenneth watched his brother for a moment, then sat back. 'Oh well, serves me right for being nosey. Let's change the subject. How's this new project thing coming along?'

'Oh, I'm still working on it.'

'I wish you'd let me look at it.'

'It isn't finished yet.'

'When will it be?'

'When it is,' Rory said, frowning. He put the fork down. 'I don't know. Look; it's sort of a personal story . . .

'Ah,' Kenneth said.

Rory leaned forward over the table, closer to his brother. 'Look,' he said, glancing round towards the french windows that led to the bar. 'I've had a few more ideas . . . well, I've thought about . . . areas I didn't think I could use that I now think I can, and I want to develop that stuff, and –'

'*What* stuff?' Kenneth said, laughing in exasperation and throwing his arms wide. 'Just tell me what *sort* of stuff!'

Rory sat back, shaking his head. 'I can't say. Really.' He glanced up at Kenneth. 'But things . . . things might start to happen soon, anyway. I can't say any more for now.' Kenneth shook his head sadly. 'They might have happened by now if you'd just let me see this . . . opera, TV series, pop-up-book, whatever the hell it is; *and* if you'd let me talk to a few people. I mean, if it's just that you're too close to it and you don't want *me* to look at it, there are people I know who're good at that sort of thing; they can see the wood from the trees; they could –'

'Aw, come on, Ken,' Rory said, a pained expression crossing his face. He ran a hand through his short, straight hair. 'This is my show; this is the way I want to do it. Just let me, all right?'

'I don't know, Rore,' Kenneth said, sitting back. 'Sometimes you play your cards so damn close to your chest I don't think you can see them yourself. You should open up a bit more, share your problems. Share some secrets.'

'I do,' Rory said, biting his lip and looking down at his glass.

'Rory,' Kenneth said, sitting forward and lowering his voice to conspiratorial levels, 'the last secret I remember you telling me was that it was you who set fire to that barn on the Urvill's estate.'

Rory grinned, stirring his finger through a little patch of moisture on the side of his glass. 'Hey, I'm still waiting to see if you tell anyone.'

Ken laughed. 'Well, I haven't. Have you?'

Rory smiled, sucking air through his teeth at the same time, clinked one thumb-nail against his glass. He glanced at his brother. 'Don't worry; my secret is safe with us.' He shook his head, then shrugged. 'Okay,' Rory sighed, trying to suppress a smile, looking away. 'There might be a job with Aunty in the offing, okay?'

'What?' Kenneth laughed. 'The Beeb? You going to be a TV star?'

'It's not definite yet,' Rory shrugged. 'And it's . . .' he frowned at his brother. 'Shit, Ken; it's just more hack-work. It's better paid, is all.'

'What *is* it though?'

'Oh, a fucking travel programme, what else?' Rory rolled his eyes. 'But anyway; we'll see, okay? It's not definite, like I say, and I don't want to get anybody's hopes up, so keep it quiet; but things might start to happen.'

'But that's *great* news, man,' Kenneth said, sitting back.

'Talking about me, I hope, boys,' Janice said, returning with their drinks on a tray.

'... said, "My *God*, Rory, I've never seen one that big!" and I said – oh; hello dear,' Rory grinned, pretending only then to notice Janice.

She sat down, smiling. 'Talking about the size of your overdraft, are we, dear?'

'Gosh-darn,' Rory said, snapping his fingers, looking at Kenneth. 'Caught telling tales again.'

'Runs in the family,' Kenneth said, taking up his glass. 'Cheers, Janice.'

'Your health.'

'Slange.'

*

They left after that drink and went back to the house at Lochgair; Rory and Kenneth cleared a tangled choke of bushes and shrubs at the rear of the garden, where Mary wanted the lawn extended. They sweated through the insect-loud afternoon, while the sun shone. Janice sunbathed, and later helped Mary and Margot prepare the evening meal.

Janice had taken that day off from the library. She and Rory left on the last train back to Glasgow that night.

It was the last time Kenneth ever saw Rory.

*

Fiona sat in the passenger seat of the car, watching the red roadside reflectors drift out of the night towards her. She was thrown against one side of the seat as Fergus powered the Aston round the right-hander that took the road out of the forest, down, into and through the little village of Furnace. She was pressed back against the seat as

Fergus accelerated again. They swung out and past some small, slower car, over-taking it as though it was stationary; headlights ahead of them glared, the on-coming car flashed its lights and she heard its horn sound as they passed, a few seconds later. The sound was quickly lost in the snarl of the Aston's engine.

'If you're driving like this to try and prove something, don't bother on my account,' she said.

Fergus was silent for a while, then, in a very controlled and even voice said, 'Don't worry. Look, I just want to get home as soon as possible. All right?'

'Everything'll suddenly get better once we're home, will it?' Fiona said. 'Kiss the kids on the head and get Mrs S to make some tea; stiff whisky for you, G and T for me. Maybe we should call up the McKeans to say we got back safely; you can ask after Julie . . .'

'For Christ's sake, Fiona –'

'"For Christ's sake, Fiona",' Fiona sneered, imitating Fergus's voice. 'Is that all you can say? You've had half an hour to think up another excuse, and –'

'I don't need,' Fergus sighed, 'any excuses. Look; I thought we had agreed to just leave this –'

'Yes, that would suit you fine, wouldn't it, Ferg? That's your way of dealing with everything, isn't it? Pretend it hasn't happened, maybe it'll go away. If we're all terribly polite and decorous and discreet, maybe the whole horrid thing will just . . .' She made a little fluttering motion with her hands, and in a high-pitched, girlish voice, said, 'Disappear!'

She looked at him; his broad, soft-jowled face looked hard and set in the dim light shining from the car's instruments. 'Well,' she told him, leaning over as far as she could towards him. 'They won't just go away, Ferg.' She tried to make him look at her. He frowned, put his head slightly to one side and lifted it, trying to look round and over her head. 'Nothing ever goes away, Fergus,' she told him. 'Nothing ever doesn't matter.' She strained over a little more.
'Fergus –' *she said.*

He pushed her away with his left hand, back into her seat.

She sat there, mouth open. He seemed to understand the silence and glanced over, a weak smile flickering on his face. 'Sorry,' he said. 'Getting in the way a bit there. Sorry.'

'Don't you push me!' she said, slapping his shoulder. She hit him again. 'Don't you ever dare push me again!'

'Oh stop it, Fiona,' he said, more exasperated than angry. 'One minute I'm in the dog-house because ... well, because I'm not all over you all the time; next second –'

'"Not all over you all the time"?' Fiona said. 'You mean not fucking *me, Fergus, is that what you mean?'*

'Fiona, please –'

'Oh.' Fiona slapped one palm off her forehead, then crossed her arms, looked away, out of the dark side window. 'Fuck; did I swear? Oh fuck. Oh what a silly fucking cow I must fucking be.'

'Fiona –'

'I said something straight. I'm so sorry. I actually said what I meant, used the sort of word you'd normally only hear from your golfing chums or your rugby pals. Or does Julie use that sort of language? Does she? Do you like her to talk dirty? Does that get you going, Ferg?'

'Fiona, I'm getting rather tired of this,' Fergus said through his teeth, his fingers gripping the wheel harder, rubbing round it. 'I'm sorry you think what you do about Julie. As I have tried to tell you, she was the wife of an old friend and I've kept in touch since she got divorced –'

'Still stuck on that, Fergus?' Fiona said, impersonating concern. 'Oh dear; we had that line back at Arrochar, I seem to recall. And what was the rest of it? Oh yes, one of her sons has leukaemia, poor little kid, hasn't he? And you've helped her and the little darling with BUPA *out of the goodness of your heart –'*

'Yes I have, and I'm sorry you choose to sneer about it, Fiona.'

'Sneer!' laughed Fiona. 'It's a joke, Fergus. Jesus, she was practically taking your zip down.'

'Oh, don't be ridiculous. It's not my fault Julie got a bit tipsy.'

'She was smashed out of her brains, Fergus, and about the only thing she remembered was that she wanted to get your trousers off. God knows why, but she seemed to associate that with pleasure.' Fiona gave a sort of strangled laugh, then put one hand up suddenly to her nose, and looked away, and sobbed once.

Fergus drove quickly on, trees flicking past like green ghosts to the right, the waters of the loch just a dark absence on the left.

Fiona sniffed. 'Trying the great silence again, eh, Ferg?' She pulled a handkerchief from her handbag on her lap, dabbed at her nose. 'Still pretending it'll all go away. Still sticking your head in your precious fucking optical-quality sand.'

'Look, can't we talk about this in the morning? I mean, when you're ...'

'Sober, Fergus?' she said, looking over at him. 'That what you were going to say? Blaming it on drink again? Is that all it was? Of course, silly me. I should have realised. Dear Julie gets drunk and for some bizarre reason suddenly starts feeling you up under the table while we're nibbling our cheese and biscuits, and making pathetic double-entendres, and attacks you outside the bathroom; totally unprovoked, of course, and it's all just the drink talking. And I'm just being hysterical, I suppose, because I've had too many of John's terribly strong G and Ts and it'll all look different in the morning and I'll come to you and say sorry and wasn't I being a silly girl last night, and you can pat me on the head and say yes, wasn't I? And we can still go for cocktails at the Frasers' and bridge at the McAlpines and tee off with the Gordons and cruise with the Hamiltons with a united front, a respectable face, can't we, Fergus?'

'Fiona,' Fergus said, face set and teeth clenched. 'I don't know,' he breathed, 'why you're making such a big thing of this. It's just one of those things that happens at parties; people do get drunk and they do *do things they wouldn't normally think of. Maybe Julie has ... or has had, in the past, a crush on me or something. I don't know. Maybe –'*

'A crush on you,' said Fiona. 'Jesus. Well, that's a better try, Ferg. But I don't think you're quite as good a liar as you think you are. And she's not that good an actress.' Fiona looked down, twisting the handkerchief in her fingers. 'Oh God, Ferg, it was so fucking obvious. I mean. I knew there was something going on; all those trips away, and getting drunk and not being able to come home, staying at one of your chums' delightful *little pied-à-terres. Oh, sorry, no, you can't phone back, he's only just got it and it hasn't had a phone put in yet. Or coming back with bruises; how you suddenly became so very clumsy or so easily marked. But at least I could still kid myself, at least I didn't have my nose rubbed in it.'*

'Fiona!' Fergus shouted, knuckles white on the steering wheel. 'For God's sake, there's nothing to have your nose rubbed in! Julie's just a friend. I haven't touched her!'

'You didn't have to, she was touching you,' Fiona said, voice quiet, looking away from Fergus, out to the darkness of the loch. A few weak lights shone on the far side, and headlights on the Otter Ferry road, two miles away across the black expanse of waves, swung out briefly, like a lighthouse beam . . . and then dimmed and disappeared. The car roared through another small village before the trees hid the view again.

Fiona kept her face away from him, looking out into the night, watching the vertical bright line of light the car threw onto the serried mass of dark conifers. Even there she could not escape him; she could see his distorted image in the slanted glass of the car's windows, dim in the background, still lit by his instruments.

She wondered how she could ever have thought that she loved him, and why she had stayed with him for so long after she'd realised that if she ever had, she did not love him now.

Of course she could say it was for the children, as people always did . . . It was true, up to a point. How terrible it was to have those easy phrases, trotted out so often in the course of gossip, or heart-to-hearts, or in magazine articles, or even court cases, become so real.

It was never the sort of thing you thought about when you were young, when you were – or thought you were – in love, and all the future shone with promise.

Problems belonged to other people. You might imagine supporting them, talking with them when they needed to talk, trying to help, but you didn't imagine that you would be the one desperate to talk (or the one too embarrassed to talk, too ashamed or too proud to talk); you didn't imagine you would be the one who needed help, not even when you told friends that of course there might be problems, or agreed with your beloved that you would always talk about things ...

Staying together for the children.

And for the adults, she thought. For the sake of appearances. God, she had thought she was above that sort of thing, once. She had been bright and free and determined and she had decided she was going to make her own way in the world, just as well as any of her brothers might. She'd been a sort of feminist before it became fashionable; never had much time for all that sisterly stuff, but she was positive she was as good as any man and she'd prove it ... And marrying Ferg had seemed like an extra boost to her life-plan. London had been exciting, but she had not shone out there, she felt, the way she had here. She had never felt any affection for the place and had made no friends there she would miss; and anyway, she would find fields to conquer up here, coming home triumphant to wed the lord of the manor.

But it had not been as she had imagined. She had expected to be the centre of things in Gallanach, but the McHoans as a family had so many other things happening to them; she had felt peripheral. The Urvills' own history, too, made her feel like something unimportant on the family tree, for all that Fergus talked of responsibility and duty and one's debt to the next generation.

She was a leaf, expendable. A twig – maybe – at best.

Somehow all her dreams had disappeared. It seemed to her now that all she had ever had had been the dream of having dreams; the goal of having goals one day, once she had made her mind up what it was she wanted.

But that had never happened. First Fergus, then the twins, then her own small part in the society of the town and the people there, and in the wider, still circumferential concerns of this wee country's middle-to-ruling classes, and in the more dissipated commonwealth of mildly powerful people who were their peers beyond that – in England, on the continent, from the States and elsewhere – took up her time, sapped her will and replaced her own concerns with theirs.

So now, she thought, I am married to a man whose touch disgusts me, and who anyway does not seem to want to touch me. She looked at Fergus's dim reflection, distorted in the glass, then tried to re-focus on her own image. Can he find me as repellent as I find him? I can't look that bad, can I? A few grey hairs, but you don't notice them; still a size twelve, and I've looked after myself. I look good in this, your standard little black number, and I still get into a tight pair of jeans . . . What's wrong with me? What did I do? Why does he have to spend half his time with that drunken, brassy bitch?

God, the best time I've had in the past five years was one night with Lachy Watt, angry at Ferg, and more surprised than anything else. They way he just took my hair in one hand, while we were standing looking up at that God-awful window in the great hall, and turned my head to him, and pulled me close; tongue down my throat before I knew what was happening, and there was something adolescent and desperate beneath all that working-class directness, but Jesus, I felt wanted *. . .*

She shook her head. That was best left out of it. Once was once; dismissible. Ever again would set a pattern. Lachy had been back one time afterwards that she knew of, a year later, and he had called, but she'd told him she wouldn't be able to see him, and put the phone down on him. No, that didn't matter.

She looked at the reflection of Fergus again, as he pulled the wheel; the car tunnelled into the forest, the wall of trees on either side a blur, their greenness more remembered than seen.

I could leave him, she thought. I could always have left him. But mother's too close for comfort; there'd be too many nearby friends, too many chances of bumping into people I'd rather not bump into; too much mitigating against the clean break; new start. God, I'm pathetic, though, that's so petty. Why haven't I the sheer drive to just get up and go, take the twins and emigrate to Oz or Canada? Or live in wild eccentricity in London or Paris?

Or I can stay, as I know I probably will. Muddle through. Look after the twins and try to make sure they negotiate the reefs of puberty and adolescence, set them up to make their way in the world, and do so without becoming just like me . . .

She looked out, into the grey sweep of road ever rushing towards them. Fergus powered the car down out of the forest, through some more houses and a few lights. The car lurched. Fergus looked over, smiled at her. She didn't know whether to smile back or not, and she wondered what that expression had meant, and what had been going through his head for the last few miles.

The car jiggled on its springs, lurched again and settled. She clutched at her seat, looking forward. The engine roared.

She looked back at Ferg, saw tears in his eyes. 'Ferg?' she said.

The car skidded a little, came straight; she glanced forward at the road, saw the corner and the trees. She clutched at the dashboard with both hands. 'Ferg!' she screamed. 'Look –!'

CHAPTER 13

I was eleven when Aunt Fiona died; I remember feeling both peeved and cheated that I was thought too young to go to the funeral. It would have been my chance to show how mature I had become, and anyway from what I'd seen on television and films, funerals looked like rather dramatic and romantic events; people dressed in black and looked sombre. They had thin, tight lips, and they sometimes wept, and there was a lot of grim clutching of other people's shoulders, and low mutterings about how so-and-so had been a good person, and that sort of thing. But under it all was the simple, joyous fact: they were dead and you weren't yet!

I hadn't got to see Aunt Fiona being buried, but I did see Uncle Fergus in hospital. I was in, too, getting my appendix out, and I went along from my ward to his room just to say how sorry I was.

He had a broken arm, some cracked ribs, and his whole face was bruised; kids with face-paints couldn't have matched all those colours. I'd never seen anything like it.

There wasn't much to say; I can't remember what I did say. He kept talking about not being able to remember anything after passing Lochgair, no matter how hard he tried. He couldn't understand why she hadn't been wearing her seatbelt. He'd thought she had been, but they said she hadn't. She hadn't. He started to cry.

*

I sat on the giant, corroded lump of concrete and steel, legs crossed, arms folded, watching the waves break on the sands below and listening to the strange, whooping, hooting sounds and hollow clanging noises produced by the fluted pipes and iron doors embedded in the fractionally tilted concrete mass.

It was a little after sunset, three days after my father's death. The sun had dipped behind North Jura, and abandoned the sky to a skeined mass of glowing clouds, sinking through the spectrum from gold towards blood-red, all against a wash of deepening blue. The wind was still warm, coming in from the south west, sharp with salt as the remnants of the rolling Atlantic swell hit the rocks nearby and sent up spray, but maybe also – well, you could imagine it, at least – containing a hint of grasses, too; something directed over the distant greenery of Ireland, or swept round from the Welsh hills along the circling wind.

The concrete block was more or less a cube, about four metres to a side, though it looked more squat than that, its lower metre buried in the sand of the small beach a few miles west of Gallanach, about level with the southern tip of Island Macaskin. The concrete and pipe-work block – four years old now, and streaked with rust and seagull droppings – was the only full-size work Darren Watt ever completed.

Darren had got his sponsorship from a cement company, which agreed to provide materials and a grant, but finding a place to put the finished piece had been tricky, and it had been Uncle Fergus, no less, who had finally come to the rescue with a site for the work;

the town council hadn't liked the idea of a gigantic concrete object the size of four garages being stationed anywhere near the town itself, and for a while it had looked like Darren was going to have real problems finding anywhere to put his concrete edifice (especially after a couple of the more pygmy-brained newspapers had taken up the story and started fuming about a ridiculous waste of public money and the outrageous despoiling of our fragile landscape with queer, arty-farty, loony-left monstrosities).

Darren had thought about playing up to this drivel by giving the thing some wonderfully pretentious title, and I recall him at a party discussing the merits of calling it The Lusitanian Coast Dialectical Kinetic/Static Object Alpha. In the end, though, he just called it Block One.

It was a three-kilometre hike from the nearest path, and even the odd yachtsperson, passing close enough to catch sight of the block, would probably have dismissed it as some old war-time ruin. Not exactly as public as Sauchiehall Street, then, but Darren had been happy. It worked; when the tide was at the right level, it produced noises like a ghost trapped in badly tuned organ-pipes, sonorous slammings as waves opened and slammed shut heavy doors like hinged manhole covers within the set tonnes of the block's hollow insides, and – depending on the waves – impressive spouts of water, bursting into the air from its rusted throats as though from some stranded cubist whale. He'd learned a lot from it, he'd said; just you wait till the next one, and the ones after that ...

I was thinking about Aunt Fiona because death and dying were on my mind, and I was going back through all the people I'd known who'd had the nerve to pop their clogs before they should have, while I was still around to miss them. Aunt Fiona was a vague memory, even though I'd been eleven when she'd died and I'd known her for so many years. It was as though by her early death the memories had lost the chance of being renewed every now and again, and instead were somehow built over, the spaces that should have been hers recycled and used-up by those of the family who were still alive.

She'd been okay; I'd liked her, from what I could remember. She'd let us play in the castle and its grounds, and she'd taken us on walks round the coast sometimes. She'd seemed young and old at once to me; of a different generation to Fergus and Lachlan, and even my father. She had seemed younger than them, never mind the real elders, like Grandma Margot; closer to us when we were children. It was a quality she'd shared with Uncle Rory.

The still absent Uncle Rory. We'd thought that – as dad's death had gone reported in a few papers, partly because of his modest fame, and partly because of the bizarre nature of his demise – Rory might hear, and finally get in touch ... but nothing had happened yet, and the funeral was tomorrow. The romantic in me wanted him to reappear at the ceremony, in the grounds of the house at Lochgair, but I doubted that he would. Too pat, too neat, too kind a thing for fate to throw up now.

I looked up at the violet sky, feeling the wind move my hair across my forehead and the nape of my neck. I could see a few stars. I stared at the heavens until my neck got sore, then said, aloud and loud,

'Well?'

Nothing.

The waves shushed across the sands. I lowered my head. Out to sea, a couple of birds flew wing-tip low across the sky-reflecting waters. I shook my head, wondering at it all.

Dad died – my Uncle Hamish seemed to be maintaining – in suspicious circumstances; God killed him.

Uncle Hamish appeared to be almost perversely upset and appalled by the implications of this supposed act; his own part in the bizarre and fatal episode troubled him less, I guessed, than the terrifying idea that there really might be, after all, a God who listens, thinks, decides and acts, just like an ordinary mortal, except more powerful. It rather indicated, I suspected, that all this time my uncle had just been playing a game, and his retributive proto-heresy was exactly as frivolous as my dad had been given to claiming. Whatever, Uncle Hamish was, in short, under sedation.

And dad was under the care of the undertaker, and would soon be under the roses at the rear of the garden in Lochgair, unchristened at the start of his life, and joined to unconsecrated ground after its end.

Some generation, I thought. If Uncle Rory was dead (and who was to say he wasn't) then Hamish, my uncle, The Tree, at that moment lying in a darkened room, moaning about a jealous God and being his brother's keeper and the divine and blinding light come from the skies and the smell of the devil and all his works and popping Valium every few hours and muttering about anti-creates and asking his wife to tell my mother that for all his atheism – so powerfully and dramatically disproved – he was sure Kenneth had been a mostly good man, and would not suffer unduly in the afterlife, even though the gates of heaven were irredeemably closed to him ... This prattling wreck, this bed-bound, hide-bound bag of gibbering nonsense was all that remained of that generation's one-time promise.

Rory gone from us for a decade, at least as good as dead; Fiona gone for want of a seat belt; and my father, drunk and angry, furiously determining to prove ... *something* by a prank barely worthy of some over-privileged Oxbridge undergraduate.

Just Hamish left, and him half-mad with an amalgamated fever of grief, guilt, and re-inoculated faith.

Some result.

*

I'd surprised myself, when Gav broke down like that, and I knew that dad was dead. I believe I actually came close to fainting. I stood, watching Gav greet, hearing Janice Rae sob into Ashley Watt's shoulder behind me, and gradually I started to feel I was no more attached to or in control of my own body than I was Gavin's. I don't mean that I stood or floated outside myself, just that I was somewhere inside me that wasn't connected with the usual channels of communication, let alone action.

I heard a noise like continual surf, and the view went sort of grey, and tunnel-like for a bit. I was suddenly aware of how delicately balanced we are on our two skinny legs, and my skin seemed to be contracting, pressing in all about me, and going cold, leaving sweat.

I wobbled, apparently; Ash took me by the shoulders and sat me down on the little chair by the table. She got Janice to make some sweet tea. I said thank you, drank the tea, shivered a bit, and then Ash dialled Lochgair for me.

The phone was engaged, but Ashley kept trying. It was a friend of mum's from the village who answered initially.

I didn't think I was crying, while I was on the phone; I felt calm and in control and I spoke quietly to my mum, who sounded trembly and yet flat-toned, and told me what had happened, but after I'd put the phone down I found that my eyes were full of tears and my cheeks wet with them. They'd dribbled round my chin and onto my chest, inside the open shirt.

'Oh dear,' I said, feeling that I ought to feel embarrassed. Ash handed me a clean tissue, and I dabbed myself dry.

'I'll drive you back,' Ashley said, squatting in front of me in the hall, my hands gathered in hers, her long face serious, eyes shining.

'You've drunk too much. We've both drunk too much,' I said. 'Anyway, you've got to get to London, start your new job.' I took a deep breath. 'Thanks, though.' I bent forward, kissed her nose.

She put her head down. I sat back in the seat again and gazed over her head at the white-painted wallpaper on the far side of the hallway.

She looked up into my eyes.

'What happened, Prentice?'

I shrugged. 'Crazy,' I said, my gaze sliding away from those sternly concerned eyes, to look at the worn hall carpet and an old red wine stain from a party two years ago. 'Just crazy.'

Ash patted my hands. 'I'll take you down in the morning, then. I can get them to hold the job. There was no rush. Only if you want.'

'I don't know,' I said, and really didn't. I bent forward, put my head between my knees and stared at the black-taped edge of the carpet under the seat and the rough floorboards beyond. I felt Ash stroke my head, her hands soft and gentle through my hair.

I didn't want to go to bed and anyway could not have slept. She stayed up with me, and we finished the real coffee and then the instant. I talked about the family, about Rory and Fiona and mum and dad. Thunder rolled over the city, just before sunrise, and I found myself laughing, sitting there on the couch, in the living room with Ashley; laughing at the thunder. She held me, shushed me.

The dawn came up dull at first, then the clouds cleared from the west and a bright blue day was there. Ashley left a note for Gav and Janice, helped me pack a bag – I couldn't decide on anything – then we left. The old 2CV, freshly pillar-box red after its latest re-spray, puttered through the near-empty streets of the bright and silent city, and rocked and rolled its way back down towards Gallanach.

The weather was perfect, the new day glorious. I talked incessantly and Ash listened, sometimes smiled and seemed always to have a kind word.

We arrived at Lochgair about breakfast-time, with the sun shining through the trees and the birds loud in the garden. Ashley stopped the car at the opened gates at the end of the drive where it entered the courtyard. 'I'll drop you here, okay?' she said.

'Oh, come in,' I told her.

She shook her head, yawned. Her long fawn hair shone in a beam of sunlight coming through the car's open side window. 'I don't think so, Prentice. I'll get home, get some sleep. Give me a call if there's anything I can do, okay?'

I nodded. 'Okay.'

'Promise?' She smiled.

'Promise,' I said.

She leaned over, put one hand behind my head and kissed my forehead. I heard her take a breath, like she was about to speak, but then she exhaled, just patted my head. I put one arm round her, held her for a moment, then pulled away, reached into the back and got my bag, opened the door and got out. 'Thanks,' I said.

'It's okay, Prentice,' she said.

I closed the flimsy door. The car revved up and turned round, one skinny front wheel poking out alarmingly from its wheel arch. The little Citroën clattered off down the drive. Ashley stuck one hand out of the window and waved; I raised my arm, and held it there as I watched the car head away under the trees through the dappling light. It paused at the main road, then turned away, its noise soon lost in the background of bird-song and wind-ruffled leaves.

The cool morning air smelled clean and fresh; I took a deep breath and rubbed my smarting eyes, feeling spaced-out from lack of sleep.

Then I picked up my bag and turned to the house.

*

It was a well-travelled country, dad told us. Within the oceanic depths of time that lay beneath the surface of the present, there had been an age when, appropriately, an entire ocean had separated the rocks that would one day be called Scotland from the rocks that would one day be called England and Wales. That first union came half a billion years ago. Some of those rocks were ancient even then; two billion years and counting, and shifting and moving across the face of the planet while that primaeval ocean shrank and closed and all that would become the British Isles still lay south of the equator. Compressed and folded, the rocks that would be Scotland – by then part of the continent of Euramerica – held within their crumpled, tortuously layered cores the future shape of the land.

By a third of a billion years ago, that part of Euramerica lay on the equator, covered by great fern forests that would be buried and folded and pressed and heated and so turn to oil and coal, in the future that was yet to come. Meanwhile the mass of rocks, afloat on the molten stone beneath, were heading slowly northwards, and sundering; the climate became hot and the rains sparse; the great dinosaurs, tree-tall and house-heavy, tramped slowly through a semi-desert while a new ocean opened to the west. After the dinosaurs had gone, and while the Atlantic still grew, the volcanoes erupted, smothering the old rock on the surface under their own vast, deep oceans of lava.

The land then held mountains higher than Everest, but they were worn down eventually by nothing harder than wind and water, until, much later still – now that Scotland was level with Canada and Siberia and the earth cooler – the glaciers came, covering the rocks with their own chill, inverted image of the old and weathered lava plains. The sheer mess of that frozen water etched the mountain rock like steel engraving glass, and pressed the roots of those fire-floating hills deeper into the dense sea of magma beneath.

Then the climate changed again; the glaciers retreated and the water they had held filled the oceans, so that the waters rose and cut what would eventually be called the British Isles off from mainland Europe, while the scoured, abraded hills to the north, set free at last from that compressing weight of ice, rose slowly back out of the earth, to be colonised again by plants and animals, and people.

On walks, on day trips and holidays, he found and pointed out the signs that told of the past, deciphering the symbols written into the fabric of the land. In Gallanach, we saw the bright seam of white cretaceous sandstone that had provided the Gallanach Glass Works with raw material for a century and a half. On Arran, he showed us rocks folded like toffee, ribboned and split; on Staffa, the even, keyboard-regular columns of cooled lava; in Edinburgh, the rubble-tailed stumps of ancient volcanoes; in Glasgow, the black, petrified remains of trees three hundred million years old; in Lochaber, the parallel roads that marked the shores of lochs dammed and un-dammed by glaciers, millennia earlier; throughout Scotland we saw hanging valleys, drumlins and corries; and in the Hebrides we walked the raised beaches where the ocean swells had crashed until the land rose, and touched rocks two and a half billion years old; half as old as Earth itself; a sixth of the age of the entire universe.

Here was magic, I remember thinking, as we drove north towards Benbecula one day, looking out at the machair, gaudy with flowers. I was just old enough to grasp what dad had been telling us, but still young enough to have to think about it in childish terms. Magic. Time was Magic; and geology. Physics, chemistry; all the big, important words dad used. They were all Magic.

I sat listening to the car's engine, as we drove; mum at the wheel, dad in the passenger seat, shirt-sleeved arm out of the Volvo's window, Lewis, James and I in the back.

The car engine made a steady growling noise, and I remember thinking it was funny that those long-dead plants had been turned into the oil that had been turned into the petrol that made the car growl. I chose to forget the absence of reptiles in those carboniferous forests, and imagined that they had been populated by great dinosaurs, and that they too had fallen into the ooze, and made up part of the oil, and that the noise the car made was like the angry, bellowing growls they would have made while they were alive, as though their last dying breath, their last sound on this planet, had been saved all these millions and millions of years, to be exhaled along a little road on a little island, pushing the McHoan family north, one summer, on our holidays.

I looked out of the open window; the machair lay dazzling under the midsummer sunshine to our left.

*

'Prentice! Prentice! Oh, Prentice; pray for your father!'

'Hello, Uncle Hamish,' I said, as Aunt Tone ushered mother and me into the bedroom where my uncle lay, propped up, splendid but demented in a pair of blue cotton pyjamas and a red silk dressing-gown decorated with blue dragons. The room was behind dim closed curtains, and smelled of apples.

'Mary! Oh, Mary,' Uncle Hamish said, seeing my mother. He clasped his hands together, holding a black handkerchief. His hair was a bit mussed and he had a stubble shadow; I'd never seen him look so disarrayed. In front of him there was a huge tray with short legs, partly covered by a quarter-completed jigsaw puzzle. I walked up to the bed and put my hand out. I clutched Uncle Hamish's still clasped hands, held them briefly, squeezed and let go.

Closer inspection revealed that Hamish was putting the jigsaw puzzle together upside-down; every cardboard flake was grey, turned the wrong way up.

Mum gave Hamish a brief hug and we sat down on a couple of chairs on either side of the bed. 'I'll make some tea,' Aunt Tone said, and quietly closed the door.

'And biscuits!' shouted Uncle Hamish at the closed door, and smiled broadly at first mum and then me. After a moment, though, his face seemed to collapse and he looked like he was about to weep.

The door opened again. 'What's that, my dear?' Aunt Tone asked.

'Nothing,' Uncle Hamish said, the mouth-only smile suddenly there again, then fading just as quickly. The door closed. Hamish peered down at the jigsaw puzzle, toyed with a couple of the pieces, looking for a place to fit them into what he had already completed. The squint bottom edge of the puzzle, some small spaces between joined pieces, a few tiny flecks of cardboard – half grey, half coloured – gathered like dust along the raised edges of the tray, and a small pair of collapsible scissors lying on the bedspread near the pillows, indicated that Uncle Hamish had – not to put too fine a point on it – been cheating.

'Thank you, both, for coming,' he said, absently, still fiddling with the grey pieces. He sounded bored, like he was talking to a couple of factory workers summoned to his office for some formality of business. 'I appreciate it.' I exchanged looks with my mother, who appeared close to tears again.

Mum had done pretty well till now; we'd both cried a bit when Ashley had deposited me at the gates of the house at Lochgair, but since then she had coped pretty well. We'd visited the good lawyer Blawke that first day, and the next day he'd actually made a house-call, a concession which, extrapolating from the attitude of his secretary when she rang us up to tell us the sacred presence was on his way, we ought to have treated with the sort of awe and respect the average person reserves for royalty and major religious figures. I was a little surprised he didn't kneel and kiss the door-step when he unfolded himself from his Merc.

The undertaker had been dealt with, a few reporters fended off, Lewis – in London – reassured that there was nothing he could do up here for now, and told not to cancel his gig dates, and James, on a school trip in Austria, finally contacted. He would arrive the day of the funeral; one of his teachers would come back with him.

Dad's study proved to be a wilderness of papers, disorganised files, chaotic filing cabinets, and an impressive-looking computer that neither mum nor I knew how to operate. The afternoon I got back mum and I had stood looking at the machine, knowing there might be stuff in it we'd need to look at, but unable to work out what to do with the damn thing after switching it on; the relevant manual had disappeared, mum had never touched a keyboard in her life and my computer expertise was confined to having a sound tactical sense of which alien to zap first and a leechlike grip on continuous-fire buttons.

'I know just the person,' I said, and rang the Watts' house.

Twenty-four hours before the funeral, Aunt Tone had rung and said could we possibly come and see Uncle Hamish? He'd asked to see us.

And so here we were. Mum sat on the far side of the bed, her eyes bright.

I cleared my throat. 'How are you, Uncle Hamish?' I asked.

He looked at my mother, as if he thought she'd talked, not me. He shrugged. 'Sorry to drag you out here,' he said. His voice was flat, emotionless. 'I just wanted to say how, how sorry I am, and I want you all to forgive me, even though I didn't ... didn't encourage him. He insisted. I told him not to do it.' He sighed and tried to press one of the cardboard pieces into place on the puzzle without success. 'We were both a little the worse for wear and,' he said. 'I did try. I tried to stop him, tried to talk to him, but ... but ...' He stopped talking, tutted in apparent exasperation and took up the little scissors. He trimmed a couple of finger-nail sized bits of cardboard off the piece and forced it into place. 'Don't make the damn things right any more,' he muttered.

I began to wonder at the wisdom of leaving Uncle H with a pair of scissors, even small ones.

He looked at me. 'Headstrong,' he said brightly, then looked down at the puzzle. 'Always was. Good; liked him; brother after all, but ... there was no sense of God in him, was there?' Hamish looked at mum, then me. 'No sense of something greater than him, was there, Mary?' he said, turning back to mum. 'Proof all round us; goodness and power, but he wouldn't believe. I tried to tell him; saw the minister yesterday; told him he hadn't tried hard enough. He said he couldn't force people to go to church. I said, why not? Did in the old days. Why not?' Uncle Hamish took up another piece of grey cardboard, turned it this way and that. 'Good enough then, good enough now; that's what I told him. For their own good.' He grunted, looked displeased. 'Idiot told me not to blame myself,' he said, staring grimly at the puzzle-piece, as though trying to pare bits off it with just the sharpness of his stare. 'I said I don't, I blame God. Or Kenneth for ... for goading ... inciting Him.' Uncle Hamish started to cry, his bottom lip quivering like a child's.

'There, Hamish,' mum said, reaching out and stroking one of his hands.

'What exactly happened, Uncle Hamish?' I asked. Sounded to me like the man had cracked completely, but I still wanted to see if he could come up with more details.

'Sorry,' sniffed Hamish, wiping his eyes then blowing his nose into the black hanky. He put the hanky in his breast pocket, clasped his hands on the edge of the tray holding the jigsaw, and lowered his head a little, seeming to address the centre of the puzzle. His thumbs started to circle each other, going round and round.

'We had a few drinks; we'd met in the town. I'd been at the Steam Packet, meeting with some people. Showed them round the factory in the morning. Just paperweights. Man from Harrods. Nice lunch. Thought I'd look for a present for Antonia's birthday, bumped into Kenneth coming out of the stationer's. Went for a pint; bit like the old days, really.'

'Here we are,' Aunt Antonia announced from the door, appearing with a tray full of crockery. There was a pause while tea was poured, biscuits dispensed. 'Shall I stay here, dear?' Aunt Tone asked Hamish.

I thought she looked worse than mum did. Her face was drawn, there were dark shadows under her eyes; even her brown, bunned hair looked greyer than I remembered.

Her husband ignored her, talking on as before, though now having apparently shifted his attention to the cup of tea Aunt Tone had placed in front of him on the puzzle tray. His thumbs were still circling each other.

'Went to the Argyll Lounge; good view of the harbour from there. Drank pints. It was like when we were younger. Had a cigar. Good chat, really. Rang the office, said I was playing truant. He rang Lochgair. We were going to go for a Chinese meal, just for old time's sake, but we never got round to it. Thought it would be fun to go on a bit of a pub-crawl, so we went on to the Gallery bar, in the Steam Packet. That was where we started talking about faith.'

Uncle Hamish stopped talking, took up his cup of tea, sipped quickly from it without raising his gaze from the tray, then replaced the cup in the saucer. 'He called me a crack-pot,' Hamish said. His eyebrows rose up his forehead; his voice rose too. Then it fell again as he said, 'I called him a fool.'

Hamish looked quickly, furtively, at my mother. 'Sorry,' he mumbled, and looked forward at the tray and the puzzle again. He sighed; his thumbs kept going round. 'I told him Christ loved him and he just laughed,' Hamish complained. 'He refused to see; he refused to understand. I told him he was like a blind man, like somebody who would not open their eyes; all he had to do was accept Christ into his life and suddenly everything would fall into place. The world would look a different place; a whole new plane of existence would open up. I explained that all we did here was merely a preparation for the next life, where we would be judged, punished and rewarded.' Hamish shook his head, face radiating dismay. 'He went all snide, asked me when exactly I'd had the brain by-pass operation.'

(God – or whatever – help me; at that point, despite it all, I had to stifle a guffaw. I coughed, and dabbed at my suddenly brimming eyes with a tissue.)

Hamish rattled on. 'I told him that only religion gave any meaning to life; only God, as an absolute, gave us a . . . peg to hang our philosophies on. What was the meaning of life, otherwise? He said, What meaning? He said, How long is a piece of string? and, What colour is the wind?' Uncle Hamish shook his head again. 'I told him faith was love, the most beautiful thing in the world. He said it was nonsense, surrendering our humanity. Humanity!' Hamish scoffed. 'Religion gives us rules; it can keep people from doing wrong; it helps us be good. But he wasn't having it, would not listen. "Religion is politics," he told me, several times. As though repeating it made it true. "Religion is politics! Religion is politics!" Blasphemed. We left the last bar – can't even remember which one it was, to be honest – and we were walking back here, for a nightcap, I think, coming along Shore Road – I left the car in the Steam Packet Hotel car park, of course – and we had some argument about the Shore Street Church. He said he liked it, liked the architecture, but it was really a testament to the skill of humans, not to the glory of God, and just a symbol. I said it was the house of God, and he'd better not trespass.' Hamish looked up at mum for a moment. 'He was walking along the wall, you see.'

Mum nodded. Hamish was already staring at the tray again.

'He said what was any church or temple but a giant, hollow idol? I told him he was sick; he said he was infected with reason. I said Reason was his God, and it was false; it was the true idol.' Hamish sighed. 'The street was wet; there had been rain. I remember noticing that . . . Kenneth shouted at me, told me. . .' Hamish shook his head. '. . . he said; "Hamish; all the gods are false. Faith itself is idolatry."'

Uncle Hamish swivelled his big, grey head and gazed gloomily at me. His eyes looked cold and jelly-like; they reminded me of frog-spawn discovered in some ditch. '"All the gods are false. Faith itself is idolatry,"' Uncle Hamish breathed, staring at me. I shivered. 'Can you credit that, Prentice?' He looked down, away from me, shaking his head.

Hamish returned his gaze to the puzzle tray. His thumbs kept circling. 'I can't remember exactly what he said,' Hamish whispered, and then sighed. 'But he jumped off the wall and ran over to the church. He started climbing.'

I heard my mother sob once, very quietly.

'I had to climb over the wall,' Hamish breathed, 'Gate was locked. By the time I got there he was out of reach. I thought he was shinning up a drainpipe. Just assumed. Heard rumbles, I think, but . . . didn't think anything of it. No flashes, that I can remember. Kenneth was yelling and swearing and shouting imprecations; calling down all sorts of punishment; I was trying to get him to come down; told him he'd fall; told him the police were coming; told him to think of his family. But he kept climbing.'

*

I studied my hands in the pink-tinged light, turning them over and looking at the lines on my palm, the veins on the back. I tried to imagine dad, climbing up that tower, hauling himself up, hand over hand, sweating and straining in the darkness, trusting to his own strength and the cool metal strip beneath his hands.

The block beneath me was silent now; the last of the waves had retreated from it and were breaking further down the beach as the tide went out. The sky was still gaudy with crimson clouds, though much of the brightness had gone. I glanced at my watch. I ought to be jumping down off this thing and heading back to the road; it was a rough hike over the headland, and dangerous in the dark. But the red streaks of the clouds were dissolving as the sunset went on, leaving the sky clear above me. This near the centre of the year, on a clear night, it would never get totally dark. I had a while yet, but I wouldn't leave it too late; mum would worry. That would just be the cherry on it, me taking the Crow Road too.

*

Uncle Hamish took another sip of his tea, frowned at the cup and spat the tea back into it. 'Cold,' he said apologetically to his wife. He dabbed at his lips with his handkerchief. I realised only then I hadn't touched the cup that Aunt Tone had poured for me.

Hamish went on: 'There was a very strange noise, a sort of humming noise seemed to come from under my feet, from the stones of the church. Couldn't work out what it was, thought it was the drink or just the effect of looking up like that, craning my neck. But it wouldn't go away, and it got louder and I felt my hair stand on end. I shouted up to Kenneth; he was about half-way up, still climbing. Then there was a flash, a blinding flash.

'Saw a glowing red line in front of me, like a vein of burning blood, like lava, in front of me. Noise terrific. Smell of sulphur; something of that nature; smell of the devil, though I think that was just coincidence. Fell down. Half blind, thought a bomb had gone off. Heard ringing, like the church bells all going on at once.' Uncle Hamish went to sip from his tea again, then thought the better of it and put the cup back on the saucer. 'Realised it had been lightning. I still couldn't believe it; found Kenneth behind me, lying on the grass and a sort of slab thing, over a grave. Hands burned. Been climbing the lightning conductor, blew him off. Don't know if that would have killed him, but he'd landed on the stone. Dead. Blood from his head.' Hamish looked slowly over at mum, who was crying silently. 'Sorry,' he told her.

She didn't say anything.

*

'Idiot,' I whispered, sitting there on Darren's great grey concrete block. 'Idiot,' I said, and for once I wasn't talking to myself. '*Idiot!*' I shouted at the sky. 'IDIOT!' I bellowed, hands clawing at the pitted concrete surface beneath me. '*IDIOT!*' I screamed, emptying my lungs to the soft sea airs. Coughing and choking, I sat there, tears in my eyes, breathing hard. Eventually I wiped my nose on my shirt sleeve, feeling like a little kid again, and then sniffed, swallowed, and breathed slower, clenching my teeth to stop my jaw trembling.

I sat back, shivering, legs out straight in front, arms behind, hands splayed on the rough concrete. I thought about them all. Dad, falling; Grandma Margot, falling. Darren, broken against the tomb-white concrete of a council litter bin; Aunt Fiona, through the windscreen of the Aston Martin, neck snapped, into the young trees by the roadside ... and who knew what had happened to Rory? Well, in a day or two I was going to start trying to find out.

So far mum and I – with Ashley's help – had only dealt with the papers and files we had to, to deal with the legal formalities. But there was a lot more stuff to go through, and somewhere in all that bumf there might be something that would tell us about Uncle Rory, and why dad had always been so sure his brother was still alive.

But for all we knew he'd died a roadside death, too.

*

Uncle Hamish turned to me. 'Swear he was still alive.' He nodded, frowning at me. I raised my eyebrows, feeling very cold inside. Hamish nodded again. 'Still alive; he said something to me. I swear Kenneth said, "See?"' Hamish shook his head. 'Said that to me; said, "See?" without opening his eyes.' He looked down at his rotating thumbs. His frown seemed to stop them. 'That was what he said; and it was so . . . wrong; such a silly, silly thing to say, that I thought I must have only thought I heard it, but I'm sure, that's what he said. "See?"' Uncle Hamish shook his head. '"See?"' He kept shaking his head. '"See?"' He turned to me. 'Can you credit that, Prentice?'

He looked away again before I could think of what to say. '"See?"' he repeated to the tray with the ruined puzzle, and shook his head again. '"See?"'

'Excuse me.' Mum got up and left the room, crying.

Hamish stared at the cardboard puzzle. Aunt Antonia sat at the end of the bed, staring hollow-eyed at her silent husband. The tray over Uncle Hamish's legs started to vibrate. I could see the duvet over Uncle Hamish's thighs shaking. The bed began to squeak. My uncle stared, appalled, at the tray on his lap, as the little grey pieces of the up-turned puzzle migrated across the vibrating surface of the tray, gradually collecting against one edge.

The spasms in Uncle Hamish's legs seemed to grow more severe; the cup of tea I'd put on the bedside table near my right elbow showed a concentric pattern of standing ripples. I suddenly thought of the scene in *The Unbelievable Prevalence of Bonking*, when the tanks enter Prague. Uncle Hamish made a strange keening noise; Aunt Tone patted his feet under the duvet and rose from the end of the bed.

'I'll get your pills, dear.'

She left the room. Hamish turned to me, his whole body shaking now, the puzzle on the tray starting to break up as the tray bounced up and down beneath it. 'Jealous,' Hamish croaked through clenched teeth. 'Jealous, Prentice; jealous! Jealous! Jealous God! Jealous!'

I got up slowly, patted his trembling hands and smiled.

*

I've always had this fantasy that, after Uncle Rory borrowed his flat-mate Andy's motorbike and headed off into the sunset, he crashed somewhere, maybe coming down to Gallanach; came off the road and fell down some gully nobody's looked in for the last ten years, or – rather more likely, I suppose – crashed into the water, and there's a Suzuki 185 GT lying just under the waves of Loch Lomond, or Loch Long, or Loch Fyne, its rider somehow entangled in it, reduced by now to a skeleton in borrowed leathers, somewhere underwater, perhaps between here and Glasgow; and we all pass it every time we make the journey, maybe only a few tens of metres away from him, and very possibly will never know.

I know that dad – who had indeed assumed that Rory had been on his way here – drove the Glasgow road a few times, immediately after Andy and then Janice raised the alarm, looking for some sign of an accident, a skid mark, a damaged fence or wall, always wondering if maybe his brother was lying unconscious or paralysed in a field or a ditch somewhere, invisible from the road . . . But all he ever found were road cones, assorted litter and the occasional dead sheep or deer.

Whatever; neither dad nor the police ever found any trace of Rory or the bike. No unidentified bodies turned up that could have been his, and no hospitals received any unknown coma victims fitting his description.

I don't think any of us ever mentioned suicide, but I at least considered the possibility that he had killed himself. Rory had been depressed, after all; his one success had been a travel book written a decade earlier, and everything else he'd tried since had failed to live up to that; he had recently failed to become a TV presenter – a job he'd thought beneath him but which he needed for the money (and so had been all the more galled when he hadn't been chosen) – and maybe, too, he'd finally admitted to himself he was never going to write his magnum opus . . .

Hell, his life just wasn't going anywhere special; people kill themselves for poorer reasons.

I reckoned the chances of him being under the waves somewhere improved significantly if he had committed suicide; he could have picked his spot to drive straight at a wall or a crash barrier, maybe on top of a cliff. Could be anywhere. I could think of a few places, further north in the Highlands, which would be perfect. If he'd tied himself to the bike somehow . . .

But why go to the effort of doing that in the first place? It wasn't as though there was some big insurance sum involved, or any funny business with wills or family money. Rory had inherited some capital when grandad died, held in trust until he was eighteen; he'd used that up travelling round India the first time, then lived off the success of *Traps* and – later – the declining advances and journalistic commissions he'd received after that. When he'd disappeared he'd had a small overdraft.

Maybe he'd been murdered. I'd thought of that years ago, even on the evening we'd heard he was missing. I had been playing down on the shore of Loch Gair with Helen and Diana Urvill, and when we came back for our tea there was a police car in the courtyard of the house.

A *police car*! I recall thinking, getting all excited.

Of course, in my fantasy I was the one who discovered Rory's evil murderer and brought him to justice, or fought with him and watched him fall off a cliff or into a combine harvester or under a steam-roller or whatever.

Only I couldn't see that anybody had had much of a motive. It had crossed my mind that it might have something to do with *Crow Road*; somebody wanted to steal the idea and keep Rory out of the way, but it wasn't even as though there was much to steal. Notes and poems; wow.

I stood up on the silent concrete block and dusted my hands off. The disappearing clouds were the colour of dried blood in a sky gone close to purple. More stars were coming out. A contrail blazed pink overhead, as a plane headed for America. I looked at my watch; I had to go. I'd told mum I'd be back for supper in an hour or so. We were expecting Lewis and Verity that evening; they were flying up from London, where Lewis had been working, and they would hire a car at Glasgow. They might be back when I returned.

*

'Shouldn't have mentioned you,' Uncle Hamish said, as I walked to the door of the dim bedroom. I turned back. He was still trembling. It hurt me to look at him, the way it hurts to hear nails scraped down a blackboard. 'Shouldn't have said anything about you, Prentice,' he said, the words whistling out between his clenched teeth. I could hear Aunt Tone's footsteps coming up the stairs in the hall outside. 'Shouldn't have said, Prentice; shouldn't have said.'

'Said what, uncle?' I said, hand on the door knob.

'That you were closer to me; that I'd won you, saved you from his heathen faith!' Uncle Hamish's eyes stared at me from a shaking, ash-grey face.

I nodded and smiled at him. 'Oh well,' I said. The door opened and I got out of the way of Aunt Tone, bearing pills and a glass of water. 'See you tomorrow, Prentice,' she whispered to me. She patted my arm. 'Thank you.'

'It's all right. See you tomorrow, Aunt Tone.'

Outside, on the landing, I looked down the stairs to where my mother was standing by the front door, putting on her jacket. I leant back against the closed bedroom door for just a second, and – looking at nothing in particular – said very quietly to myself, 'See?'

*

I went to the land-side edge of the concrete cube, and faced back at the remains of the sunset, trying to work out how I was going to feel seeing Lewis and Verity again, after the way I'd behaved at New Year. But search as I tried, I could find no trace of dread or jealousy; I was even looking forward to seeing them again. Something of the coldness that had settled over me in the last few days seemed to have spread to the way I felt about Verity. It felt like all my jealous passion had dissipated like the clouds overhead.

I thought about jumping down onto the beach, but that might have been asking for another family tragedy, so I climbed down, walked to the end of the shallow scoop of bay and set off through the grass by the side of the burn, heading back to Gallanach through the calm summer gloaming.

*

. . . He told us about the plants on the islands, too; how the open, glorious machair, between the dunes and the farmed land, was so dizzily sumptuous with flowers because it was the place where the acidic peat and the alkali sands produced a neutral ground where more plants could flourish in the sunlight. And just the names of those plants were a delight, almost a litany; marsh samphire, procumbent pearlwort, sand-spurrey, autumnal hawkbit, cathartic flax, kidney vetch, germander speedwell, hastate orache, sea spleenwort; eyebright.

We learned about the people who had made Scotland their home: the hunter-gatherers of eight or nine thousand years ago, nomads wandering the single great wood and stalking deer, or camping by the edge of the sea and leaving only piles of shells for us to find; the first farmers, just beginning to clear the land of the blanket of thick forest a few millennia later; the neolithic people who had built the tomb of Maes Howe before the pyramids were constructed, and the stone circle at Callanish before Stonehenge, in the thousand-year summer of the third millenium; then came the Bronze Age and Iron Age people, the Vikings and Picts, Romans and Celts and Scots and Angles and Saxons who had all found their way to this oceanically marginal little corner of northern Europe, and left on the place their own marks; the treeless slopes themselves, the roads and walls, cairns and forts, tombs, standing stones, souterrains, crannogs and farms and houses and churches; and the oil refineries, nuclear power stations and missile ranges, too.

He made up stories, about the secret mountain, and the sand-drowned forest, the flood that turned to wood, the zombie peat, and the stone-beings that drilled for air. Sometimes the location for, or the subject of, a story would have some basis in fact; the secret mountain was a real hill on which grew a flower that grew nowhere else in the world. There had indeed been great storms that had moved whole ranges of sand dunes inland, drowning forests, and villages ... And peat *was* un-dead, the surrounding rocks' acidity, the chill Atlantic airs and ever-likely rain conspiring to prevent the corpses of the dead plants from decomposing.

Other stories were pure fantasy, the result of a kind of child-like quality in him, I think. If you looked at certain stands of trees from a distance, especially in a glen, and when in full leaf, they did look like great bulging torrents of green water, bursting from the depths of the earth and somehow frozen. There was a sort of visual naïvety at work there that verged on the hallucinogenic, but it did, I'd argue, make a warped sort of visual sense. Magmites – the people who lived in the mantle of the earth, beneath the crust, and who were drilling up for air the way we were drilling down for oil – must just have appealed to that part of him that loved turning things around. Opposites and images fascinated him, excited him; magicked inspired absurdity from him.

I think Uncle Rory would have given almost anything to have tapped the lush gravidity of that source as well.

Telling us straight or through his stories, my father taught us that there was, generally, a fire at the core of things, and that change was the only constant, and that we – like everybody else – were both the most important people in the universe, and utterly without significance, depending, and that individuals mattered before their institutions, and that people were people, much the same everywhere, and when they appeared to do things that were stupid or evil, often you hadn't been told the whole story, but that sometimes people did behave badly, usually because some idea had taken hold of them and given them an excuse to regard other people as expendable (or bad), and that was part of who we were too, as a species, and it wasn't always possible to know that you were right and they were wrong, but the important thing was to keep trying to find out, and always to face the truth. Because truth mattered.

I suppose we all want to pass on our beliefs; they seem even more our own than the genes we transmit ... but maybe they are largely inherited too, even if sometimes what you inherit is the exact opposite – the reversed image of what was intended.

Sometimes I felt he was trying to brain-wash us; that he wanted us to be images of himself, thinking the way he thought, doing what he would have done, as if that would help him cheat death, make him less mortal somehow. Then all his parables and laws seemed like megalomania, and his reasoned certainties like dogma.

Other times he seemed genuinely altruistic, and on occasion I thought I could sense something like desperation in him, trying so hard to equip us as best he could for the vicissitudes of life, while the world changed all around us so fast that some of his ideas and theories – which had seemed so important to him in his life, and so crucial for us to know in turn – became irrelevant; were proved wrong, or just shown to be not so important after all.

My mother was different, and always had been. I don't think she ever really laid down the law like that, not even once; she just got on with things. We knew we were loved, and we knew when something we'd done was disapproved of, but she trained us by example, and let us make mistakes. The only idea I think she could ever be accused of trying to put into our heads was the welcome realisation that whatever happened to us, she'd be there.

I'm not sure that it wasn't the more effective method in the end, and – in its own way – more confident, too.

*

Half an hour after I'd left Darren's post-post-modernist concrete block I stood in the dusk light beneath the dun on the hill of Bac Chrom, within sight of the track at last, the lights of Slockavullin village beneath me, the eastern edge of Gallanach a thin grid of orange sparks to my right, the main road to Oban and the north busy with lights of white and orange and red, and the dark landscape below full of soft undulations, littered with chambered cairns, cup and ring marked rocks, standing stones, tumuli and ancient forts.

All the gods are false, I thought. Faith itself is idolatry.

I looked into that ancient, cluttered darkness, wondering.

CHAPTER
14

'So anyway, bro, how are things?'

Lewis shook his head slowly and deliberately. He held up his whisky glass and studied it from close range, focusing with explicit care, one eye at a time. I formed the impression he was attempting to fix the tumbler's image in his memory so he'd know the identity of the receptacle to blame come the following morning. I was so drunk at the time this actually seemed like quite a smart idea, and I would probably have attempted to do the same thing myself if I'd thought I was remotely capable of coordinating my hand, eyes and brain to that degree. The only reason I could get my drinking hand and my mouth in roughly the same place at approximately the same time at this stage in the evening was because I'd had so much recent practice at it. And even that comparatively simple system wasn't a hundred per cent any more; I'd missed my mouth twice already and spilled small amounts of whisky onto my chin and shirt. I'd carried it off with dignity, though.

Lewis looked like he was going to sleep. Either that or the superior intellect of the whisky glass had hypnotised him. I knew the problem.

'Lewis?' I said.

'Wha – what?' he looked at me, confused.

'I was saying,' I said. 'How are things?'

'Oh,' he said, and sighed. 'I don't know.' He frowned. 'Verity said to me just yesterday ... she said, "Lewis, I don't think we understand each other any more." '

'What did you say?' I sipped my whisky carefully.

'I said, "Whadaya mean?",' Lewis snarled.

Then he burst out laughing. It must have been infectious laughter because I started laughing too, and then we were both laughing, but we couldn't have been that drunk because we didn't over-do it. Five minutes later – well, maybe ten, absolute max – we'd stopped laughing almost entirely.

'Really?' I said, wiping my eyes.

Lewis shook his head. 'Na, course not. Everything's ... was pure dead brilliant, actually.'

'Good,' I said, and drank. I meant it too, but even as I realised that I meant it, I thought: ah, it's just the drink. I'll be worse in the morning. Still, I looked up at Lewis and said, 'I think I'm better.'

'Better ...?' Lewis began, giggling.

'Better than ... yesterday, Mr Creosote?' I started to laugh.

'Better get a bucket –' Lewis howled, but couldn't manage the rest of the line, because by then we were on the floor. I laughed until my ears hurt.

*

I stood beneath the larches in the rain, holding an umbrella, wearing a kilt and feeling a little self-conscious. The stand of dripping trees had gone yellow and dropped their needles during the last few weeks, turning the ground beneath them a dully shining blond that seemed like a tinted mirror to the ash-bright expanse of overcast sky. I touched the plain black obelisk, slick and cold in the chill October rain. Behind me, the noise from the marquee – an increasing choir of chattering voices – was slowly drowning the patter of the drizzle as it fell through the twigs and branches above onto the sodden ground; a busy, buzzy, shared excitement displacing what the solitary soul perceived as a sort of tranquil gloom.

What guy? I thought. What is Ash going to show me; who? (And already thought I might have guessed.) Shit, I didn't like the sound of this.

The rain came on harder and I listened to it drumming on the taut black skin of the umbrella, remembering remembering.

*

'Remember the River Game?'

'Remember the *Black* River Game?'

'Ha!'

We were digging dad's grave, waist deep in the rich black earth of Lochgair, partially shielded from the house by the dense mass of rhodie bushes and tall tangles of wild roses. Jimmy Turrock, the council workman sent from the municipal cemetery to dig the grave officially, and who'd been in the same class as Lewis at school, was sitting against the wheel of his miniature earth-mover, arms folded, head back, mouth open, snoring. That morning over breakfast, Lewis and I had decided we'd dig the hole ourselves. If nothing else, it would take our minds off our hangovers, which were industrial strength.

The River Game was something dad made up himself. He did it for Lewis and me. The first version was roughed out in a big sketch book, while he tinkered with the rules. When he was happy with it all, he got a big bit of white cardboard from a display company in Glasgow, drew out the playing surface, painted it, sprayed it with lacquer and edged the board with black tape. He'd bought various

Lego packs and made the ships and the cargoes out of those. The rules were typed, the cards were printed on labels and they were stuck onto the back of ordinary playing cards. We were presented with the result as a sort of extra present to be shared between Lewis and me for Christmas 1981. James was still a bit young; he'd only have chewed the ships and choked on the cargoes.

Lewis – who had asked for and got a television for his room, and a new Walkman – had the good grace to express gratitude. I was still celebrating having finally worn down dad's resistance to having a computer in the house, and was therefore far too busy kicking pixel and re-staging the attack of the Imperial AT-ATs on the rebel snow trenches to be bothered sparing more than the most cursory glance at what was, when all was said and done, a lump of amateurishly painted cardboard, a handful of non-motorised and very basic Lego bits, a few adulterated cards and what looked suspiciously like an exam paper. 'Yeah; great, dad. Got any more PP9 batteries for this wee car? The one out your calculator didn't last long,' was about as enthusiastic as I got about the game for most of the festive period.

Later, I deigned to play.

The River Game was based on trade; dad had wanted something that would distract us from all the war games Lewis and I played: soldiers, with our friends in the woods, battles with our toys, wars on friends' computers. He really wanted something non-capitalistic as well as non-military, but the River Game was going to be just his first effort; he would – he told us – be working on something much more right-on, once he had the time to spare. He'd see if we liked the River Game first.

You had two or three ships; you sailed them from a port on one side of the board to a port on the other side through what was either a big loch or lake choked with islands, or a piece of territory with an awful lot of waterways snaking through it, depending how you chose to look at it. You picked up cargo at the second port and sailed back. The cargo was worth a certain amount when you got back to your home port, and with the money you could buy more ships, configured for speed or capacity. There were at least half a dozen major routes from one port to the other, and basically, the shorter the route you took, the more hazardous it was; there were whirlpools, channels prone to rock falls, stretches of river where the sand-banks changed all the time, and so on. The weather had a chance to change every few moves, and how much the different types of cargo were worth depended on ... Oh, what your opponents had chosen to carry, what the weather was, whether the month had an 'r' in it; I can't remember it all.

It was quite a fun game, mildly addictive, with a reasonable balance of skill and luck, and Lewis and I eventually got quite a few of our friends playing it, but the truth is it improved dramatically when Lewis – with my help – drew up an extra set of rules which let you build *warships*!

We played that game for weeks before dad caught us at it in the conservatory, one rainy May day, and asked how come there were all these ships with funny-coloured cargoes clustered so close together and surrounded by wrecks where there were no hazards.

Oops.

We called it the Black River Game (Dad even objected to the title). He had been working on a new improved version of the original game that involved using some of the money to build railways across the board; you laid track, you built bridges, dug tunnels, coped with rock falls and marshes and recalcitrant land owners, and the first one to finish his or her railway was, in effect, the winner. But he stopped work on this sophistication when he found us acting out furiously destructive naval engagements on his painstakingly crafted board. He didn't take it away, though. I think for a while he was trying to develop another non-combative game that he'd defy us to turn martial, but it stayed at the development stage and never did see the light of day.

I stopped digging for a moment, wiped some sweat from my brow with the hem of my T-shirt, which was lying on the ground at the head of the grave. I leant on my shovel, looking at Jimmy Turrock's up-ended face while he snored. Lewis stopped digging for a moment too, breathing hard.

I said, 'We disappointed him, though, didn't we?'

Lewis shrugged. He took a handkerchief from his back pocket and wiped his face. 'Oh, Prentice, come on; boys will be boys. Dad knew that.'

'Yeah, but he expected better of us.'

'Dads always do, it's traditional. We turned out not too bad.'

'Neither of us did as well as he expected at Uni,' I said. I'd told Lewis – though not my mother – that I was fairly certain I'd failed my finals.

'Well, for a start, he didn't know about you,' Lewis said, scraping some earth off the blade of his spade. 'And he was smart enough to know degrees aren't everything. Come on, we're not in prison, we're not junkies and we're not Young Tories.' He waggled his eyebrows. 'It's no small achievement.'

'I suppose,' I said, and started digging again. (Pity he'd mentioned prison; another thing I hadn't told Lewis about was that I'd been nicked for shop-lifting. Not that I'd be going to prison, but it's the thought that counts.)

Lewis kept on digging. 'We could have done worse,' he insisted.

'We could have done better,' I said, shovelling another load of earth out of the pit.

Lewis was silent for a while, then said, quietly, 'Better than ... yesterday?'

I laughed in spite of myself (and in spite of the grave, and my aching head and still bruised heart). 'Shut up,' I said, 'please.'

Lewis shut up. I encountered another rhodie root and attacked it with the hacksaw, then took up the spade again, blinking sweat out of my eyes and waving a couple of flies away.

Lewis muttered almost inaudibly as he dug; 'It's only *waffer* thin ...'

We snorted and guffawed for a while, then took a break for yet more Irn-Bru, sitting at the edge of the grave, legs dangling into it, with Jimmy Turrock still blissfully – and vocally – in the land of nod across the grave in front of us.

I drank deeply from the bottle, passed it to Lewis. He finished it, grimaced, looked at the bottle. 'You know, I've finally realised what this stuff reminds me of,' he said, and belched heavily. I followed suit, trumping his sonorous burp with one that disturbed a few drowsy crows from nearby trees and even had Jimmy Turrock stir in his sleep.

'What?' I said.

'Chewing gum,' Lewis said, screwing the cap back on the bottle and chucking it into the grass near the council earth-digger.

I nodded wisely. 'Yeah, right enough.'

We sat there, silent for a while. I looked at Jimmy Turrock's spotty, open-mouthed face and his wispy red hair. His snores sounded like somebody forever trying to start a badly-tuned buzz-saw. I listened to it for a while, and watched a couple of flies buzzing around in a tight but complicated holding pattern in front of his mouth, as though daring each other to be the first to investigate inside. After a while they broke off, though, and settled for exploring the rough landscape of Jimmy's checked shirt. My head hurt. Come to that, almost everything hurt. Ah well, self-inflicted wounds.

Jimmy Turrock snored on, oblivious.

*

Lewis and Verity had arrived the night before, an hour after I'd got back from my sunset visit to Darren's sea-side sculpture. Their plane had been late and they'd had problems hiring the car, so they arrived nearly two hours later than we'd expected. Rather than phone from the airport, Lewis had hired a mobile along with the car but then when they'd tried to use it, it hadn't worked. The upshot was that mum and I had been getting into a fine panic, and I'd been dreading watching the news: '... and we're just getting reports of an incident at Glasgow airport ... details still coming in ...'

I mean, statistics tell you family tragedies oughtn't to come in quite such close succession, but Jeez; it gets to you, when somebody dies as unexpectedly as dad. Suddenly everybody you know seems vulnerable, and you fear for them all. Every phone-call sends your heart racing, every car journey anyone takes you want to say, Oh God be careful don't go above second gear have you thought of fitting air-bags is your journey really necessary be careful be careful be careful ... So there we were; mum and I sitting watching the television, on the couch together, side by side, holding hands tightly without even realising it and watching the television but not taking in what we were watching, and dreading the sound of the phone and waiting waiting waiting for the sound of a car coming up the drive.

Until I heard it, and leapt over the couch and hauled open the curtains and the car drew up and Lewis waved at me as he got out and I whooped, 'It's them!' to my mum, who smiled and relaxed and looked suddenly beautiful again.

There was a big three-cornered hug in the hall; then mum saw Verity standing by the door, taking a very long deliberate time to take her jacket off and hang it up; and so she was brought into the scrum too, and that was the first time, I realised, that I'd ever actually embraced her, even if it was just one arm round her slim shoulders. It was all right.

Then the phone rang. Mum and I jumped.

I got it. Mum took Lewis and Verity into the lounge.

'Hello?'

'Hello!' shouted a voice of immodestly robust proportions. 'To whom am I talking?' the booming voice demanded. It was Aunt Ilsa. We'd left a message at the only contact address we had for her, two days earlier. She was in Ladakh, a place so out of the way it would take several international airports, a major rail terminus and substantial investment in a network of eight-lane highways to promote it to the status of being in the middle of nowhere.

'It's Prentice, Aunt Ilsa.' There was a satellite delay. I was talking to what I suspected was the only satellite ground station between Islamabad and Ulaan Baatar. There was a lot of noise in the background; it sounded like people shouting, and a mule or something.

'Hello there, Prentice,' Aunt Ilsa bellowed. 'How are you? Why did you want me to call?' Perhaps, I thought, she'd been taking steroids and they'd all gone to her vocal chords.

'I'm . . . there's –'

'– ello?'

'– some bad news, I'm afraid.'

'What? You'll have to speak up, my dear; the hotelier is proving refractory.'

'It's dad,' I said, thinking I might as well get this over with as quickly as possible. 'Kenneth; your brother. I'm afraid he's dead. He died three days ago.'

'Good God! What on earth happened?' Aunt Ilsa rumbled. I could hear shouting. The thing that sounded like a mule went into what appeared to be a fit of coughing. 'Mr Gibbon!' roared Aunt Ilsa. '*Will* you control that fellow!'

'He was struck by lightning,' I said.

'Lightning?' Aunt Ilsa thundered.

'Yes.'

'Good God. Where was he? Was he on a boat? Or –'

'He was –'

' –golf course? Mr . . . hello? Mr Gibbon had a friend once who was struck by lightning on a golf course, in Marbella. Right at the top of his back-swing. Bu –'

'No; he was –'

' –course it was an iron.'

' –climbing,' I said.

' –number seven, I think. What?'

'He was climbing,' I shouted. I could hear what sounded like a fight going on at the other end of the phone. 'Climbing a church.'

'A *church*?' Aunt Ilsa demanded.

'I'm afraid so. Listen, Aunt Ilsa –'

'But he wouldn't be seen dead near a church!'

I bared my teeth at the phone and growled. My aunt, the unconscious humorist.

'I'm afraid that's what happened,' I said as evenly as I could. 'The funeral is tomorrow. I don't suppose you can make it, can you?'

There was a noise of some Ladakhian confusion for a while, then, *fortissimo*; 'I'll have to leave you now, Lewis –'

'Prentice,' I breathed through gritted teeth.

' –Our yak has escaped. Tell your mother our thoughts are with her at –'

And it was goodbye downlink.

I looked at the phone. 'I'm not sure you have any to spare, aunt,' I said, and put the phone down with a feeling of relief.

'I need a drink,' I said to myself. I strode purposefully towards the lounge.

*

Lewis had been marginally more sensible than me, later on, that night before the funeral; he'd gone to bed one whisky before I had, leaving me in the lounge alone, at about three in the morning.

I should have gone then too, but I didn't, so I was left to get morose and self-pitying, re-living another evening in this room, another whisky-connected two-some over a year earlier.

'But it's not *fair*!'

'Prentice, –'

'And don't tell me life isn't fair!'

'Aw, *think*, son,' dad said, sitting forward in his seat, clutching his glass with both hands. His eyes fixed on mine; I looked down, glaring at his reflection on the glass-topped coffee table between us. 'Fairness is something we made up,' he said. 'It's an *idea.* The universe isn't fair or unfair; it works by mathematics, physics, chemistry, biochemistry ... Things happen; it takes a mind to come along and call them fair or not.'

'And that's it, is it?' I said bitterly. 'He just dies and there's nothing else?' I could feel myself quivering with emotion. I was trying hard not to cry.

'There's whatever he left behind; art, in Darren's case. That's more than most get. And there's how people remember him. And there might have been children –'

'Not very likely in Darren's case, was it?' I sneered, grabbing at any opportunity to score even the smallest rhetorical point over my father.

Dad shrugged, staring into his whisky. 'Even so.' He drank, looked at me over the top of the tumbler. 'But the rest,' he said, 'is just cells, molecules, atoms. Once the electricity, the chemistry, stops working in your brain, that's it; no more. You're history.'

'That's defeatist! That's small-minded!'

He shook his head. 'No. What you're proposing is,' he said, slurring his words a little. He pointed one finger at me. 'You're too frightened to admit how big everything else is, what the scales of the universe are, compared to ours; distance and time. You can't accept that individually, we're microscopic; here for an eye-blink. Might be heading for better things, but no guarantees. Trouble is, people can't believe they're not the centre of things, so they come up with all these pathetic stories about God and life after death and life before birth, but that's cowardice. Sheer cowardice. And because it's the product of cowardice, it promotes it; "The Lord is my shepherd". Thanks a fucking lot. So we've to live like sheep. Cowardice and cruelty. But everything's okay, because we're doing the Lord's work. Fuck the silicosis, get down that mine and work, nigger! Aw shucks; sure we skinned her alive and threw her in the salt pans, but we were only doing it to save her soul. Lordy lordy, gimme that old time religion and original sin. Another baby for perdition ... Shit; original sin? What sick fuckwit thought that one up?'

Dad drained his glass and put it down on the glass-topped table between us. 'Feel sorry for yourself because your friend's dead if you want, Prentice,' he said, suddenly calm and sober. 'But don't try to dignify it with what's supposed to be metaphysical angst; it's also known as superstitious shit, and you weren't brought up to speak that language.'

'Well, thanks for the fucking censorship, dad!' I yelled. I jumped up and slammed my own glass down. The table top cracked; a single big flaw crossed, deep and green and not quite straight, like a dull ribbon of silk somehow suddenly embedded in the thick glass, from one edge of the table to the other, almost underneath our tumblers.

Dad stared at it then snorted, chuckling. 'Hey, yeah! A symbol.' He shook his head, glum, muttering as he sat back: 'Hate the fuckers.'

I hesitated, looking at the cracked glass, instinct – or training – telling me to apologise, but then did what I'd intended to do, and set about storming out of the room.

'Just fuck off, dad,' I said before I slammed the door.

He looked up, pursed his lips and nodded, as though I'd asked him to remember and put the lights out before he went to bed. 'Yup; okay.' He waved one hand. 'Night.'

I lay in bed seething, thinking of all the smart things I should have said, until I fell into a troubled sleep. I woke early and left before anybody else was up, driving my hangover back to Glasgow and shouting at caravans that got in my way, and that was the last meaningful, full and frank exchange of views with my dad that I ever had.

*

'I wish he hadn't died right now,' I said. I didn't look at Lewis. I was still looking at Jimmy Turrock, asleep against the wheel of his council digger. 'I wish I could – I wish we could have started talking again.' One of the two flies exploring the cotton landscape of Jimmy's shirt suddenly buzzed up to his forehead. His snoring hesitated, then went on. 'It was so stupid.' I shook my head. 'I was so stupid.'

'Yeah,' Lewis said after a bit. 'Well, that's just the way it is, Prentice. You weren't to know.' I heard Lewis sigh. 'There was something I wish I'd told him, too. Could have said, over the phone, end of last week.'

I looked at Lewis. 'Oh yeah?'

Lewis looked awkward. He crossed his arms and sucked at his bottom lip. He glanced at me. 'Were you really that ... you know; keen on Verity? I mean; are you?'

I kicked my heels against the sides of the grave, checked out a couple of tree roots we'd have to tackle before we could dig much deeper. I shrugged. 'Ah, it was just infatuation, I suppose. I mean, you know, I'll always like her, but ... all that stuff at New Year ... that was ... well, partly the drink, but ... mostly just sibling rivalry; sibling jealousy,' I said. We both grinned. He still looked awkward. This time, instead of sucking his bottom lip, he bit his top one.

I knew, just like that.

'You *are* getting married,' I said, gulping.

Lewis looked at me with wide eyes. 'She's *pregnant*?' I spluttered, contralto.

Lewis's mouth was hanging open. He shut it quickly. He wiped his face with the hanky; his eyebrows and eyes registered surprise.

'Um, both,' he said. 'Almost certainly.' He rung the hanky out over the hole, but it didn't drip (still, though, we would leave a fair amount of sweat in our father's grave).

Lewis nodded and his smile was flickering, uncertain. I hadn't seen him look so unsure of himself since the time when he was sixteen and I *almost* had him convinced the Boxer Rebellion had been about underpants.

'Fooof,' I said.

Seemed as appropriate as anything. I stared over at Jimmy Turrock, blinking.

Lewis was making a clicking noise with his mouth. He cleared his throat. 'Wasn't exactly planned, to tell the truth, but ... well; I mean, we both, you know; want it, so ... And, well, you know how I feel about marriage and all that stuff, but ... Fuck it, it just keeps things simple.'

He sounded almost apologetic.

I shook my head and, turning to him with a big smile, I said, 'You total bastard.' I put my hands on my hips. He looked concerned, but I guess my grin must have looked sincere. 'You total, complete and utter bastard; I hate you,' I told him. 'But I hope you're disgustingly happy.' I hesitated, just a little, then I hugged him. 'Obscenely happy,' I said. Probably have cried but I was pretty cried out by that stage.

'Man.' He breathed into my shoulder. 'I didn't know how you'd take it.'

'In the neck,' I said, pushing him away. 'Told mum?'

'Wanted to wait till after the funeral. Mind you, I was going to wait till then to tell you, too, so maybe Verity's spilling the beans right now.'

'So when's the big event?'

'Which one?' Lewis smiled; embarrassed, I do believe. He shrugged. 'We thought October, and the sprog thinks March.'

I let out a long, shuddering sigh, head feeling a bit swimmy. 'Marriage, eh?' I said, shaking my head again. I looked him down and up, hoisted one brow. 'Think you'll take to it?'

Lewis grinned. 'Like a lemming to water.'

I laughed. Eventually I laughed so loudly I woke Jimmy Turrock, who looked at me – sitting on the edge of my father's grave on the day of his burial, guffawing away fit to wake the living – with undisguised horror.

Like a lemming to water. Lewis knew as well as I did the maligned little buggers are perfectly good swimmers.

*

James arrived back about mid-day. He was ... well, pretty distressed, and all the fragile defences mum, Lewis and I had been constructing for the past few days – Lewis and I joking, mum staying quiet and keeping busy – crumbled. James seemed to blame dad, blame us; blame everybody. He was ugly with anger and he was like a racing outboard in the calm little pond we'd been trying to create; the house felt hellish and we all started snapping at each other. Outside, at the back of the garden, we could hear the council digger, excavating the rest of the hole. The engine revved up and down; it sounded like a machine snoring. James wished us all dead and ran up to his room and slammed the door. It was a relief to get back out to the grave and help Jimmy Turrock apply the finishing touches.

Then it was time to get showered and changed and wait for the hearse and the mourners. The funeral was suitably grim, despite the sunshine and the warm breeze. The words Lewis said over the grave sounded awkward and forced. Mum looked white as paper. James stood, mouth twisted, furious; he stalked off the instant the coffin touched the bottom of the grave. I threw some earth down onto the pale wood of the lid, putting back a little of what I'd helped dig out.

But it passed, and the people who came – a good hundred or more – were kind. We were busy in the house afterwards, feeding and watering them, and then that passed too.

*

My big brother and his intended asked me to be their best man the day after dad's funeral. I'd slept, fitfully, on the idea, but finally said yes. It had already been agreed between the two families that the wedding would be held at Lochgair. Lewis and Verity stayed another day after that, then left to go back to London so that Lewis could resume his gigs. He was almost ashamed when I saw him next, when he confessed that nobody thought his delivery had altered a bit; he was just the same on stage after dad's death as he had been before. The only thing he changed was that he stopped telling the joke about the uncle that dies in an avalanche on a dry ski-slope.

I told him not to worry about it; you had to be a different person on stage. The person he was up there would only change if he told a story about dad dying. Maybe a routine based on the idea of an atheist getting struck by lightning while climbing a church tower would be therapeutic for him, one day.

Lewis had the decency to be appalled at the idea.

Mum and I went through dad's papers, and were able, after Ashley's tuition, to work the computer and access the information it held.

Dad's will, which had been written at the time of Grandma Margot's death, had turned up in the strongbox hidden under the study floorboards. The strongbox had been no big secret; we all knew about it. It was just something to make any burglar's job more difficult. Mum had already seen the will when she had opened the strongbox the morning after dad's death, in the company of one of her friends from the village. She had only looked at the first paragraph, which confirmed that dad wanted to be buried in the grounds of the house. She'd been too upset to look at any more of it, and had put the will back under the floor.

So we opened the strongbox again, divided the papers, took a desk each, and looked at what we had. Mum had given the pile with the will in it to me. I read it first, and my heart sank after I'd scanned quickly through it and got to the end.

'Oh no,' I said.

'What's wrong?' she asked from the main desk in front of the window.

'It's the will,' I said, turning it over, looking at the last part again, looking over the page but still failing to find what I was looking for. 'It hasn't been witnessed or anything.'

Mum came over and stood behind me. She took the four hand-written sheets from me, frowning. Her skin was pale and her eyes looked dark. She wore black jeans and a dark blue shirt and her hair was tied back with a piece of blue ribbon. She handed the will back to me. 'I think it's all right,' she said slowly. She nodded. 'I'll call Blawke to make sure. He'll need to look at it anyway.' She nodded again, walked back to sit in her seat and started reading through the papers she had in front of her. Then she looked up at me. 'You phone him, would you?'

'All right,' I said and watched her bend to the papers again. She appeared to read for a few moments; I almost wanted to laugh, she seemed so unconcerned. She looked up again after a few seconds and just sat there, looking out through the open velvet curtains at the back lawn.

She sat like that for a full two minutes, unmoving, face unreadable. I smiled; I wanted to weep, to laugh. Eventually I said softly, 'Mum?'

'Hmm?' She turned to me, a hesitant smile on her tin face.

I held the will up from where it lay on the desk. 'This is dad's will.' I managed a smile. 'Don't you want to know what it says?'

She looked confused, then embarrassed, and put her hand to her mouth. 'Oh, of course. Yes. What does it say? Let's see.'

I pulled my seat over alongside hers.

*

The good lawyer Blawke opined that the will was perfectly legal; under Scottish law, a hand-written will did not have to be witnessed. He even came out and looked at it personally, which made two visits in one week. Truly our cup of honour ranneth over.

'Yes,' the lawyer Blawke said, reading the will as he sat in the front lounge. 'Well, I can't see anything wrong with it.' He looked unhappy. 'Unarguably his writing ...'

He studied it again.

'Yes,' he nodded, finally. 'I actually warned him against doing this, some time ago, but he seems to have got away with it.' The heron-like lawyer seemed sad that the will was litigation-proof. He smiled weakly, and mum offered to re-fill his whisky glass.

The will – expressed with a brevity and a lack of ambiguity the best lawyers would have been proud of, and the rest alarmed at – left the house, grounds and so on to mum, along with a two-fifths share in both the residue of dad's savings and any money made after his death. Lewis, James and I had one-fifth shares each. There were specified amounts to an almost archetypal spread of right-on causes: CND, Amnesty International and Greenpeace. Ten grand each. Ten grand! I was initially stunned, fleetingly annoyed, then ashamed, and later vaguely impressed. Mum just sighed, like she'd been expecting something like that.

I confess to having experienced a sensation of relief on discovering I had not been written out of dad's will; I wouldn't have blamed him. I think and hope that that feeling was engendered more by a desire to feel I'd still been loved – despite everything – than by avarice. I didn't think there would be all that much to go round after those donations, anyway.

Dad's agent, his accountant and the lawyer Blawke worked it out between them (though I checked their figures later). The good lawyer summoned us all to his office a fortnight after dad's death. Only James wouldn't come. Lewis flew up specially.

It had all, indeed, been just about as simple as it had looked. Blawke told us the sums involved and I was pleasantly surprised. The donations to right-onnery seemed much more in proportion now; I can only claim that I had spent (what at least seemed like) so long living on bread and cottage cheese and fish suppers in Glasgow – measuring my money in pennies and reluctantly-parted-with pounds – that I had an excuse for not being able to imagine that the thirty K dad had salved his conscience with when he'd written the will had actually been quite a small part of the modest fortune he'd built up over the years.

Dad had left over a quarter of a million pounds, after the government had taken its cut.

My share came to well over forty thousand smackeroos. The likelihood was that for the next few years at least, I'd bank about fifteen grand per annum, which might or might not tail off, abruptly or gradually, depending on how well dad's stories held up against the tests of time ... not to mention the likes of Thomas the Tank Engine, the Teenage Mutant Ninja Turtles, and whatever other delights the future of the children's fiction market held.

Anyway, suddenly I was, if not quite within range of the mountains of Rich, certainly well into the foothills of Comfortable. It entirely made up for the discovery, a few days earlier, that the estimate I had made of my chances of passing my final exams had been considerably more accurate than any of the conclusions I had drawn in the course of them. I had distinguished myself by failing, a result the department prided itself on happening only rarely.

My initial reaction had been to cut my losses on the honours front and see if I could take an MA instead; a re-sit would mean a whole extra year at university. But that sentiment had only lasted for a day. In the turmoil of feelings and fortunes dad's death had produced, the prospect of another year's study, with the framework and time scale that would provide – especially if I applied myself, as I thought I would now be able to – seemed suddenly a relief rather than a chore.

At any rate I still had a little time to decide what to do, and the money would make the choice easier. A return to Glasgow need not now also mean a return to the joys of sharing a flat with Gav, Aunt Janice, and their sonically extrovert passions.

We stood, the three of us, mum, Lewis and I, on the pavement outside the Main Street offices of the lawyer Blawke, in Gallanach.

I was still thinking, *Forty grand?* and trying not to look too stunned. Mum was slowly putting on her black leather gloves.

Lewis and I looked at each other.

Lewis wasn't doing too badly himself, down in London, but he too had looked pretty surprised when Blawke told us the sums that were heading our way. Mum hadn't really shown any reaction; she'd just thanked the good lawyer politely and asked after his wife and family.

'Fancy a drink?' Lewis said to me. I nodded. I felt slightly faint. 'Mum?' Lewis said.

She looked round at him, small and neat in her dark blue coat. It was a bright, warm day and I could see the silver in her dark brown hair. She looked so delicate. I felt like I was in my early teens again, mum seemingly getting shorter and shorter with each season that passed.

'What?' she said. I found myself sniffing the air; I was downwind, but all I could smell was Pear's soap and Lewis's Aramis. Mum seemed to have stopped wearing perfume.

'I think a drink, to steady our nerves,' Lewis said to her.

'Aye,' mum said, looking thoughtful. She gave a thin wee smile and nodded at us. 'Aye, he'd have liked that.'

And so we went to the Lounge of the Steam Packet Hotel, looking out over the tourist-crowded pier and the packed car park. The water was bright amongst the hulls of the moored yachts, and the Mull ferry was a black shape in the distance, heading away.

We drank vintage champagne and fifteen-year-old malt. I suspected dad would have approved.

*

Lewis had to head back to London that night. Mum and I had been busy for a week, tidying up all the loose ends an unexpected death leaves, especially when the deceased is somebody as socially and professionally entangled as dad.

Then mum had gardened while I'd sorted through less urgent papers; printing out everything on the disks, searching out all the rest of the stuff on stories, and sending it – or copies – to dad's literary executor, his editor in London. I had become modestly PC-computerate (Ashley had given me a grounding in the basics, though PCs were not really her field). I'd even learned how to change the toner cartridge in the photocopier without making a mess.

On one of the earliest computer disks dad had used, dated shortly after he'd finally joined the computer age and bought the Compaq, in 1986, I found copies of some of Rory's poems; dad must have been putting them onto the system from the drafts Rory had left. I printed those out. It didn't look like dad had been very impressed with the poems, or he'd presumably have transcribed them all onto the computer (they weren't on the hard disk or backed up onto another floppy either – another indication my father had regarded them as relatively unimportant), but at least I again had something Rory had written. I was still hoping more of Rory's papers would surface somewhere.

Dad's old diaries turned up in a cardboard box at the back of a cupboard. Mum glanced at them, handed them to me. They looked pretty boring, frankly: 'M&I to Gal; shops, prom walk, back; did VAT.' and 'me Glasg car 1040 LHR 1315 F'furt; late, missed others. tel. L'gair Din in room, TV' were two of the more exciting and informative entries for last year. Dad's ideas books – A4 pads, usually – were where the interesting stuff was. We'd look at the diaries later.

Then, one day, at the back of dad's oldest and most decrepit filing cabinet, I'd discovered treasure. It was in the form of three tatty, falling-apart Woolworth folders stuffed with old exercise books and shorthand-pads, bulging manila envelopes stuffed with old tickets, timetables and assorted scraps of paper, as well assorted sheets of paper of various sizes, some stapled together, most loose, some typed and some hand-written, and all the work of

Uncle Rory. There was one sealed envelope, too.

Here were all the poems I'd seen before and more, typescripts of all the travel pieces, and the progenitor of *Traps*; Rory's India journal; tattered, battered, stained and torn and littered with doodles and little hand-drawn maps and sketches. A fold-out map of India was stapled to the inside back cover of the first exercise book, and on it Rory's spastically erratic route round the country was picked out in blue Biro. The back cover of the second book was covered with little faded train and bus tickets, attached to the cheap, fibrous blue paper with rusting staples. The last exercise book had only one ticket stapled to the rear cover: Rory's Air India ticket home. Some of the pages were stained with what looked like saffron, and I swear one book still smelled of curry.

I'd sat down there and then and begun to read, flicking through the thin, brittle pages of the journal, smiling at the spelling mistakes and the awkward, amateurish drawings, looking for passages I remembered.

I'd looked at the other stuff too, and found one play – another martial yarn about death and betrayal, and apparently nameless – which contained not only the passage about the fate of soldiers which I'd read in the delayed train back in January, in the rain on the line at the back of Crow Road, but which also ended with the lines I'd heard first a few weeks before that, in Janice Rae's flat. In Janice Rae's bed, in fact.

And all your nonsenses and truths, I'd read.

'Your finery and squalid options,' I'd said quietly, to myself.

Rory's climax-delaying mantra was all there, right down to the last, three-word line. But, given the situation the narrator was in at that point, the lines took on an extra resonance, and an irony I had not been able to appreciate before. The section was circled with red ink and under that last line was written a note in large letters:

USE FOR END CR.

Gradually though, as I'd looked at it all, my feeling of quiet elation faded as I realised there seemed to be nothing else in any of the folders that seemed to relate to *Crow Road*. All I found was one cryptic note scribbled in pencil on the inside flap of what looked like the most recent of the three tatty files. It said:

"CR: !B killsH!!? (save)
(jlsy? stil drwnd)"

B and H. I vaguely remembered these abbreviations from the notes I'd lost. I shook my head, cursing my own idiot negligence, and Uncle Rory's frustrating delight in abstract abbreviation.

... Jlsy. Well, *that* was a recurring theme in Rory's work.

... Stil drwnd. But Hell, I thought H got crshd btwen crge & tr!

'Fuck it,' I'd said, and closed the file. I'd turned the bulky, heavy, sealed manila A4 envelope over in my hands for a while, then opened it. Computer disks. (That was a surprise. As far as I knew Uncle Rory had never possessed a computer.) Eight big floppy computer disks each in their own brown paper envelopes. Hewlett-Packard Double-sided Flexible Disks, Recorder # 92195A (Package of 10 disks). Well, yes; of *course* there would have to be two missing. They were numbered 1 to 8 in black felt-tip, and that was the only indication they weren't brand new and unused. The write-protect holes were still taped over.

I'd looked over at the Compaq, sitting on dad's desk, but the big, somehow already old-fashioned looking disks wouldn't even have fitted into the Compaq's drive if you'd folded them in half.

Making a mental note to call Ashley in London about the disks some time, I put them back in their manila envelope and the envelope back in its faded folder, and spent a fair while after that just leafing through Uncle Rory's India journal, smiling sadly at it all and becoming almost as willingly lost in it as it seemed Rory had in the pungent, teeming wastes of India itself ... until mum called me from the foot of the stairs, and it was time for tea.

*

A few days later, I'd travelled back up to Glasgow by train; we'd got all the immediate matters regarding my father's death sorted out. It had been a perfect day; summer-warm and spring-fresh, the air winter-clear, the colours more vivid than in autumn.

I'd felt a sort of shocked calm settle over me as I'd travelled, and been able to forget about death and its consequences for a while.

The familiar route had looked new and startling that day. The train had travelled from Lochgair north along the lower loch, crossed the narrows at Minard, and stopped at Garbhallt, Strachur, Lochgoilhead and Portincaple Junction, where it joined the West Highland line and took the north shore of the Clyde towards Glasgow. The waters and the skies blazed blue, the fields and forests waved luxuriously in a soft, flower-scented breeze and the high hill summits shimmered purple and brown in the distance.

My spirits had been raised just watching the summer countryside go past – even the sight of the burgeoning obscenity of the new Trident submarine base at Faslane hadn't depressed me – and when the train had approached Queen Street (and I'd been making very sure I had all my luggage with me) I'd seen something sublime, even magical.

It had been no more than that same scrubby, irregularly rectangular field of coarse grass I'd sat looking at so glumly from the delayed train in the rain that January. Then, the field's sodden, down-trodden paths had provided an image of desolation I had fastened onto, in my self-pity, like a blood-starved leech onto bruised flesh.

And now the field had burned. Recently, too, because there was no new growth on the brown-black earth. And yet the field was not fully dark. All the grass had been consumed save for a giant green X that lay printed, vivid and alive, on the black flag of the scorched ground. It was the two criss-crossing paths through the wedged-in scrap of field that still shone emerald in the sunlight. The flames had passed over those foot-flattened blades and consumed their healthier neighbours on either side while they themselves had remained, made proof against the blaze and guaranteed their stark survival just by their earlier oppression.

I'd stood there, in the act of taking my bags down from the luggage rack. And smiling to myself, I'd said, 'See?'

*

Dad hadn't specified any memorial; all his will had said was that he wanted to be buried somewhere in the grounds of the house. There was some discussion, and eventually mum decided on a plain black marble obelisk with his name and the relevant dates on it.

I stood there, dressed in my slightly preposterous Highland finery, half-way through this wedding in the rain and remembering the funeral in the sunlight a season earlier, and I thought again how damn ugly that dark monument had turned out, then I shook my head and turned, and walked back to the lawn and the marquee. The ground was squelchy and I had to tread carefully to avoid getting mud on my thick white socks. The kilt swung against my knees.

I wondered if Ash was back yet.

*

'What what what? Come on, Prentice! My first chance to snog tongues with your brother as a married man and you're dragging me away waving . . . ha! ha! *Where* did you get *these*?'

The hall of the Lochgair house was swarming with people, crowding in, laughing, brandishing presents, shaking hands, demanding drinks, slapping Lewis on the back, hugging Verity, talking quietly to my mother, wandering through the press of people greeting each other and bumping and smiling and talking away and generally making me feel I might have arranged the reception line a little better; it had been a relief to spot Ashley struggling through the crowd at the front door, remember the computer disks, dash upstairs to get them and then down to intercept her and haul her into the lounge.

'Found them in dad's study,' I told Ashley, holding the disks out to her. She put a gaily wrapped package down on a chair, took one of the big disks from me and slid it out of its paper wrapper, grinning.

Then she looked up, frowned and stepped back, arms wide. 'Prentice,' she said, voice deep with censure. 'You haven't said how stunning I look yet. I mean, come now.'

Ash wore loose black pants and a shimmery silver top; hair back-swept and piled up. The glasses had been replaced by contacts. 'You look great,' I told her. I nodded at the disk in her hand. 'Think you can do anything with that?'

Ash sighed and shook her head. 'I don't know. Haven't you got the machine they ran on?'

I shook my head. 'I asked my mum about it; she thinks they might have been Rory's.'

'That long ago, eh?' Ash tapped the disk sleeve dubiously, as though expecting it to crumble to dust at any second.

'I didn't know until today he even had one; I mentioned to mum I'd ask you about these, and she said Rory did have a computer, or a word processor or whatever. Got it out in Hong Kong about a year before he disappeared.'

'Hong Kong?' Ash looked even more dubious.

'Some sort of … copy; clone? Of an … well, mum said an Orange, but I guess she means Apple. She remembers him complaining that it – or the program or whatever – didn't come with proper instructions, but he got it to work eventually.'

'… Uh-huh.'

'Dad left it in the flat Rory shared in Glasgow when he took Rory's papers away. Wouldn't have a computer in the house, at the time.

'Wise man.'

'I'm going to try and track down the guy Rory shared the flat with, but I reckon the machine's been chucked out or whatever long ago, and I just thought, could you ... you know ... you might know somebody who perhaps could be able to ... to decode what's on there?' I shrugged, suddenly feeling awkward. Ash was now looking at the disk as though fully anticipating that creepy crawlies were about to start emerging from it. 'I mean,' I said, clearing my throat, suddenly feeling hot and sweaty. 'There might not be anything on them at all, but ... I just thought ...'

'So,' Ash said slowly. 'Let me get this straight: you don't know the machine, but it's probably some ancient nameless Apple clone from the dark grey end of the market, almost certainly using reject chips; it probably had a production run that lasted until the first month's rent fell due on the shed the child-labourers were assembling them in, it used an *eight-inch drive* and ran what sounds like dodgy proprietorial software with more bugs than the Natural History Museum?'

'Umm ... Yeah. That about sums it up.'

Ash nodded a few times, lips tight, weighing the disk in her hands. 'Right.' She nodded at the ones I still held. 'Okay. Can I take these?'

'Sure.' I handed them to her and she turned for the door.

'See you later,' she said, heading into the crowded hall. I went after her; she was excusing her way to the front door.

'Ash!' I said, squeezing through after her. 'Not now! Come and enjoy the party!'

'Don't worry,' she said, glancing back. 'I shall return. I'll drop these at home so I don't forget to take them back to London; I know people who might be able to help ... but I just remembered I forgot something; something for you. Left it at mum's.' She looked out the door; it was starting to rain. 'Shit.'

There was an old giant brass cartridge case by the hall hat stand which held our assorted umbrellas and walking sticks; I lifted a brolly from it. Ash turned to me, a worried expression on her face as she said, 'I saw that guy again. I'll show you. Give my present to the happy couple!'

'What guy –?' I said, but she was already sprinting through the still-arriving guests for the little red 2CV, parked a good fifty metres down the car-crowded drive, the disks held tight to her chest. I watched her high-heels flashing over the gravel, and the other guests turning to look at her, then there were more people to greet and hands to shake.

I took the brolly myself eventually and went for a walk up the garden to dad's grave, just to get away from the crowds for a bit.

*

Back in the house, I dodged one of the waitresses from the Lochgair Hotel, carrying a huge tray with champagne flutes out of the kitchen towards the marquee; I waved at mum, splendid in black with white stripes and standing talking to Helen Urvill, and went through to the hall. I put the umbrella in the old cartridge case. Then I thought maybe I should open it out and dry it, like you're supposed to, so I hauled it out again and left it opened in the hall.

'Prentice,' Verity said, coming down from upstairs.

She was enfolded in white silk; a creation of some clothes-designer friend of hers in Edinburgh. Technically it was a blouse, medium-length skirt and jacket, but when she wore it it looked like a single piece, and handsome it was too. She was hardly showing yet, but the outfit would anyway have disguised an almost full-term pregnancy. She wore white leggings, and high-heels that made her taller than me. She also wore the fulgurite necklace; mum had guessed both that Verity would want to wear it, and that she might think it best not to, in case the association hurt, so she'd made a point of telling Lewis she thought Verity ought to wear it, if it suited the outfit she had chosen. Verity's hair was as short-cropped as ever, but she looked none the worse for that, and the little white micro-hat she wore, complete with thrown-back, white fish-net veil, sat well on her too. She came up to me, took me by the shoulders and kissed me on the cheek.

'That was a great speech; thanks,' she said. She was still holding my shoulders, and squeezed them. She looked the way you're supposed to look, both when you're pregnant and on the day of your marriage; glowing, radiant, suffused with joy. Still had perfect skin. She put on a convincingly upper-class English accent as she said, 'You've been en ebserloortly soopah byest men, my deah.'

I put my hands lightly on her still slim waist and made a small bowing motion. 'Any time,' I said, and grinned.

She laughed, shaking her head. She stepped back, folded her arms, looked me up and down and said, 'And so smart.'

I curtsied, fluttering my eyelashes.

She laughed again and held out her hand. 'Come on; let's find my husband. He's probably flirting with the bridesmaids by now.'

'I thought that was my job,' I said, taking her arm in mine as we went towards the rear of the hall. I heard the front door open behind us. I turned and looked, stopped, then turned back to Verity. 'I'll take a rain check on that, shweetheart.'

Verity smiled at Ashley Watt, shaking a glistening waterproof she'd just taken off, and nodded. 'Well, there's appropriate, today.' She winked at me and walked off.

Ashley met me at the foot of the stairs, brandishing a VHS cassette. 'Got it. Take me to your video.'

'Walk this way,' I told her, heading up the stairs two at a time.

'Do I get to look up your kilt?' she said from behind.

'Not if you're lucky.'

I switched the lights on in the study; we tended to keep the curtains closed. There was a TV and video in the study. I switched it all on and put the cassette in the machine.

'Cool,' Ashley said, standing hands on hips in the middle of the study, heels neatly over the centre of dad's Persian rug, bunned hair directly beneath the big brass and stained-glass light fixture, hanging extravagantly beneath an ornate plaster ceiling rose. She swivelled, surveying the book-case walls, the maps, the prints and paintings and various interesting bits and pieces scattered around shelves, tables, desks and the floor.

'Bit cluttered for my taste,' I said, starting the tape and watching some end-credits. 'Dad found it conducive enough.'

'Fast forward,' Ash said. The screen scrolled quickly, then the BBC Nine O'Clock news started flashing before us. Ash turned away, so I let it roll.

Ashley crossed to an over-crowded book case; there was an empty crystal bowl perched on a pile of loose papers on top of the book case, and Ashley tapped the bowl very gently with one finger. She took her hand away, held it in the air near the ice-coloured ornament, and clicked her fingers. She bent her head towards the bowl, seemingly listening for something. I frowned, wondered what she was up to.

She turned and faced the bowl, went 'Ah,' in a high-pitched voice, then listened again, head tilted, smiling this time.

'Ashley, what exactly are you doing?'

She nodded at the bowl. 'Crystal; you can make it ring by producing the right noise.' She grinned like a little girl. 'Good, eh?' She looked behind me. 'That's you,' she said, nodding at the screen.

I hit Play. We stood, watched.

'... talked to Rupert Paxton-Marr of the *Inquirer*, one of the journalists held by the Iraqis, and asked him how he'd felt,' said the BBC man in Amman.

I couldn't resist a thin smile, one journalist asking another how he felt.

Rupert Paxton-Marr was a tall, blond, blue-eyed man with exactly the jaw-line I'd have chosen for myself, given the opportunity; sickeningly handsome, he had an accent to match. 'Well, Michael,' he said. ('Air, hair lair,' I said to myself.) 'I don't think we were really in much danger; clearly international attention has fixed on Iraq, and I think they knew we knew that, and accepted we were ... weren't a threat to them. Umm ... our driver had taken a wrong turning, and that was that. Of course, one does remember what happened to, ah, Farhzad Bazhoft, but I don't think you can let that stop you; in the end one has a job to do.'

'Thank you, Rupert. And now, reporting fr –'

I hit Stop and turned to Ashley, standing beside me. She was still looking at the blank screen where the little green zero symbol sat in one corner, wobbling almost imperceptibly. She had sucked her cheeks in and her lips were pursed. There was a whoop of laughter from somewhere downstairs. Ash nodded slowly, looked at me. 'That's ma boy,' she said.

'You're sure about that?' I said.

'I'm sure.' She looked serious. She looked pretty good, too, now I looked properly; I couldn't remember ever seeing Ashley wearing make-up, and you'd have thought that not having had the practice she'd be crap at it, but she looked great; maybe a little over-enthusiastic with the dark stuff round the eyes, but why quibble? She nodded. 'Don't look at me like that; I'm really sure.'

'Sorry. I believe you,' I said. I spun the tape back, to play it again. Ashley put one hand on my arm and rested her chin against the shoulder of my Prince Charlie jacket.

'Turn the sound down,' she said. 'That guy's voice is like chewing on silver paper.'

I turned the sound down. The noise of people laughing and talking in the marquee came through the double glazing and the heavy burgundy of the velvet curtains. I heard an amplified voice outside say, 'Testing.' It was probably Dean Watt; he and his band had been hired by Lewis and Verity to play during the afternoon (for the evening they'd booked a more traditional wheech-your-partner fiddle and accordion band).

I ran the clip again. 'Definitely, officer,' Ashley said, tapping the top corner of the TV. 'Recognise him anywhere, even with his clothes on.'

I switched the TV off and ejected the cassette. I stood for a moment, rubbing my chin.

'Whoops,' Ashley said, and delicately rubbed a little of that transferred make-up from the black shoulder of my jacket.

I waited till she'd finished, then went to dad's desk, unlocked a lower drawer and took out a slide tray; one of those plastic things that holds a few hundred transparencies. 'So, when you saw this guy, Paxton-Marr,' I said, opening the tray and putting the lid on the desk, 'in Berlin, in this hotel, in the jacuzzi ...' I looked up at Ashley, standing sceptically by the TV, one elbow resting on it as she watched me. 'What was the hotel called again?'

'I told you,' she said. 'I can't remember. I called June, and neither could she. It's probably the only place she ever stayed and forgot to nick a towel or yet another emergency sewing kit or whatever.' Ash shrugged. 'Frankly, Prentice, I was stoned out of my brains most of the time I was there. All I can remember is it had a big pool in the basement with a jacuzzi at one end, and they did really good breakfasts.' She sighed. 'Excellent hopple-popple.' Her eyebrows flicked once.

'Hopple-popple?' I grimaced.

'Scrambled eggs,' Ash smiled. 'Take me to Berlin and I'll find it for you. It was somewhere near the zoo.'

I put the tray down on the desk, went over to Ashley, holding out a little piece of cardboard; it was the front cover off a book of matches, torn off the piece that held the matches.

'Wasn't the Schweizerhof, was it?' I asked her.

She looked steadily into my eyes for a little while, then took the piece of card, looked at it and turned it over.

'Twenty-seven eleven eighty-nine,' she muttered. She nodded and handed me the cover back. 'Yeah,' she said, frowning. 'Yeah; it was. That was the place.'

I put the little torn bit of cardboard back in the slide tray. It was the second last one, out of about forty of them.

'What's the significance of the date?' Ashley asked, coming over to the desk. Outside, I could hear the sound of an electric guitar chord and a few drum beats.

'I think that was when dad received it.' I picked the latest torn cover out of the tray. 'This one arrived just after he died.' We both sat on the edge of the desk; Ashley looked at the little piece of glossy cardboard.

'Woo,' she whistled. 'Amman Hilton. Spooky, or what?'

'Yeah. Spooky as fuck,' I said, tapping the cover with one fingernail. 'And I'm *sure* I recognise that guy Paxton-Marr, too. From Glasgow, or Edinburgh, or here. I've met him. In the flesh, I think.'

Ash put her elbow on my shoulder. 'And damn firm, tanned flesh it was too, let me tell you,' she said.

I looked into those grey eyes, smiling. 'But not as firm and tanned as your programmer from Texas.'

Ash laughed, skipped off the desk. 'Systems Analyst. And you're right; they breed them bigger and better in Texas.'

Music started up in the marquee. *Kiss The Bride.* Ash stood on the Persian rug again, putting one hand to her ear. 'Hark; it's young brother and his pals.' She frowned. 'Doesn't sound like a Mark E Smith or Morrissey track to me.' She shook her head. 'Tsk. How are the mighty fallen.' She put her head down so that, if she'd been wearing glasses, she'd have been looking over them at me. 'Want my advice?'

'Mm-hmm,' I nodded.

'Come on and dance. We can sort – or you can sort – this out later, when you've had time to think.' She struck a dramatic, arguably dance-inspired pose and held out one hand. 'Hey baby, let's boogie!'

I laughed, shut the match-book covers away and locked the desk drawer.

'That's it, laddy,' Ashley said, holding my arm as we went to the door. 'You put that key in yer sporran.'

'At least I know down there it's safe from interference,' I told her. She smiled. I locked the study door too.

'By the way, by the way,' Ash muttered into my ear as we headed along the landing for the stairs, 'got a gramme of the old Bogotá talcum powder about my person. Fancy a toot, later?'

'What, the real thing?' I grinned. 'I thought speed was your poison.'

'Normally,' she nodded. 'But this is a special occasion; I splashed out.'

'You wee tyke,' I said. I pulled her closer as we walked, held her tight. 'You just stick with me, kid, all right?'

'Whatever you say, ma man.'

We did kick-steps down the stairs. Risky, when you're wearing a kilt as it is meant to be worn, but invigorating.

*

I danced with Ashley, and with Verity, and with Helen Urvill, and with mum, cutting in on Lewis after he'd persuaded her onto the floor. Most of the time though she just sat, surrounded by family and friends, watching us all with an expression that, to me at least, spoke of a kind of stricken joy; a surprise that such pleasure could still exist – and she feel even remotely a part of it – when dad was not here to share in it all.

I am not a natural dancer but I made an exception for Verity's wedding. I grooved and sweated and drank and made a point of doing the old red blood cell impression, circulating; bathing in, soaking up and transmitting onwards the oxygen of family news and gossip from cell to cell . . .

'Where are you off to next, Aunt Ilsa?' I asked the lady in question, during our waltz. Aunt Ilsa – even larger than I remembered her, and dressed in something which looked like a cross between a Persian rug and a multi-occupancy poncho – moved with the determined grace of an elephant, and a curious stiffness that made the experience a little like dancing with a garden shed.

'Canada, I think, Prentice. Churchill, on Hudson's Bay. To observe the arctic bear.'

I confess I had to re-process that sentence a couple of times as we danced, before working out that she did not intend to study the region naked (an image I found rather alarming), but was merely using a more pedantically accurate term for a polar bear.

'Super.' I smiled.

*

Uncle Hamish sat at the table with the rest of the family and got slowly drunk. I danced with Aunt Tone, and asked after her husband's health.

'Oh, he's getting better all the time,' Aunt Tone said, glancing at him. 'He hasn't had the nightmares for weeks now. I think going back to work helped him. Fergus was very understanding. And he's had a lot of long chats with the minister. People have been very kind, altogether. You haven't talked to him?' Aunt Tone looked at me critically.

'Not for a bit.' I gave her a big smile. 'I will, though.'

*

Uncle Hamish watched the dancing. He lifted his whisky to his lips, sipped at it, then shook his head with such slow deliberation I caught myself listening for the creak. 'No, Prentice. I have been foolish, and even vain. I did not pay sufficient heed to the scriptures. I thought that I knew better.' He sipped his whisky, shook his head. 'It was vanity; my theories, my beliefs about the hereafter; vanity. I have renounced them.'

'Oh,' I said, disappointed. 'No more anti-creates?'

He shook, as though a chill had passed through him. 'No, that was my mistake.' He looked at me straight for the first time. 'He punished both of us, Prentice.' Uncle Hamish flicked his gaze towards the roof of the marquee. 'Both of us,' he repeated. He looked away again. 'God knows we are all his children, but he is a strict father, sometimes. Terribly, terribly strict.'

I put my head on my hand and looked at my uncle as I considered this idea of God as child-abuser. Hamish started to shake his head again before he'd sipped his whisky, and I experienced a brief feeling of excited horror, waiting for the resulting catastrophe; but he just stopped in mid-shake, sipped, then shook his head slowly again. 'Aye; a strict father.'

I patted his arm. 'Never mind.' I said, helpfully.

*

I danced with Aunt Charlotte, Verity's still-handsome and determinedly superstitious mother, who told me that the newly-weds would surely be happy, because their stars were well-matched.

Exhibiting a generosity of spirit I rather surprised myself with, I agreed that certainly the stars in their eyes seemed to augur well.

*

I bumped into the smaller than life-size Mr Gibbon near the bar at one point; I was in such a gregarious, clubbable mood I actually enjoyed talking to him. We agreed Aunt Ilsa was a wonderful woman, but that she had itchy feet. Mr Gibbon looked over at Aunt Ilsa, who had – I could only imagine by force – got Uncle Hamish up for a dance. Together they were having the same effect on the dance floor as a loose cannon manned by hippos.

'Yes,' Mr Gibbon said, sighing, his eyelids fluttering. 'I am her kentledge.' He smiled at me with a sort of apologetic self-satisfaction, as though he was the luckiest man alive, and tip-toed off through the crowds with his two glasses of sherry.

'Kentledge?' I said to myself. I'd have scratched my head but my hands were full of glasses.

*

'Prentice. Taking a breather too, eh?'

I had stepped outside the marquee for a breather, late on, after the hoochter-choochter music started and the place got even warmer. I looked round in the shadows and saw Fergus Urvill, Scottishly resplendent in his Urvill dress tartan. Fergus came into the light spilling from the open flap of the marquee. He was smoking a cigar. The rain had ceased at last and the garden smelled of earth and wet leaves.

Fergus glittered; crystal buttons sparkled on his jacket; black pearls of obsidian decorated his sporran, and the skean dhu stuck into the top of his right sock – a rather more impressive and business-like example of the traditional Highland-dress knife than mine, which looked like a glorified letter opener – was crowned with a large ruby, glinting in the light against the hairs of his leg like some grotesquely faceted bulb of blood.

'Yes,' I said. 'Yes, getting my breath back.'

Fergus looked into the marquee. 'They're a handsome couple, eh?'

I glanced in, to see Lewis and Verity, hand in hand, talking to some of Verity's relations. Lewis had changed into a dark suit and a bootlace tie; Verity wore a dark skirt and long, gold-coloured jacket.

I nodded. 'Yes,' I said. I cleared my throat.

'Cigar?' Fergus said, digging an aluminium tube from one pocket of his jacket. I shook my head. 'No,' Fergus said, looking at me tolerantly. 'Of course you don't, do you.'

'No,' I said. I grinned inanely.

I was surprised at just how uncomfortable I felt in his presence, and how hard it was both to work out precisely why I felt that way, and to disguise the fact. We talked for a little while. About my studies; going better now, thank you. And about flying. Fergus was learning to fly; up at Connel, the air field a few miles north of

Oban. Oh, really? Yes. Hoped to be going solo by the end of the year, if all went according to plan. He asked me what I thought of the Gulf crisis and I, quailing, said it all kind of depended how you looked at it.

I think I made him feel as awkward eventually as I had from the start of the conversation, and I took the opportunity of a new reel beginning to head back into the marquee, to join in another swirling, riotous dance.

*

Ashley, Dean and I retired to my room in the house during the supper interval, while people got their breath back and the band – four oldish guys mysteriously called the Dougie McTee Trio – tried to get drunk.

We snorted some coke, we had a couple of Js, and in response to a single question from Dean, I told them both all about the River Game; its history, every rule and feature, a thorough description of the board, an analysis of the differing playing styles of myself, Lewis, James, dad, mum and Helen Urvill, some handy tips and useful warnings, and a few interesting excerpts from certain classic games we'd played. It took about ten minutes. I don't think I repeated myself once or left anything out, and I finished by saying that all of that, of course, wasn't to mention the secret, banned version; the Black River Game.

They both stared at me. Dean looked like he hadn't believed a word I'd said. Ashley just seemed amused.

'Aye. Good coke, isn't it?' she said.

'Yep,' Dean said, busy with mirror and blade again. He glanced at his sister and nodded at me. 'For God's sake, Ash, stick that number in his mouth and shut him up.'

I accepted the J with a smile.

*

The three of us kick-stepped down the stairs.

'Hoy, all that stuff about that game,' Dean shouted as we three swung into the marquee, where an Eightsome Reel of extravagant proportions and high decibel-count was in its Dervish phase. 'That gospel, aye?'

I frowned deeply as I looked at him. 'Oh no.' I shook my head earnestly. 'It's *true*.'

*

Later, I sat alone at a table, quietly drinking whisky, watching them all. I'd lowered my head; one hand lay flat, palm-down, on the table. I felt very calm and deadly and in control; shit, I felt like I was Michael Corleone. The tunes and laughs and shouts washed through me, and the people, for that moment, seemed to be dancing about me, for me. I felt . . . pivotal, and drank a silent toast to Grandma Margot. I drank to my late father. I thought of Uncle Rory, wherever he was, and drank to him. I even drank to James, also absent.

James was coming down only slowly from his peak of anger. Even now, he was still so sullen and difficult to get on with that it had almost been a relief when he'd said he didn't want to be involved in the wedding. He'd gone to stay with some school pals at Kilmartin, a little north of Gallanach, for the weekend. I think mum was unhappy he wasn't here today, but Lewis and I weren't.

I drank some more whisky, thinking.

A marriage.

And a little information.

Not to mention more than a little suspicion.

All it had taken was one blurred face, glimpsed far away by somebody else, seen soundless for a second on a fuzzed TV in a noisy, crowded, smoky pub in Soho, one Friday evening – just one tiny example of all the inevitable, peripheral results of a confrontation in a distant desert – and suddenly, despite all our efforts, we were back amongst the bad stuff again; shrapnel from the coming war. Although, of course, I couldn't be sure.

Mum went past, dancing with Fergus Urvill, who was sweating. Mum looked small, next to him. Her expression was unreadable. *Jlsy*, I thought, and drank to Uncle Rory.

*

Lewis and Verity left at midnight in a taxi. None of that let's-make-a-mess-of-the-car nonsense for them. The taxi was supposedly heading for Gallanach; only mum and I knew they were actually booked into the Columba in Oban, and heading for Glasgow and the airport tomorrow.

The four-man trio played; the dancing continued. Mum left with Hamish and Tone; she was staying with them tonight. I was in charge of the house. I danced until my legs ached. I talked until my throat hurt. The band, and the bagpipe players who'd joined in with them, stopped playing at about two. Dean and I fed some home-made compilation tapes through the PA, and the dancing went on.

Later, after everybody had either left or crashed out in the house, Ash and I walked out along the shore, by the calmly lapping waters of Loch Fyne, in a clear, cool dawn.

I remember babbling, high and spacey and danced-out all at once. We sat and stared out over the satin grey stretch of water, watching low-flying seagulls flapping lazily to and fro. I treated Ash to bits of Uncle Rory's poetry; I knew some of it by heart, now.

Ash suggested heading back and to the house, and either having some coffee or getting some sleep. Her wide eyes looked tired. I agreed coffee might be an idea. The last thing I remember is insisting I had whisky in my coffee, then falling asleep in the kitchen, my head on Ash's shoulder, mumbling about how I'd loved dad, and how I'd loved Verity, too, and I'd never find another one like her, but she was a heartless bitch. No she wasn't, yes she was, no she wasn't, it was just she wasn't for me, and if I had any sense I'd go for somebody who was a kind and gentle friend and who I got on well with; like Ash. I should take up with Ash; I should fall in love with her, that's what I ought to do. Only if I did, I muttered into her shoulder, she'd be sure to fall for somebody else, or die, or get a job in New Zealand, but that's what I ought to do, if only things worked that way ... Why do we always love the wrong people?

Ash, silent beneath me, above me, just patted my shoulder and laid her head on mine.

*

Mum woke me in the late afternoon. I moaned and she put a pint glass of water and two sachets of Resolve down on the table near my head. I tried to focus on the water. Mum sighed, tore the sachets open and tipped the powder fizzing into the glass.

I checked things out with the one eye that would open. I was in my room at Lochgair, on my bed, still mostly clothed in shirt and kilt and socks. My head felt like it had been recently used for a very long and closely contested game of basketball. Somebody had stolen my real body and replaced it with a Prentice-shaped jelly mould packed full of enhanced-capacity pain receptors firing away like they were auditioning for a Duracell commercial. Mum was dressed in faded jeans and an old holed sweater. Her hair was tied back and she wore violently yellow rubber kitchen gloves which were doing horrible things to my visual cortex. A yellow duster dangled from her hip pocket. I couldn't think what else to do, so I moaned again.

Mum sat down on the bed, put a hand on my head and ran my curls through her rubber-clad fingers.

'What's that you've got in your hair?' she said.

My brain cells? I wondered. Certainly it felt like they'd been squeezed out of my ears. Damn rim-shots. Not that I could share this insight with my mother, for the simple reason that I couldn't talk.

'What is it?' mum said. 'This black stuff?' She rubbed her fingers together in my hair, the rubber gloves squeaking horribly. 'Oh, stop moaning, Prentice. Drink your water.' She sniffed at her fingers. 'Hmm,' she said, rising and heading for the door. 'Mascara, eh?'

I looked up, monocular, at the closing door, grimacing.

Massacre?

CHAPTER
15

I sipped my Bloody Mary, looking down at huge, white, piled-up clouds so bright in the mid-day sunshine they looked yellow. The plane had just levelled out and there was a smell of food; they were serving lunch further forward in the cabin. I watched the clouds for a moment, then looked at my magazine. I was on my way to London, a couple of torn-off match-book covers in my pocket, hoping to confront Mr Rupert Paxton-Marr.

*

'Thanks mum ... Ash?'

'Yo, Prentice. How's it hanging?'

'Oh, plum.'

'Still wearing the kilt, eh? Look, I've had some word from –'

'How about you?'

'Eh?'

'How are you?'

'Oh, rude health. Verging on the obscene. Listen; my computer wizard's been in touch.'

'What? About the disks?'

'Cor-rect.'

'What's on them? What do they day? *Is* there anyth –'

'Hey ... hold your horses. Had to get the stuff *to* him first.'

'Oh. Where is he?'

'Denver.'

'*Denver*?'

'Yup.'

'Denver *Colorado*?'

'... Yes.'

'What, in America?'

'Yeah, Northern Hemisphere, The World, The Solar System ...'

'Okay, okay, so he's ... hey, is this your Texan programmer? Has he moved states?'

'Systems Analyst, for the last fucking time, Prentice, and no, it isn't him; just a guy I exchange E-mail with sometimes.'

'Right. And he's got the disks?'

'No, of course he hasn't got the disks.'

'What? Then –'

'He has the information that was held on them. Well, on the one that held anything. Seven were blank; not even formatted.'

'Ah, right. I see ... so what does it say? What is on it? Was it all Rory's –'

'It's a little more complicated than that, Prentice.'

'Oh.'

'I've got a message on my screen here from him. Thought you might be interested in it.'

'Oh; you're at work. Hey, have you seen the time? You're working late, aren't you?'

'Yes ..., Prentice. Do you want to hear the message?'

'Will I understand it?'

'You'll get the gist of it.'

'Okay.'

'Right. I quote: "I thought your man up there in the misty glens might like to know –"'

'"Misty glens"? That's sounds a bit patronising.'

'Prentice; shut up.'

'Sorry.'

'"... might like to know what our game plan is with respect to your word-processed file(s). As we don't yet know what geek program this mutant *No-namo*-brand clone was running, we have had to resort to extreme measures to access the data. Dr Claire Simmons of London University, who picked up the disks, will use a vintage Hewlett Packard TouchScreen (which has compatible eight-inch drives) in the establishment's Museum of Computing to extract the raw binaries, *sector by sector*, praying all the while that somebody has posted an ediger to Usenet that she can use to strip off the physical addressing; she will then attack the content one word at a time, swapping bytes as needed and inverting bits if none of it looks like ASCII, stripping the eighth bits if they're in the way or un-encoding the lot if we can't do without them, and unload the result to a Prime mini-computer (another indestructible antique) somewhere on the campus network. She moves all this to her Iris, double-encrypts it and E-mails it via Internet (off JANUS or BITNET to nsfnet-relay.ac.uk, probably) via Cornell to an account I'm not supposed to have on the Minnesota Supercomputer Center's Cray-2 (currently the biggest and quickest compute-server short of a Connection Machine at the high end, so I might as well use *it* to do the decryptions and perhaps take my own first whack at demangling before moving the data along). From there I download via a dedicated T3 line to an SGI 380SX-VGX at one of AT&T's Bell Labs (the one in Boulder, I think – another unofficial account) from where I can further download – and filter out certain offending control characters – to a Mac II at my office. Then I dump the results onto a floppy and bike them home to tinker with in my basement, which is where the *hard* work starts." ... Get all that, Prentice?'

'Yeah. Basically what he's saying is, it's a piece of piss.'

'Absolutely. A doddle.'

'Great. So when can we expect to see some results?'

'No idea. Don't forget the guy's doing it for fun, and he's a busy man. No promises, but he sounds confident. I'll call him in a week if he doesn't get in touch first.'

'Tell him I'll fax him a crate of champagne or something.'

'Certainly. So, when ...? Ah shit. Fucking decollator's jammed again. Gotta go attend the print, Prent.'

'Okay. Bye. Oh, and thanks.'

'...'

*

I now had a better idea of what Rory had been doing in the days before his disappearance. It looked like he had been working on *Crow Road* between the time he'd come back from London after seeing his friends and the evening he disappeared, on the motor bike he'd borrowed from his flat-mate. That was what he'd been doing, stuck in his room in the flat in Glasgow; finally actually writing something on his bizarre contraption of a computer.

He'd done it, he'd stopped writing notes and started on the work itself.

I'd talked to a retired policeman who at the time had looked – briefly – into what had happened to Rory. The police hadn't come up with anything; they'd interviewed Janice Rae, and Rory's flat-mate Andy Nichol, and looked at the papers Rory had left with Janice. There was no suicide note, so they'd decided the papers weren't relevant. Apart from checking the hospitals and eventually listing Rory as a Missing Person, that had been that.

The only useful information I'd got from the police was that Rory's flat-mate had left local government and joined the civil service a few months after Rory had disappeared. I'd tracked Andy Nichol down at a tax office in Plymouth and called him there, but apart from saying he'd heard a lot of keyboard-clattering noises coming from Rory's room during the days before Rory had borrowed his bike and disappeared, he'd only been able to confirm what I already knew. He did say he'd tried working Rory's Neanderthal computer after dad had said he could have it, but he couldn't make the beast work; he'd sold the machine and the two blank disks that had come with it to a friend in Strathclyde University. It had been chucked out years ago.

... Whatever; after those few days work, Rory had suddenly upped and offed, and never came back. Maybe the stuff on the disks would give me a clue why he'd suddenly done that. If there *was* anything useful there; that clattering noise didn't prove anything... I'd seen *The Shining*.

*

The cloud cover started to break up over the midlands; I chomped through my lunch. The starter was smoked salmon. I thought of Verity and Lewis, on honeymoon in the Bahamas, and – with just a tinge of sadness – silently wished them well.

*

I saw Ashley come into the pub. She stood near the door, looking round, that strong-boned head swivelling, those grey eyes scanning. She didn't see me on the first sweep; I was mostly hidden by other people. I watched her take a couple of steps forward, look round again. She was dressed in a dark, skirted suit, under the old but still good-looking jacket I remembered her wearing at Grandma Margot's funeral. Her hair was gathered up and tied; she wasn't wearing her glasses. Her face looked tense and forbidding. She seemed harder, more capable and more self-contained than I recalled her being in Scotland.

In those few moments, in the noise and smoke of a pub by the river, a quarter mile from the Tower, in the great, cruel, headless monster that was London after a decade of Hyaena rule, I wondered again at my own feelings for Ashley Watt. I knew I didn't love her; she didn't make me feel anything like the way I had about Verity, and yet I'd been – I realised – looking forward to seeing her, and now that I had seen her, just felt, well . . . happier, I guess. It was all puzzlingly simple. Maybe – to lapse into the humdrum continuum for a moment – she was the sister I'd never had. I remembered the mascara mum had discovered in my hair after the wedding, and wondered if the position of honorary sibling was one Ashley would entirely welcome.

I tried to remember Ashley's tone when I'd rung her, a couple of days ago, to say that I was coming down (this about a week after I'd had my own personal info-dump on the workings of the world computer network). I had already called Aunt Ilsa and arranged to stay with her and Kentledge Man, and I'd wondered at the time if I'd detected the merest hint of reproach in Ashley's voice when I'd told her I would be staying in deepest Kensington. At any rate, she'd told me there was a sofa-bed and a spare duvet of indeterminate tog value at the flat she shared in Clapham, in case Aunt Ilsa went on some sudden expedition to Antarctica and forgot to tell her Filipino maid, or whatever. She'd added that the two girls she shared with really wanted to meet me (I felt pretty sure the person they really wanted to meet was Lewis).

I raised my hand as Ashley's gaze passed again over where I stood; she caught the movement, and that city-hard expression changed instantly, relaxing and softening as she smiled broadly and walked over.

'Hiya, babe.' She punched my shoulder, then gave me a big hug. I hugged right back. She smelled of *Poison*.

'How are you?' I asked her.

She put one fist on her hip and held her other hand up in front of my face, fingers spread. 'Drinkless,' she grinned.

*

'You got *off*?'

'Yeah,' I said, swirling the remains of my pint round in my glass.

Ash shook her head. 'I thought you were going to plead guilty.'

'I was,' I confessed. I shrugged, looked down. 'I got a smart lawyer. She said it was worth fighting. Ended up in a jury trial, eventually.'

Ash laughed. 'Well done,' she said. She lowered her head until she could look into my eyes. 'Hey, what's the matter?'

'Well,' I said, trying not to smile. 'I *did* do it after all; it seems wrong I got off because I dressed in a suit and I could afford an expensive advocate and people in the jury had heard of dad and felt sorry for me because he'd died. I mean if I'd come from Maryhill and I wasn't reasonably articulate and didn't have any money, even if I *had* just forgotten I hadn't paid for the book, I bet everybody would have told me to plead guilty. Instead, thanks to the money, I had an advocate who'd probably make God look just a little lacking in gravitas, and discovered a talent for lying through my teeth that promises a glittering career as a *Sun* journalist.'

Ash leaned conspiratorially forward over the small table we were crouched round, and quietly said, 'Easy, boy, you're on their turf.'

'Yeah,' I sighed. 'And don't drink the tap water.' I looked around the place, all crowds and smoke. The English accents still sounded oddly foreign. 'No sign?' I asked.

Ash looked round too, then shook her head. 'No sign.'

'You sure he drinks here?'

'Positive.'

'Maybe he's been sent away, back to the Gulf.'

Ash shook her head. 'I spoke to his secretary. He's having some root canal work done; he's here till the end of next week.'

'Maybe I should have just arranged to see him.' I sighed. 'My new-found talent as a con-man might have come in useful. I could have said I had pictures of Saddam Hussein torturing a donkey or something.'

'Maybe,' Ash said.

We had discussed this sort of thing. Ash's first idea was simply that she should ring him up, tell him she'd seen him on television and heard he worked in London; she was here too, now, and did he fancy a drink sometime? But I wasn't sure about this. If he'd been reluctant to give Ash his name in Berlin, and thought even there that he'd already said too much, he might be suspicious when she rang up. So I felt; so my – by now rather paranoid – feelings suggested. A chance meeting seemed more plausible, or at least it had when I'd been talking to Ash from dad's study in Lochgair. Now I wasn't so sure.

'How's your wizard?' I asked her.

'Eh?' Ash looked confused for a moment. 'Oh; Doctor Gonzo? Still working on the files. They weren't just weird shit, they were corrupted weird shit; where did your dad keep those things; inside a TV? But anyway; he's still hopeful.'

'Doctor *Gonzo*?' I said, tartly.

'Don't look like that, Prentice,' Ash chided. 'This guy's knocking his pan in for you for nothing. And he has got a doctorate.'

I smiled. 'Sorry.'

'Oh, and supposing the good Doctor can decipher all that corrupted crap you presented him with, what format do you want these files in eventually anyway, you ungrateful wretch?'

'How d'you mean?'

'I mean what program do you use on the Compaq?'

'Oh, Wordstar,' I nodded knowledgeably.

'Version? Number?'

'Ah . . . I'll have to come back to you on that one. Look; just ask him to print it out and send it to me. Would that be okay?'

She shrugged. 'If you want. Or you could get a modem; E-mail's about a zillion times faster.'

'Look, I'm still not all that comfortable around computers that don't come with a joystick and a "fire" button; just . . . just ordinary airmail and real paper will be fine.'

Ash grinned, shook her head. 'As you wish.' She stood up. 'Same again?' she asked, clinking my glass.

'No,' I said. 'I'll have a half.'

'Any particular sort?'

'Na, anything.'

I was alternating pints and whiskies on principle; they keep giving you your old glass back down here.

I watched Ash weave her way to the bar.

I still felt nervous about meeting this guy Paxton-Marr, but all-in-all, I told myself, things weren't so bad. Those of us most affected by dad's death were – with the possible exception of Uncle Hamish – bearing up pretty well, I might yet find out what Uncle Rory had written, I didn't have to worry about money, I had no criminal record, and I was being a good young(ish) adult again, attending diligently to my studies. Mostly I stayed in Glasgow during the week, and went back to Lochgair at weekends, unless mum – sometimes accompanied by James – came to stay with me. I had got filthy drunk just once since dad had died, and then with good reason; it had been the day Thatcher resigned. Bliss was it, etc., even if the Tapeworm Party was still in power.

The lawyer Blawke had found me a place to rent for the year I needed to be in Glasgow. It was part of the property of a Mrs Ippot, who'd died rich but intestate at a sourly ripe old age, having throughout her life promised part, or all, of her sizeable fortune to various individual relations and combinations of relations within her extensively and antagonistically divided family, in a blizzard of contradictory letters, and with what appeared to be a profound lack of consideration for the litigious chaos that was bound to ensue. Mrs Ippot, in short, had been the sort of client probate lawyers have wet dreams about.

My own theory was that Mrs I had actually thoroughly detested every single one of her relatives, and had hit on a nicely appropriate way of confounding all of them. By Jarndyce out of Petard, Mrs Ippot's lawyer-infested legacy had ensured that her rebarbatively consistent family would suffer years if not decades of self-inflicted hatred and frustration as the increasing legal fees gradually corroded the monies she had left; a tortuously slow method of telling your relatives from beyond the grave exactly what you thought of them that makes giving all the loot to a cats' home look positively benign in comparison.

And so I stayed in the late Mrs Ippot's enormous town house in Park Terrace, overlooking Kelvingrove Park and the River Kelvin running through it. The museum and art gallery sat red, huge and stately to the left, its sandstone bulk crammed with the silt of time and human effort, while on the hill to its right, skirted by the black outlines of trees, the university soared with self-impressed Victorian fussiness into the grey autumnal skies, positively exuding half a millennium's experience in the collation and dissemination of knowledge.

The high ceilings and vast windows of Mrs Ippot's former home appeared to have been the work of an architect anticipating the design of aircraft hangars; the interior was cluttered with paintings, rugs, chandeliers, life-sized ceramics of the smaller big cats, small statues, large statues and objets d'art of every imaginable description, all interspersed with heavy, dark, intricately gnarled wooden furniture that gave the appearance of being volcanic in origin. The house's inventory – drawn grimly to my attention by a spotty clerk who obviously resented the fact I was younger than he was – came in three volumes.

I christened the place Xanadu, but never did find any sleds.

My friends, of whom I saw less these days, suggested parties when they first heard about the place. On seeing it, they usually agreed with me that to mount a serious whoopee on the premises would be to invite cultural catastrophe on a scale usually only witnessed during major wars and James Last concerts.

One of my pals – graduated, employed; moving on to better things – sold me his old VW Golf, and I drove down to Lochgair most weekends, usually on a Thursday night as I didn't have any classes on a Friday. James and I helped mum, who was redecorating the house. She was talking about knocking down the old conservatory and putting in a new one, perhaps covering a small swimming pool. She had also formed the idea of building a harpsichord, and then learning to play it. We took tea at the Steam Packet Hotel on occasion, and James kept an Ordnance Survey map on which he inked in all the walks we undertook, on the hills and through the forests around Gallanach.

Mum and I had started going through dad's diaries. Some were pocket size, some were desk diaries; a couple of early ones were effectively home made. They went back to when he'd been sixteen. I'd suggested Mum read them first in case there was anything embarrassing in them, though I think in the end she just skimmed them. They weren't the stuff of scandal, anyway; the entries we'd sampled when we first discovered them in the box at the back of the cupboard were about as revealing as they ever got; really just appointments, notes on what had happened that day, where dad had been, who he'd met. If there was a single indiscretion recorded there, I never found it. The same went for any but the most basic observation or idea; he'd kept those in the A4 pads.

It was at the bottom of the box containing dad's diaries, in an old presentation tin which had held a bottle of fifteen-year-old Laphroaig, that I found Rory's diaries; little pocket books, usually a week-per-two-pages. Dad must have filed them separately from the other papers.

I got very excited at first, but then discovered that Rory's diaries were even more sparse – and considerably more cryptic – than my father's, with too many initials and acronyms to be easily understood, and too full of week- and even month-long gaps to form a reliable impression of Rory's life. There was no diary for the year he disappeared. I'd tried to make sense of Rory's diaries, but it was uphill work. The entry for the day of my birth (when Rory had been in London) read:

K r; boy 8£. *Prentis*?!? M ok Eve, pub.

The entry for the next day read: "vho" in shaky writing, and that was all. "ho" and "vho" (or sometimes h.o. and v.h.o.) often followed entries regarding pubs or parties the night before, and I strongly suspected they stood for hungover and very hungover. K meant Kenneth and M Mary, pretty obviously. ok was itself (its opposite was nsg, which stood for Not So Good; he'd spelled it out the first time he'd used it, following a "48hr h.o." after Hogmanay the previous year). A small r meant "rang"; a telephone call. And I had indeed weighed in at eight pounds.

I found a few mentions of "CR" – I even recognised some of the notes I'd read the previous year; he must have jotted them down in his diary first before transferring them to his other papers. But there was nothing to provide any new answers.

The one thing that stayed with me as a result was not a solution to anything, but rather another mystery. It was on a page at the back of the last diary, the diary for 1980; a page headlined by the mysterious message:

JUST USE IT!

... a page covered with notes, some in pencil, some in ball-point, some in very thin felt-tip, but a page which held the only instance anywhere in all the papers I had where Rory had made an effort not just to alter or score out some words or letters, but to obliterate them. It read:

show Hlvng pty wi C?" (whoops): 2 close??

The symbols just before the H and C had been obliterated by a heavy black felt-tip marker, but the original note had been written with a ball-point, and by holding the page up to the light at just the right angle, I could see that the first letter had been an F and the second an L.

F and L. Those abbrevations didn't turn up anywhere else in Rory's notes for either *Crow Road* or anything else that I knew of. Rory *never* crossed stuff right out; he only ever put a line through it.

Why the big deal with the felt-tip? And who were F and L? And why that "whoops"? And what was too close to what?

I found myself cursing Uncle Rory's inconsistency. F in the diaries sometimes meant Fergus (aka Fe), sometimes Fiona (also Fi), and sometimes Felicity, a girl Rory had known in London, also recorded as Fls, Fl or Fy (I guessed). The only L in the diaries seemed to be Lachlan Watt, though he – mentioned on the rare occasions when he came back to visit from Oz – was LW, more usually.

Some nights at Lochgair, after long evenings spent poring over those little, thin-paged diaries on the broad desk in dad's study, trying to make sense of it all, and failing, I'd fall asleep in my bed with the symbols and acronyms, the letters and numbers and lines and boxes and doodles and smudges all swirling round in front of me even after I'd put the light out and closed my eyes, as though each scribbled sign had become a mote of dust and – by my reading – been disturbed; lifted from the page and blown around me in a vortex of microscopic info-debris, chaotic witnesses of a past that I could not comprehend.

I found one thing which – after a little puzzled thought – I could comprehend, but which I hadn't been expecting, in Uncle Rory's 1979 diary. Stuck to the inside back cover with a yellowing stamp hinge was an old, faded, slightly grubby paper Lifeboat flag, without its pin.

The sentimentalist in me was reduced almost to tears.

*

In Glasgow I had taken to sitting in churches. It was mostly just for the atmosphere. Catholic churches were best because they felt more like temples, more involved with the business of religious observance. There was always stuff going on; candles burning, people going to confession, the smell of incense in the air . . . I'd just sit there for a while, listening but not listening, seeing but not seeing, there but not there, and finding solace in the hushed commerce of other people's belief, absorbed in the comings and goings of the public and the priests, and their respective professions of faith. A father would approach me, now and again . . . but I'd tell him I was just browsing.

I walked a lot, dressed in my Docs and jeans and a long tweed coat that had been my father's. Uncle Hamish sent me thick letters full of original insights into the sacred scriptures, which I dipped into sometimes when I couldn't sleep. I never got further than page two of any of them. I frequented the Glasgow Film Theatre, and installed a video and a TV in the lounge. I bought a ghetto-blaster which usually lived in the flat's kitchen (and so became known as the gateaux-blaster) but which I would take walkabout with me sometimes, at least partly for the weight-training which transporting the brute from room to room provided. I'd stand and look at time-dark paintings, or run a finger over the line of some cold, marble animal, while the tall, glittering rooms resounded to the Pixies, REM, Goodbye Mr Mackenzie, The Fall and Faith No More.

*

'He's here,' Ash said, coming back with the drinks. She sat down.

I looked around. I saw him after a while. A little shorter and a little younger-looking than I'd expected, from the tape I'd seen. He was talking to a couple of other guys; they were all dressed in grey trench coats, and one had put a hat down on the bar that at least looked like it ought to be called a fedora. I wondered if the other two were also journalists.

Rupert Paxton-Marr; a foreign correspondent, his meticulously-trained, razor-sharp mind ready in an instant to describe a place as 'war-torn' and bring home to us all events and disasters in far away places, to talk of people tearing at the rubble with their bare hands, to reveal that only with dawn did the full extent of the devastation become apparent, and even – in the very best traditions of British popular journalism – to ask people who'd just seen their entire family duly butchered, burned, crushed or drowned, *How do you feel?*

Ash seemed contemplative, eyeing me with a steady gaze. 'Well . . .' I said, feeling my heart beat faster and my palms start to sweat. I took the two torn match-book covers out of my pocket. 'Think I'll go see what he has to say for himself.'

'Want me to come?' Ash started to move in her seat.

I shook my head. Then bit my lip. 'Shit, I don't know. All the way down here, I was just going to go up to him and say, "You send these to my dad?", but now I don't know. It feels a bit weird.' I looked over at the three men. 'I mean,' I laughed. 'They're even wearing trench-coats!'

Ash looked briefly over too. 'Hey,' she said, smiling. 'They're on wine; they're not just knocking back whiskies and heading off. They'll be here a while yet. Sit and think for a moment.'

I nodded, took a deep breath and drank some whisky.

I thought about it some more. Then I said, 'Okay. Maybe we should go together. You could sort of introduce . . . I could go out and pretend to just come in . . . Hell; I could just tell him the truth . . . I don't know.' I closed my eyes, appalled at my own lack of gumption.

Ash got up, putting a hand on my shoulder. 'Sit here. I'll tell him I've just recognised him. You come over later; just mention the match-books. Don't show them, not at first. How does that sound?'

I opened my eyes. I shook my head and said, 'Oh, I don't know, good as anything.'

'Right.' Ash went over to the men. She pulled something from the back of her head as she went, and shook her long fawn hair down. It was the length of the jacket. I smiled to myself. That's my girl, I thought.

I saw them look her up and down. Rupert smiled, then looked mystified as she talked, animated, hands waving. Then he laughed, his tanned, handsome face smiled and he looked her up and down again. The expression changed just a little, though, after that, as though something else had occurred to him. He looked a little more wary. So it appeared to me, anyway. He held out one hand, seeming to make introductions. Ash nodded. He pointed to the bar; she shook her head, then nodded back at me.

Rupert Paxton-Marr gazed above me, then dropped his gaze. He looked at me then back at Ashley. She was talking to him. His expression went through puzzlement, maybe concern, then went wary again, finally cold, studiously expressionless. He nodded, leaning back against a post supporting the front of the bar. Ash glanced back at me, her eyes opening wide for an instant, then she turned back to the men.

I started to get to my feet.

Rupert's expression didn't change as I walked over. Two couples passed in front of me, weaving their way between the tables. When they'd passed, Rupert was already on his way to the door, mouth smiling broadly, one hand alternately waving and pointing at his watch as he backed off. By the time I got to where Ash and the two guys in the trench coats were standing, he'd made it out to the street.

I stood there, frowning at the door Rupert Paxton-Marr had exited through. Something about the way he'd moved as he'd backed off had left me with an uncanny feeling of déjà vu.

Ash looked surprised. So did the two guys. One of them looked me up and down. 'Jesus Christ,' he said. 'How'd you do that? Usually only women with toddlers screaming "Daddy!" in tow have that sort of effect on Rupe.'

Remember, remember, I thought to myself, and smiled. I turned to the man and shrugged. 'It's a gift,' I told him.

'He owe you money or somefink?' the second man said. They were both about thirty, lean and clean-cut. Both were smoking.

I shook my head.

Ash laughed loudly. 'No,' she said, holding her hands out to the two men. 'It's just that the last time we all met up, we all got filthy drunk – didn't we, Presley? – and Rupert thinks Presley here –'

Presley? Ash was indicating me when she said the name. *Presley*? I thought.

'. . . thinks that Rupert tried to proposition him. Which he didn't, of course, but it was all a little embarrassing, wasn't it, dear?' Her happy, smiling face looked demandingly at me.

I nodded dumbly as the two men looked at me as well.

'Embarrassing,' I confirmed.

Ash was beaming smiles all over the place like a laser gone berserk. 'I mean,' she said, tossing her hair. 'Rupert isn't gay, is he? And Presley ...' She looked suddenly sultry, voice slowing, going a little deeper. 'Here ...' She took an extra breath, her gaze flickering down from my face to my crotch and back, '... *certainly* isn't.'

Then she seemed to collect herself and directed a broad smile to the two men. They looked suitably confused.

*

'*Presley*? *PRESLEY*?' I yelled as we walked rapidly along Thomas More Street. 'How *could* you?' I waved my hands about. A light drizzle was falling out of the orange-black sky.

Ashley strode on, grinning. She held a small umbrella; her heels clicked. 'Sorry, Prentice; it was just the first thing I thought of.'

'But it isn't even very *different* from Prentice!' I shouted.

She shrugged. 'Well then, that's probably why it was the first thing I thought of.' Ash laughed.

'It's not funny,' I told her, sticking my hands into my pockets, stepping over some empty pizza containers.

'It wasn't funny,' Ash agreed, almost prim. 'It's your reaction that is.' She nodded.

'Great,' I said. 'There are two guys going around now who think my name is Presley, but to you it's just a hoot.' I stepped on a wobbly paving stone and jetted dirty water up my chinos. 'Jeez,' I muttered.

'Look,' said Ash, sounding serious at last. 'More to the point, I'm sorry I fucked that up. I don't know *why* he dashed off like that. All I said was I'd a friend with me. I didn't even say you wanted to meet him or anything. It was weird.' She shook her head. 'Weird.'

We had escaped from the pub after finishing our drinks and

chatting – awkwardly on my part, easily on Ashley's – with Rupert's two friends (Howard and Jules); a stilted conversation whose most useful result seemed to have been a general agreement that old Rupe was a lad, eh?

'Doesn't matter,' I told her. I saw a taxi coming with its light on and suddenly remembered I was rich. 'I know where I saw him, now.'

I stepped into the road and waved.

'You do?' Ash said from the kerb.

'Yep.' The cab pulled in. Things were looking up; my usual Klingon Cloaking Device – which has tended to engage automatically on the rare occasions I have felt rich enough in the past to afford a taxi – seemed to have been de-activated. I held the door open for Ashley.

'So; you going to tell me, or be all mysterious?' she said as she got in.

'I'll tell you over dinner.' I sat beside her and closed the door. 'Dean Street, Soho, please,' I told the driver. I smiled at Ashley.

'Dean Street?' she said, eyebrow arching.

'Amongst many other things, I owe you a curry.'

*

When I was fifteen I had my first really bad hangover. On Friday nights I and some of my school pals used to meet at the Droid family house in Gallanach; we'd sit in Droid's bedroom, watching TV and playing computer games. And we'd drink cider, which Droid's big brother purchased for us – for a small commission – from the local off-licence. And smoke dope, which my cousin Josh McHoan, Uncle Hamish's son, purchased for us – at an exorbitant commission – in the Jacobite Bar. And sometimes do speed, which came from the latter source as well. Then one night Dave McGaw turned up with a litre of Bacardi and he and I finished it between the two of us, and the next morning I was woken up by my dad to a strange and horrible new feeling.

vho, as Rory would have written. nsg at all.

There had been a phone-call for me; Hugh Robb, from the farm near the castle, reminding me I'd agreed to come and help with making the bonfire for Guy Fawkes' night. He was coming out to pick me up.

This, of course, was not really what I needed (any more than I needed dad lecturing me on how unsound a custom it was to build bonfires on November the fifth and so celebrate religious bigotry; didn't I know it had been an anti-catholic ceremony, and the effigy burned on the fire used to be the Pope?), but I couldn't admit to mum and dad I'd been drinking and had a hangover, so I had to get dressed with my head pounding and my insides feeling distinctly unwell. I waited outside on the porch steps, taking deep breaths in the cool clear air and wishing the hangover would just go away. Then I suddenly thought maybe it wasn't a hangover; maybe this pounding in my head was the first symptom of a brain tumour ... and so I ended up praying that I *did* have a hangover.

Hugh Robb was a big, amiable Scotch Broth of a lad; he was a full year older than I was but we were in the same class at school because he'd been kept back a year. He arrived in a tractor hauling a trailer full of branches and old wood and I rode with him in the cab, wishing that the tractor had better suspension and that Hugh could have thought of something else to talk about other than the prolapsed uterus of one of the farm's cows.

Round the hill from the castle there was a big east-facing field; it was surrounded by trees on all sides but the slope gave it a view towards Bridgend. I still thought of it as the ponies' field because it was where Helen and Diana's ponies had been stabled originally before they'd been moved to a more level paddock west of the castle.

Hugh and I unloaded the broken planks and the great bare grey branches from the trailer. We worked together for a bit, then I continued to stack the wood while Hugh went to collect some more. He made a couple of trips, dumping what looked like about a tonne of wood each time before announcing he was off to another farm where they had even more wood.

I let the tractor disappear, bumping along the track towards the castle, then collapsed back in the huge pile of branches awaiting my attention. I lay, spread-eagled and half-submerged on the springy mass of grey, leaf-nude wood and stared up at the wide blue November sky, hoping the bass drum inside my head would hit a few thousand rest-bars reasonably soon.

The sky seemed to beat in time to the throbbing inside my head, the whole blue vault pulsing like some living membrane. I thought about Uncle Rory and his discovery that it was not possible to influence TV screens from afar by humming. I wondered – as ever – where he was; he'd been gone a couple of years by that time.

A bird swung into view over the trees behind my head, and I lay there and I watched it; broad, flat-winged, flight feathers at the square wing-tip ruffling like soft fingers, the small, quick head flicking this way and that, the brown-grey body between the soft density of wings tilting and turning as it glided the cool air, tail feathers like a rich brown fan.

'Beauty,' I whispered to myself, smiling despite the pain in my head.

Then suddenly the buzzard burst and sprayed across the sky; it fell plummeting, limp and trailing feathers, to the ground. A double crack of sound snapped across the field.

The bird fell out of sight behind me. I blinked, not believing what had happened, then rolled over, looking through the mask of branches at the trees edging the field where the sound of the shots had come from. I saw a man holding a shotgun, just inside the trees, looking to one side then the other, then running out into the field. He wore green strapped wellies, thick brown cords, a waxed jacket with a corduroy collar, and a cloth bunnet. One more prick in a Barbour jacket, but this one had just shot a buzzard.

He gazed down at something in the grass, then smiled. He was tall and blond and he looked like a male model; enviable jaw line. He stamped down on the thing in the grass, looked around again then backed off, finally turning and walking smartly back into the woods.

I should have shouted, or taken the bird to the police as evidence – buzzards are a protected species, after all – but I didn't. I just watched the Barbour disappear into the trees, then rolled over and breathed, 'Fuckwit.'

He was at the firework party the following night, laughing and talking and sharing a dram from Fergus's hip flask. I watched him, and he saw me, and we looked at each other for a few moments before he looked away, all in the furious, writhing light of the pyre that I had put together, and which contained – pushed in near its now blazing centre – the corpse of the bird he had killed.

CHAPTER
16

We stood beside the observatory dome, on the battlements of Castle Gaineamh, facing into a cool westerly breeze. Lewis, in cords and a grease-brown stockman's coat, looked through the binoculars, his black hair moving slightly in the wind. Verity stood at his side, face raised shining to the winter blue sky, bulky in her thermal jacket, her ski-gloved hands clasped thickly under the bulge of her belly. The plain beyond the woods below, holding Gallanach and cupping the inner bay, was bathed in the deep-shadowed sunlight of late afternoon. Wisps of cirrus moved high above, tails trailing up, promising clear weather. A two-coach sprinter moved in the distance, on the viaduct at Bridgend, windows glinting in the sunlight. I took a deep breath and could smell the sea.

The unopened air-mail packet from Colorado, lodged next to my chest between shirt and jacket, make a crinkling, flexing noise, giving me a funny feeling in my belly.

'No sign?' Verity asked.

Lewis shook his head. 'Mm-mm.'

Verity shivered. She hunched her shoulders, bringing them up and in towards her neck. 'Brr,' she went. She linked arms with Lewis.

'Ah,' he said, protesting, still looking through the field glasses, though now at a slight angle.

Verity tutted, and with a gorgeously pretended scowl moved away from her husband and stepped over to me. She slid an arm round my waist, snuggling. I put an arm round her shoulders. She rested her head against my arm; I looked down at her. She was growing her hair a little. The sides of her head weren't actually shaved any more. She smelled of baby oil; Lewis had what sounded like the enviable job of smoothing it over The Bulge, in an attempt to fend off stretch marks later. I smiled, unseen, and looked back to the north.

'Is that what-do-you-call-it?' Verity said, nodding.

'No, that's thingy-ma-bob,' Lewis said, just as I said,

'Hey; well remembered.'

'Dunadd,' Verity said patiently, ignoring both of us. She was looking at the small, rocky hill a kilometre to the north. 'Where the footprint is.'

'Correct,' I said.

Lewis glanced at us, grinned. He lowered the binoculars a little. 'Can't see it from here, but that's where it is.'

Dunadd Rock had been the capital of Dalriada, one of the early and formative kingdoms in Scotland. The footprint – looks more like a bootprint, actually, just a smooth hollow in the stone – was where the new king had to place his foot when he made his vows, symbolically – I suppose – to join him to the land.

'Can I have a look?' Verity said. Lewis handed her the glasses, and she leant against the stone battlements, supporting her belly. Lewis stood behind her, chin lowered onto her shoulder.

'Right at the summit, isn't it?' Verity asked.

'Yep,' Lewis said.

She looked at Dunadd for a bit. 'I wonder,' she said, 'if you had one of your feet planted there, when you gave birth . . .'

I laughed. Lewis went wide-eyed, drawing up and back from his wife. She turned round, grinning wickedly at Lewis and then me. She patted Lewis's elbow. 'Joke,' she said. 'I want to be in a nice warm birthing pool in a nice big hospital.' She turned back to the view. Lewis looked at me.

'Had me fooled,' I shrugged. 'Runs in the family, after all.'

'Can you see that stone circle, too?' Verity said, lifting the binoculars to gaze further north.

Earlier that day, Helen Urvill, Verity and Lewis and I had been behaving like tourists. The land around Gallanach is thick with ancient monuments; burial sites, standing stones, henges and strangely carved rocks; you can hardly put a foot down without stepping on something that had religious significance to somebody sometime. Verity had heard of all this ancient stoneware but she'd never really seen it properly; her visits to Gallanach in the past had been busy with other things, and about the only place she had been to before was Dunadd, because it was an easy walk from the castle. And of course, because we had lived here most of our lives, none of the rest of us had bothered to visit half the places either.

So we borrowed Fergus's Range Rover and went site-seeing; tramping through muddy fields to the hummocks that were funeral barrows, looking up at moss-covered standing stones, plodding round stone circles and chambered cairns, and leaning on fences staring at the great flat faces of cup-and-ring marked rocks, their grainy surfaces covered in the concentric circular symbols that looked like ripples from something fallen in a pond, frozen in stone.

*

'Did I ever tell you about the time I used to be able to make televisions go wonky, from far away?'

It was a bright and warm day, back in that same summer Rory had come out to the Hebrides with us. Rory and I were walking near Gallanach, going from the marked rocks in one field to the stone circle in another. I remember I had a pain in my side that day and I was worrying that it was appendicitis (one of the boys in my class that year had almost died when his appendix had ruptured). It was just a stitch, though. Uncle Rory was a fast walker and I'd been intent on keeping up with him; my appendix waited another year before it needed taking out.

We had been visiting some of the ancient monuments in the area, and had started talking about what the people who'd built the cairns and stone circles had believed in, and that had led us on to astrology. Then suddenly he mentioned this thing about televisions.

'Making them go *wonky*?' I said. 'No.'

'Well,' Rory said, then turned and looked behind us. We stood up on the verge as a couple of cars passed us. It was hot; I took off my jacket. 'Well,' Rory repeated, 'I was . . . a few years older than you are now, I guess. I was over at a friend's house, and there was a bunch of us watching *Top of the Pops* or something, and I was humming along with a record. I hit a certain deep note, and the TV screen went wavy. Nobody else said anything, and I wondered if it was just coincidence, so I tried to do it again, and after a bit of adjusting I hit the right note and sure enough, the screen went wavy again. Still nobody said anything.' Rory laughed at the memory. He was wearing jeans and T-shirt and carried a light jacket over his shoulder.

'Well, I didn't want to make a fool of myself, so I didn't say anything. I thought maybe it just worked on that one particular television set, so I tried it at home; and it still happened. The effect seemed to work from quite a distance, too. When I stood out in the hall and looked into the lounge, it was still there, stronger than ever.

'Then we were going up to Glasgow, mum and I, and we were

passing a shop window full of TVs, and so I tried this new gift for messing up TV screens on them, and hummed away to myself, and all the screens went wild! And I was thinking Great, I really can do magic! The effect is getting stronger! I could appear on TV and do this! Maybe it would make everybody's screens go weird!'

'Wow,' I said, wanting to get home and try this myself.

'So,' Rory said. 'I stopped in my tracks and I asked mum. I said, "Mum; watch this. Watch those screens." And I hummed for all I was worth, and the pictures on the screens went wavy. And mum just looked at me and said, "What?" And I did it again, but no matter how hard I tried I couldn't get her to see the effect. Eventually she got fed up with me and told me to stop being silly. I had screens going mental in every TV shop we passed in Glasgow that day, but nobody else seemed to be able to see it.'

Rory grimaced, looking across the edge of the plain beyond Gallanach to the little rocky hill that stuck up from the flat fields.

'Now, I wish I could remember just what it was that made the penny drop, but I can't. I mean, usually a beautiful assistant says something stupid and the clever scientist says, "Say that again!" and then comes up with the brilliant plan that's going to save the world as we know it ... but as far as I remember it just came to me.'

'What?' I said.

Rory grinned down at me. 'Vibrations,' he said.

'Vibrations?'

'Yeah. The vibrations I was setting up in my own skull – actually in the eyeball, I suppose – were making my eyes vibrate at about the same frequency as the TV screen flickers. So the screen looked funny, *but only to me*, that was the point. And it made sense that the further away you were from the screen – as long as you could still make it out, of course – the more pronounced the effect would appear.' He looked down at me. 'You see?'

'Yeah,' I said, 'I think so.' I studied the road for a bit, then looked up, disappointed. 'So it doesn't really work after all?'

Rory shook his head. 'Not the way I thought it did, no,' he said.

I frowned, trying to remember how we'd got onto this. 'What's that got to do with what we were talking about?' I asked.

Rory looked at me. 'Ah-ha,' he said, and winked. He nodded at a gate set in the low wall facing the road; beyond were the standing stones. 'Here we are.'

*

'Here we are.' The stair-door creaked open; I went to help Helen. She handed me a tray with four pewter mugs. The mulled wine steamed; it smelled wonderful. 'Mmm, great,' I said. Helen took my hand and stepped out through the little half-size door onto the battlements. Her broad face was tanned and her body looked lean and fit after some early-season skiing in Switzerland. She wore Meindl boots, an old pair of leather trousers that had belonged to her mother, a cashmere sweater and a flying jacket that looked distressed enough to have seen action over Korea, if not Greater Germany. Her hair was shining black and shoulder length.

She took a mug. 'Help yourself,' she said. 'Any sign of him?'

'Nope,' I said. I held the tray out to Lewis and Verity, who made the appropriate noises and took a mug each.

Helen nodded at the corner of the airmail package inside my jacket. 'Still incubating that, Prentice?'

I grinned. 'Yeah.'

We stood there sipping the hot, spicy wine, looking north.

*

'Prentice? Ash. He's done it.'

'Who? Doctor Gonzo?'

'Yeah; printing it out now; mail you the hard copy tomorrow morning; he'll E-mail it to me too, I'll download the files and stick them on a disk your Compaq'll accept and bring it with me next week when I come up for Hogmanay ... unless you got a modem yet, did you?'

'No, no I didn't.'

'Okay; that'll be the arrangement, then. Sound all right to you?'

'Yeah; great. I'll write back to say thanks. He, ah ... say what the files actually were in the end?'

'Text.'

'That all he said?'

'Yep. Prentice, he hasn't read whatever he found; well, probably not more than the first few lines to check they were in English, not gibberish. Once he'd cracked it I don't think he was really interested in what was actually written there. But it is text.'

'Right. Text.'

'Should get to you in a few days, airmail.'

*

The big envelope from the States had arrived in the mail this morning, five days after Ash had called; the return address was Dr G, Computing Science Faculty, University of Denver, Co. I'd stared at the thing as it lay there on the front door mat, my mouth gone oddly dry. I had a slight hangover, and had decided – as I gingerly picked the disappointingly slim package up – that I'd open it after breakfast. Then after breakfast I'd thought maybe I should leave it until later, especially when Verity rang and invited me over to the castle.

It was the last day of 1990; a full twelve months after that fateful party when Mrs McSpadden had sent me down to the cellar for some more whisky. We were all back here for the usual round of parties and visits and hangovers. I was mostly looking forward to it all, even though I was still trying to find reasons not to ask Fergus the things I knew I ought to ask him about Mr Rupert Paxton-Marr. But then, maybe I oughtn't to ask them at all. Maybe what was in this airmail package would relieve me of the need to ask any questions (I told myself). I kept coming back to the distinct possibility that maybe I was making something out of nothing, treating our recent, local history like some past age, and looking too assiduously, too imaginatively for links and patterns and connections, and so turning myself into some sort of small-scale conspiracy theorist.

I had been immersed in my studies all term, and everything seemed to be going well. My professor, reading my tutorial papers and essays, had gone beyond noises of encouragement and vicarious complacency to a sort of uncomprehending peevishness that I'd contrived to fail so spectacularly the year before.

Meanwhile, in the history that we were currently living through, it looked like a war was going to start in just over two weeks, but – apart from a kind of low background radiation of species-ashamed despair because of that – personally I felt not too bad. Mum appeared to be holding out, despite Christmas and New Year traditionally being a bad time for the bereaved. She had actually started building the much talked-about harpsichord, turning a spare bedroom at Lochgair into a workshop which at the moment looked suitably chaotic; James had mostly rejoined humanity, to the extent that several times over the last few weekends before Christmas he'd taken his Walkman phones off long enough to have what could, with only a little generosity, be described as a conversation. Lewis was doing well, Verity was almost disgustingly healthy (apart from the occasional sore back and a bladder that appeared to have become inordinately susceptible to the sound of running water), and I actually looked forward to seeing Lewis and Verity now, much to my own amazement; there was still a distant pang when Verity smiled at me ... but it was more remembered than real.

I looked at my watch. In four hours I'd be setting off for Glasgow Airport, for Ashley. She was booked on a late flight and I'd volunteered to go pick her up. She'd be working until half-five in London this evening, and it would have been pushing the old

2CV a bit to get to Scotland – let alone here – in time for the bells.

I scanned the skies to the north, watching for movement. I was looking forward to the drive, even if it was at night and I wouldn't be able to see the scenery.

The wind gusted a little and I supped my mulled wine. The woods – evergreen and deciduous-bare – swept down to the fields and then the town; forests rose on the hills to the east.

'Anybody heard the news today?' Lewis asked.

'Nothing special happening,' Helen said.

I guessed she'd got an up-date from Mrs McSpadden, who tended to keep the TV on in the kitchen these days.

'All quiet on the desert front,' breathed Lewis, taking up the glasses again and looking north towards Kilmartin.

'You sure he'll come that way?' Verity asked.

Lewis shrugged. 'Think so.'

'Said he would,' Helen confirmed.

Verity stamped her feet.

'Hey,' Helen said. 'I never asked you, Lewis; you got any Gulf jokes?'

Lewis made an exasperated noise, still looking through the binoculars. 'Na. I heard a couple of crap Irish ones, and the usual suspects in different disguises, but there hasn't been anything good. I was trying to work on a routine about if the Stealth bomber worked as well as it did in Panama, the B-52 as it did in Viet Nam and the marines as effectively as they did in Lebanon, then Saddam had nothing too much to worry about, but it wasn't funny enough.' He brought the glasses down from his eyes for a moment. 'In fact, it wasn't funny at all.'

'I know a girl from school who's out there,' Helen said. 'Nurse.'

'Yeah?' Verity said, stamping her feet again.

'Ha!' Lewis said suddenly.

'You seen him?' Verity said, clutching Lewis's arm.

He laughed, glancing down at her. 'No,' he said, and grinned at me. 'But guess who got called up as a reservist?'

I shrugged. 'I give in.' I didn't think I knew anybody in the forces.

Lewis smiled sourly. 'Jimmy Turrock. Used to be a bandsman. They're the stretcher-bearers in war time.'

I frowned, not recognising the name. 'Jimmy –?' I began. Then I remembered.

'The grave-digger!' I laughed.

'Yeah,' Lewis said, turning away again, raising the glasses. 'The grave-digger.'

I felt cold inside and my smile faded. 'Wow,' I said. 'Some sense of humour the army has.'

'Work experience,' Lewis muttered.

'Who's this you're talking about?' Verity asked.

'Guy helped us bury dad,' Lewis said.

'Oh,' she said. She hugged Lewis.

'You going to go if they call you up, Prentice?' Helen Urvill said, not looking at me.

'Hell no,' I said. 'Which way's Canada?'

'Yeah,' muttered Lewis. 'Shame dad's dead; maybe he could have got us into the equivalent of the National Guard, if we have one.'

'Traffic wardens?' I suggested. Lewis's shoulders shook once.

'You really wouldn't go?' Helen said to me, one eyebrow raised.

'I might send them some blood if they ask me nicely,' I told her. 'In an oil can.'

'I suppose we can't use the telescope, can we?' Verity said suddenly, nodding at the white dome to our right. 'As well as the binoculars I mean.' She looked at each of us.

'Nup,' Helen said.

'Too narrow a field of view,' Lewis said.

'And upside down,' I added.

Verity looked over at the dome. There was a smile on her face. 'Do you remember that night we met in the dome?' she said, looking up at Lewis. 'We hadn't seen each other since we were kids ...'

Lewis handed the glasses to Helen, who held them one-handed, straps dangling. Lewis hugged his wife. 'Of course I do,' he said, and kissed her nose. She buried her face in his coat. I looked away, thinking about the drive up to the airport this evening.

Maybe I should allow another half-hour or so for the journey, just in case of hold-ups. And of course they were building new bits onto the airport at the moment; could be a problem parking, and tonight was bound to be busy. I'd leave early, no sense in leaving late and having to hurry. I had taken to driving a bit slower and more carefully these days. Mum still worried, but at least I could reassure her with a clear conscience.

I sighed, and the package against my chest flexed again. I looked down at it. Hell, this was silly; I ought to read the stuff. Waiting until I got back to the house and was sitting at the desk in the study was just putting it off.

'How's the wonderful world of Swiss banking these days anyway, Hel?' Lewis asked.

'Oh, wacky and transparent as ever,' Helen said. They started talking about Zürich and London, and I sat down on the slope of slated roof, behind them. I pulled the airmail package out and opened it carefully. Verity looked back at me and smiled briefly, before turning back to Helen and Lewis to share some joke about the Hard Rock Café. My hands felt clammy as I slid the sheets of paper out of the thick white envelope. This is daft, I thought. It probably *is* gibberish, or Rory's job application for that travel programme presenter's job; a CV for the TV. Nothing important, nothing revelatory.

The first sheet was a letter from the good Doctor, arcane with acronyms and abbreviations, telling me how he'd deciphered the binary mush he'd been sent and turned it into what I held in my hands. He sounded like a likeable guy, but I kind of just glanced at the letter. I went on to the print-out.

There were about fifty or sixty pages of single-space laser print. The first twenty or so pages were taken up with pieces I recognised:

articles and poems and the nameless play Rory had apparently decided to cannibalise for the end of *Crow Road.* Then came three passages of prose.

I glanced up at the others; Helen and Verity were still talking, Lewis was looking through the binoculars towards Gallanach. I started reading, and my mouth went dry.

I raced through each of the passages, my eyes bulging, hands shaking. The voices of the others, the cool December air and the chill slates under my backside seemed like they were all a million miles away, as I read what Uncle Rory had written.

'D'you know where the twins were conceived?'

'No idea,' he said, and belched.

'Fucking McCaig's Folly, that's where.'

'What, Oban?'

'The very place.'

'Good grief.'

'You don't mind me saying this, I mean talking about Fiona like this, do you?'

'No, no.' He waved one hand. 'Your wife; you talk about her. No. no, that's bad, that sounds bad. I'm all for women's lib.'

'Might have bloody known. Might have bloody known you would be. Bloody typical, if you ask me. You're a Bolshie bastard, McHoan.'

'And you are the unacceptable face of Capitalism, Ferg.'

... That was how the first passage began. I finished it and realised my mouth was hanging open. I closed it and started, dazed, the next passage:

'Henriss ... never liked him either; fat lipped beggar ... queer, y'know; thass wha he's singing you know; d'you know that? "Scuse me while I kiss this guy ..." disgussin ... absluley disgussin ...'

'Fergus, do shut up.'

' "Scuse me, while I kiss this guy" ... bloody poofter coon.'

'I'm sorry about this, Lachy.'

'That's okay, Mrs U. You no going to put your seat belt on, no?'

'No; not for short journeys –'

'Lachy? Lachy . . . Lachy! Lachy; I'm sorry about your eye . . . really really sorry; never forgave myself, never . . . here, shake . . .'

'Holy fucking shit,' I whispered, when I finished it. Suddenly my hands felt very cold. I looked at the slates I was sitting on, then over at the dome of the observatory, gleaming in the low winter sun.

'You okay, Prentice?' Verity said, frowning at me from the battlements.

I nodded, tried to smile. 'Fine,' I gulped. I turned to the third and last passage.

Fiona sat in the passenger seat of the car, watching the red roadside reflectors as they drifted out of the night towards her; she was thrown against one side of the seat as Fergus powered the Aston around the right-hander . . .

. . . And on through to the end:

. . . 'Look –!'

And that was all. I looked up, brain reeling.

'Yo,' Helen said, looking through the binoculars. She bent at the knees and put her mug down on the stones under her feet, then rose smoothly again.

'You see him?' Verity said, turning, still hugged within Lewis' arms, to look out over the battlements.

'Could be,' Helen said. She handed the field glasses over to Lewis.

'Yeah, might be,' he said. It was Verity's turn next with the binoculars.

I swallowed a few times, put the sheets of paper back in their envelope. I stood up and walked over to the others, in a kind of trance.

Verity shook her head. 'Na, I can't see the damn thing.' She handed the glasses to me. 'You're looking pale, Prentice. You sure you're okay?'

'Fine,' I croaked, not looking at her. I took the binoculars. 'Thanks.'

I'd seen the speck unaided by that time. Once I'd found it again the binoculars enlarged the dot into the frontal silhouette of a high-winged light aircraft, flying more or less straight towards us, its body pointed a little to the south west to compensate for the wind. It waggled in the air a little as it flew down the glen, encountering a gust high above Kilmartin.

'Christ,' Lewis said. 'It's a Mig on a bombing run; everybody down!'

I handed the glasses back to Helen, who didn't look particularly amused. She frowned at me. 'You okay, Prentice?'

'Fine,' I said.

'You should have loaned your dad your jacket,' Lewis told Helen.

'Doesn't fit him,' Helen said, binoculars at her eyes. I watched the dot of the plane drift closer towards us through the northern sky.

'You were in a sleeping bag,' I heard Lewis say softly to Verity. He was holding her from behind, chin on the crown of her head. I must have missed what they'd said earlier. I felt weird; I was glad the battlements were too high to fall over if I fainted.

Verity smiled. 'I remember. We were all smoking and playing cards and taking turns to look at the stars, and we got the munchies.' She frowned. 'There was Diana and Helen, and ... what was that guy's name?' She glanced round and up at Lewis. 'Wayne somebody?'

'Darren somebody,' Lewis said. He accepted the glasses from Helen, held them with one hand and balanced them on Verity's head. 'Hoy, stand still.'

'Sorry, *sir*,' she said.

'Darren Watt,' I said. The plane was closer now but harder to see; it had dropped below the level of the hills behind and was no longer silhouetted against the sky. You could still see it with the naked eye, though. It glinted, once.

Verity nodded. Lewis tutted in exasperation. 'He was the gay guy, wasn't he?' Verity said.

'Yup,' Lewis said. 'Sculptor. Good, too; fucking shame, that was.'

'Oh God,' Verity said. 'Of course, he died.'

'Bike crash,' Helen said, scooping up her mug of cooled wine from the flagstones, and draining it.

The plane was flying over Gallanach now. I thought I could hear its engine. I remembered standing here once with mum, years ago. Fergus and dad were shooting at clay pigeons in a field to our right somewhere, and I remembered hearing the flat Crack ... Crack noise of the guns, and thinking they sounded just like one plank falling on top of another. Blam! indeed. *Remember, remember* ...

Verity laughed, making Lewis tut again. 'You were doing your radio impressions,' she said, 'that night. Remember?'

'Of course,' Lewis said.

'Why was I in a sleeping bag?' Verity said, frowning at the approaching plane.

'You were in the cupboard.' Helen smiled. She waved out across the chill afternoon air above Gallanach. I looked back at the plane, which was switching its lights on and off.

'Oh,' Verity said. 'Yeah; the wee cubby hole.'

'Ah ha,' Helen said, as Lewis waved too, still watching through the binoculars, now elevated above Verity's head. 'But it was really a secret passage.'

'*Was* it?' Verity asked, glancing at Helen.

'Yeah. Di and I used to take the bit of wood off at the back and get into the attic. Wander all over.'

'Anything interesting in there?' Lewis asked. The plane was in a shallow dive, angling towards us a few hundred metres away.

'Just pipes and tanks,' Helen shrugged. 'There was a loft door into mum and dad's room.' She smiled. 'When we started getting interested in sex, we used to pretend we'd get up there one night and see if we could catch them at it, but we were too frightened.' Helen laughed lightly. 'Had us giggling ourselves to sleep a few nights, though. And anyway, Ferg had put a bolt on it.'

The little white Cessna roared overhead, waggling its wings. Lewis and Verity and Helen all waved. I stared up, seeing the single tiny figure waving in the cockpit. The plane banked, circled round the hill the castle stood on and came back over, lower, engine loud and echoing in the woods beneath.

I made myself wave.

Oh dear fucking holy shit, I thought.

The plane waggled its wings again, then straightened out over Dunadd as Fergus took the Cessna – his Christmas present to himself – back north to its home at Connel.

'That it?' said Verity.

'Yup,' Helen said.

'What did you expect?' Lewis asked. 'A crash?'

'Oh . . .' said Verity, heading for the door to the stairs. 'Let's get back in the warm.'

Blam! *Remember, remember.* Amman Hilton. Look –! JUST USE IT! Kiss the *sky*, you idiot . . .

'Prentice?' Lewis said, from the little door. I looked over at him. 'Prentice?' he said again. 'Wake up, Prentice.'

I'd been staring after the departing plane.

'Oh,' I said. 'Yeah.' On still shaky legs, I followed the others down from the wind-blown battlements and into the warm bulk of the great stone building.

*

'So the televisions weren't going wonky at all,' I said, still struggling to understand.

'That's right,' Rory said. 'It just looked like it, to me only.' He plucked a long piece of grass from beside one of the standing stones and sucked on the yellow stalk.

I followed suit. 'So it was in your head; not real?'

'Well ...' Rory frowned, turning away a little and leaning back on the great stone. He folded his arms and looked out towards the steep little hill that was Dunadd. I stood to one side, watching him. His eyes looked old.

'Things in your head can be real,' he said, not looking at me. 'And even when they aren't, sometimes they ...' he looked down at me, and I thought he looked troubled. 'Somebody told me something once,' he said. 'And it sounded like it had really hurt him; he'd seen something that made him feel betrayed and hurt by somebody he was very close to, and I felt really sorry for this person, and I'm sure it's affected them ever since ... but when I thought about it, he'd been asleep before this thing had happened, and asleep again afterwards, and it occurred to me that maybe he'd dreamed it all, and I still wonder.'

'Why don't you tell him that?'

Rory looked at me for a while, his eyes searching mine, making me feel awkward. He spat the blade of grass out. 'Maybe I should,' he said. He nodded, looking out across the fields. 'Maybe. I don't know.' He shrugged.

*

I stood there, back at the same stone my Uncle Rory had rested against, a decade earlier. I'd left the castle and driven here to the stone circle shortly after we'd come down from the battlements. There was still plenty of time to get back to Lochgair for dinner before I had to set off for Glasgow, and Ash.

I leant against the great stone, the way Rory had when he'd talked about the man betrayed, the man who'd seen – or thought he'd seen – something that had hurt him. I looked ahead, out over the walls and fields and stands of trees. I shivered, though it wasn't especially cold.

'See?' I said, quietly, to myself.

Maybe Rory had been looking at Dunadd that day, as I'd assumed at the time. But beyond Dunadd, just a little to the right on this line of sight, I could see the hill where Gaineamh castle stood, its walls showing blunt and steel grey through the naked trees.

*

'Prentice!'

'... Yeah?'

'Food! Come on, it's getting cold!'

Mum had been calling from the bottom of the stairs. I was sitting at the desk in the study, curtains open to the darkness, just the little desk light on, its brass stalk gleaming, its green shade glowing. I looked back down from my reflection in the dark computer screen, first to my watch – still half an hour before I had to leave to pick up Ashley – and then to the thin, battered-looking pocket diary lying opened on the desk.

Fri F @ Cas, L.Rvr, trak, hills. Bothy;
fire, fd, dnk, js. (F stnd) rt in clng!
guns. F nsg. trs & scrts. F barfd
WELCOME TO ARGYLL!

I saw her hair first, shining tight-tied in a spotlight somewhere down the domestic arrivals concourse. I hadn't seen Ashley Watt for about six weeks, after that night in London when I'd seen but not talked to Rupert Paxton-Marr. Ashley was dressed in the same business-like suit she'd worn that night, and carried a big shoulder bag. Her smile was broad.

'Ash. Great to see you.' I hugged her, lifting her off her feet.

'Woo!' she laughed throatily. 'How ya doin, Presley?'

I winced, dramatically, but still offered to carry her bag.

*

'Prentice; you read a couple of things your uncle wrote and suddenly you're accusing people of murder? Come on.'

'Haven't you looked at the files Doctor Gonzo sent over?'

'Of course not; not my business, Prentice.' Ashley sounded indignant. 'Oh; before I forget,' she said, reaching for her jacket on the back seat and digging into a pocket. She took out a little three-inch Sony disk and handed it to me. 'Present from Colorado. Yours to tinker with.'

'Thanks,' I said, putting the disk in my shirt pocket. 'I might, too; the spelling mistakes have been annoying me.' I moved my head. 'The stuff's in that envelope on the back seat.'

'You don't want me to read it *now*, do you?'

'There's a torch.'

'Am I allowed to finish building the spliff first?'

'Okay, but then read.'

I'd waited till we were out of Glasgow before I'd told Ashley about the horrible ideas concerning Fergus that I just couldn't get out of my head.

Most of the journey from Lochgair up to Glasgow I'd spent thinking, trying to work out what might be true and what false in the fragments of writing that Rory had left on disk. The rat in the ceiling and the confession of something over-seen; that was what had taken me back to stand amongst the standing stones that afternoon, after I'd left the castle.

And remembering what Rory had said to me there had taken me back to that 1976 diary entry.

rt in clng! F nsg.

trs & scrts

And the 1980 diary with the words JUST USE IT!, and the L that had been changed to a C; the L *must* stand for Lachlan Watt and the F for Fiona. That was the secret Fergus had told Rory, that night in the bothy; the story of Fergus waking up after being brought home from Hamish and Tone's party and crawling through the castle roof-space to see his wife in bed with Lachy Watt. That was the party that Fiona and Lachlan had left together.

Of course, all I had was Rory's fictionalised word for any of it.

So I'd asked my mum, over dinner.

'Did Fiona . . . leave a party with somebody else?' she repeated, looking mystified.

'It's just something in one of Rory's poems,' I said. '. . . Not earth-shakingly important or anything, but there's an odd sort of note that . . . well, I just wondered if you knew, or had heard . . .' I shrugged, sipping my glass of water.

Mum shook her head, helping herself to some more peas. 'The only time I ever saw Fiona leave a party with somebody else, Fergus was there too. In body, at least.'

'Uh-huh?' I said.

. . . scrts . . .

*

I owed the last, absurdly simple part of the theory to a stag that had suddenly run onto the road while I was zapping down Glen Croe, between the Rest-and-be-Thankful and Ardgartan. One moment the road ahead was clear in the headlights, next second Wha! Something dark brown looking big as a horse with huge antlers like some twisted aerial array came belting out of the forest across the road and leapt the downhill crash barrier. I slammed the brakes on, nearly locking the wheels. The beast disappeared into the darkness and the car swept through the single cloud of steamy breath it had left behind.

I'd come off the brakes and accelerated again almost immediately, shaking my head and muttering curses at all kamikaze deer, and feeling my heart-beat start to slow again after my fright. I'd adjusted my seat belt and looked over at the passenger's seat. Something had moved there, when I'd braked.

I'd left the airmail envelope holding the print-out of Rory's pieces sitting on the passenger seat, because I wanted Ashley to read them. The envelope had slipped forward under the deer-induced sharp braking, plonking down into the passenger footwell. I'd tutted, waited for the straight along the side of Loch Long, checked for traffic, then reached over, retrieved the package from the footwell and put it back on the seat.

And that had set me pondering.

I'd passed through Arrochar in a daze, thinking, of course!

*

Ashley read the relevant passage while we travelled the new, fast stretch of the Loch Lomond road.

'Yeah,' she said slowly. 'Mm-hmm.' She put the sheaf of papers down, switched off the torch, looked at me, then lit the J. 'So this is Rory's idea of what happened just before Fergus and Fiona crashed?'

'Yeah.'

'And is this Rory indicating your Aunt Fiona fucked my Uncle Lachy?' she sounded almost amused.

'Right,' I said. I glanced at her.

'Kind of fanciful, isn't it?' she said. 'Jeez, he was hardly ever here, and they didn't really move in the same social circles.'

'Damn,' I breathed. 'Maybe you should have read the other two bits first.'

'Hmm.' Ashley drew smoke in, handed the J to me.

I took a small toke. 'Yuk; what's this?'

'Herbal mixture,' Ash said. 'No point giving up fags and then smoking tobacco in Js.'

'Hmm,' I said, handing the number back.

'So what are you saying, Prentice? Did I miss something?'.

'Maybe.' I shook my head, letting the car slow as we approached Tarbet. 'Or maybe I'm reading too much into it . . . want to read the other two bits?

Ash sighed, accepted the J back and switched the torch back on.

We passed Tarbet, accelerating over the shallow neck of land to Arrochar, pottered through the village at less than forty, then gathered speed again as we curved round the head of Loch Long, passing the place where I'd retrieved the airmail package from the footwell a couple of hours earlier.

'Yeah, but what *did* Fergus tell Rory?' Ash said, finishing that part.

'Read the next bit,' I said. I waved my hand when Ash offered me the joint.

The road started to climb along the dark shoulder of the hillside towards the Rest-and-be-Thankful, leaving the old road still down in the floor of the glen. I kept a careful look out for Mad Stags From Hell crashing across the road, but none appeared.

'Woof,' Ash said, closing the last page. 'Horny stuff towards the end there.' She switched the torch off again. 'You think that last bit is what Fergus told Rory in the bothy, if it really happened?'

'Yeah,' I said. 'There's a diary entry to back it up, and there *is* a way through the castle's attic from the observatory to the master bedroom, and a loft door. Helen mentioned it just today.'

'But Prentice!' Ash laughed, coughing. 'All you've got is Rory's ... written word for it!'

'It's all circumstantial, I know. Although mum does remember the party at Hamish and Tone's, and Lachy did help Fiona take Fergus home.'

'Wow,' Ash said, tartly.

'So anyway, what's happened is: Fergus has spilled these beans to Rory, who's spent years trying to come up with some creative ideas for his big project and failed dismally, then decided Just Use It; use the one spectacular piece of real-life drama only he and Fergus know about; he's written this sort of diary piece about the time they were in the bothy together; another, more fictionalised bit about what Fergus actually saw; and then a third passage that ... well, that's the point.' I glanced over at her. 'I was hoping you might see the same thing I did in that last bit, the bit in the car. I think that was what Rory was writing just before he borrowed the bike and went to see Fergus, because of what he had started to suspect, when he was writing that.'

'Went to see Fergus?'

'Yes.' I looked over at her. 'And Fergus killed him.'

'*What*? And Fergus *killed* him?' Ash said, voice high. 'Why, Prentice?' She opened the window a crack and threw the roach out.

'I'll come to that,' I said, holding up one finger. We were passing Loch Restil now; I was still watching out for stags.

Ashley shook her head. 'Prentice, have you been reading crime novels instead of your history books?'

I gave a small laugh. 'No. The worst crimes are always in the history books, anyway.'

Ash undid her hair, reached into her bag and started to brush her hair with a long-tooth comb. 'Hmm,' she said. 'Okay. So keep going.'

'Right,' I said. 'That guy Paxton-Marr. He'd been sending dad those match-book covers . . . I mean *match-book* covers, right?'

'Yeah, so?'

'So he knows Fergus; Fergus was getting the guy to send them, making dad think Rory was still alive, farting around all over the world. Why should Fergus want to do that?'

'I don't know, but what's so special about match-book covers?'

I looked over for a moment; her face was pale in the lights of an on-coming car. 'That bit in the bothy,' I told her. 'Rory tells Fergus he accidentally set fire to a barn on the estate when he was a kid. I think the only other person Rory'd ever told about that was dad, who thought that nobody else knew. So when these match-book covers came from all over the world, he thought it was a secret sign from Rory.'

Ashley was silent for a while, then sighed. 'What fertile imaginations you have in your family.'

'Yeah,' I said. 'I'm afraid so.'

We rounded the long left-hander into Glen Kinglas, where Verity had almost lost the back-end of the Beemer a year earlier. The long straight disappeared into the darkness. A few tiny red sparks in the distance were tail lights. I had another shivery feeling of déjà-vu.

Ashley tapped her fingers on the dashboard, then ran them through her hair. After a while she said, 'And what did Rory suspect?'

'Murder. His sister's murder.'

Ash took her time before answering. 'You think Fergus killed your Aunt Fiona *as well*?''

I nodded. 'You guessed it.'

'She was already dead when they had the crash?'

'Hmm, I hadn't thought of that,' I admitted. I came off the power. I checked the mirror; there was nothing following us, and no headlights in front. 'No, I believe Rory got it right in that bit he wrote, and she was alive when they crashed; I was thinking of something else.'

'What?' Ash said.

I braked smoothly as though we were approaching a sharp corner, not on a long straight. From the corner of my eye, I could see Ash looking at me. I changed down to second gear, let the engine brake the car. I reached over and hit the little red release button on Ashley's seat belt, then I slammed the brakes on. The Golf skidded briefly along the road on locked wheels. I heard Ashley shout something. Her hands went out in front of her. She shot forward, harder than I'd intended and went 'Oof!' against the dashboard, blonde hair flying. Her head hit the screen.

The car juddered to a stop.

I stared in horror.

Ash sat rubbing her forehead. She glared at me. She was holding her chest just underneath her breasts with her other hand. She glared at me. 'What the *fucking* hell was that for, Prentice?'

'Oh shit,' I said, hand to mouth. 'Oh God, are you all right?' I checked the mirror, put both hands to my mouth. 'I didn't mean to actually hurt you.'

'Well you actually did, you idiot.' She looked down at her seat-belt anchorage, then at the buckle. One side of the belt was still wrapped round her. I sat staring at her, my back against the driver's door, my heart pounding. Ashley patted her forehead, studied her fingers, then scowled at me and sat back in her seat, re-fixing her seatbelt. She waggled her shoulders, sticking her chest out a little and grimacing through the screen at the dark grey length of road exposed to the headlights. 'You complete fool, Prentice; I may never dance the rhumba again.' She looked at me, then pointed forwards. 'Drive.'

'God, I'm sorry,' I said. I got the car moving again.

Ash patted her chest and inspected her forehead in the mirror on the back of the sun-visor, using the torch she'd been reading with. 'No lasting damage done, I think,' she said, snapping the torch off and the visor shut.

'I'm really sorry,' I said. I rubbed my hands on my trousers, one at a time. 'I didn't mean –'

'Enough,' Ash said. 'I promise I won't sue, okay?'

'Yeah,' I said, shaking my head. 'But I'm really –'

'You think,' Ash interrupted, 'that your Uncle Fergus killed his wife by driving off the road and undoing her seat belt just before they hit?'

I took a deep breath. 'Yes.'

'Slow down, will you?' Ash said.

'Eh?' I said, slowing. We hadn't been going particularly fast.

Then I realised. 'Oh. Yeah,' I said, feeling even worse. 'I pick my places, don't I?'

Ash didn't reply; we both watched, silent, as the Golf dawdled past the parking place at the Cowal road junction where Darren Watt had died.

'Shit,' I said. 'Oh God, I'm doing an awful lot of apol –'

'Forget it,' Ash said. 'Let's get home.'

I shook my head. 'Oh shit,' I said miserably.

*

The lights of Inveraray were off to our right, steady across the dark waters of Loch Shira as we rounded Strone Point, when Ash spoke again. 'Bit of a risky way to top your wife, isn't it?'

'Convincing, though. And maybe ... Don't laugh,' I said, glancing over at her. 'Maybe the perfect crime.'

Ash looked at me dubiously. 'Oh dear, Prentice. Really.'

'I'm serious,' I said. 'He banged his head; he doesn't remember the last few miles of the drive. He even asked to be hypnotised, though they never did. Short-term memory gone, see? Hell, if he did it just on the spur of the moment, maybe even *he* isn't sure he meant it. He told me himself that he thought Fiona had been wearing a seat belt. I saw him just after the crash, while I was in hospital too, getting my appendix out. So nobody – maybe not even him – will ever know. It's fucking perfect. Risky but perfect, if it does work.'

We stopped at traffic lights by the ornate, hump-backed bridge that took the road over the Aray. I sat staring at the red light; Inveraray sat ahead, round the side of the little bay, white buildings glowing in the sodium twilight of the street lights.

'But if he doesn't know he did it,' Ash said, putting the sun visor down again and checking her forehead in the mirror in the lights of the on-coming stream of traffic, 'why would he kill Rory anyway?'

I shrugged. 'Maybe he *does* know he did it; but even if he doesn't, he might guess that he did. Maybe he was afraid Rory would publish something too close to the truth, maybe Rory was threatening to tell people about his theory; the police, for a start. Maybe neither murder was premeditated; maybe Fergus just reacted, both times. I don't know.'

'Hmm,' Ash said. She sat looking baffled for a bit, then shook her head. The lights changed and we crossed the bridge.

'If I'm right,' I said, 'Fergus probably had thought about killing her before he did. Maybe he only actually decided then and there, on the road that night; but he must have thought about it. Like I say; even if he isn't sure he did it himself, he knows he might have. I mean how hard do you have to think about something, how seriously, before it becomes something you could do, in the heat of the moment?'

'I give in,' said Ash. 'You tell me.'

'Jeez,' I said. 'When I was feeling really bad last year I used to lie awake at night thinking that if there was some way of killing Lewis, quickly, painlessly, with no way of being found out, I might just do it, especially if I knew somehow that Verity would turn to me afterwards –'

'Oh for God's sake, Prentice,' Ash said, turning her head to watch downtown Inveraray slide past. A minute later we were out, accelerating down the darkness of the loch side.

'Look,' I said. 'I was pretty fucked-up. I mean, I'm not saying it wasn't my own fault, Ash; I know it was. I'm not looking for sympathy. I'm just trying to explain that some crazy stuff can go through your head sometimes through love, or jealousy, and maybe, if it's triggered by something ... I mean if somebody had actually given me a method of killing Lewis like that I'd probably have been horrified. I hope I couldn't even have thought about doing it any more once I knew it was possible. It was just a fantasy, a kind of warped internal therapy, something I day-dreamed about to make me feel better.' I shrugged. 'Anyway, that's the case for the prosecution.'

Ash sat, mulling, for a while.

'So,' she said. 'Have you checked out whether Fergus was alone the night Rory may or may not have gone to see him? I mean this whole thing falls to pieces if your uncle –'

'He was alone, Ash,' I told her. 'Mrs McSpadden had gone to visit relatives in Fife that weekend. Mum and dad had suggested the twins came and stayed with us. Fergus brought them over about tea time; I remember talking to him. He had a couple of drinks and then he left. So he was alone in the castle.'

Ash looked at me. I just shrugged.

'Okay,' she said eventually. She rested her elbow on the door, and tapped at her teeth with one set of nails. Her skirt had ridden up a little, and I stole the occasional glance at her long, blackly shining legs.

'So,' she said later when we were in the forest, away from the loch side and a few kilometres out of Furnace. 'What is to be done, Prentice?'

'I don't know,' I confessed. 'There's no body ... Well, there is Aunt Fiona's, but that's neither here nor there. But Rory's still missing, in theory. I suppose I could go to the boys in blue with what I've got, but Jeez, can you imagine? Right, sonny, so you think this wee story that ye've read means yer uncle wiz kilt ... Ah see. Would you mind just putting on this nice white jaikit? Aye, the sleeves are a wee bitty on the long side, but you won't be needing yer hands much in this braw wee room we've got for you with the very soft wallpaper.'

We curved down into Furnace, the road finding the loch shore again. I could sense Ash looking at me, and chose not to look back, concentrating on checking the mirrors and the instruments. Eventually she took a breath. 'Okay. Supposing Fergus did kill Rory, what did he do with the body?'

'Probably hid it,' I said. 'Not too near the castle ... He had plenty of time; all night. He had a Land Rover; he could have got the bike in the back. Bit of a struggle maybe, but Fergus is a biggish lad, and a 185 Suzi isn't that heavy. It did occur to me he could have driven the bike himself with the body lashed to his back looking like a pillion. It's a bit Mezentian, but possible. But then he'd have had to have walked back from wherever he left it ...' I looked over at Ashley, who was staring at me with a worried, even frightened expression. I shrugged. 'But I think he took it up to one of the lochs in the hills, in the Landy; used the forestry tracks and dumped body and bike together into the water. There are plenty of places. The forest to the south of the castle, on the other side of the canal ... It's just full of little lochs up there, and there are tracks to most of them; it's the obvious ... What's the matter?' I asked.

'You're right into all this, aren't you?'

'What do you expect?' I laughed, a strange, tight feeling in my belly. 'What if I'm right? Jeez, this guy might just have killed two of my close relations; wouldn't *you* be kind of interested?'

Ash breathed out. 'Oh dear, Prentice,' she sighed, shaking her head and staring out of the window at the night as we swept through the forest towards Lochgair. 'Oh dear, oh dear ...'

*

We pulled up outside the Watt house in Bruce Street before eleven. Ash looked in the visor mirror again. She frowned and held her hair away from her face, turning her head from side to side. 'Can't see a bruise,' she said.

I looked over. 'No, I think you're all right there.' I spread my hands. 'Look, I'm really sorry –'

'Oh, shush,' Ash said. She nodded at the house. 'Coming in?'

'Just for a minute. I'd like to ask a favour of your mum.'

'Yeah?' Ash said, reaching into the back for her flight bag. 'Let me guess; you want to get in touch with Uncle Lachy.'

I turned the engine off and killed the lights. 'Aye; I wondered if she might let me have his phone number in Australia. I'd like a wee word with him.'

'Yeah, I bet you would.'

We got out of the car and walked up the path towards the door.

*

I had a brief chat with Mrs Watt, gracefully refused a dram, and left after five minutes. A shower scattered raindrops in bright cones under the street lights as I drove away. I went up Bruce Street then took a couple of lefts onto the Oban road where it ran along the side of what had been the Slate Mine wharf.

When I saw the building site, I pulled in and stopped the car.

The site was lit with a sort of hollow orange dimness by the nearby sodium lamps. It was here I'd come with Ashley that night after Margot's percussive cremation; we sat here on the Ballast Mound, the World Hill. It was the night she'd told me about Berlin, the Jacuzzi, and the man who'd hinted there was some trick being played on somebody in Gallanach. She'd given me that piece of the Berlin Wall, shortly after we'd sat together here. The developers had been going to level the mound the following day, preparatory to putting up some new houses.

But it looked like they hadn't got very far.

The old wharf was derelict again; levelled all right, and with foundation trenches dug, but no more. Little wooden stakes were stuck into the ground near a few of the trenches; loose bits of wet string tied to them lay straggled across the ploughed-up ground. There were no earth movers or dumper trucks on the site any more, just a couple of loose piles of bricks, the bottom few layers already overgrown by weeds. A picket fence round the site had been knocked flat almost all the way round, and the developer's sign-board hung flapping in the breeze, secured at only one corner to a rickety, lop-sided framework.

Gone bust, I supposed and, with a look at where the Ballast Mound had been, drove away.

CHAPTER 17

The line went dead. Twenty thousand kilometres away – and a lot more than that if you took the satellite route my words had – a man put the phone down on me. I listened to the electronic buzz for a while, then replaced the onyx handset in its gold cradle.

I put my hands between my knees, looked out through my own reflection in the study windows to the darkness of the park and the string of orange lights along Kelvin Way, and felt a cold, sick feeling coiling in my belly. I was running out of excuses for doing nothing.

If Lachlan Watt had said '*What*?' or '*How dare you*!' or something like that; even if he'd just denied it – indignant or amused – and perhaps especially if he'd asked me to repeat what I'd just said, I'd have had some doubt. But to put the phone down ... Did that make sense? I mean, you're living quietly in Australia, the phone goes, and somebody you last remember as a kid in Scotland has the nerve to ask if you ever slept with his aunt in her marital bed. Do you put the phone down without another word if the answer's No?

Maybe you do. Everybody's different. Maybe I still didn't know enough. I lowered my head to the green leather surface of the antique desk and banged my head softly a couple of times, my hands still clasped between my knees.

I'd been putting this off for days. And anyway weeks had passed. First, Ashley's mum hadn't had Lachy's number, then she got it off somebody else in the family, then it turned out it was an old number (I hadn't tried it anyway) and he'd moved, then there was a delay getting the new number, and when Mrs Watt did phone up with it, I'd dithered. What was I supposed to say? How did I broach the subject? Come right out with it? Talk round it? Hint? Accuse? Make up some story about a just-discovered will, with a bequest to the one man she'd been unfaithful with? Or the one she'd most enjoyed being unfaithful with? Should I pretend to be a lawyer? A journalist? Offer money? I fretted for days and could have gone on doing so for months.

I'd stayed in Glasgow that Thursday night, completing a paper on the effect of industrial growth on the drive towards the unification of Germany in the eighteenth century; it wasn't actually due in until the following Friday, but I reckoned that slamming the blighter in a whole seven days early would keep the Prof. happy.

I'd turned one of the late Mrs Ippot's first-floor reception rooms into a study, moving a giant oak and leather desk over to the window with the help of Gav and Norris; I'd bought a PC similar to but faster than the machine at Lochgair and plonked it roughly in the middle of the mega-desk, where it looked a bit lost, but clashed nicely. For the essay on German unity, I'd surrounded the computer with a dozen delicately beautiful pieces of Meissen pottery. Whether they had any positive effect on the worth of the paper I don't know, but they were a lot more soothing to look at while I was searching for inspiration than a blinking cursor.

I'd finished the paper about 2am and printed it out. I thought about getting in the car there and then, dropping the paper through the letter-box of a pal who'd take it in to the department for me tomorrow, and then heading for Lochgair. But I was tired, and I'd already told mum I'd be down in the morning; I didn't want to wake her by arriving in the middle of the night.

So I'd had a whisky and gone to bed.

The main bedroom in Mrs Ippot's expansive town house contained a canopied four-poster about the size of a double garage, the sleeping surface of which was about the same height as a mini's roof. The posts were telegraph-pole thick; highly polished mahogany carved into representations of fairies, elves and gnomes, all stacked like little caryatids. I liked to imagine they were the work of an Amerindian totem-pole maker who'd read too much Tolkien.

The centre-piece of the bedroom was a vast chandelier cut from ruby-coloured Murano glass; it hung like a glistening spray of frozen blood from the centre of a gilt-smothered ceiling whose few flat patches were covered in paintings of cherubs and fawns cavorting in a sylvan landscape that appeared to be equal parts Rubens and Disney.

The walls of the room, when not hidden from view by the bed's luxurious (but Islamically abstract) brocade side curtains, were covered with huge Rococo canvases of Venus in various guises, settings and ages, though all shared the same state of déshabillé and a rotundity of figure that must have required the painterly equivalent of soft-focus to appear so leniently attractive.

Where the walls did not glow with acres of flesh, they reflected that golden voluptuousness with great gilt-frame mirrors which almost visibly strained the walls they hung on, and which, I couldn't help but notice, also provided rather a good view from and of the silk-sheeted bed. I'd understood Mrs Ippot had been elderly and frail when she died, but I rather hoped she'd had more fun in the bed than just lying there contemplating the condign punishment I'd decided she had devised for her immediate family (certainly *I* had yet to share the space between those sheets with anybody, though the bedroom's sheer scale and stateliness did lend masturbation an air of solemnity and arguable dignity the apprehension of which had previously quite passed me by). Even the bedside tables were Chippendale; one of them was topped with a large cut-crystal Venetian vase which I kept fruit in, when I remembered. Otherwise it played host to the little lump of concrete that had been part of the Berlin Wall, which Ashley had given to me over a year earlier.

The bedroom also contained the greater part of Mrs I's collection of camphor-wood chests; a few too many, perhaps. Despite the visual and tactile splendour, olfactorily it was like sleeping in a chemist's.

However, the sad truth is that being surrounded by art treasures designed to excite the eye, gladden the gland and animate the avarice does not guarantee a full night's kip. I'd woken at about half-six, lain there restlessly for a bit, then given up trying to get back to sleep and got up to have some toast and a cup of tea.

I'd put the TV on in the kitchen and found we were at war.

*

I sat and watched it for a while; heard the CNN guys in Baghdad, saw the reporters report from Saudi airfields, listened to the studio pundits gibber about surgical strikes and pinpoint accuracy, and discovered that, these days, war is prosecuted, not waged. Actually, both words struck me as possessing greasily appropriate connotations in the circumstances.

'Fuck it,' I said to myself. What was telephoning somebody you hardly know on the other side of the planet and asking them impertinent questions about their sex life, compared to this gratuitous malfeasance? I strode up the stairs to the reception-room study, determined to make the phone call.

I settled on the direct approach and the truth about myself.

And Lachy Watt put the phone down on me.

Maybe he just wanted to get back to the TV and watch our exciting Third World War for a bit.

*

I'd stayed in the Lochgair house over Hogmanay itself. We had plenty of drink in, and mum and I had prepared loads of food, but not many people actually visited after the bells. Verity went to bed about ten past midnight after struggling to stay awake from about ten o'clock. She had a very small glass of whisky at the bells. Some people from the village came in about one, Aunt Tone and Uncle Hamish arrived about two for half an hour of strained conversation, and some of James's pals called in after four, but mostly it was just mum, Lewis, James and I together. James conked out about six, but Lewis and I were determined to see the dawn come up just on principle.

We sat in the conservatory, talking and listening to CDs on the gateaux blaster, which I'd brought down with me from Glasgow because it sounded better than the Golf's own sound system (which anyway didn't include a CD player). We were drinking whisky, chasing it with pints of mineral water; pacing ourselves. Lewis felt we were both starting to nod off at one point and so suggested a game of chess. I mooted for the River Game, but we'd have had to have dug the board and everything out and read through all the rules, so we decided chess would be simpler.

'I've been too sensible,' I told him, while pondering a pawn exchange.

'Sensible?' Lewis sounded surprised. '*You*?'

I grinned. 'Well ... Look at me; I'm studying, I'm living quietly, I'm coming home to mother each weekend ... I even bought a sensible, reasonably cheap car. All that money I got ...' I shook my head. 'I'm twenty-two; I should have blown it all on floozies or dangerous drugs, or just took off round the world, or bought a Ferrari.'

'You can't buy a Ferrari for forty grand,' Lewis said, chin in hands, studying the board.

'I didn't say it had to be a new one.'

Lewis shrugged. 'Well, you've still got most of the dosh. Go ahead; go do some of that stuff.'

'Yeah, but I sort of promised mum I'd get this degree.'

'Okay, so wait till the summer and *then* do it.'

'But mum'll just worry if I get a fast car.'

'So take off round the world.'

'Yeah. Maybe. I might.'

Lewis looked up at me. 'What are you intending to do, anyway, Prentice?' He grimaced, stretched, rubbed his face. 'I mean, are you still just going to wait and see who's recruiting graduates and then take what sounds like the best job, or have you settled on something yet? Something you actually want to do?'

I shook my head. 'Still open, that one,' I said. I took the pawn Lewis had offered. He looked vaguely surprised. 'I still like the idea of just *being* a historian,' I told him. 'You know, ideally. But that means staying in academia, and I don't know if that's what I want. Somehow I don't think they let you go straight from graduation onto prime-time TV with a twenty-six part dramatised history of the world.'

'Sounds a little unlikely,' Lewis agreed, taking my pawn. 'You given up on the diplomatic service?'

I smiled, thinking back a year to Uncle Hamish's party. 'Well, I'm not sure I'm cut out for that. I've met some of those people, they're bright . . . But in the end you have to do as you're damn well told by fuckwit politicians.'

'Ah! Politics, then?' Lewis said.

I bit my lip, looking the length and breadth of the board, trying to work out if the bishop I wanted to move next was going to cause any problems in its new position. 'Na, I should have started by now anyway, but . . . shit; you have to make deals. You have to lie, or come so damn close to lying it makes little difference. It's all so fucking expedient, Lewis; they all have this thing about my enemy's enemy is my friend. "He may be a son-of-a-bitch, but he's our son-of-a-bitch." I mean; good grief. What a crock of shit that is. I despair for our species.'

'Not politics, then.'

'I wonder if Noam Chomsky needs an assistant,' I said.

'Probably got one,' Lewis said.

'Yeah,' I sighed. 'Probably.'

Lewis looked quizzical. 'Everything else all right?'

'Yeah,' I said, feeling awkward. 'Why?'

He shrugged, studied the board again. 'I don't know. I just wondered if there was anything . . .'

'Hi guys.'

We both looked over to see Verity, hair in spiky disarray, face soft with sleep, wrapped in a long white towelling dressing gown, padding into the conservatory holding a glass of milk.

'Morning,' I said.

'Hi there, darlin,' Lewis said, swivelling so she could sit on his lap. She put her head on his shoulder and he kissed her forehead. 'You okay?'

She nodded sleepily. Then she straightened, drank some milk and ruffled Lewis's hair. 'Might get dressed,' she said, yawning. 'Been having nightmares.'

'Aw,' Lewis said tenderly. 'You poor thing. Want me to come to bed?'

Verity sat on Lewis's lap, rocking back and forth a little, her bottom lip pouting. She frowned and said, 'No.' She smoothed Lewis's hair again. 'I'll get up. You finish your game.' She smiled at me, then looked up. 'Nearly dawn.'

'Why, so it is,' I said. Beyond the glass of the conservatory there was just the faintest hint of grey in the sky over the house.

Verity waved bye-bye and went off, head down, rubbing her eyes, back into the house.

I moved the bishop. Lewis sat and thought.

I had won a knight and another pawn for the bishop when Verity came back. She was washed and dressed; she looked fabulous in leggings and a black maternity dress with a black leather jacket over the top. She stood at the doors, clapped her hands together and – when we appeared quizzical – waved some keys at us and said, 'Fancy a drive?'

We looked at each other and both shrugged at the same time.

We took Lewis and Verity's new soft-top XR3i – roof down, heater up full – out into the grey-pink dawn and drove through Lochgilphead and then into Gallanach and just cruised about the town, waving at the people still walking around the place and shouting Happy New Year! at one and all. Lewis and I had brought the whisky, just in case we met anybody we felt we ought to offer a dram. So we started with each other, and all that water during the night must have done us the power of good because the whisky tasted great.

(I'd looked back at the castle, as we'd passed the hill on the outskirts of Gallanach, feeling guilty and ashamed and nervous because I still hadn't done anything about my suspicions, but telling myself that I *still didn't have any real* evidence, and anyway I was off-duty now; this was the season to have fun, after all. Hogmanay; let's-get-oot-oor-brains time. And, naturally, an end-of-year truce. Hell, it was traditional.)

'Let's go down Shore Road and drop some whisky on that grave dad hit!' Lewis shouted suddenly. 'Mr Andrew McDobbie 1823–1875 and his wife Moira 1821–1903 deserve to be thought of at this time!'

'Ugh, you ghoul,' said Verity.

'No,' I said. 'It's a great idea. Verity; to the church!'

Which is how we came to find Helen Urvill and Dean Watt wandering through Gallanach along Shore Road, arm in arm. Dean was playing – necessarily softly – on his Stratocaster, while Helen held a bottle of Jack Daniels. They were being followed by a bemused-looking dog.

'Happy New Year!' shouted Dean Watt, and struck a chord. There ensued a great deal of Happy New Years; the mongrel that had been following Helen and Dean joined in by barking.

There were lots of hugs and handshakes and kisses too, before Helen Urvill yelled, 'Yo Verity!' as she hung on Dean's shoulder and breathed bourbon fumes at us. 'You sober, girl?'

'Yep,' Verity nodded briskly. 'Want a lift anywhere?'

Helen swung woozily round to look at Dean, who was fiddling with a machine-head. 'Well, we were heading back for the castle ...' She frowned deeply, and her eyes flicked around a bit. 'I think ...' She shrugged; her thick black eyebrows waggled. 'But if you're *going* somewhere ...'

'Let's go somewhere,' Verity said to Lewis, who was in the passenger's seat. 'Somewhere further.' She nudged Lewis.

'Okay,' Lewis said. 'Got a full tank; where we going to go?'

'Oban!'

'Boring!'

'Glasgow!'

'What *for*?'

'How about,' I suggested, over the noise of the barking hound. 'That bit north of Tighnabruaich, where you can look out over the Kyles of Bute? That's a nice bit of scenery.'

'Brilliant!' Lewis said.

'Great idea!'

'Let's go!'

'Get in, then.'

'And let's take the dog.'

'Is it car-trained?'

'Who cares? We can point it over the side if it comes to it.'

'Fuck it, yeah, let's take the mutt.'

'Might not want to come,' Dean said, and handed the Fender to Lewis, who put it at his feet with the neck by the door, while Dean knelt down by the side of the dog, which was sniffing at the rear wheel of the Escort.

'Course it wants to come,' Helen said, with the conviction only the truly drunk can muster. 'Not a dog been born doesn't like sticking its nose out a car window.'

'Here you go,' grunted Dean, lifting a puzzled-looking canine of medium build, indeterminate breed and brownly brindled coat into the car and onto my lap.

'Hey, thanks,' I said, as Helen clambered in beside me and Dean squeezed in on her far side. 'So it's me that gets to find out if this beast's shit-scared of driving.'

'Ah, stop whining,' Helen said, and pulled the fishy-smelling dog away from me to plonk it in Dean's lap.

'All set?' asked Verity.

'I wonder if its wee eyes'll light up when the brakes go on?' Dean said, trying to look into them.

'All set!' Helen yelled, then yodelled lustily as we performed a U-turn and went smoothly back through the town. Helen offered me some Jack Daniels, which I accepted. We still shouted Happy New Year! at people, and the dog barked enthusiastically in accompaniment; it didn't seem in the least discomfited when we left Gallanach and headed through Lochgilphead and away.

We stopped briefly at Lochgair. I ran into the house. Mum was up, washing dishes. I kissed and hugged her and said we'd be a few hours. Not to worry; Verity was bright as a button and so sober it ought to constitute a crime in Scotland at this time on a Hogmanay morning. She told me to make sure nobody else drove, then, and be careful. She made me take a load of sandwiches, dips and God-knows what, two bottles of mineral water and a flask of coffee she'd just made, and I staggered out the house and had to put most of it in the convertible's rather small boot, but then that was that and off we went through the calm, brightening day, playing lots of very loud music and munching through the various bits and pieces of food I hadn't stashed in the boot. Dog liked the garlic dip best.

*

'I don't give a fuck what colour he is; a man who can't pronounce his own name shouldn't be in charge of the most destructive military machine the world has ever seen,' I heard Lewis say, while I sat looking at Dean Watt, and thought, Shit, not again.

'She did, did she?' I said, trying to look pleased. 'Well. Good for her. Nice chap, is he?'

Dean shrugged. 'Okay, ah suppose.'

We were sitting on the rocks beyond the car-park crash barrier at the viewpoint above West Glen, overlooking the Kyles of Bute. The island itself stretched away to the south, all pastel and shade in the slightly watery light of this New Year's morning. The waters of the sound looked calmly ruffled, reflecting milky stretches of the lightly clouded sky.

Damn, I thought.

Ashley had got off with somebody at Liz and Droid's party. Dancin and winchin, as Dean had put it. Then gone off together. And suddenly I felt like it had happened again. Maybe not quite as stylish as jumping off your uncle's Range Rover into your future husband's arms, but just as effective. My heart didn't exactly go melt-down this time, but it still wasn't too pleasant a feeling.

Dean seemed happy to adjust his Strat and pick out the occasional tiny, tinny-sounded phrase; Lewis and Verity and Helen were arguing about the coming war. Or at least Lewis was ranting and they were having to listen.

'Aw, Hell,' Lewis said. 'I'm not arguing he isn't an evil bastard . . .'

Ashley, I thought, staring out into the view. Ashley, what was I thinking of? Why had I taken it so slow? What had I been frightened of? Why hadn't I said anything?

Hadn't I known what it was I wanted to say?

'– democracy and freedom, what Our Brave Boys are actually going to be fighting for is to restore the nineteenth century to Kuwait and defend the seventeenth century in Saudi Arabia.'

Now I thought I knew what I wanted to say, but it might already be too late. The knowledge and the provenance of its uselessness were the same; a feeling of loss I couldn't deny. Did that mean I was in love with her? If I was, it felt quite different from what I'd felt for Verity. (Verity sat at Lewis's side, huddled in her leggings and leathers and wearing Lewis's startlingly bright skiing jacket, all orange and purple and lime; she looked like a little psychedelic blonde Buddha perched on the tartan car rug.) Something calmer than that, something slower.

'– ternational law is only so goddman sacrosanct when it isn't something awkward like the World Court telling America to quit mining Nicaraguan harbours.'

But perhaps I was wrong about Ash being interested in me, anyway. Ashley was the one I remembered talking to in the Jac that evening after Grandma Margot's cremation; she was the one who kept telling me to tell Verity I loved her. If you love her, tell her. Wasn't that what she'd said? So if Ashley felt anything for me beyond friendship, why hadn't she said anything to me? And if she did feel anything, what was she doing going off with this friend of Droid's?

'– next time the US wants to invade somewhere and see what happens; out'll come that good old veto again. Heck, we got *lots* of practice using that. *We'll* do it if the Yanks don't. Panama? This place with the ditch? You don't like the guy in power any more after paying him all that CIA drug money over the years? Ah, why not? On you go. Seven thousand dead? Never mind, we can hush that up.'

Could I finally be right, and a woman was taking up with somebody else to make me feel jealous? I doubted it. Maybe she had been patiently waiting for me to tell her how I felt, or make some sort of move, and now she was fed up waiting, so all bets were off. But why should she have been so passive? Was Ashley that old-fashioned? Didn't sound like it; from what she'd told me, it was her who went after that Texan systems analyst, not the other way round. If she'd fancied me at all she'd have said or done something about it before now, wouldn't she?

'– resolutions are fine, unless they're against Israel, of course, in which case, Aw sheeit; you guys just stay in them Golan Heights, and that Gaza Strip. Shoot; them Palestinians probably weren't – aw, gosh-darn; did I say shoot them Palestinians? Well, hell no, we won't mention that. Twenty-three years the Israelis have been ignoring UN resolutions and occupying foreign territory; south, east and north. Hell's teeth, they'd probably invade the Mediterranean if you told them the fish were Palestinian. But does the US lay siege to them? Impose sanctions? Like fuck, they *bank-roll* the place!'

Maybe she did think of me as a brother. All those times I'd rambled drunkenly away to her about how much I loved Verity and what a hard time I was getting from everybody, and how wonderful Verity was, and what a poor, hard-done-by kid I was, and how much I loved Verity and how nobody understood me, and how wonderful Verity was ... How could you expect anybody to listen to all that moronic, self-pitying, self-deluding crap for so long and not think. Poor jerk?

'– we paid him to fight the Iranians for us, but now the scumbag's getting uppity, so we'll pay other scumbags like Assad to help fight *him*, and it'll all happen –'

Unloading all that stuff on Ash; most people would have told me to fuck off, but she listened, or at least didn't interrupt ... but what must she have been thinking? The response just couldn't be, Oh, he's so sensitive, or Oh, what a deep capacity for lurve this young fellow has ... *Poor jerk*. That about covered it. Or just, *Jerk*.

'– a modern day Hitler it's Pol Pot; even Saddam Hussein hasn't obliterated two million of his own people. But does the West mount a crusade against *that* genocidal mother-fucker? No! We're *supporting* the vicious scumbag! The United fucking States of America and the United fucking Kingdom think he's just the bee's knees because he's fighting those pesky Vietnamese who had the *nerve* to beat Uncle Sam –'

But maybe she hadn't really got off with this guy. Maybe it was all a mistake, maybe there was still a chance. Oh shit, I thought, and watched a seagull glide smoothly through the air below us, over the tops of the trees and the bundled rocks that led down to the distant shore.

'Oh,' said Verity suddenly, and clutched her belly, and looked wide-eyed at Lewis, who was in full flight over the vexed sands of Kuwait, and apparently quite beyond verbal interception.

'– Sabra and Chatila; ask the Kurds in Halabja –' He stopped dead, looked at his wife, who was still clutching her belly, looking pleadingly at him.

Lewis's jaw dropped and his face went white.

Verity hugged herself, put her head between her knees and started to rock back and forth. 'Oh-oh,' she said.

Lewis staggered to his feet, hands flailing, while Verity's shoulders started to quiver. The dog, which had been snoozing at Lewis's feet, jumped up too.

'Verity, what's wrong? Is it –?' began Helen, leaning over and putting an arm on Verity's shoulders.

'Who's the least drunk?' Lewis hollered, gaze oscillating rapidly between the car parked a few metres behind us and his wife, sitting rocking back and forth and shaking. The dog barked, bouncing up on its front feet, then sneezing.

'Oh! Oh! Oh!' said Verity, as Helen hugged her.

'Aw Christ,' said Dean. 'Verity, you're no about to drop, are ye?'

Lewis stood with his hands out, fingers splayed, eyes closed, on the rock. 'I don't believe this is happening!' he yelled. The dog barked loudly in what sounded like agreement.

Helen Urvill, her face down at Verity's knees – where Verity's head was still wedged – suddenly slapped Verity across the back and rolled away, laughing.

Dean looked confused. I felt the same way, then realised.

Lewis opened his eyes and stared at Helen lying laughing on the rock.

Verity rose quickly and gracefully, her face pink and smiling.

She stepped up to Lewis and hugged him, rocking him, her face tipped up to his as she giggled. 'Joke,' she told him. 'It isn't happening. I keep telling you, this baby's going to be born in a nice warm birthing pool in a nice big hospital. Nowhere else.'

Lewis sagged. He might have fallen if Verity hadn't held him. He slapped both hands over his face. 'You unutterable ... minx!' he roared, and put a hand to each side of Verity's grinning face, holding her head and shaking it. She just giggled.

So we sat and had some coffee and sandwiches.

'*Damn* fine coffee,' muttered Lewis.

Well, he had a tartan shirt on.

*

We drove back later; I watched buzzards and crows and gulls stoop and wheel and glide across the under-surface of thickening grey cloud. We were all very tired save Verity, and I must have fallen asleep because it came as a surprise when we had to stop to put the top up, in Inveraray, when the rain came on. It was a cramped, claustrophobic journey after that, and the dog whined a lot and smelled.

We got to Lochgair; I staggered into the house, collapsed into my bed and slept for the rest of the day.

I kept missing Ashley after that. Whenever I rang the Watt house she was out, or asleep. She rang me once, but I'd been out walking. Next time I called she had caught the train for Glasgow, en route for the airport and London.

Tone and Hamish's usual post-Hogmanay soirée had been even more subdued than usual. Hamish had given up drink, but apparently found his heretical ideas on retribution more difficult to jettison, and so spent most of the evening telling me – with a kind of baleful enthusiasm – about a Commentary he was writing on the Bible, which cast new light on punishment and reward in the hereafter, and which had great contemporary relevance.

I drove back to Glasgow on the fifth of January. After New Year's Eve, watching Fergus show off his new plane, I hadn't visited the castle again.

*

Two weeks later, after I had had my abbreviated conversation with Lachlan Watt in sunny Sydney, I set off for Lochgair at nine that Friday morning, listening to the war on the radio for as long as I could, until the mountains blocked out the signal.

War breaks out amongst the oilfields and the price of crude plummets. From being an ally so staunch he can missile American ships and it passes as an understandable mistake, and gas thousands of Kurds with barely a gesture of censure (Thatcher promptly increased his export credits, and within three weeks Britain was talking about all the lovely marketing opportunities Iraq represented; for chemicals, presumably), Saddam Hussein had suddenly become Adolf Hitler, despite more or less being invited to walk into Kuwait.

It was a war scripted by Heller from a story by Orwell, and somebody would be bombing their own airfield before too long, no doubt.

From Glasgow to Lochgair is a hundred and thirty-five kilometres by road; less as the crow flies, or as the missile cruises. The journey took about an hour and a half, which is about normal when the roads aren't packed with tourists and caravans. I spent most of the time shaking my head in disbelief at the news on the radio, and telling myself that I mustn't allow this to distract me from confronting Fergus, or at the very least sharing my suspicions with somebody other than Ash.

But I think I already knew that was exactly what would happen.

And Ash ... God, the damn thing may be just muscle, merely a pump, but my heart really did seem to ache whenever I thought of her.

So I tried not to think about Ashley Watt at all, utterly unsure whether by doing so I was being very strong, or extremely stupid. I chose not to make an informed guess which; my track record didn't encourage such honesty.

*

Mum dropped her laser-guided bombshell over lunch that day. We were sitting in the kitchen, watching the war on television, dutifully listening to the same reports and watching the same sparse bits of footage time after time. I was already starting to get bored with the twin blue-pink glowing cones of RAF Tornadoes' afterburners as they took off into the night, and even the slo-mo footage of the exciting Brit-made JP-233 runway-cratering package scattering bomblets and mines with the demented glee of some Satanic Santa was already inducing feelings of weary familiarity.

On the other hand, such repetition left one free to appreciate the subtler points in these reports that might otherwise have gone unnoticed, such as the fact that the English *could* pronounce the soft *ch* sound, after all. The little rascals had only been teasing us all these years, saying 'Lock' Lomond and 'Lock' Ness! Why, it must be something genetic, we'd all thought. But no! Places like Bah'rain and Dah'ran were rolled confidently off the tongue by newsreader after newsreader and correspondent after correspondent as though they'd been using the technique for years.

Unfortunately, rather like a super-gun, there appeared to be a problem traversing such a sophisticated phonetic delivery system, and while the Arabian peninsula obviously lay in the favoured direction, nowhere unfortunate enough to be located to the north of London seemed able to benefit from this new-found facility.

'Oh,' mum said, passing the milk across the kitchen table to me, 'assuming we're all still alive next Friday, Fergus has asked me to the opera in Glasgow. Is it all right if we stay with you?'

I watched the lines of tracer climb above Baghdad, impotent

spirals of light twisting to and fro. I felt frozen. Had I heard right? I looked at my mother.

She frowned. 'Prentice, are you okay?'

'Wha–?' I said. I could feel the blood draining from my face. I put the jug down, feeling as white as the low-fat it contained. I tried to swallow. I couldn't talk, so I settled for clearing my throat and looking at mum with a interrogatory expression.

'Fergus,' mum said tolerantly. 'Invited me to the opera in Glasgow, next Friday. May we stay with you? I assume there's room . . . I do mean separate rooms, Prentice.' She smiled. 'Are you all right? You're not worried about the war, are you? You look white as a sheet.'

'I'm fine,' I waved one hand weakly. Actually I felt sick.

'You look sick,' mum said.

I tried to swallow again. She shook her head. 'Don't worry, Prentice. They won't conscript you; you're far too Bolshie. I really wouldn't worry.'

'Hg,' I said, almost gagging.

'Is that all right? Are we allowed to stay with you? Does your lease, or whatever, cover that?'

'Ah,' I said at last. 'Yeah.' I nodded, finally swallowing successfully. 'Yeah, I think so. I mean, of course. Yes. Why not? Loads of room. What opera? What are you going to see?'

'Macbeth.'

Macbeth! 'Oh,' I said, trying to smile. 'That's Verdi, isn't it?'

'Yes, I think so,' mum said, still frowning. 'Would you like to come? It's a box, so there should be room.'

'Um, no thanks,' I said. I didn't know what to do with my hands, which seemed to want to shake. Finally I shoved them in the pockets of my jeans.

'You sure you're all right, Prentice?'

'Of course!'

Mum tipped her head to one side. 'You're not upset because I'm going out with Fergus, are you?'

'No!' I laughed. 'Why, are you?'

'We've partnered each other at bridge a couple of times. He's a friend, Prentice, that's all.' Mum looked puzzled.

'Right. Well,' I said. 'Yes, of course there's room. I'll ... no problem.'

'Good,' mum said, and clicked a couple of sweeteners into her tea. She was still looking at me strangely. I turned and watched the war for a while. Jumping Jesus, now what?

*

I sat at dad's desk. It took longer to write down what I suspected than I'd thought it would. I started with pen and paper, but my writing looked funny and I kept having to dry my hand. Finally I used the computer and printed out what I'd typed. I put the sheet of paper in an envelope and left it lying in the top right drawer of the desk. I wished dad had had a gun, but he hadn't. I settled for the old Bowie knife I'd had since my Scouting days, sticking the leather sheath down the back of my jeans. I changed into a T-shirt and a shortish jumper so that I could get at the knife quickly, feeling frightened and embarrassed as I did so.

Mum was in what had been a spare bedroom, constructing the harpsichord. When I stuck my head round the door, the room stank of varnish and the sort of old-fashioned glue you'd rather not know the original source of. 'I'm just going up to the castle, to see Uncle Fergus,' I said. 'You reminded me: there are some pieces of Lalique in the house I'm staying in. I thought I'd have a talk to Fergus about them, see if he fancied bidding for them when the contents are eventually auctioned.'

Mum was standing at the work-bench, dressed in overalls, her hair tied back. She was polishing a piece of veneer with a cloth. 'Pieces of what?' she said, blowing from the side of her mouth to dislodge a wisp of hair that had escaped the hair clasp.

'Lalique. René Lalique. Glass; you know.'

'Oh, yes.' She looked surprised. 'Fergus'll see them on Friday, won't he?'

'Well, they're in storage in the cellar,' I said. 'I haven't actually seen them. They're in the inventory. I took a note of them. But I thought if he did want to look at them, maybe I could look them out in time for Friday.'

'Oh.' Mum shrugged, tipped oil from a bottle onto the brown-stained cloth. 'Okay, then. Say hello from me.'

'Yeah,' I said. I closed the door.

I walked away thinking I should have said more, should have said ... well, the conventional things you tell people when you're going in fear of your life. But I couldn't think of a way to say them that wouldn't sound ridiculous and melodramatic. I'd closed off the letter I'd left in the desk with quite enough of that sort of thing, I thought.

I took the Golf out of Lochgair, along the Gallanach road. The Bowie knife was an uncomfortable lump down and across the small of my back, its wood and brass handle cold on my back at first, then warming.

I stopped and made a phone call in Lochgilphead.

'Mr Blawke, sorry to trouble you at home –'

Ostensibly I was just checking out whether it was all right for me to mention the Lalique to Fergus, before the expensive French glass-ware was included in any auction, but really I was making sure the lawyer Blawke knew where I was going.

It wasn't until I was at the foot of the castle driveway that I realised all this time I'd just been assuming Fergus would be there. As I hesitated, hands shaking on the wheel, it occurred to me there was probably a good chance he wasn't. I hadn't checked, after all, and Fergus frequently went away for the weekend; maybe he wasn't at the castle. Relief coursed through me, along with an annoying current of shame that I felt so relieved.

I took the Golf up the drive.

The gravel circle in front of the castle held five cars, including

Fergus's Range Rover. 'Oh God,' I said to myself.

I parked the Golf behind a Bristol Brigand which sat half on the gravel and half on the grass. I walked up to the doors and rang the bell.

'Prentice!' Mrs McSpadden roared. 'Happy New Year to you.'

'Happy New Year,' I said, realising only then that I hadn't seen Mrs McS since the turn of the year. I was permitted to kiss the formidable ramparts of one of Mrs McS's cheeks. 'Is Uncle Fergus in?' I asked. *Say, No*, I thought, *Say, No*!

'Aye, he is that,' she said, letting me into the castle. 'I think they're playing billiards. I'll take you up.' She stood aside to let me into the entrance hall with its glassy-eyed audience of stags' heads.

'Actually, it's sort of personal,' I said, smiling faintly, aware I was blinking a lot.

Mrs McS looked at me oddly. 'Is that a fact? Well, then, would you wait in the library?'

'Ah . . . all right,' I said.

We walked through the hall. 'Isn't this Gulf thing terrible?' Mrs McSpadden shouted, as if trying to be heard there. I agreed it was terrible. She showed me into the library, on the other side of the lower hall from the kitchen entrance. I stood in there nervously, trying to breathe normally, letting my gaze flick over the ranked rows of impressive, dark leather spines. I wished my own was half so noble and upright. The room smelled of leather and old, musty paper. I went to look out one of the room's two small windows, at the garden and the wood beyond. I adjusted the knife down the back of my jeans so that I could get at it easily.

'Prentice?' Fergus Urvill said, entering the library. He closed the door behind him. He was dressed in tweed britches and a Pringle jumper over a checked country shirt, with thick socks and brogues. He brushed some grey-black hair away from his face. His jowls flexed as he smiled at me, lifting a little from the collar of his shirt.

I cleared my throat.

Fergus stood there, his arms folded. After a moment he said,

'What can I do for you, young man?'

I moved from the window to the large wooden table that filled the centre of the room, and put my hands lightly on its surface to stop them shaking. A seat back pressed into my thighs.

'Fergus ...' I began. 'I wondered ... I wondered if you knew where ... where my Uncle Rory might be.'

Fergus frowned, then one eye closed and he sort of cocked his head. Still with his arms folded, he leaned forward a little. 'Sorry? Your uncle –'

'Uncle Rory,' I said. Maybe a little too loudly, but at least my voice didn't sound as shaky as I'd expected. I lowered it a little to say, 'I thought you might have an idea where he is.'

Fergus stood straight again. The frown was still there around his eyes, but his lips were smiling. 'You mean Rory, who disappeared ...?'

'Yes,' I nodded. My mouth felt dry and I had to fight to swallow.

'I've no idea, Prentice.' Fergus scratched behind one ear with one hand. He looked mystified. 'Why do you think I might know?'

I felt myself blinking too much again, and tried to stop it. I took a breath.

'Because you got a man called Rupert Paxton-Marr to send match-book covers to my dad.' My hands were shaking even though they were planted on the surface of the table. I pressed down harder.

Fergus rocked back a little on his brogues. His frown-smile intensified. 'Rupert? Sending your dad ... what?' He looked a little amused, a little confused, and not nervous in the least. *Oh God, what am I doing?* I thought.

Of course, I hadn't thought to bring any of the match-book covers with me. 'Match-book covers,' I said, my dry throat rasping. 'From all over the world, so that dad would think Rory was still alive.'

Fergus looked to one side and unfolded his arms, sticking his hands in his pockets. He looked up at me. 'Hmm. Would you like a drink?' he said.

'No,' I told him.

He moved to the other end of the table, where there was a small wooden desk like the top of a lectern. He opened it and took out a squat decanter and a crystal glass. He took the glittering, faceted stopper out of the decanter and poured some of the brown liquid into the glass, frowning all the time. 'Prentice,' he said, shaking his head and mating stopper and decanter again. 'I'm sorry, you've lost me. What are you ... what is ... what do you think is going on? Rupert's sending, or was sending Kenneth ...?'

'Match-book covers, from hotels and restaurants and bars in various parts of the world,' I told him, as he stood, relaxed, one hand in pocket, one hand holding the glass, his face scrunched up in the manner of one trying hard and with some sympathy to understand what another is saying. 'Somehow,' I struggled on, 'they were meant to convince dad that Rory was still alive. But I think he's dead.'

'Dead?' Fergus said, drinking. He nodded at the seat I was standing over. 'Aren't you going to take a seat?'

'No thanks,' I said.

Fergus shrugged, sighed. 'Well, I can't imagine ...' The frown came back again. 'Has Rupert *told* you he was doing this?'

'No,' I said.

'And are you sure it wasn't Rory?' Fergus shrugged. 'I mean, was it his handwriting?'

'There wasn't any handwriting.'

'There wasn't ...' Fergus shook his head. He smiled, an expression that looked to be half sympathy and half incomprehension. 'Prentice, I'm lost. I don't see ...' His voice trailed off. The frown returned. 'Now, wait a moment,' he said. 'You said you thought I might know where Rory is. But if he's dead ...?' He stared, looking shocked, into my eyes. I tried hard not to look away, but in the end I had to. I looked down at the table-top, biting my lip.

'Prentice,' Fergus said softly, putting his glass down on the table. 'I've no idea where your uncle is.' There was silence for a while. 'Rupert is an old school friend of mine. He's a journalist who goes all over the world; he's out in Iraq at this moment, in fact. I haven't seen him for a couple of years, though he used to come and shoot on occasion. He is a bit of a practical joker at times, but ...' Fergus looked thoughtful. He shrugged. 'Rory did tell me something once about setting fire to a barn on the estate once; accidentally, when he was very young. That might tie in with these match boxes ...' He shook his head, inspected the contents of his glass. 'But I don't *think* I ever mentioned that to Rupert.'

I felt sick. 'Nothing about ... some pieces of writing makes any sense, does it?'

'Writing?' Fergus said, tilting his head, one eye narrowing. He shook his head. 'No. Whose writing?'

'Rory's. Based on something that you saw here; up in the roof-space of the castle, and which you told Rory when you were in that bothy together. The night you shot the rat.'

Fergus had leaned forward again. He looked totally bemused. Finally he jerked upright and laughed. He looked at the glass he held. 'Maybe I should lay off this stuff. You're making less and less sense as you go along here, Prentice. Rory and I did spend a night in a bothy once, on the estate. But there wasn't any ... rat.' He smiled and frowned at the same time. 'Or any shooting. I don't think we even had guns with us; we were fishing some of the out-of-the-way lochans and streams.' He sighed, giving the impression of patient weariness. 'Is this something you've read?'

'Yes,' I conceded.

'What, in your father's papers, since his death?' Fergus looked as though he felt pity for me.

I nodded, trying not to look down from his gaze. 'Sort of,' I breathed.

'And who is meant to have seen what?' He raised one finger to his mouth, bit briefly at a nail and examined it.

'None of that makes any sense to you, does it?' I said. 'No ... confession, revelation? Nothing to do with Lachy Watt?'

Fergus looked hurt. He swirled the glass, drained it. 'That was a very long time ago, Prentice,' he said quietly.

He looked at me more sorrowfully than accusatorily. 'We were only children. We don't always appreciate the seriousness of what we do ...' He glanced at his empty glass ... 'when we're younger.'

He put the glass on the table.

I couldn't match his gaze, and lowered mine again. I felt dizzy.

I heard Fergus take in a breath. 'Prentice,' he said, eventually. 'I was quite close to Kenneth. He was a friend. I don't think we saw eye-to-eye on anything really, but we ... we got on, you know? He was a gifted man, and a good friend, and I know I feel the loss. I can imagine how you feel. I ... I've had my own ... What I mean is, it isn't an easy thing to cope with, when somebody that close dies so suddenly. Everything can look ... Well, everything can look very black, you know? Nothing seems right. You even resent other people their happiness, and, well, it just all seems very unfair. It is a terrible strain to be under; don't think I don't appreciate that. And just now, when the world seems ...' He took another deep breath. 'Look, old son –'

'I'm sorry,' I said, stopping him. I smiled shakily. 'Uncle Fergus; I'm very sorry I came here. I've been silly. I don't know what I was ...' I shook my head, looked briefly down. 'I don't know what I was thinking. I've not been getting much sleep recently.' I smiled bravely. 'Watching too much television, maybe.' I waved one hand round a little, as though flailing out for something just beyond reach, then shrugged. 'I'm sorry,' I concluded.

Fergus looked serious for a moment. Then he gave a small smile. He crossed his arms again. 'Oh well. I think everything looks a bit sort of mad, really, at the moment, doesn't it?'

'A bit,' I agreed. I sniffed, wiped my nose with a paper hanky.

'Sure you won't have that drink?' Fergus said.

I nodded, stuffed the hanky back into my jeans. 'No thanks, I have to drive. Better be getting back.'

'Right you are,' Fergus said.

He saw me to the door. He patted me on the shoulder as I stood in the doorway. 'Don't worry, Prentice, all right?'

'Yeah,' I said.

'Oh, and I don't know if your mother's mentioned it –'

'Opera; Friday.' I smiled.

Fergus smiled too, jowls wobbling. 'Ah, she has.'

'Yes. No problem,' I said.

'Jolly good. Well, that's all right then.' He offered me his hand.

We shook. 'Thanks, uncle,' I said. He nodded, and I walked down the steps and across the gravel to the Golf.

He waved goodbye from the steps, looking concerned but encouraging.

I let the Golf trundle down to the bottom of the hill, where the drive levelled out and joined the tarmac single-track which swept round the base of the hill towards the main road between Gallanach and Lochgilphead. At the junction I stopped. I just sat there for a while. I raised my right hand and looked at the palm for a while, then spat on it and rubbed it hard on the side of my thigh. I tore the knife and its sheath out from my jeans and threw them down into the passenger footwell. I looked in the rear-view mirror, where I could just see the reflection of the top of the castle – its battlements and silver observatory dome – through the limbs of the leafless trees.

'Guilty as charged, you bastard,' I heard myself say. Then with a quick look either way, I revved up, slipped the clutch and sent the VW screaming along the road away from the castle.

*

The courtyard was empty and the house storm doors were shut when I got back to Lochgair. I parked the Golf in the yard and got out; my hands were shaking. I felt like getting furiously drunk. I stood there, breathing hard in the calm air, listening to gulls crying above the drive down towards the loch, while crows crackled in the trees around the house like some drunken chorus, scornful. My heart was thudding now and my trembling hands were slick with sweat. I had to rest back against the side of the car. I closed my eyes. The cries of the birds were replaced by a roaring noise in my ears.

Jesus, I thought, if this was how I felt, how must Fergus be reacting, if I was right, and he was guilty? Now would be the time to watch him, study him. But I could barely have walked just then, let alone drive back to the castle, even if I had been able to summon up the courage to return.

Eventually I felt better again, and instead of going into the house, went for a walk through the woods and the forest and up into the hills, and sat on an old ruined wall on the hill topped by the cairn where dad had told us about the mythosaurs, all those years ago. I looked down to the trees and the loch in the pastel light cast by the bright, gauzy overcast, while the mild wind freshened. I replayed that scene in the castle library time after time after time, imagining that I remembered every word, every movement, every nuance of tone and phrasing, every millimetric increment of body language, trying to work out whether I was being terribly sensitive and acute, or just insanely fanciful and paranoid.

Sometimes I thought it was perfectly obvious that Fergus was utterly genuine, and all my ideas, all my suspicions were demonstrably ludicrous. Of course the man was innocent; I was insane. Guilty as charged, indeed; who was I to judge?

Other times it was as though his every inflection and gesture shrieked artifice, lies, deception. Very good deception, cunningly deployed lies and artful artifice, but everything false all the same.

He had reacted just as you would expect somebody to react. But was that the way somebody actually would react? I didn't know, and could not decide.

I got so angry and confused at it all I threw my head back and screamed at the grey sky, roaring full force, all noise and no meaning till my lungs emptied and my throat ached. I doubled up, coughing and spluttering, eyes watering, feeling marginally better but looking round guiltily, hoping nobody had heard or seen. Only a couple of crows answered, harsh voices calling from the trees beneath.

I'd chosen a vantage point from which I could watch the road and the house, and only went back down there when I saw mum's Metro turn off the loch road from Gallanach and flicker like a green ghost as it moved up the drive, half-obscured by the trunks and branches of the bare, grey oaks.

*

I suppose I was uncommunicative with James and my mother that evening; I spent most of the time in dad's study, reading and re-reading the three pieces Rory had written about himself, Fergus, Aunt Fiona and Lachlan Watt. I looked through some of Rory's diaries, gritting my teeth at the impenetrable paucity of their desiccated information. I turned on the Compaq and looked at the letter I'd written that morning. Damn; found a spelling mistake that had got through the spell-checker; 'saw' where I'd meant to type 'was'.

I started drinking whisky after dinner, sitting at the desk in the study at first, craning over its leather surface, sifting through the various papers and diaries, my eyes getting sore. I nearly spilled my whisky into the Compaq at one point, so I turned off the little green-shaded light on the desk and went over to the couch, taking all the bits and pieces with me. I switched on the standard lamp behind me and lay lengthwise on the couch, surrounded by paper. I had the TV on with the sound turned down most of the time, using the remote to turn it up whenever it looked like there was something interesting coming in from the Gulf. I heard James go to bed about eleven-thirty. Mum looked in to say good-night about twelve. I waved, wished her pleasant dreams and kept on reading.

I woke up just after two with the whisky glass balanced on my chest and my eyes feeling gritty. I finished the whisky even though I didn't really feel like it, then went to bed. I drank some water before I fell asleep.

*

The clock said 4:14 when I woke up, my bladder just at that point where it might or might not be possible to fall asleep again without having to go for a pee (it didn't usually wake me with so poor an excuse). I lay there for a bit, listening to soft rain hitting the bedroom window. Maybe that was what had woken me. I turned over to go to sleep again, then suddenly started to wonder if I'd turned the computer off. I had the feeling that I had, but I couldn't actually remember doing so. Fuck it, I thought; it would be safe enough. I rolled over onto my other side.

But my bladder had woken up properly in the meantime and was demanding attention. I sighed, swung out of bed, not bothering with my dressing gown even though the house had grown a little chilly by now. There was an orange night-light plug in a socket in the corridor; I decided to save my eyes from the shock of putting on any more powerful illumination and navigated the anyway familiar route to the bathroom by the plug's pale orange glow.

I sat in the darkness, peeing. A sort of quarter-erection had made it advisable to sit down. I smiled, remembering Lewis's spiel about trying to pee when you had a full bladder and a full erection at the same time. I flushed the toilet, washed my hands and drank some water from the tap. Mum must have been varnishing some part of the harpsichord earlier, judging by the smell in the corridor. I padded along to the study.

I could just make out the dim shape of the desk and computer on the far side of the room when I opened the study door. I couldn't hear the Compaq's fan running, or see a light on, but I went over to it anyway. I stood with my thighs against the wood and leather back of the desk's chair, and leant forward, pressing the computer's disk eject button in case I had switched it off but had left a disk in it. No disk. I yawned, straightened, and rubbed the inside of my right fore-arm where it had brushed against the glass shade of the little desk light. The shade had been hot.

There was a little red dot glowing on the dark screen of the computer monitor; must be the reflection of the TV on the other side of the room. Ha; so I had left it –

I froze, suddenly wide awake.

Why was the light shade hot?

The little red light reflected on the screen winked out, as though suddenly obscured.

I threw myself back from the desk, just starting to sense movement behind me; I fell backwards as something dark scythed past in front of my face and a noise like the wind terminated in a splintering crash. Somebody – just a silhouette in the dim vague shadows of the room, lit only by the feeble light spilling from the hall night-light – stumbled forward, just behind where I had stood, arms reaching in front of them, pulling something long and dark and thin out of the wrecked back of the seat. The figure started to turn as I landed heavily on my back on the rug; I kicked out at their nearest knee, wishing I was wearing my Docs. Or anything, come to that.

I felt my heel hit their leg. 'Huh!'

Sounded male; he staggered a little, then came forward at me, one arm raised as I started to roll, suddenly feeling very vulnerable and naked. A smashing noise sounded from overhead; metal and glass. I kept rolling, pushing up with my hands and leaping to my feet. Glass was falling from the ceiling as something thudded into the floor where I'd lain. I was at the man's side as he staggered forward, raising the bar or jemmy or whatever the hell it was from where it had struck the carpet. I kicked him in what I hoped was the kidneys and watched him stumble to one side, then something banged into the top of my head and hit my shoulder, confusing me. My feet crunched over something hard on the rug as I staggered. More light from the hall, as I stood swaying, dazed, and the attacker recovered. I could see him better now; all in black. Gloves, balaclava. His build . . .

'Uncle Ferg?' I heard somebody whisper. It sounded like me.

'Prentice?' said a woman's voice, distantly, worriedly, from the corridor.

I watched the man in front of me seem to hesitate, arm raised. I was falling. I staggered backwards, trying not to fall, crashing into a filing cabinet.

'Prentice!' mum screamed, somewhere. Then; 'James! Get back!'

The dark figure looked towards the hallway, where the light was. I nearly fell round the side of the filing cabinet, then pulled myself up on some shelves, staring back at the black-dressed man in the middle of the room. There was movement at the study door; sparks flashed in the middle of the ceiling. I clutched at something on the bookshelf; graspable, heavy enough; an ashtray or bowl. I threw it, heard it hit his body and clunk to the floor. He still stood there, maybe only for a second or so, but it seemed like an eternal hesitation, while he glanced from me to the hallway again. I thought I heard a door slam. I roared, shouting incoherently the way I had on the hillside that afternoon as I stumbled from the shelves, past the filing cabinet and nearly fell over the desk while he came forward at me, arm raised again; I picked up the computer's keyboard from the desk, hauling it bursting free and swinging it as hard as I could at him as he brought his arm down.

There was a terrific, bone-ringing crash that seemed to infect the whole world, like an electric shock and a thunder-clap and an earthquake all at once. There was an odd pattering and clinking noise from every part of the room. I stood, holding nothing, blinking in the darkness while somebody moved stumbling away, obscuring light.

I felt weird. My feet and arms and head felt buzzy and sore, but when I felt my head I couldn't feel any blood. Feet felt slippy. I heard the phone on the desk make a noise, and picked it up, still dazed.

'Which service?' said a man's voice.

'Police!' I heard my mother shout.

'Sorry,' I mumbled. I put the phone down, pushing myself away from the desk. I tripped on the pale remains of the keyboard. Its lettered keys lay scattered about the floor like teeth. I stubbed my toe on something, bent down and picked up a long steel bar. I limped to the top of the stairs in time to see the front door slam shut.

My head felt buzzy again; I went into the kitchen, found the broken door lock and two full red plastic petrol cans sitting on the kitchen table, then got back out into the hall, still holding the steel bar even though it was beginning to feel very heavy, and shouted, 'Mum? Mum; it's all right! I think ...' before I had to sit down at the kitchen table, because my tongue had suddenly become a clapper in the bell of my skull, and my head was ringing. I put my arms on the table and rested my head on them while I waited for the echoes in my head to go away.

'Welcome to Argyll,' I told myself.

The kitchen light was painfully bright when it went on. Mum brought me my dressing gown and put a blanket over my shoulders and made me drink heavily sugared tea, and I remember thinking, Sugared tea; dad must have died again, and mumbling something about having a flag in my foot when mum washed them and put bandages on them, and wondering why she was looking so upset and James so frightened; then police came. They seemed very large and official and asked me lots of questions. Later, Doctor Fyfe appeared looking slightly dishevelled, and I recall asking him what he was doing up at this time in the morning, and how he was these days. Old ticker holding out all right, was it?

CHAPTER
13

e were on the battlements; I faced into the cool north wind. I waited to feel the dizziness of déjà-vu, but didn't. Maybe too much had happened, or not enough time had passed.

*

'Well, whatever the heathen equivalent is,' Lewis said. 'Will you?'

'Of course,' I said. I looked down into the small pink face bundled inside the old family shawl; Kenneth McHoan had his eyes tightly closed and wore an expression of concentration on his features that implied sleep was a business of some deliberation. One of his hands – the thumb so small it could have fitted on just the nail of one of my own thumbs – was held up near his chin; the tiny fingers made a slow waving motion, like a sea anemone in a stray current, and I jiggled up and down a little, cradling the sleeping child and going, 'Shh, shh.'

I glanced at Verity, sitting beside Lewis, her arm round his waist. She looked up from her son's face for a moment.

'Uncle Prentice, the Godfather.' She smiled.

'An offer only a churl could refuse.'

*

'People have their own absorption spectra, Prentice,' said Diana Urvill, as she took a Corning turn-of-the-century cut glass plate out of the display case in the castle Solar and – after wiping the plate with a lint-free cloth – handed it carefully to me. We both wore white gloves. I took the plate – like an immense ice crystal with too many angles of symmetry – and placed it on the table, on the topmost sheet of foam. I folded the translucent padding over – thinking how much it looked like prawn crackers – secured it with tape, then found a suitably sized box and placed the plate in the centre, on a bed of small white expanded-polysytrene wafers that looked like flattened infinity symbols.

I lifted one of the giant sacks of the wafers and filled the box to the brim with them, covering the wrapped-up plate, then closed the box and took the little card Diana had left on the table and taped it to the side of the box where it could be read. Then I put the box on a five-high pile near the door; the stacking limit was six, so it completed that column.

'Absorption spectra?' I said sceptically, as we started to repeat the whole process with a Fritsche rock crystal ewer.

Diana, dressed in baseball boots, black tracksuit bottoms and a UCLA sweatshirt, her black hair tied in a pony tail, nodded, and breathed on the ewer before polishing it. 'Things they get absorbed in. Interests, that sort of thing. If you could take a sort of life-spectrum for everybody, of all the things they believed in and took an interest in and became involved in – all that sort of stuff – then they'd look like stellar spectra; a smooth band of colour from violet to red, with black lines where the things that meant something to those people had been absorbed.'

'What an astronomical imagination you have, Diana,' I said. 'Getting enough oxygen up on Mauna Kea, yeah?' I grinned.

'Just a pet theory, Prentice.' She finished polishing the ewer. 'Better than believing in,' she said, and handed me the elaborately carved jug, 'crystals.'

'Well, that's true, in a very un-Californian way, isn't it?' I filled the inside of the ewer up with little polystyrene beads from another giant sack, a broad smile on my face as I remembered.

*

She cried out and the crystal sang in reply.

Later, we exchanged signals.

*

'Help me fold these sheets, will you?'

*

The day after all the excitement at Lochgair, I sat at the dining table with what looked like a turban on my head. It was a towel wrapped round one of those sealed liquid containers you freeze and put in cool boxes.

I signed the statement.

'Thank you, sir.'

'Davey, stop calling me "sir", for God's sake,' I breathed. Constable David McChrom had been in my class at school and I couldn't bring myself to call him "officer". His nickname had been Plooky, but that might have been carrying informality a little too far.

'Ach, second nature these days, Prent,' he said, folding the papers and standing up. He looked depressingly fresh and well-scrubbed; joining the police force seemed to have done wonders for his skin condition. He lifted his cap from the table top, turning to my mother. 'Right. That's all for now, Mrs McHoan. I'll be getting back, but if you think of anything else, just tell one of the other officers. We'll be in touch if we hear anything. You all right now, Mrs McHoan?'

'Fine, thanks, Davey,' mum smiled. Dressed in jeans and a thick jumper, she looked a little dark around the eyes, but otherwise okay.

'Right you are, then. You look after that heid of yours, okay, Prentice?'

'As though it were my own,' I breathed, adjusting my towel.

Mum saw him out.

The CID were still in the study, looking for fingerprints. They'd be lucky. I looked out of the dining-room window to where a couple of policemen were searching the bushes near the kitchen door.

My, we were being well looked after. I doubted a roughly equivalent fracas in one of the poorer council estates would have attracted quite such diligent and comprehensive investigation. But maybe that was just me being cynical.

My head hurt, my feet hurt, my fingers hurt. All the extremities. Well, save one, thankfully. Most of the damage came from the central light fixture in the study ceiling. It was part of that – a large, heavy, brass part of it – which had hit me on the head, and it was the shattered glass of its shades which had cut my feet as I'd stumbled around the study. My fingers hurt from the impact of computer keyboard and steel tyre-iron.

The desk drawers had been levered open. The back of the desk's matching chair had taken the full force of a blow with the tyre-iron, the light fixture had been hit accidentally by the same implement and the ceiling rose damaged, the Compaq's keyboard was wrecked and the kitchen door needed a new lock. I felt I could use a new head.

Nothing had been stolen, though I'd noticed that all the papers I'd been looking at earlier that night – and which I'd left scattered round the couch – had been neatly gathered together and piled on one end of the desk, under a paperweight. The envelope I'd left in the desk's top right drawer that morning was still here. The police didn't open it. Apart from the damage, and that one contrary act of tidiness, it looked like our attacker had taken nothing, and left behind him only the petrol and the tyre-iron.

I wanted to phone Fergus; ask him how he was. Good night's sleep? Any aches and pains? But mum had been fussing over me after Doctor Fyfe had said I'd need watching for a day or two and I wasn't being allowed to do very much. Somehow I lacked the will, anyway.

They'd asked me if I had any idea who it might have been, and I'd said No. I didn't say anything to my mother, or anybody else, either.

What could I say?

I was certain it had been Fergus – his build had been right, and even though I'd been dazed, I swear he did hesitate when I spoke his name – but how was I supposed to convince anybody else? I shook my head, then grimaced, because it hurt. I couldn't believe I'd been so stupid, not even thinking that he might try and steal or destroy whatever evidence he thought I had. 'Is this something you've read?' I whispered to myself, remembering what Fergus had asked me. 'In your father's papers, after his death?'

Jeez. I felt myself blush at my naïvety.

Mum continued to fuss, but I got better through the day.

After the CID boys finished in the study, I photocopied all Rory's papers – though I had to drag a chair over to the photocopier and sit down to do it – then, before the police left, and after much pleading, got mum to drive into Gallanach and deposit the parcelled originals in the bank. She came back with a new lock for the kitchen door. I hadn't been able to persuade her that a little holiday – in Glasgow, maybe – would be a good idea, so while she was away I rang Dean Watt and asked if he and Tank Thomas fancied coming to stay at Lochgair for a few days. Tank was a quiet and normally docile friend of the Watts', two metres tall and one across; I'd once seen him carry a couple of railway sleepers, one over each shoulder, without even breaking sweat.

James – who'd earlier been appalled that he'd only missed the first two periods of school while the police interviewed him – arrived back at four, glowing with glory. Apparently his part in the night's events – which I'd thought consisted largely of sticking his head round his bedroom door and being told to get back in again (and doing as he was told, for once) – had gained something in the translation at school; I suspected the gains involved the single-handed beating-off an attack by an entire gang of ninja assassins while mum and I slept.

I told mum about Dean and Tank, but she wasn't having it, and rang Dean up to cancel the protection I'd arranged. The police had promised to keep an eye on the house over the next few nights, after all; a patrol car would check up the drive. This didn't sound like much good to me, but mum seemed reassured.

Old Mr Docherty, a leathery-faced octogenarian with wispy white hair who was one of our neighbours in the village, arrived at tea-time and offered to come over with his shot-gun and sit up all night. 'Ah've nuthin tae steal maself, Mrs McHoan, and Ah'd rather make sure you and the bairns were all right. Canny have this sort aw thing going on in Lochgair, ye know. Be Glasgow people, Ah tell ye. Be Glasgow boys.'

Mum thanked him, but refused. He seemed happy when we asked him to help us fit the new lock on the kitchen door. Lewis was all set to come up from London when we told him what had happened, but mum persuaded him we were fine, really.

Fretting for something else to do, I rang up Mrs McSpadden at the castle and related all that had happened, and twice told her how I suspected the raider had been after Rory's papers, which I'd copied and deposited in the bank. 'In the bank, Prentice,' she repeated, and I could hear her voice echoing. 'Good idea.'

I asked after Fergus and Mrs McSpadden said he was fine. He and his friends had been out fishing that day.

To my own amazement, I slept soundly that night. James said lights came up to the drive twice. I had to go and see Doctor Fyfe that day, and mum insisted on driving me into Gallanach, despite the fact I felt fine. Doctor Fyfe gave me permission to go back to Glasgow that evening, providing I took the train and stayed with friends.

I stayed the extra night instead, and left by car in the early hours, taking Rory's diaries and the copies of his papers with me. I phoned Mrs McSpadden from Glasgow and told her that, too, and discovered that Fergus had gone to Edinburgh for a couple of days. On impulse, I told her I'd remembered something more from the attack, and I'd be going to the police in a day or two, once I'd checked on something.

*

Back at university, I attended lectures – hobbling a little on my cut feet – and I studied, though I had headaches on the Monday and the Tuesday night. I made sure Mrs Ippot's house was securely locked each night, and closed all the shutters. I rang mum three or four times each day. Mum said Fergus had sent a huge bouquet of flowers to the house, when he'd heard what had happened. He'd phoned from Edinburgh and advised getting an alarm system fitted, and knew a firm in Glasgow who'd do it cost price, as a favour to him. Wasn't that sweet of him? Oh, and I hadn't forgotten she and Fergus would be coming to Glasgow for the opera at the end of the week, had I?

I said of course not.

I put the phone down, numb, my thoughts racing in a kind of aimless short-circuit as I wondered what on earth I was going to do.

And, naturally, I followed the war like a good little media-consumer.

The clichés were starting to come out. It was hardly possible to open a newspaper, turn on a television or listen to a radio programme without having rammed down the relevant orifice some witless variation on the facile adage concerning truth being the first casualty of war; a truism that is arguably a neat piece of propaganda itself, implying as it does that the majority of the military, politicians and media have any interest in, respect for or experience with disseminating the truth even in times of profoundest peace.

I started inventing reasons for not putting mum and Fergus up on the Friday. I would be ill. I would have a bad cold. I would discover that the tenancy agreement specified I couldn't have anybody else to stay over-night at the Ippot house. The electricity had been cut off due to a computer error. A gas leak. Serious structural deficiencies caused by the weight of mirrors and chandeliers. Anything.

I stopped watching the war at Tuesday lunch-time because if I'd carried on the way I had been, the history we were living through was going to stop me getting my degree for the history that had been and gone.

Ash rang on the Tuesday evening. I told her everything that had happened, at the castle and Lochgair. She didn't seem to know what to make of it all; she said maybe I ought to go to the police. She sounded low, and said things weren't too good at work, though she wouldn't be more specific.

Meanwhile, the sound of her voice was pulling me apart; it filled me with elation at the same time as it plunged me into despair. I wanted to shout Look, woman, I think I'm falling in love with you! I am! I do! I love you! Honest! I'm sure! Well, almost certain! ... but you couldn't; I couldn't. It wasn't the sort of equivocal thing to shout at any time, and even if I had been completely sure how I felt, I probably couldn't have told her, not just then. I got the impression it wasn't the sort of thing she wanted to hear anyway. She sounded like she just wanted to keep her head down for the moment; keep things quiet, uncomplicated; just cool out. Recently banged-on-the-head nutters raving down the phone at her suddenly declaring undying passionate love for no apparent reason was probably the last thing she needed. I *was* sure about that. Well, fairly certain.

So it was a desultory kind of phone call. I felt pretty depressed myself at the end of it. I didn't ask her about her love-life.

I put the phone down feeling the same way I had a year earlier, the day I'd been travelling from Gallanach to Glasgow after Hogmanay, and I'd pretended to be asleep when the train stopped at Lochgair. Remembering that cowardice and that shame, I almost picked the phone up again to call Ash back, and my hand reached out a couple of times, and I debated with myself, muttering, my face contorting with silly expressions, and I told myself I was acting like a madman, and I really wanted to make that call and I really ought to, but I was terrified to do it as well, even though I knew that I should . . . shouldn't I? Yes; yes I should; yes I definitely ought to, it was obvious, clear definite. I should.

But in the end I didn't.

At least there was always work to be done. I'd submerged myself in my studies with a feeling of almost orgasmic relief. The very fact the past can be taken or left made me want to accept it; the sheer demanding immediacy of the present made it repulsive.

And so everything returned to a sort of normality, which didn't last, of course.

*

On Wednesday, the 23rd of January 1991, shortly after noon, Fergus Walter Cruden Urvill left Gaineamh Castle in his Range Rover and travelled north through the town of Gallanach and the village of Kilmartin, passing Carnasserie Castle and the cairn and standing stone at Kintraw, crossed the thin flood plain of the Barbreck River above Loch Craignish, travelled inland again to rejoin the shore at the cut-off for the Craobh Haven marina development, and then curved past the village of Arduaine, skirting Loch Melfort before passing through Kilmelford and entering the forest that led to Glen Gallain and then down to the shore of Loch Feochan and the twisting road heading for Oban. The Range Rover passed through the town a little before one o'clock and continued north to Connel, waited for the traffic lights to change at the old bridge over the Falls of Lora, then crossed, negotiated some road-works and finally turned left off the road a little further on, entering the thin strip of level coastal ground that was the Connel airstrip.

Fergus Urvill parked the Range Rover in the airfield car park. He talked to one Michael Kerr, from the village of Benderloch a couple of kilometres up the road from the field. Kerr was repairing the car-park fence; Mr Urvill said he wanted to use the telephone in the Portakabin that served as the airfield office. Michael Kerr said that Mr Urvill seemed in a good mood, and told him that he would be flying out to one of the Outer Herbrides ('the Utter He-Brides,' were his exact words), where an old school friend lived. He was going to surprise this friend and take him a bottle of whisky for a belated Hogmanay. He showed Michael Kerr the bottle of Bowmore whisky he was taking with him, in a small leather suit-case which also contained some clothes and toiletries. The only thing Kerr noticed that was out of the ordinary was that Mr Urvill grimaced a couple of times, and flexed his shoulders oddly. Kerr asked the older man if he was all right, and Fergus said yes, but it felt like a couple of ribs were acting up a little. An old injury; nothing to worry about.

Mrs Eliza McSpadden, the housekeeper at the castle, had confirmed that Mr Urvill had complained of chest pains the night before, and had taken some Paracetamol painkillers. He had taken a box of the tablets with him that morning, when he drove to

Connel. He had said he would be away for a couple of days, and – apparently on impulse as he was about to get into the car – asked Mrs McSpadden to prepare some of her Cullen Skink soup for his lunch on the Friday. He wouldn't need more as he would be dining with Mrs Mary McHoan in Glasgow that evening, before the opera. The Colonial restaurant in Glasgow later confirmed that they had a booking for two for the Friday evening in Mr Urvill's name.

When Mr Urvill came back out of the airfield office, it was about one-thirty. Michael Kerr helped him check the Cessna aircraft. The plane taxied to the end of the runway, faced into a wind and then took off into a five-knot south-westerly breeze, in good visibility under a five-thousand-foot cloud-base of light overcast. The forecast said the breeze would freshen and veer to the south east that evening, and the following few days would be bright and clear with a steady southerly wind of force three or four.

*

The Cessna was spotted by the British Army radar base on the island of St Kilda flying into an area that was restricted for missile testing. The light aircraft was flying at an altitude of two thousand feet on a bearing of 320°, which would take it towards Iceland. There was no radio response from the plane, and an RAF Nimrod, on patrol over the North Atlantic, was diverted to intercept.

The Nimrod rendezvoused with the light aircraft at 1516 GMT. It decreased speed and flew almost alongside, a little above and ahead of the Cessna for twenty-five minutes, attempting to make radio and visual contact. The Nimrod crew reported that the single occupant of the plane seemed to be unconscious, slumped back in his seat.

At 1541 GMT the Cessna's engine started to cut out and the plane – presumably out of fuel – began to lose altitude. The engine stopped altogether less than a minute later. The plane pitched forward, causing the pilot's body to slump over the controls, whereupon the aircraft went into a steep dive and started to spin. It fell into the sea, impacting at 1543.

The Nimrod circled, dropping a life raft and reporting the position of the wreck to nearby shipping. The plane sank twenty minutes later, as the sun was setting. There was little visible wreckage. An East German trawler picked up the Nimrod's liferaft during the following morning.

The crew of the Nimrod reported that at no time had the figure on board the light aircraft shown any sign of consciousness.

*

'Hello?'

'Prentice?'

'Speaking. Is –?

'It's Ashley. I just heard about Fergus.'

'Ashley! Ah ... Yeah. I heard this afternoon. I was going to call; I don't have your work number.'

'Well?'

'Well, what?'

'Do you know any more than what's been on the news?'

'Well, mum went up to the castle to see if Mrs McSpadden needed a hand, and she said she seemed kind of shell-shocked; kept talking about soup.'

'Soup?'

'Soup. Cullen Skink, specifically.'

'Oh.'

'Yeah, well, apparently Fergus seemed in good spirits, but he'd had some chest pains, the night before. Anyway, he drove up to Connel to fly out to the Hebrides to see some chum of his out there, and next thing we know he's dive-bombing the Atlantic and forgetting to pull up. Unconscious, apparently.'

'Hmm ... so what do you think?'

'Well, I don't know. Mum said she asked Mrs McSpadden who he was going to see, and she said she didn't know who it could have been. The police had already asked her that, apparently; they said they would make enquiries.'

'Right. You think it was a heart attack?'

'I don't know. Umm . . .'

'What?'

'Well, apparently Mrs McSpadden said Fergus had a phone call the night before. She took it initially, then handed the phone to him.'

'Yeah? And?'

'Whoever it was, they were Scottish, but it was an international phone call; a satellite call. Mrs McSpadden thought she recognised the voice but she wasn't sure.'

'Hmm. Recognised the voice.'

'Yeah. Did . . . I mean, did she know Lachy?'

'Yes. Yes, she did. They both worked behind the bar in the Jac, about . . . twenty years ago, maybe.'

'Ah-ha.'

'Ah-ha indeed.'

I took a deep breath. 'Look, Ash, I've been mean –' I heard a noise in the background.

'Shit, that's the door. What?'

The breath sighed out of me. 'Ah . . . nothing. Take care, Ash.'

'Yeah, you too, bye.'

I put the phone down, put my head back, looked up at the plaster stalagtites that formed the ceiling frieze in the study of the Ippot house, and howled like a dog.

*

The Strathclyde Police received a telephone tip-off at their headquarters in Glasgow that a drug ring was using Loch Coille Bharr – just south of the Argyllshire village of Crinan – as a hiding place for cocaine, at 1325 on January the 23rd. The tip-off was quite specific, talking of weighted, water-tight plastic cylinders towed behind yachts coming from the Continent and transferred to the loch to await pick-up by dealers from Glasgow. The loch was cordoned off that day and police divers started searching the south end of the loch the following morning, while policemen in small boats used grappling hooks to drag the rest.

No drug-packed cylinders were ever found, but on the second day one of the boats snagged something heavy. A diver went down to free the line from what was expected to be a water-logged tree.

He surfaced to report that the line had hooked onto the rear wheel of a motor-bike which had, tied to it, the remains of a body.

The bike and the body were brought to the surface that evening. The corpse had decomposed and been eaten by fish, to the point of being a skeleton held together more by the clothes it still wore than by the few pieces of connective tissue left. The clothes suggested the deceased had been a male, but the police weren't sure of the skeleton's sex until the body was examined in Glasgow the following day.

What they did know was that the bike – a Suzuki 185 GT registered in 1977 – had been reported stolen by its owner in Glasgow in 1981, after it had been loaned to a friend and never returned. Probably that alone would have led to the police coming to Lochgair to see us, but one of the local policemen with a long memory had already put two and two together when he'd heard the make and model of the bike.

The corpse carried no identifying papers, but dental records matched. We knew then it was Rory.

The skeleton had been found wearing a crash-helmet, but it must have been put back on after Rory had been murdered; according to the pathologist's report, he'd been killed by a series of blows to the back of the head with a smooth, hard, spherical or nearly spherical object, approximately nine centimetres in diameter. He was probably unconscious after the first blow.

And so, after the coroner had released the remains following the inquest in late February, Uncle Rory's bones came back to Lochgair at last, and were laid to rest at the back of the garden, under the larches, between the rhododendrons and the wild roses, at the side of his brother. The stone-mason added Rory's name and dates to the black marble obelisk, and we held a small ceremony just for the immediate family and Janice Rae. It fell to me to read out the words Rory had, apparently, intended to close *Crow Road* with, by way of a funeral oration.

The passage came from Rory's nameless play, and began: 'And all your nonsenses and truths . . .'

Janice cried.

I remarked to Lewis that the way things were going in our family it might work out cheaper in the long run if we bought our own hearse.

I do believe he was shocked. Or maybe he just wished he'd said it.

Technically the case remained open and Rory's murderer was still being sought, but beyond briefly interviewing mum, Janice and Rory's old flat-mate Andy Nichol, the police took no further action. I never did find out just how good at adding-up that policeman was.

*

The firm Ashley Watt was working for in London went into receivership in the last week of January. She was made redundant, but remained in the city looking for another job.

*

The war ended, in a famous victory. Only their young men died like cattle, and there was even talk of the US making a modest profit on the operation.

*

Verity's baby was born – bang on time – on March the 2nd, in London, in a warm birthing pool in a big hospital. The boy was registered as Kenneth Walker McHoan; he weighed three and a half kilos and looked like his father.

Lewis, Verity and young Kenneth travelled up to Lochgair two weeks later.

*

The lawyer Blawke read Fergus Urvill's will in Gaineamh Castle on the 8th of March. I had been asked to be present, and travelled down by train – the Golf was in for a service – with feelings of bitterness and dread.

Helen and Diana, solemnly beautiful in black, both looking tanned – Helen from Switzerland, Diana from Hawaii – sat together in the tall-ceilinged Solar and heard that they were to inherit the estate, with the exception of various pieces of glass held in the castle, which – as the twins had already known – were to be donated to the Glass Museum attached to the factory. Mrs McSpadden – sitting hunched and crying with what was, in retrospect, a quite baffling quietness – received the sum of twenty-five thousand pounds, and the right either to live on in the castle, or receive a similar amount if the property was sold or if she was asked to vacate her apartments by the twins or their heirs. Fergus had asked to be buried in the old castle garden, but as they never did recover the body a monument was decided on instead. A memorial service would he held in Gallanach at a later date.

The Range Rover was part of the estate, but the Bentley Eight had been willed to my father. Fergus had changed his will after dad's death – following promptings by the good lawyer Blawke – and so the car and its contents passed to me instead, which came as something of a surprise.

There were various other bits and pieces – bequests to charities and so on – but that was the gist of it.

The lawyer Blawke handed me the keys to the Bentley after the reading, while we were standing around awkwardly drinking small sherries dispensed by a quietly tearful Mrs McSpadden and I was still in a slight daze, thinking, What? Why? Why did he give me the car?

I talked to the twins. Helen just wanted to get away, but Diana had decided to stay on for a while; I agreed to come and help her pack stuff away in a few days time. Fergus's personal effects were going to be stored in the cellar, and of course the glass had to be packed up to be taken to the museum. The twins said they still hadn't decided what to do with the castle long-term, and I got the impression it depended on what Mrs McSpadden chose to do.

I said my good-byes as soon as I decently could. I had intended to take mum's Metro straight back to Lochgair; I'd told Helen and Diana that I'd probably come back that afternoon with mum, to take the Bentley away. But for some reason, when I got out of the castle doors, I didn't go crunching over the gravel to the little hatchback but turned and went back into the Solar and asked if I could take the Bentley to Lochgair instead, and come back for the Metro later.

Diana told me the garage was open, so I walked round to the rear of the castle where the garage and outhouses were. The Bentley sat inside the opened double garage, burgundy bodywork gleaming like frozen wine. I opened the car, wondering why the will had mentioned the contents of the Eight as well as the vehicle itself.

I got in and sat in that high armchair of a driver's seat, smiling at the walnut and the chrome and breathing in the smell of Connelly hide. The car looked showroom-clean; un-lived in. Nothing in the door pockets, on the back seats or the rear shelf; not even maps. I hesitated before opening the glove box. I was just paranoid enough to think maybe there was a bomb wired to that or the ignition, but, well, that didn't seem very Fergus-like, despite it all. So I opened the glove box.

It contained the car's manual – I'd never seen one bound in leather before – the registration documents, and a cardboard presentation box I recognised as coming from the factory gift shop.

I took it out and opened it. There was a paperweight inside, which was what the box was meant to contain, but the big lump of multi-coloured glass was a little too large for the cardboard insert that went with the box. When I looked at the base it was an old limited edition Perthshire weight, not a Gallanach Glass Works product at all.

I left the paperweight lying on the seat and got out, checked the car's boot – carefully, thinking of the end of *Charley Varrick* – but that was in concourse condition too.

I went back to the driver's seat and sat there for a while, holding the paperweight and gazing into its convexly complicated depths, wondering why Fergus had left this lump of glass – not even from his own factory – in the car.

Then I weighed the glassy mass in my hand, and clutched it as you might a weapon, and took another, evaluating look at it, and realised. It was spherical, or nearly spherical, and probably pretty well exactly nine centimetres in diameter.

I almost dropped it.

I shivered, and put the paperweight back in the presentation case, put that in the glove-box, and – after the car did not blow up when I turned the ignition – drove its quietly ponderous bulk back to Lochgair.

*

Fergus's memorial service was held a week later, at the Church of Scotland, on Shore Street in Gallanach, mid-Argyll. Kind of a traumatic location for the McHoans, and I wouldn't have gone myself – it would have felt too much like either hypocrisy or gloating – but mum wanted to attend, and I could hardly not offer to escort her.

We put some flowers on the McDobbies' grave, where dad had died, then went in to the church, each kissing the sombrely beautiful twins.

I stood listening to the pious words, the ill-sung hymns and the plodding reminiscences of the good lawyer Blawke – who must be becoming Gallanach's most sought-after after-death speaker – and felt a furious anger build up in me.

It was all I could do to stand there, moving my mouth when people sang, and looking down at my feet when they prayed, and not shout out some profanity, some blasphemy, or, even worse, the truth. I actually gathered the breath in my lungs at one point, hardly able to bear the pressure of fury inside me any longer. I tensed my belly for the shout: Killer! Fucking MURDERER!

I felt dizzy. I could almost hear the echoes of my scream reflecting back off the high walls and arched ceiling of the church ... but the singing went on undisturbed. I relaxed after that, and looked around at the trappings of religion and the gathered suits and worthies of Gallanach and beyond, and – if I felt anything – felt only sorrow for us all.

I looked up towards the tower. *All the gods are false*, I thought to myself, and smiled without pleasure.

I talked to a red-eyed Mrs McSpadden after the service, walking down through the gravestones towards the road and sea, under a sky of scudding cloud; the wind tasted of salt. 'Aye,' Mrs McSpadden said, in what was for her almost a whisper. 'You never think it's going to happen, do you? We all have our little aches and pains, but when I think about it, if I'd just said something when he mentioned a sore chest that night to go to the doctor ...'

'Everybody hurts, Mrs McSpadden,' I said. 'And he had broken those ribs, in the crash. Anybody would have assumed it was just those.'

'Aye, maybe.'

I hesitated. 'Mum said he'd had a phone call from abroad, the night before?'

'Hmm? Oh, yes. Yes, he did. I thought I . . . Well, yes.'

'You don't know who it was?'

'No,' she said slowly, though I saw her frown.

'It's just that a friend of mine from university who's abroad at the moment had been going to call Fergus, to ask permission to visit the factory – he's writing a dissertation on the history of glass making – and I haven't heard from him for a while; I wondered if it might have been him, that's all.' (All lies of course, but I'd tried to ring Lachy Watt in Sydney and found that the phone had been disconnected. Ashley's mum didn't know where he was now, and I did still want to know what had finally driven Fergus to do what he had.)

'Oh, I don't know,' Mrs McSpadden said, shaking her large, florid head. A big black bead of glass glittered at the end of her hatpin; a stray strand of white hair blew in the gusting wind.

'You didn't hear anything that was said,' I prompted.

'Och, just something about putting somebody up. I was on my way out the door.'

'Putting somebody up?'

'Aye. He said he hadn't put anybody up, and that was all I heard. I suppose he must have been talking about people who'd stayed at the castle, or hadn't stayed; whatever.'

'Yes,' I said, nodding thoughtfully. 'I suppose so.' I shrugged. 'Ah well. Perhaps it wasn't who I was thinking of after all.'

Or maybe it was. Maybe if Mrs McS had heard one more word before she'd closed that door, it would have been the word 'to'.

'Come to think of it,' Mrs McSpadden said, 'I'd just been talking about you, Prentice, when the phone went.'

'Had you?'

'Aye; just mentioning to Mr Urvill what you'd said about remembering more details of when your house was burgled.'

'Really?' I nodded, putting my gloved hands behind my back and smiling faintly at the grey and restless sea beyond the low church wall.

*

'*Canada*?' I said, aghast.

'I've got an uncle there. He knows somebody working in a firm installing a system I know a bit about; they swung the work permit.'

'My God, when do you go?'

'Next Monday.'

'Next *Monday*?'

'I'll be going up to Gallanach tomorrow, to say goodbye to mum.'

'Flying?'

'Driving. Leaving the car there. Dean can use it.'

'Jesus. How long are you going to Canada *for?*'

'I don't know. We'll see. Maybe I'll like it.'

'You mean you might *stay*?'

'I don't know, Prentice. I'm not making any plans beyond getting there and seeing what the job's like and what the people are like.'

'Shee-it. Well, can I see you? I mean; I'd like to say goodbye.'

'Well, you going to Gallanach this weekend?'

'Umm ... Would you believe that this weekend I was intending to drive a Bentley to Ullapool, get a ferry to the island of Lewis, drive to the most north-westerly point on the island I could find and throw a paperweight into the sea? But ...'

'Well, don't let me stop you. I've got plenty of family to see, goodness knows.'

'But –'

'But I'm flying out from Glasgow on the Monday morning. You can put me up in this palace you're living in, if you like.'

'Sunday? Yeah. Let me think; can't get a ferry on a Sunday, but I can get to Ullapool on Friday, travel over; back Saturday. Yeah. Sunday's fine. What time do you think you'll get here?'

'Six all right?'

'Six is perfect. My turn to take you for a curry.'

'No it isn't, but I accept anyway. I promise not to throw brandy all over you.'

'Okay. I promise not to act like an asshole.'

'You have to *act*?'

'Gosh, you know how to hurt a chap.'

'Years of practice. See you Sunday, Prentice.'

'Yeah. Then. Drive carefully.'

'You too. Bye.'

I put the phone down, looked up at the ceiling, and didn't know whether to whoop with joy because I was going to see her, or scream in despair because she was going to Canada. Caught between these two extremes, I experienced an odd calmness, and settled for a low moan.

*

I was starting to think that maybe the Bentley wasn't really me. People gave me funny looks when I drove it, and I had already been stopped by some traffic cops on Great Western Road the day I drove the beast back from Lochgair to Glasgow. Is this your car, sir? they'd asked.

With hindsight, perhaps saying, Gosh, I thought you only did this to black people! wasn't the most politic reply to have made, but they only kept me waiting for an hour while they checked up on me and scrutinised the car. I spent the time sitting in the back of the police car thinking of all the worthy causes I could give the proceeds of the Bentley's sale to (I certainly wasn't going to keep Fergus's blood-money). The African National Congress and the League Against Cruel Sports were two names that suggested themselves as fit to spin Ferg's remains up to near turbo-charger speeds in his watery grave. Thankfully the Bentley's tyres were nearly new and the lights, like everything else, were all in perfect working order, so the boys in blue had to let me go.

Anyway, it felt right that it was the monstrous burgundy-coloured Eight I took to the Hebrides rather than the Golf.

I started out on the Friday morning and took the A82 to Inverness, then crossed to the west coast and Ullapool. The drive confirmed that the Bentley would have to go. It hadn't been as unwieldly as I'd imagined it might be, but I just felt embarrassed in the thing. There hadn't been anything in Fergus's will to say I couldn't do what I wanted with the car, so what the hell, I'd sell it.

I caught the afternoon ferry to Stornoway. I stayed in the Royal Hotel that night, read history books about ancient wars and long-gone empires, and dipped into our currently interesting times via the television. I stationed the paperweight on the bedside table, as though to guard me through the night.

*

At ten o'clock the next morning I stood in a strong wind and light drizzle, wrapped in my dad's old coat, near the lighthouse at the Butt of Lewis – trying to think of a good joke about *that* to tell my brother – and wishing I'd brought a brolly. I hadn't been able to decide whether this really was the most north-westerly point of the island – there was a place with the appropriate name of Gallan Head that might have done as well – but in the end I thought maybe it didn't really matter that much, and anyway this headland was easier to get to.

There were some cliffs, not especially high. I had the paperweight in my pocket, and I took it out, feeling suddenly self-conscious and foolish even though there was nobody else around. The wind tugged at the coat and threw light, soaking spray into my eyes. The sea was tarnished rolling silver and seemed to go on forever into the light grey watery expanse of spray and air and cloud.

I hefted the glass ball, then threw it with all my might out to sea. I don't think it would have mattered especially to me if it had hit the rocks and shattered, but it didn't; it just disappeared into the greyness, heading towards the piling, restless waves. I think I saw it splash, but I'm not sure.

I had been thinking about saying something, when I threw the paperweight into the sea; 'You forgot something,' had been the line I'd been toying with on the drive up, through the peat-smoke smell. But it seemed trite; in the end I didn't say anything.

Instead I stood there for a while, getting wet and cold, and looking out at the waves and thinking of that wreckage, lying out there on the floor of the Atlantic, a few hundred kilometres to the northwest, far beneath the surface of that grey receiving sea.

Was Fergus Urvill anywhere, still? Apart from the body – whatever was left of him physically, down there in that dark, cold pressure – was there anything else? Was his personality intact somehow, somewhere?

I found that I couldn't believe that it was. Neither was dad's, neither was Rory's, nor Aunt Fiona's, nor Darren Watt's. There was no such continuation; it just didn't work that way, and there should even be a sort of relief in the comprehension that it didn't. We continue in our children, and in our works and in the memories of others; we continue in our dust and ash. To want more was not just childish, but cowardly, and somehow constipatory, too. Death was change; it led to new chances, new vacancies, new niches and opportunities; it was not all loss.

The belief that we somehow moved on to something else – whether still recognisably ourselves, or quite thoroughly changed – might be a tribute to our evolutionary tenacity and our animal thirst for life, but not to our wisdom. That saw a value beyond itself; in intelligence, knowledge and wit as concepts – wherever and by whoever expressed – not just in its own personal manifestation of those qualities, and so could contemplate its own annihilation with equanimity, and suffer it with grace; it was only a sort of sad selfishness that demanded the continuation of the individual spirit in the vanity and frivolity of a heaven.

The waves surged against the cliffs, thudding into the rock and being reflected. The shapes of their energy charged back into that wild, disturbed water, obliterated and conserved at once.

It seemed to me then that it was this simple; individual life has no momentum, and – just as dad had said – the world is neither fair nor unfair. Those words are our inventions, and apply only to the results of thought. To die as Darren had, and as my father had, and perhaps as Rory had, with what might have been great things still to do, and much to give and to receive, was to make our human grief the greater, but could not form part of any argument. They were here, and then they weren't, and that was all there was.

My father had had the right of it, when I'd been so upset at Darren Watt's death; it had been a sort of petulance I had felt towards the world, an anger as well as a sadness that Darren had died so soon (and so uglily, so sordidly; a litter bin, for fuck's sake). How dare the world not behave as I expected it to? How dare it just rub out one of my friends? It wasn't fair! And, of course, indeed it was not fair. But that was beside the point.

Well, the old man had been right and I had been wrong, and I just hoped that he'd known somehow that I would come to my senses eventually.

But if he had gone to his grave – via the McDobbie's – thinking that his middle son was a credulous fool, and likely to stay that way, well, that hurt me; hurt me more than I could say, but there was no fixing that now. It was over.

*

I turned and left and caught the ferry back to Ullapool from Stornoway that afternoon, drinking cups of styrofoam coffee and eating greasy pies while I stood out on deck watching the beating waves.

We'd seen dolphins following the ship once, coming back this way past the Summer Isles after a holiday, one day many years ago;

mum and dad and Lewis and James and me.

But that was then.

I was back in Glasgow six hours later. I slept well.

*

And so we went back to the Anarkali restaurant on that Sunday night, Ashley Watt and I, and we had a meal that was almost identical to the one we'd had before, on the summer night when dad had died, except we got along just fine this time, and Ashley didn't throw any brandy over me, and I didn't act like a complete asshole, and as I sat there, talking about all the old times and about the future, again I didn't know whether to laugh or cry, because it was so good to see her, but she was going away tomorrow, flying off across that wide grey ocean I'd stood looking at just the day before, flying away to Canada and maybe going to stay there, and I didn't know whether to ask about any men in her life or not – even though I knew from Dean that the guy she'd gone off with at Hogmanay had only been a one-night thing – and I still didn't feel I could tell her how I felt about her because she was going to go away now, and how could I suddenly say I love you when I'd never said it to anybody in my life before? How could I say it now especially, the night before she was due to leave? It would look like I was trying to make her stay, or just get her into bed. It would probably wreck this one precious evening that we did have, and upset her, confuse her, even hurt her, and I didn't want to do any of that. And through it all I knew there must have been a moment when I could have told her, some time in the past, some time over the last few months, when it would have been the right time and the right place, and it would have felt like the most natural thing in the world to say and do, but somehow, in the heat of things, just during the complexity of events – and thanks to my own stupidity, my hesitation, my indecision; my negligence – I'd missed it, and that, too, was gone from me; over.

So I just sat there, across from her, looking into her soft-skinned face all glowing in the candle-light, that long, thin nose rising straight above her small, smiling red mouth as if together they made an exclamation mark, and I felt lost in the grey sparkle of those eyes.

We walked out into the cool March night. It was fair but it had been wet and the pavements shone. Ashley stood on the steps as I put on the old tweed coat that had been my dad's. She wore a black dress and the old naval jacket with the turned-over cuffs I remembered from Grandma Margot's funeral. She leant against some railings, watching me button my coat up, and with her left foot she clicked her toe and heel as if in accompaniment to some song I couldn't hear.

I looked down at her tapping black shoe as I adjusted my collar. 'Morse code?'

She shook her head, long fawn hair spilling over her dark shoulders.

We went arm in arm down the steps. 'What was that film that had a dancer tapping out insults at somebody?' I said.

'Dunno,' Ash said, click-clicking her feet as we walked.

'Was it *Dead Men Don't Wear Plaid*?' I scratched my head. I wasn't wearing gloves and I could feel Ashley's warmth through her jacket. She smelled of *Samsara*, which was a departure for her, I thought.

'Maybe,' she said, and then she laughed.

'What?'

'I was just remembering,' she said, squeezing my waist. 'Mrs Phimister's class. Remember? The French teacher? We were in the same class.'

'Oh yeah,' I said. We turned onto Woodlands Road.

'You hated her because she'd confiscated a radio or something, and you used to tap out insults in morse code.' Ash laughed loud.

'God, yeah,' I said. 'That's right.'

'"Fuck off you old cow", was the witticism I recall best," Ash said, still snorting with laughter.

'Jeez,' I said, pulling away from her a little to look into her eyes. 'You mean you could decipher it?'

'Yeah,' Ash said, with a sort of friendly scorn.

'You rotter!' I laughed. 'You absolute cad-ess. You cad-ette; I thought that was my secret. I only told people later, after I'd left school, and then nobody believed me.'

'Yeah,' Ash said, grinning at me. 'I knew. A couple of times I almost got detention because I was giggling so much. Nearly wet my knickers trying not to laugh. Got some very stern looks from Mrs Phimister.' She laughed again, throwing her head back.

'I didn't even know you *knew* morse code,' I said. 'I learned it in the scouts. Where did you learn it?'

'My grandad taught me,' Ash said, nodding. 'We used to sit and pass messages at meal times by clinking our cutlery off the plates. Mum and dad and the others always wondered what we found so hilarious about yet another helping of shepherd's pie and chips.'

'And you never said!' I shook my head. 'You rascal!'

She shrugged, looked down at her black, medium-high heels as she did a little tap-dance. 'You didn't like me; what was the point?'

'I didn't like any girls,' I told her. 'In fact I wasn't that keen on any of the boys either. Come to think of it, I felt mostly contempt even for my friends.'

'Yeah,' Ash said, leaning over towards me so that her grinning face was almost on my chest. 'But you didn't break *their* noses with a boulder disguised as a snowball, did you?'

I stopped in my tracks.

Ash gave a little squeal as she staggered, suddenly losing support on one side. She steadied and turned. She faced me, looking puzzled, from a metre or so away. I just stood there open-mouthed.

'You knew that was me?'

'Course I did.' She frowned and smiled at the same time.

'Another secret gone!' I exclaimed, waving my arms. 'I've felt guilty about that for years!'

Ash tipped her head to one side.

'Well, not all the time,' I said. 'I mean, on and off.'

She raised one eyebrow.

'Okay,' I said, slumping a little. 'Mostly off. But I did feel bad about it. I really did. I always felt bad about that.'

Ashley shook her head gently and came forward, took my arm and led me along the street. 'Never mind,' she said. 'I never told anybody. And I forgave you.'

'Really?' I said, putting my arm round her again, 'When?'

'At the time. Well, after it stopped hurting, anyway.'

We turned the corner into Woodlands Gate. I shook my head. 'Why didn't you ever say you knew it had been me?' I asked her.

She shrugged. 'The subject never really arose before.'

I shook my head again. 'Good grief,' I said. 'All this time. Good grief.'

*

Ashley had been ravenous when she'd arrived at the house in Park Terrace a little after seven that Sunday evening, so she'd just dumped her bags and we'd gone straight out to the restaurant. When we got back after the meal, I showed her round the place. We opened a bottle of Graves I had in the kitchen – after first agreeing that of course we shouldn't – and then walked from room to room while I did my guided tour bit and pointed out the more interesting or valuable works of art, while we sipped our wine and the statues gleamed and the chandeliers glittered and the paintings glowed and the carpets spread before us like gigantic blow-ups of oddly symmetrical printed circuits.

Ashley shook her head a lot. When she saw the main bedroom she laughed.

We went back to the kitchen. She demurred when I offered to top her glass up. 'I should go to bed now,' she said, pulling a hand through her hair. She put her glass down on an oak working surface. 'Take some water in a big glass and get to me bed . . .' she said. 'Do you mind?' She looked at me.

I shrugged. 'No, of course not. There's glasses in the bathroom, beside your room.' A terrible sadness settled on me then, and I had to swallow hard a couple of times. I drank, to hide it, then said, as matter-of-factly as I could, 'What time do you want up tomorrow?'

'About seven should do.'

'Right,' I said, looking at my glass. 'Right. Seven. I'll bring you tea and toast, all right?'

'Fine.'

'Okay then,' I said.

I looked up and she was smiling. She looked at her watch. 'Well,' she said, and flexed her brows. 'Night-night.'

She came forward, put one hand on my shoulder, kissed my cheek.

I put my hand on her hip, let my head nuzzle towards hers a little. She put her arm round my waist and I turned to her, hugged her, my lips at her neck, kissing delicately. She pushed her head against mine, and we started to turn to each other at the same moment, as she put her arms round me; the kiss just seemed natural after that.

It went on for some time. Ashley seemed to loosen and grow more tense at the same time; her mouth appeared to want to swallow mine, her hands grabbed my curls, nails scratching at my scalp. I pulled on her hair, kissed and licked her neck. She dug her nails into the small of my back through my shirt. We kissed again and I kneaded her backside, then pulled the dress up while she wriggled a little to make it easier, and I found skin, stockings, her knickers, and pushed my hands inside, gripping her smooth, warm bum. She pulled herself up against me.

'This,' she said, breaking off, breathing hard, while her hands stroked the nape of my neck and her gaze flicked from my mouth to my eyes and back again, 'this might be better suited to that ridiculous bedroom, what do you think?'

I nodded. 'Good idea.'

'Bring the wine.'

'Better yet.'

*

It was something. On that monumentally ostentatious bed of the late Mrs Ippot's, Ashley and I made love like we'd done it for years and then been apart for years and just met up and hadn't forgotten a thing.

A couple of times, lying there panting afterwards while we trickled with sweat and licked at each other, or were stroking and caressing and thinking about starting all over again, she laughed.

'The room?' I said, first time.

'No,' she said, shaking her gorgeous head, all tawny hair and flushed face. 'It's just you and me; I never thought this was going to happen.'

And, later, when she cried out, I heard the crystal bowl on the table by the side of the bed ring, pure and faint, as if in reply.

*

It was later still, when we'd put the lights out and had agreed just to cuddle, exhausted and drained, but had not been able to merely cuddle, and so had coupled once more, and I still lay on top of her, inside her, while she breathed and I breathed and our hearts gradually slowed down again, that I did what I'd done before in that situation, flexing whatever muscle it is in the male genitals or the associated support systems that briefly fills the slowly detumescing penis with blood again, sending a small pulse of socketed touch into Ashley's body. She gave a little exhalation half-way between a sigh and a laugh, and then squeezed back with her vaginal muscles, like a hand round me.

There was a pause, and I thought I felt her go very still for a second, and then she squeezed me again; two quick grippings in succession. There was a pause, and I responded, but she dug her fingers into the small of my back as though to stop me, and so I relaxed.

She squeezed again, four times, the second pulse longer than the other three. Another pause, during which I realised – it was morse! Then another four pulses, the second one short and the others long.

I. L. Y.

I had raised my head away from her shoulder while I concentrated on what she was doing in there; now I lowered my face to her skin again. I laughed, very lightly, and after a moment so did she, and then I sent the same signal back, with a single long pulse at the end: I.L.Y.T.

And I swear the sending made the signal all the truer.

And that falling was followed by two more shared fallings, as we fell apart, and then asleep.

*

I woke and she was dressed, standing by the bed, a beatific smile across her face, which was washed and glowing and framed by neatly combed hair. I struggled to get up on one elbow.

'Ash?'

She put one hand to the back of my head and kissed my lips. 'I have to go,' she said.

'What? But – you mean to *Canada*?'

'Prentice, I promised. I have to.'

I felt my jaw drop. I rolled onto my back for a second, then sat bolt upright. 'But last night!' I said, spreading my arms wide.

Ashley smiled even more broadly and climbed half onto the bed, one black-stockinged knee on the crumpled sheets. She kissed me. 'Was wonderful,' she said, 'but I have to go.'

'You can't!' I slapped myself on the forehead with one palm.

'This can't be happening! It's a dream! Stay!' I reached out to her, held her face between my hands. 'Ashley! Please! Stay!'

'I can't, Prentice. I said I'd go. I promised.'

'I'm serious!' I said. 'I don't –'

She put one soft hand gently to my mouth, shushing me, then kissed me long and tenderly. 'I'm going, Prentice,' she said, 'but it doesn't have to be for ever.'

'Well, how long?' I wailed.

She shrugged, stroked my shoulders with her hands. 'You get this degree, okay? If you still want me then, well . . .'

'Promise?' I said, in what was meant to be a terminally sarcastic manner, but came out pathetically.

She smiled. 'I promise.'

'Oh my God!' I said, looking at the clock by the crystal bowl. 'I don't believe this!' Maybe, if I could just stall her . . .

'There's a taxi waiting,' she told me. 'It's all right.' She smoothed some hair away from my eyes, her touch like silk.

'But I was going to drive –'

'You rest,' she said. 'You probably had too much wine last night, anyway. The taxi really is waiting.' She slipped her hand under the covers, held my penis as she kissed me, then slipped away as I fell forward, trying to embrace her, hold her, keep her.

'Ashley!' I said desperately. She was at the door.

'Yes?' she said.

'I didn't dream that . . . signal last night, did I?'

She laughed. 'Nope. Meant every letter; every word. With all my heart.' One brow flicked. 'Amongst other organs.' She tipped her head to one side, eyebrows raised. 'And you?'

'The same,' I gulped.

She looked down at the floor, then back at me, still smiling. 'Good. Well, we can take it from there, okay?'

'I'll write every day!' I told her.

'Don't be ridiculous,' she laughed, with one shake of her head. 'Just pass those exams.'

'They'll be over by mid-June,' I said, more to keep her there in my sight for a few seconds longer that for any other reason.

'Then I'll be back in mid-June,' she said.

She pulled her black gloves from her jacket pockets and put them on. 'Bye, Prentice.' She blew me a kiss.

'Bye,' I gulped. She closed the door. I flopped back, stunned, staring at the glittering red chandelier.

I jumped out of bed as the front door banged closed; I tore downstairs bollock-naked and waved to her from one of the drawing room windows, which went from about human knee level to giraffe's head level.

She saw me; I could see her laughing. She pushed the window down and waved, and pointed to my groin and made a shocked expression as the cab started away. The driver saw me too and looked amused and shook his head. The cab drove off around the curbed terrace. I opened the window and leaned out, waving, and Ashley pushed the cab's window right down and stuck her head and arms out and blew me kisses through her wildly waving, slip-streamed hair all the way until the cab rounded the corner and disappeared.

*

I sat down on the parquet, staring at the white gauziness of the huge net curtains, all my muscles complaining, my head pounding, my penis tingling, my flesh goose-pimpling against the cool wood of the floor. I shook my head. I collapsed back, banging my already internally abused head on a Persian rug. The carpet's pile was luxuriously deep however, so it didn't hurt as much as it might.

I looked up at the ornately carved wooden ceiling, not entirely sure what to think. Then I started to laugh, lying there in the enormous room, naked, tummy wobbling, laughing like an idiot and hoping the resemblance ended there.

'Oh well,' I said, laughing, to the ceiling. 'Here's hoping.'

*

'Good; you're getting sensible,' mum said. She walked carefully towards me, the big blue sheet folding and drooping between us. She took the sheet's other two corners from me.

'*Getting*?' I said indignantly.

Mum smiled, folded the sheet over twice more and put it on top of the tumble drier. I pulled another sheet down off the old clothes pulley that hung under the ceiling of the utility room. We took an end each, stood apart, pulled the sheet taut.

'Mm-hmm,' she said, tugging at the sheet again. 'I think selling the Bentley is very sensible.' She folded the sheet over, hand to hand; I did the same. We pulled it taut again. Mum looked thoughtful. 'Maybe we should sell that ancient thing sitting in the garage out there, as well.'

'The Lagonda?' I said. We folded the sheet over again.

'Yes,' mum said, walking towards me again. 'It's just a waste of space at the moment.'

'You mean you weren't thinking of going in for classic car restoration after you've finished the harpischord?'

Mum smiled as she took the sheet from me. 'Well, actually that had occurred to me, but ...' She wrinkled her nose. 'No; I don't think so.'

'Well, we won't get much for it in the state it's in at the moment.' I pulled another sheet down.

'I'm not bothered about the money,' mum said. She folded the sheet away, shot me a mischievous look. 'And besides, whose fault is it the car's in the state it is, anyway?'

'What?' I said. I stood looking at her.

Mum took the sheet from me and put two of its corners in my hands as she backed off, pulling it tight. She smiled. 'It was you who tipped the big dresser down onto it in the garage that time, wasn't it?'

She pulled the sheet; it flew out of my fingers, billowing over the floor of the room like some slow motion wave. I ran after it, catching it. I retrieved the corners, untwisted the sheet and studied the amused expression on my mother's face. She tugged the sheet again and I held onto it this time.

I'm ashamed to admit that it even occurred to me to deny it, albeit briefly. I grinned sheepishly as we folded the sheet over. 'Yeah, guilty as charged, but it was an accident.' I shook my head. 'How did you work that out?'

She walked towards me, took the sheet from me. 'Found a bit of broken glass in your underpants when I was washing them,' she said, and gave a tiny laugh as she turned away to place the sheet on the drier.

I looked up at the ceiling. 'Oh dear,' I said.

Mum turned round, standing there in her jeans and blouse, glowing with what might well have been self-satisfaction. She reached up and pulled a last sheet down off the pulley, handing one end to me. 'Yes. Well, we'll draw a discreet veil over that little incident, shall we?'

I nodded, pursed my lips. 'Might be best,' I agreed. I coughed, pulled the sheet taut with her, and with a textbook expression of interested interrogation, asked, 'And how is the harpsichord-construction project going, anyway?'

'Well –'

*

It didn't end there, either. Nobody had thought to tell me, but obviously it was open season on Prentice's ignorance. If you were female, anyway.

'Well,' I said. 'I think my absorption spectrum must be hazy.'

'No,' Diana said. 'I think it's much like anybody else's.' She took a Waldglas beaker out of the display cabinet and glanced at me. She may have seen a hurt expression because she shrugged and smiled and said, 'Okay, maybe yours has a few more black lines.

You were always interested in all sorts of stuff, weren't you?'

I shrugged. 'It runs in the family.'

'Fact is,' Diana said, breathing on the knobby green glass, 'it's probably thanks to you I spend so much of my life fourteen thousand feet above Hawaii looking for I-R stars.'

'It is?' I said.

'Yeah,' Diana said, smiling at the glass as she polished it. 'You remember the night there was Helen, me, you, Lewis and Verity and ... Darren? We were up in the observatory?'

'I remember,' I said.

'You got really stoned and started gibbering about how fantastic the universe was?'

I shook my head. 'I don't remember that,' I confessed.

'Well, you were pretty ripped,' Diana said. She handed me the beaker. 'But you were coherent, mostly, and you were *really* enthusiastic. I mean you even shut Lewis up; you just raved about how amazing astronomy was. You meant cosmology, but what the heck. You were just bubbling with it.' She brought a second Waldglas beaker out of the cabinet.

'Huh.' I filled the beaker with polystyrene beads, found a box big enough to hold the two beakers and put the first one carefully into its bed of little white infinity symbols. 'Well, I'll take your word for it.'

'Oh, you were just so *fascinated* with it all. Especially with stellar evolution. That had obviously really blown your mind. "We are made of bits of stars!" you shouted.' Diana laughed a little. 'You'd been reading about all that stuff and it just tickled you pink. You told us about how the sun and the solar system were made out of the remnants of older stars that had blown up; how the elements that made up the world had been made in those ancient stars, and that meant our bodies, too, every atom. Jeez, I thought *you* were going to explode.' She handed me the second beaker.

'Hmm,' I said. 'Well, I sort of remember that, I think.'

Actually, I wasn't sure I really did at all. My recollection of that evening got very hazy after the bit where Verity had pretended to tell me my fortune.

'"We are made from bits of stars! We are made from bits of stars!" you kept yelling, and went through it all: super novae scattering heavy atoms; the debris swirling through space, other novae and supers sending shock-waves through the debris, compressing it; stars forming, planets; geology, chemistry; life.' Diana shook her head. She extracted a thin, delicate, old-looking flute of a wine glass from the display case. 'And Jeez, you made me feel ashamed. I mean, dad had built the observatory for us; it was a present, in a way. And we hardly used it. We went up there to smoke dope. And here you were, knew all about this stuff, and actually made it sound interesting. You were really gone on the idea that we were stuck down here on this one little planet and still just savages really, but we'd glimpsed the workings of the universe, worked out from light and radiation what had happened over the last fifteen billion years and could talk sensibly about the first few seconds after the big bang – even if the jury has gone back out on that idea nowadays – and could predict what would happen to the universe over the next few billion, and understand it ...' Diana held the wine glass up to the light, and cleaned it with the cloth. 'You were pretty scathing about religion, too; tawdry and pathetic in comparison, you said.' She shrugged. 'I didn't necessarily buy that, but you made me ashamed not to have used the telescope more. And so I did, and then I got some books on astronomy, and found out a lot of it was about maths, which I was good at anyway, though somehow the fact astronomy was about numbers and equations as well as stars and telescopes hadn't occurred to me. But anyway, that was the start of it, I was hooked. Been a star-junkie ever since, Prent, and it's all your fault.'

She flashed a shocked expression at me and handed me the glass.

I shook my head. 'You as well, eh?'

'Hmm?' Diana said.

'Nothing,' I breathed, running a hand through my hair. 'Shit, I never knew.' I looked mockly serious. 'This is something of a responsibility, Diana. I trust you haven't had cause to regret your decision.'

'Not at all, Prentice.' She closed the now empty cabinet, and took off her white gloves. 'I mean, maybe I'd have settled on astronomy anyway, without your one-man show. Whatever; it's been fun. Cold at nights and a long way from the beach, and the air's a bit thin ... but it's the skies that really take your breath away.' She nodded. 'You should visit, come see it all some time.'

'I'd like to,' I said. 'People allowed to come and look round?'

Diana folded her arms and rested her back against the display cabinet. 'It can be arranged.'

'There's somebody I'd like to take there.'

Diana smirked. 'Yeah? Somebody special? Who's that?'

'Oh ... friend of mine. In Canada at the moment.'

'Ashley, huh?'

I felt myself blush. 'Well, yeah,' I said, trying not to grin too much.

Diana nodded, still smiling. 'It'd be great to see you both out there. You two sort of an item these days?'

I shrugged, felt myself blush again. 'Sort of. I hope so. I think so.'

Diana laughed, which was good to hear; I didn't think she had laughed since Fergus died. 'Yeah, I think so.'

*

Verity and Lewis brought young Kenneth to the castle that day, so that Mrs McSpadden could go all gooey over him. She did. Diana seemed equally charmed. Kenneth just slept.

Diana broke open a bottle of twenty-five-year-old Macallen, which was older than any of us (well, except Mrs McS, but she'd gone back to the kitchen by then), and an awful lot older than Kenneth.

'Let's wet his head,' Diana said.

'Can we go up on the roof?' I said. It just seemed like a good idea.

So we climbed up there, into a bright March afternoon with a keen blue sky and a smell of wood-smoke on the westerly breeze. We sat on the slates and drank our whiskies and took turns holding the baby, who was still fast asleep.

'You having him christened?' Diana asked Verity softly, peering down at the infant's tiny scrunched-up face. She rocked him to and fro.

'Well, I think mum and dad would rather he was, but I'm not bothered one way or the other. Lewis isn't too keen, are you my love?'

Lewis showed his teeth. 'Over my dead body, actually.' he said.

'See?' Verity said to Diana, who was smiling broadly and holding the boy close, sniffing him. She just nodded.

Verity glanced at Lewis, then said, 'Prentice?'

'Yo?'

'We'd like you to be his godfather. Would you be?' She actually looked as though she thought I might refuse. Lewis was grinning at me.

I cleared my throat. 'Well . . . in terms of the actual title, I'm sort of taking a long hard look at my previous statements about the existence or non-existence of a supreme being at this moment in time, re-appraisal-wise,' I said, a suitably pained expression on my face as Diana handed the baby to me.

Lewis laughed.

Anyway, it was agreed, and then we thought the little blighter ought to have at least a semblance of a christening, so Lewis dabbed his finger in his whisky and reached over and put a tiny drop of the spirit on his son's head, and said, 'There; that's all he's going to get.'

'Kenneth Walker McHoan,' I said, cradling him with one arm and raising my glass in the other hand.

We drank the lad's health. Then Diana threw her glass away over the battlements towards the woods. Lewis, Verity and I all looked at each other, then followed suit, and heard a couple of the tumblers smash somewhere in the trees beneath. Young Kenneth opened his eyes at that point, looked woozily up at me and let out a small, plaintive cry. I laughed and kissed his tiny nose, then handed him back to his mother so she could feed him.

I stood up then and went to the battlements, and held the ancient rough stones beneath my hands. I looked out over the woods and the plain and the fields; to Gallanach, with its quays and spires and serried streets, and out to the crumpled hills beyond, the brindle of forests to the east and the glitter of waves to the west, where the ocean was. I thought of Ashley, on the other side of that ocean, and wondered what she was doing right now, and hoped that she was well, and happy, and maybe thinking of me, and then I just stood there, grinning like a fool, and took a deep, deep breath of that sharp, smoke-scented air and raised my arms to the open sky, and said, '*Ha*!'

COMPLICITY

Iain Banks

A few spliffs, a spot of mild S&M, phone through the copy for tomorrow's front page, catch up with the latest from your mystery source – could be big, could be very big – in fact, just a regular day at the office for free-wheeling, substance-abusing Cameron Colley, a fully-paid-up Gonzo hack on an Edinburgh newspaper.

The source is pretty thin, but Cameron senses a scoop and checks out a series of bizarre deaths from a few years ago – only to find that the police are checking out a series of bizarre deaths that are happening right now. And Cameron just might know more about it than he'd care to admit . . .

Involvement; connection; liability – *Complicity* is a stunning exploration of the morality of greed, corruption and violence, venturing fearlessly into the darker recesses of human purpose.

'A remarkable novel . . . superbly crafted, funny and intelligent' *Financial Times*

'A stylishly executed and well produced study in fear, loathing and victimisation which moves towards doom in measured steps' *Observer*

'Compelling and sinister . . . a very good thriller' *Glasgow Herald*

'Fast moving . . . tightly plotted' *Sunday Times*

THE WASP FACTORY

Iain Banks

Enter – if you can bear it – the extraordinary private world of Frank, just sixteen, and unconventional, to say the least.

'Two years after I killed Blyth I murdered my young brother Paul, for quite different and more fundamental reasons than I'd disposed of Blyth, and then a year after that I did for my young cousin Esmerelda, more or less on a whim. That's my score to date. Three. I haven't killed anybody for years, and don't intend to ever again. It was just a stage I was going through.'

'A mighty imagination has arrived on the scene'
Mail on Sunday

'There's no denying the bizarre fertility of the author's imagination: his brilliant dialogue, his cruel humour . . .'
Irish Times

'Read it if you dare. Weirdly talented'
Daily Express

'A brilliant book, barmy and barnacled with the grotesque'
New Statesman

'*The Wasp Factory* is a first novel not only of tremendous promise, but also of achievement, a minor masterpiece'
Punch

☐ The Wasp Factory	Iain Banks	£6.99
☐ Walking on Glass	Iain Banks	£6.99
☐ The Bridge	Iain Banks	£6.99
☐ Espedair Street	Iain Banks	£6.99
☐ Canal Dreams	Iain Banks	£6.99
☐ Complicity	Iain Banks	£6.99
☐ Whit	Iain Banks	£6.99

Abacus now offers an exciting range of quality titles by both established and new authors. All of the books in this series are available from:

Little, Brown and Company (UK),
P.O. Box 11,
Falmouth,
Cornwall TR10 9EN.

Fax No: 01326 317444.
Telephone No: 01326 317200
E-mail: books@barni.avel.co.uk

Payments can be made as follows: cheque, postal order (payable to Little, Brown and Company) or by credit cards, Visa/Access. Do not send cash or currency. UK customers and B.F.P.O. please allow £1.00 for postage and packing for the first book, plus 50p for the second book, plus 30p for each additional book up to a maximum charge of £3.00 (7 books plus).

Overseas customers including Ireland, please allow £2.00 for the first book plus £1.00 for the second book, plus 50p for each additional book.

NAME (Block Letters) ....

....

ADDRESS ....

....

....

☐ I enclose my remittance for ....

☐ I wish to pay by Access/Visa Card

Number ☐☐☐☐☐☐☐☐☐☐☐☐☐☐☐☐

Card Expiry Date ☐☐☐☐